Geralyn Dawson's
"Bad Luck" books are irresistible!

Romantic Times BOOKreviews
loves the Bad Luck Brides…
"Everything you love about the Bad Luck series is beautifully rolled into Kat and Jake's love story: madness, mayhem, humor, adventure, passion, steamy love scenes and the ties that bind a family together. Dawson touches the heart with a story that captures the meaning of trust and love in a relationship and leaves you eager for the next installment."
—*Romantic Times BOOKreviews* on *Her Scoundrel*

"Dawson…dishes up plenty of adventure, sexual tension, love and laughter, poignancy and even a tear or two. You'll be gloriously satisfied with the return of the McBrides!"
—*Romantic Times BOOKreviews* on *Her Bodyguard*

Praise for *The Bad Luck Wedding Night…*
"Wonderful! Delightful! Entertaining!"
—*romrevtoday.com*

and *The Bad Luck Wedding Cake…*
"A delicious gourmet delight! A seven-course reading experience."
—*Affaire de Coeur*

"Warm and delicious enough to satisfy the sweet tooth of any reader. Geralyn Dawson leaves me hungry for more!"
—Teresa Medeiros, bestselling author of *A Kiss to Remember*

and of course, *The Bad Luck Wedding Dress*
"Utterly charming—one of the most appealing books I've read. I loved it!"
—Patricia Potter, author of *Beloved Impostor*

Also by Geralyn Dawson

Her Scoundrel
Her Bodyguard
Give Him the Slip
My Long Tall Texas Heartthrob
My Big Old Texas Heartache
The Pink Magnolia Club
The Bad Luck Wedding Night
Sizzle All Day
Simmer All Night
The Kissing Stars
The Bad Luck Wedding Cake
The Bad Luck Wedding Dress
The Wedding Ransom
The Wedding Raffle
Tempting Morality
Capture the Night
The Texan's Bride

GERALYN
DAWSON
HER
OUTLAW

HQN™

ISBN-13: 978-0-373-77196-7
ISBN-10: 0-373-77196-7

HER OUTLAW

This edition published by arrangement with Harlequin Books S.A.

www.HQNBooks.com

Printed in U.S.A.

To my readers
Who just can't get enough Bad Luck.

HER
OUTLAW

PROLOGUE

Edinburgh, 1896

*I'*VE FOUND HIM. *After all this time. He isn't dead, after all.*

Fate has delivered Alasdair MacRae to me.

Hamish Campbell absently played a ten of hearts, his gaze resting on the faint scar beside MacRae's right eye. The result, he knew, of a cut from a signet ring during a backhanded blow. A mistake, that. One of youth and impatience and a temper slipped beyond control. It remained the biggest regret of his life.

Now, Fate had delivered this second chance literally to his table, and the card player could barely contain his glee.

The predator within began to plan. How to best take advantage of the moment? Subtlety was called for. Secrecy, too. It wouldn't do to have the prey catch his scent before the prize was within his grasp.

And such a prize it was. The Sisters' Prize. A treasure beyond measure. It should be his. It *would* be his.

What once was lost, now was found. Alasdair MacRae was the key.

CHAPTER ONE

London, 1897

EMMA MCBRIDE TATE WANTED to be wicked.

It was an itch that demanded to be scratched. A yearning deep in the marrow of her bones. She wanted to throw off the bonds of convention and revert to her childhood ways. She wanted to be bad again, if only for a little while.

How sad that the most daring thing she could think to do was to sneak off from London's Savoy Hotel and window shop by herself while her sister and grandmother indulged in an afternoon nap.

"Emma, you wild woman, you," she grumbled beneath her breath as she strolled down a busy street.

Once upon a time, she'd been a true mischief maker. The eldest of three sisters dubbed the McBride Menaces by the citizens of Fort Worth, Texas, she'd led her siblings in shenanigans ranging from mild pranks to out-and-out crimes. She'd released sneezing powder into the ventilation system at church and flown her arch-enemy Charlotte Russell's bloomers from the county courthouse flagpole. She'd robbed her first train by the age of twelve and kidnapped a man before the same year was out.

Then, at the ripe old age of nineteen, she'd sneaked her

fiancé, Casey Tate, into her bedroom at Willow Hill for a little not-so-innocent play.

For the first twenty years of her life, Emma lived like a hellion, a spitfire, a Menace—but when pneumonia claimed Casey's life three months into their marriage, her mischief died with him. For the last ten years, the closest she'd come to true adventure was watching her sisters experience it.

And she was tired of it. She was tired of the monotony of her life, tired of teaching school, tired of being the Widow Tate. The Menace in her was stirring, and once again, she craved excitement and adventure. She craved wickedness.

She was a restless Texan in London, strolling Oxford Street on a springtime afternoon looking for trouble.

She found it.

At a shop across the street, a man held a door open for a trio of doddering elderly ladies. He was tall and muscular with shoulders as broad as the Brazos River beneath his dark gentleman's jacket. He wore his thick black hair short, his face clean shaven. His square jaw, chiseled cheekbones, and thin, straight nose gave him a masculine beauty that any woman would admire.

But it was his eyes that stole Emma's breath. Set deep beneath raven brows, the color a unique silver-gray, they radiated power. Danger. And they were focused on her.

Yes, trouble with a capital *T.*

Awareness skittered along her nerves. She felt like a fluffy, feminine rabbit pinned by a sleek, strong, gray-eyed mountain cat. Her mouth went dry, her knees a little weak.

The moment ended when a boxy omnibus rattled down the street and broke the line of sight. By the time the vehicle passed, the man had disappeared.

Emma sighed with a mixture of relief and disappointment. A man like that would likely offer more adventure than she needed.

She continued her stroll. Springtime weather had brought shoppers and sightseers out in force. Women's perfumes clashed on the breeze as conversations buzzed. Emma grinned down at a rosy-cheeked infant, then smiled at the uniformed nanny pushing the perambulator. Stopping to buy a bouquet of yellow daisies from a flower girl on a corner, she eavesdropped on a conversation about Sarah Bernhardt's performance in *La Samaritaine.*

The aroma of baking bread caught her notice, and as she contemplated following its aroma to its source, a display in a variety store's plate glass window caught her eye. Emma halted in her tracks. "Oh, my."

"It's awful, isn't it?" came a male voice from behind her.

Emma glanced over her shoulder and caught herself just before she said "oh, my" a second time.

It was him. Trouble. Standing close enough for her to smell the sandalwood in his scent.

Her pulse spiked. "Excuse me?"

He gestured toward the window, and that's when Emma noticed the ice cream cone he held in his right hand. Eating on the public street? A rule-breaker, then. Of course.

Her mouth watered.

"The mannequin. Not exactly an effective sales tool, in my opinion. What could the designer have been thinking?" He took a long lick of his ice cream cone, and Emma forced herself to look away. Darned if her neck didn't tingle as if he'd licked her.

"The mannequin looks like a donkey," she observed. "All it's lacking is a tail."

She noted Trouble's lack of a British accent—lack of any accent, actually—and wondered about his origins before turning her attention to the figure in the window. It was obviously supposed to represent a woman wearing a fashionable travel bonnet and a gray traveling cloak. But the…wings—for lack of a better term—on the bonnet, the model's exceedingly long face, and the way the ill-fitting bustle gave the figure a four-legged look rather than two made the result comical. Emma could just imagine what her sisters would say if they were standing here with her.

"Aha," said the man. "Your smile brims with mischief. I insist you share your thoughts."

Emma laughed. She had no business talking to a stranger on the street, but she so enjoyed the zing of excitement that resulted. "I was thinking of my sisters. One of them would surely dare me to sneak inside and pin a tail on the mannequin."

Amusement lit those intriguing gray eyes. He took another bold lick of his cone, then reached into his jacket pocket and drew out a red silk scarf. A woman's red silk scarf. Holding it out to her, he boldly challenged, "Do it."

"What?" Emma took a step back, giving a shaky little laugh.

"I'll stand for your sisters. What's your name, my dear?"

She shouldn't… "Emma. Emma Tate."

"I'm Alasdair. Dair. And I'm daring you, Emma." He twisted his wrist, waving the bright red scarf in front of her face. "Sashay into Blankenship's and pin the tail on the donkey."

Temptation stirred. Needs long suppressed rose up within her. Emma focused on the scarf, circling her lips with her tongue. "Why should I take such a risk?"

His voice was smooth and mellow as aged whiskey. "Why, for the prize, of course."

She jerked her gaze up. He stared at her mouth. "Prize?" she croaked out.

"Do you like…ice cream, Emma?" He took a big bite of his chocolate cone.

Emma shivered. At this particular moment, she absolutely craved ice cream. Her blood stirred, her senses grew acute. With the stranger's gray-eyed gaze holding her spellbound, she felt more alive than she had in years.

She should leave. Right now. She should turn away, march back to the Savoy, take a seat in the rocker beside the fireplace, and read a book.

Instead, she indulged herself and allowed the brazen buried within her to flutter back to life. "Yes. Yes, I do."

He grinned at her, tossed her the scarf.

Emma caught it, wrinkled her nose at the cloying feminine perfume wafting from the silk. Lifting her chin, she said, "I prefer strawberry ice cream, please."

He gave her a two-fingered salute as she walked boldly into the store.

Blankenship's offered a variety of feminine fripperies, and as Emma greeted a salesclerk and pretended to shop, the female in her couldn't help but compare the quality of the merchandise to that which could be found at home. As she'd discovered so often during her forays into London shops, the handwork on the ready-made dresses couldn't compare to what her mother produced. Emboldened by a sense of American superiority, Emma casually made her way closer to the window display.

He stood where she'd left him. His eyes made contact with hers through the window glass, holding her captive as he slowly licked a dribble of ice cream off his thumb. Emma flushed and tried to concentrate on the task at hand.

This would be easier if Mari and Kat were here to run interference for her and keep the male salesclerk distracted, but Mari was back in Texas with her husband Luke Garrett, happily swelling with her third pregnancy, while Kat was snoozing at the Savoy. However, judging by the salesclerk's obvious lack of enthusiasm for his job, she expected him to lose interest in her if she "just browsed" long enough. With scarves on her mind, she hovered over that display, clucking her tongue, tsking and sighing and showing no sign of making up her mind.

From the corner of her eye, she saw Dair shaking his head at her selections. The man didn't care for drab colors. *How interesting he paid any attention to me, then.*

Stop it. She wasn't being drab now, was she? Drab women didn't play silly pranks because a handsome gentleman with a wicked smile dared it of them.

On the other side of the window glass, he sucked the tip off the cone. Emma's nipples tightened.

She forced her attention back to the display table.

The entrance of a pair of potential customers into the shop offered the opportunity she'd waited for. "I simply can't decide between the teal and the peacock," she declared, removing two scarves from the table. "I must see them both in the sunlight."

The clerk glanced her way. "Um, madam, it is not allowed to take items from the store prior to purchase."

"Oh, la," she said gaily. "I'm not going outside. Just over here to the window."

Since the window stood well away from the door, the salesclerk paid her little mind as she approached the display with the two scarves in hand. On the other side of the large window, Alasdair took another long lick of his cone and nodded toward the teal. It was a pretty color, Emma thought. Maybe once the bet was done, she'd buy it.

Finding a beam of sunlight, she held the silk cloths up and made a show of continuing her clucking and sighing. Within moments, the salesclerk dismissed her completely, turning all his attention toward the women dawdling over expensive handbags. Seeing her chance, her heart pounding, mischief humming in her blood, Emma yanked a pin from her hat and slid the red silk scarf from her pocket as she slipped into the window display. Within seconds the "donkey" sported a tail.

Giggles bubbled, threatened to erupt from within her, so Emma beat a hasty retreat from the shop, commenting on poor dye quality as she sailed empty-handed past the annoyed but clueless salesclerk. Out on the sidewalk, a glance at the window had the laughter escaping, spilling out on a wave of glee she'd not experienced for years. What a fun, foolish bit of childishness. It made her feel young again. Made her feel free again.

Wanting to share her pleasure, she glanced around for the man called Alasdair.

She didn't see him. She turned completely around, staring at the crowd. No tall, dark, scandalous stranger. No wicked grin or suggestive twinkle in Trouble's eyes. He wasn't there.

Bet he's in the ice cream shop. Anticipation thrummed inside her, and it had little to do with strawberry ice cream. She fixed her gaze upon the shop's doorway and waited for him to appear.

And waited.

And waited.

Until the bubble of excitement inside her finally popped.

A welcher, Emma thought as her joy evaporated. She'd made a bet with a welcher. "Why that sorry, no-good—"

"Miss Emma?"

She turned to see a sandy-haired young man wearing a smeared white apron holding an ice cream cone. A strawberry cone. "Yes?"

"Gentleman asked me to give this to you." He handed over the cone. "Said to offer his apologies, that important business called him away. It's strawberry ice cream with pecan sprinkles. Fellow said to tell you he thought you'd enjoy nutty things."

Emma folded her arms. Her foot took to tapping. *Humph.* Business. She doubted it. More likely he'd been waiting on his wife or girlfriend…or, recalling the perfume on the scarf, his mistress…and he didn't want to be caught flirting with another woman. The cad.

Grumpily, she accepted the cone and indulged in bad manners by taking a taste right where she stood. The ice cream was rich and sinfully delicious, and he'd been right about the pecans. They were an appropriate way to top off a nutty adventure.

A bark of laughter and some feminine giggling brought her attention back to Blankenship's display window, and witnessing the results of her prank banished the last of her pique.

It *was* funny. It had been fun. Funny and silly and a right fine dare.

Emma smiled and savored another taste of strawberry ice cream. She would enjoy relating this story to her grandmother and sister. She'd enjoy remembering the look in that handsome man's eyes as he licked his ice cream cone and watched her. As an adventure, this had been an acceptable start.

Emma turned back toward the Savoy, her steps light, a smile lingering on her lips as she enjoyed her prize while she strolled. She couldn't wait to see what would happen next.

SEATED AT A TABLE INSIDE the tea shop across the street from Blankenship and Barrows, Dair MacRae winced with regret as he watched the beauty take a bite from her ice cream cone and sashay away. She'd had an air about her that appealed to him. She'd seemed so…alive.

He hadn't mistaken the interest in her eyes, the encouragement in her smile. He'd have liked to have seen the game to its end, but the woman he'd come to meet had arrived a few minutes early and duty had called. She wouldn't have approved of his actions, and at this point, he couldn't afford to offend her.

A waitress served the pie and tea he'd ordered, then asked if they needed anything more. "Sister Mary Margaret?" he asked.

"I'm fine, thank you, Alasdair," the middle-aged nun responded. "The lemon pie here is such a treat. Are you certain you don't want a piece?"

"I'm certain. I've already indulged my sweet tooth today." He dismissed the waitress with a nod, then got down to business. The hesitation he'd noted in her eyes was giving him a bad feeling. "Your note said you have news for me, Sister?"

"Yes." Her bow-shaped lips dipped into a frown. "Yes, I do, and I fear it's news you'd rather not hear. Alasdair, it tears at my heart to say this, but I'll not be able to fulfill my end of our agreement. I cannot move to Texas and become the new director of the Piney Woods Children's Home."

Dair stiffened. "What?"

"I cannot accept the position."

"But you've already agreed to take it." She'd agreed to his proposition two weeks ago. She'd been excited about the move. "What happened? If it's the money, I'll—"

"It's not the money. You've been very generous and Mother Superior was grateful for the donation." The nun reached across the table and touched his arm. "Alasdair, I've been asked to oversee St. Stephen's Orphanage in Derby. It's where I grew up. I could not say no."

"Sure you can," Dair said, his voice tight. "You can't back out on me, Sister. We have an agreement. I'm counting on you. The children are counting on you."

"I know, and I am sorry to disappoint you." Her light blue eyes gleamed with sincerity. "If it were any other position, I could refuse, but St. Stephen's is my heart. You understand that, I'm sure."

It was a low blow. He did understand, but it didn't mean he had to like it. The good-hearted nun had just put him in a hell of a bind.

Dair drummed his fingers on the table. "Tell me you've found a replacement willing to go in your place. Tell me she'll be joining us in a few moments so that I can conduct an interview."

Sister Mary Margaret attempted a smile, but didn't quite pull it off. "I'm afraid that's not the case. It's not easy to find a trustworthy person willing to uproot herself and move to another country to accept a job of such great responsibility. I've been unable to find a replacement to recommend."

"There must be someone, Sister."

"You should try an agency, Dair."

"No. They don't do a thorough enough investigation into their employees' backgrounds. Besides, I need a personal referral from someone I trust implicitly."

"Alasdair, I know it's important to you to personally choose the right person for this job. I discovered early on in our acquaintance that you have a deep-seated need to control events. But wouldn't it be easier to find the perfect employee in Texas?"

"I'd have to *be* in Texas for that, and making the trip at this juncture simply isn't feasible."

"If this is so important to you, why not?"

"It's complicated, Sister. Just know that I would go if it were possible." The problem needed to be solved from here.

Dair's mind raced. What could he do to change her mind? "I'll double the salary. You could send the extra back to St. Stephen's. You'd be helping both causes."

Her fork slipped from her fingers and clattered to her plate. "But you've already offered a salary far beyond fair."

"It's obviously not enough if you're willing to turn down the position." He'd just have to work a little harder, a little longer, to obtain the extra funds. "Plus, I'll increase the endowment by twenty percent."

That was a lie, of course—he didn't have the funds for that unless he swallowed his pride and asked his friend, Jake Kimball, for help—but she wouldn't know it until it was too late. If he got her to Piney Woods, she'd stay. "I need you, Sister. Please reconsider."

She listened, but another half hour of his most persuasive arguments netted him nothing more than a vow to keep looking for a replacement, and the promise that she'd pray for him. He didn't figure either one would do him much good.

Frustration rode his shoulders, and an all too familiar headache nudged at his brain as he exited the bakery and joined the crowd of shoppers strolling along the sidewalks. Worry had him feeling mean and malicious, so he indulged himself by calling on old talents to pick a few wealthy men's pockets. He managed surprisingly good results. Gentlemen carried more in their pockets these days than they had when he supported himself with the practice.

He worked the streets and fought off the headache until a tingle at the back of his neck warned him that he'd caught somebody's notice. Casually glancing around, he attempted to identify the spy.

There. A ragamuffin boy of about ten. One of London's legion of homeless children, no doubt. Carefully, Dair set his trap.

He led the boy into an alley, then hid behind a wooden crate. When the boy walked by, he grabbed him by the scruff of the neck. The kid squealed as Dair pushed his back against the wall, his feet dangling a foot off the ground. "Hello, boyo. I think it is time you and I had a bit of a chat, don't you?"

"Let me go, mister. I didn't do nothin'."

"I beg to differ. You've been watching me. Why?"

Bravado rang in the boy's tone. "Maybe I'm thinking to hook what you've been busy snitchin'."

"If you have the hands to take it from me, little one, it's yours. First, though, I'll have an answer to my question." He tightened his grip on the boy slightly and smiled a threat. "Why are you dogging my heels?"

The boy's eyes rounded. He'd understood Dair's warning. "It's a job. He's paying me."

"Who is paying you? To do what?"

"Watch. That's all. I'm to watch what you do and report. But don't worry, mister. I won't tell about the dippin' you've been doin', I swear."

Dair gave him a little shake. "How long? How long have you been watching me?"

"Today's me first day. I promise. The regular fella couldn't work today, so I'm filling in. Me mom is sick and she cain't work and we need the money for the little ones."

The regular fellow? Damnation. "Who hired you?"

"I don't know his name!" The boy rattled off a lengthy explanation that netted Dair little useful information beyond the fact that someone was going to some effort to track his movements. Why?

The most obvious, and disturbing, reason was that someone might have made the connection between Alasdair MacRae and the Highland Riever. But if that were the case, why was he still walking freely around London?

How had he missed being under surveillance?

It couldn't be the police following him. He wouldn't have missed them. So, who was it? What had the watchers witnessed? The Riever at work? Or even worse, Dair's…incidents? For just a moment, he closed his eyes.

Then the boy squirmed and tried to escape. Dair tightened his hold. "Listen up. I've a message to pass along to your employer. I request a face-to-face meeting. Tell him to name a time and place and deliver it to my current residence. I trust he already has that information."

"Yessir. I'll pass it along, sir. I certainly will."

Dair grabbed the day's ill-gotten gains from his pocket

and tucked the cash into the boy's shirt pocket. "After that, I suggest you find a different line of work. If I catch you within eyeshot again, you'll not get off so easy."

"Yessir. Thank you, sir. You'll never see me again, sir."

The boy's face was alight with gratitude at the windfall. Nevertheless, the moment his feet touched the ground, he scampered off.

Dair left the alley brooding, the headache continuing its persistent, though thankfully slight, throb. Hadn't this day gone from heaven and the delightful Miss Emma straight to quitting-nun and spying-urchin hell?

He needed to take this one problem at a time. First, the Piney Woods Children's Home. He need not panic. Just because Sister Mary Margaret refused him didn't mean his plans were for naught. He still had time to find the perfect person for the job. After all, Sister Mary Margaret surely wasn't the only woman in the world looking to do good works. Dair simply didn't meet too many of them.

He ordinarily concentrated his attention on women who liked to be bad. Women like the darling, daring, delectable Emma Tate.

Regarding the other problem, perhaps the boy's employer would contact him. If not, Dair would put his own people to work. Angus Fraser had his finger on the pulse of London. If anyone could find out who was watching Dair and why, Angus could.

Hearing someone shout his name, he looked up. Jake Kimball waved him over to a cab. "I've escaped the mayhem at Bankston House and I'm headed to Gaylords for a nice, quiet meal. Care to join me?"

Dair didn't hesitate. He climbed into the cab and settled back against the soft leather seat with a sigh.

Kimball's brow arched. "So what has you looking like a boy who's lost his favorite slingshot?"

Dair was willing to share only one of his immediate problems with his friend. "I need a woman."

"Can it wait until after supper, or I shall I drop you off at Fanny's along the way?"

One corner of Dair's mouth lifted in a rueful grin. "I lost my nun, Jake."

Kimball frowned and pursed his lips. "Hmm. I didn't figure you for a man who entertained those sorts of fantasies. Did she have one of those wooden rulers?"

This time Dair chuckled out loud. "I've a project in the works that requires the services of a trustworthy woman of good character, superior morals and keen intelligence. Do you have any idea where I can find such a paragon?"

"Actually, I might." Jake waved and winked at a pretty woman strolling along the sidewalk. "You could follow my lead and do what I've decided to do."

Dair knew that Jake had a project of his own that required a woman's touch. He'd recently assumed guardianship of his own set of orphans—his late sister's children. "You found a governess?"

"No. I've realized that the children don't need a governess. They need permanence. They need love. What the children need is a mother."

Surprised, Dair gave his friend a long look. Though they'd known each other for years and considered one another a good friend, both Dair and Jake kept parts of their lives private. Still, Dair knew Jake Kimball well enough to assume that he had something…different…in mind when it came to providing said mother. "And where do you propose to find one of those?"

Jake Kimball flashed his pirate's grin. "I intend to advertise for one."

Oh, those poor children. "All right, Kimball," Dair said with a sigh. "What crazy scheme have you cooked up this time?"

CHAPTER TWO

"COME WITH ME, EMMA," a man's voice whispered in her ear. His lips nuzzled the sensitive skin of her neck. His large hand cupped the fullness of her breast, his thumb dragging with exquisite slowness across her nipple. "Come with me."

A hand shook her shoulder. "Wake up, Emma!"

Emma clung to sleep, clung to her dream. She didn't want to awaken. *Come with me.*

Sharp fingernails sank into her skin, shook her again. "Emma! It's time to get dressed. We don't want to be late."

In her room at the Savoy Hotel three days after her ice cream escapade, Emma opened her eyes to her youngest sister's impatient glare. The remnants of her dream evaporated as reality intruded, and she recalled the business before them. Yes, she *did* want to be late. She wanted to be entirely too late. "This is such a bad idea."

"You're not backing out, so just hush," Kat McBride said.

Sitting up, Emma took a good look at her sister. Always the actress, Kat was costumed and ready for the farce—a buxom, gray-haired woman wearing an ugly dress and wire-rimmed glasses that failed to hide the gleam of excitement in her eyes. Emma flopped back down on her bed. "I can't believe I agreed to do this."

"I can't believe you're acting like such an old fuddy," Kat responded, tugging her sister from the bed and onto her feet.

"Really, Em. Where's your sense of adventure? Don't tell me you used it all up playing pin-the-tail-on-the-mannequin the other day. That was an amusing prank, true, but this plan…it's McBride Menace material."

Emma scowled at Kat. "We're not children anymore. We need to think before we act. I was lucky I didn't get caught."

"Oh, stop being realistic. That totally spoils the mood."

Emma rubbed her eyes and took a longer look at the woman literally beaming with excitement. Was this really her youngest sister? The same sister who'd seldom shown enthusiasm for anything in the years since tangling with a bigamist liar who'd "married" her, got her with child, then died at the hands of an outlaw? The same Kat McBride who'd hardly smiled since losing her daughter in a wagon accident? Why, Emma could hardly believe it.

"You know what?" Kat continued. "You're right. We're not children anymore. But then neither is our grandmother. I'd like to think we at least can be as adventuresome as Monique Day."

"Oh, my." As adventuresome as Monique? There was wicked, and then there was Monique. Their grandmother changed men and lifestyles at the drop of a bonnet. "This is worse than I thought."

Kat adjusted her wig, then carefully rubbed an itch at the end of her nose so as not to displace her face paint. Staring over the top of her eyeglasses, she added, "It'll be exciting, Emma. You'll see. Now, go put on your dress. The yellow one, remember? You look delicious in that gown."

An hour later, standing in a line of women outside of Bankston House in St. James Square, Emma recalled her sister's comment and smothered a snort. "You were wrong, Kat."

"Hmm?" Kat frowned down at her bosom and surreptitiously shifted the stuffing.

"Standing in line with a dozen other women competing for the chance to marry a man I've never met, all the while accompanied by my younger sister who is dressed in a wretched disguise is not exciting. It's humiliating. Demeaning, even."

"*Wretched?* I'll have you know this is a wonderful disguise." Kat smiled smugly and patted her prodigious, well-padded bosom. "People get out of my way. You're approaching this entire exercise with the wrong attitude. Maybe it could be considered demeaning if you truly were here in answer to Jake Kimball's advertisement for a wife, but we're here for a bigger purpose."

"We're here to steal from him!"

"Shush!" Kat snapped, casting furtive glances over her shoulders. Then, lowering her voice, she added, "But only because he stole from me first."

"But what if you're wrong? What if Kimball doesn't have your necklace? What if we get caught snooping? Do they still transport felons to New Zealand?"

"I'm not wrong." Kat folded her arms. "He has it and I want it back. I'll get it back."

The item in question was one of a trio of unique jeweled pendants given to Emma, Mari, and Kat McBride years ago by an unusual woman under curious circumstances. The necklaces were the McBride sisters' most prized possessions, and Kat's had gone missing almost five years ago—shortly after Jake Kimball had tried to buy it from her.

Last week during a visit to the London Zoo, Kat stumbled across both Jake Kimball and a piece of information that led her to believe he was in possession of her prized piece of jewelry. Then, upon learning that he'd placed an advertisement for a wife in the newspaper, Kat had concocted her plan.

Kat and her concoctions. Emma shook her head and despite her best intentions, a smile played upon her lips. How long had it been since Kat concocted anything? Emma couldn't deny that this was nice to see.

"This is the best way for me to get my property back," Kat continued. "Rather than humiliated, Emma, you should feel proud. Just think. Your actions will help strike a blow against a man so boorish as to marry a stranger off the street in order to provide maternal care to five orphaned children so he can ignore the fact he's their guardian and gallivant off to the far reaches of the world. He's a scoundrel, Emma. Why…"

Having heard the tirade a number of times already, Emma tuned her sister out. Humiliation. Maybe that wasn't the right word for the emotion rumbling around inside her, after all. Actually, Emma was feeling a lot of things at the moment. Excitement. Apprehension. Guilt. Envy.

Envy? She blinked. Considered the idea. Grimaced. How pitiful was that? She was jealous that Kat was the one having all the fun.

With a little kick, Emma sent a small rock skittering across the cobblestones. It was true. The silver-eyed Dair and his scandalous dare had fueled her inner imp to life, and she was feeling green-eyed because *she* wanted to be the one wearing the disguise. Pretending to be the outrageous and outspoken Wilhemina Peters sounded so much more entertaining than playing herself—boring old widowed schoolteacher Emma Tate.

Emphasis on boring. And old. Boring and old.

She'd turn thirty this summer.

Sighing, Emma watched a child in the park across the street attempt to get a paper kite airborne. In moments of self-honesty, she admitted the milestone likely lay at the root of her discontent. Her birthday loomed like a dull gray cloud on her horizon. Or maybe more like a buzzard. A big old black buzzard.

Get a hold of yourself, Emma. Pity parties are so unattractive.

Emma eyed another rock, gave it a kick, too, then sighed again. Despite her current discontent, she didn't want to change her entire life. She enjoyed teaching. She liked living in Fort Worth. She could find a husband easily enough if that's what she wanted. Since Casey's death, she'd stepped out with a respectable number of men, and she'd been seriously courted a time or two. No one had captured her heart, however. No one fired her blood enough to risk a relationship. After having known true love in the past, Emma wasn't prepared to settle for less. She'd have powerful, vigilant and true love or she'd have none.

Right now, anyway. If she changed her mind and let it be known around town that she was looking, men would come calling again. Maybe she'd reach that point someday. Maybe she'd be willing to settle. But not yet. She wasn't there yet. All in all, life was good. She was a content woman.

Content, except for being bored. And old.

She scowled at a pigeon pecking at the grass beside the walk. Of the three McBride sisters, only she could claim that she'd never had a true adventure.

She wanted one, darn it. Was that so awful? And playing her boring old self in a scheme of her sister's making wasn't at all what she had in mind.

Besides, this plan was all Kat's idea. Kat's adventure, not

hers. Once again, Emma was relegated to a supporting role which was precisely the function she wished to forsake.

That must be the source of her peevishness. *She's* the one who'd come to England looking for adventure. Leave it to Kat to be the one to find it.

Now that's mean, Emma Tate, her conscience chastised. *Stop it. Kat has had a rough time. Her false marriage, losing her reputation. Losing her child, for God's sake!*

Emma's cynical side fired back. *My own life hasn't been a bed of roses, either. I know loss, too. Didn't I lose my husband, the love of my life, at the ripe old age of twenty? Before he'd given me the child I long for?*

True, and that was bad. No doubt about it. But in her life since then, the choices she'd made since being widowed were just that. Her choices. She'd chosen to be the good girl, the dependable one. The teacher. The babysitter. The friend. The niece. The sister. The daughter.

What happened to the woman? The companion? The sweetheart? The lover? Whose fault was it that the woman had gotten lost?

Emma sighed. Her fault. Her choice.

Maybe if she wasn't so lonely, she wouldn't feel this envy, this discontent. Maybe if the ice cream incident had ended with something more adventurous than pecan sprinkles—like say, a kiss—then she'd be more inclined to sit back and let Kat enjoy her turn at mischief. As it was, she simply couldn't summon any enthusiasm for the scheme.

Nevertheless, despite her misgivings, Emma wanted to succeed. She wanted Kat to find her necklace. Ever since it had disappeared, Emma had felt a little tug of awkwardness, of incompleteness, each time she donned her own.

"I want this to work," she announced when her sister's

diatribe finally wound down. "Honestly, I do. I just hope I can do a good job. It's been a long time since I've tried to charm a man. I'm out of practice."

"You'll do fine, Em." Kat reached over and smoothed an errant blond curl back behind her sister's ear. "You look stunning, and men always find you fascinating. While it's true there are some pretty girls here and you are older than most of them—"

"Thanks for building my confidence."

"—as long as you refrain from turning on the frost with Kimball the way you do with most men, I feel certain we'll walk away with an invitation to his house party next weekend. Just remember, Emma. That's the goal. Advance to the second round of the bride hunt."

The bride hunt. Emma had a sudden vision of a fox outfitted in a cummerbund darting across a field with hounds wearing wedding veils nipping at its heels.

She tried to keep the goal uppermost in her mind when her turn to interview arrived. After all, the sooner this task was accomplished, the sooner she could get back to her own interests. She gave her sister's hand a quick squeeze, squared her shoulders, pasted on a bright smile, and entered the Bankston House study.

A man she assumed was Kimball sat behind a large carved mahogany desk. Dark hair. Blue eyes. He was a handsome enough man for a scoundrel, she supposed.

"Good afternoon, Miss…?"

This is it. The curtain rises. You might not be the natural actress Kat is, but you can do it, Emma.

"Mrs.," she corrected. "Mrs. Tate. I've been widowed for some time now. This is my companion, Mrs. Wilhemina Peters."

The man behind the desk nodded toward "Mrs. Peters," then addressed Emma. "My condolences on your loss. I'm Jake Kimball. This is Mrs. Pippin—" he gestured toward an elderly woman seated on a sofa, then nodded toward a figure who entered the room through a side door and came to stand beside Kimball's desk "—and Mr. MacRae."

Emma smiled at Mrs. Pippin, then turned to acknowledge Mr. MacRae. The polite smile on her face slipped.

Silver eyes. Chiseled cheekbones. Alasdair.

Dair. I dare you...

Shocked, Emma didn't move, didn't breathe, didn't blink. Her heartbeat pounded. Her blood hummed. A shiver crawled up her spine. Without taking his gaze from hers, Dair MacRae propped a hip on the edge of Kimball's desk, his movement slow with a jungle cat's grace.

Then, he smiled. A slow, sensuous, secretive grin.

She tingled in response. *Oh, my. Oh my oh my oh my.*

For a long minute, they could have been the only two people in the room. The air thickened. Emma went warm. Everything feminine inside her seemed to lift and swell.

She held her breath, waiting for him to mention their earlier meeting. What would this do to Kat's plan? Were they ruined before they ever began?

Finally, Dair spoke, his voice a smooth, mellow, intimate sound. "It's a pleasure to meet you, Mrs. Tate."

Relieved, she attempted a polite nod. Feared it came off more like a twitch. Clearing her throat, she croaked, "Mr. MacRae."

His penetrating gaze seemed to see into her soul. "Alasdair, please. Or Dair. My friends call me Dair."

Though her heart continued to pound, Emma finally

managed to drag her gaze away from the man when Mrs. Pippin said hello.

While the woman and Kat exchanged niceties, Emma managed to collect herself. Apparently—for now, anyway—the game continued.

Jake Kimball offered her a wide smile. "So, Mrs. Tate. Judging by your delightful accent, I gather you're from America?"

Emma tried her best to ignore Dair MacRae's mesmerizing stare as she responded to Kimball's questions. Nervous, she tried hard not to fidget and give herself away as she told the stream of lies. Although, it would help if the silver-eyed jungle cat looked somewhere—anywhere—else.

When she stumbled over a falsehood and Kat jumped to the rescue with a lie of her own, Dair MacRae tilted his head to one side, his smoky gaze still intent, but now also considering. Emma felt compelled to reach out and smooth away the thought line in his brow.

Quickly, she sat on her hand. *What in the world is the matter with you? Remember the woman's scarf he pulled from his pocket? The way he disappeared? The man is a rogue.*

As Kimball continued his questioning, MacRae lifted a round crystal paperweight from his friend's desk and tossed it from hand to hand. His big hands matched the rest of him in size, Emma noted, yet he caught the crystal with a gentle touch. She'd always found gentleness in big men appealing. Growing up in a town full of cowboys, she saw a lot of big men. She seldom considered any of them gentle.

Not that Dair MacRae was necessarily a gentle man. Not at all. His relaxed posture failed to hide his predatory air and by nature, predators weren't gentle.

Kat launched into a sales pitch enumerating Emma's good qualities. Emma didn't appreciate being talked about as if she weren't in the room, though she guessed she'd brought it on herself. MacRae had distracted her. Was *still* distracting her. She waited on pins and needles for the words *ice cream* to come out of his mouth and undoubtedly ruin her chances to win the invitation so important to Kat.

"So you see, Mr. Kimball," her sister concluded. "It would have been foolish of Emma not to accept the bribe."

Dair MacRae's mouth silently formed the word *Emma,* then he slowly licked his lips.

Oh, my heavens. Emma shivered in response, then forced her attention back to the conversation at hand.

Jake Kimball continued to address Kat. "And her hobbies, what does she like to read?"

"History books. She's interested in foreign lands. She has a particular interest in Scotland, as her family originated in that country, and she fell in love with the Highlands during one of our visits there."

"An intelligent beauty," MacRae said. He winked at her, then added, "Scotland is one of the finest places on earth."

Emma's cheeks warmed. She didn't understand the game here. Was he not going to mention their previous meeting at all? If so, why not? Perhaps the wife she'd suspected yesterday? The mistress? Since she couldn't very well ask those questions, she replied with the first thing that popped into her mind. "You're a Scot, Mr. MacRae?"

"By blood, if not by birth. Actually, I was born in Texas, but I left there long ago. I'm a wanderer by nature."

"Oh?" A fellow Texan. Imagine that. Emma leaned forward. Maybe there was no wife, after all. No ties that bound. *Wishful thinking, Emma.* Beware. Besides, why should it matter to her anyway? "What's your favorite place to visit?"

He cocked his head and considered the question. "The islands of Hawaii are particularly appealing."

"The Hawaiian Islands?" Emma mentally pictured brilliant flowers, perfumed sea breezes, and an azure ocean lapping gently at naked lovers rolling in the sand on a deserted beach. He had dark hair and broad shoulders and…oh, stop it! "I've always been fascinated by that part of the world."

This daydreaming indulgence was getting out of hand.

While Kat and Jake Kimball continued conversing *about* her, Emma asked herself what was the matter *with* her? It's not as if she'd never received a man's attention before. To be honest, if not modest, she was accustomed to such notice. Every woman garnered attention in a male-dominated frontier town. However, it wasn't her habit to react this way to a man, especially not one she just met. What was it about Dair MacRae that sent her off into a fantasy land?

Then her eyes widened and her brows winged up as a thought occurred to her—a wicked, exciting, stimulating idea. Was this the sort of escapade she'd come to England in search of? Not an ice cream bet about a donkey tail, but a man? *This* man?

Come with me, whispered her dream man.

I dare you, Alasdair had said.

No, surely not, the practical Emma asserted. She wanted adventure without danger, didn't she? This man exuded danger, so much so that the smoldering look in his eyes sent shivers up and down her spine.

Kimball and Kat continued their back-and-forth banter

until finally, MacRae interrupted. "Excuse me, Jake, but perhaps I should mention that you've run over time with Mrs. Tate, and you have asked hardly any questions on the list."

"Oh, yes. You're right. I apologize." Kimball jerked his attention away from Kat and scanned the piece of paper in front of him. Seconds later, he looked at Emma and gently asked, "You said you've been widowed for awhile. Why have you not remarried?"

Emma's thoughts drifted back to her husband, and a sad smile played upon her lips. She and Casey had grown up together, been friends much of their lives. She'd miss him and mourn him for the rest of her life. "I loved my husband deeply. I've yet to find another man who will share with me a love that is strong, vigilant and true."

MacRae's brows arched. "Mrs. Peters" rolled her eyes and let out a soft, but audible groan. Kimball asked, "Will you not settle for less, Emma Tate?"

She opened her mouth to tell him that yes, she'd agree to the loveless marriage he promised. Somehow, though, after she sneaked a glance at MacRae, other words, surprising words, emerged. "No, I will not."

Kimball sat back in his chair. Kat gave Emma a quick, hard pinch. "Sorry," Kat said, her tone oozing innocence. "There was a fly on your arm. Just shooing it away."

"I see," Kimball said.

So did Emma, and she wanted to kick herself. By speaking from her heart, she'd ruined Kat's plan. She should have prevaricated. She should have pretended. She should have told the man an out-and-out lie.

Dismay washed through her. The McBride Menace in her was shamed. Obviously, she needed more practice at pretending. Her skills in that area weren't rusty, they were ruined. It had been years since she'd tried to be someone other than herself. Years since she'd set out to attract a man. And she'd never attempted to attract one man while lusting after another. In the same room. She'd needed more time to prepare.

She'd have needed a lifetime to prepare.

She cast a look toward her sister and silently conveyed her apology. This plan obviously hadn't worked, but they need not give up. They could try something else. Since they wouldn't be invited to Chatham Park to compete for the position of Mrs. Jake Kimball, perhaps they could gain entrance to the estate under the guise of being servants. They could forge some references, scrounge up a maid's costume or two. It could work. It'd be fun. It'd be an adventure.

Then Jake Kimball shocked her and everyone else in the room by extending an invitation to his country house.

Holy Hannah. I did it. We're in. Once her surprise waned enough for Emma to think, she rose from her seat and accepted the invitation. "Why, yes. Thank you. We'll be pleased to attend, although, I must say I'm surprised. I didn't think—"

"We didn't think you'd be so perceptive, sir," Kat said, jumping to her feet. She poked Emma in the side with her elbow. "Some men don't recognize treasure when it's right in front of their face."

"Oh, I recognize treasure," Kimball replied, addressing Kat. "You can count on that. I am a treasure hunter, after all. And just so you know, once I find a treasure, I don't give it up."

While his friend spoke, MacRae's intense stare never left Emma. *Me, too,* he seemed to say. In fact, she could almost hear his voice speaking those words in her head. It was a curious thing, like one of those moments she sometimes shared with her sisters when they seemed to read one another's mind.

But Dair MacRae wasn't her sister, and she didn't know him as well as she knew her own name. She didn't know the man at all, but she knew the man was dangerous. He wasn't her adventure.

She wanted to ask if he'd be joining them at Chatham Park. She wanted to ask him if the scarf had been his wife's.

Kimball escorted the women to the door, then bowed over their hands, one at a time. "Until the weekend."

"The weekend," Kat replied, her eyes sparkling and alive.

Alasdair MacRae moved to stand beside Kimball. He nodded to Kat, then took hold of Emma's hand. "It's been a pleasure to meet you, my dear. Until next weekend."

Yes! He'll be there!

Confound it, Emma. Get a hold of yourself.

I'd rather he get a hold of me.

Then he brought her hand to his lips and kissed it. Lightning sizzled up her arm and Emma shuddered. She managed no more than a shaky smile as they took their leave, and it wasn't until the door closed behind them that she felt freed from a sensual spell.

"We did it, Emma!" Kat exclaimed, throwing her arms around her sister and giving her a quick, hard hug before tugging her down the street away from Bankston House. "You were awful, but you're still obviously superior to most of these other women, and Jake Kimball was smart enough to recognize it. Just think, a week from now, I may well have my necklace back. Wouldn't that be wonderful, Em?"

"Yes," Emma agreed, staring at the spot on the back of her hand that still tingled from Dair MacRae's kiss.

"I'm so excited. That was fun. Wasn't that fun, Emma?"

"Yes. Yes, it was." With the stress of the interview behind her, Emma took a moment to savor the pleasure of accomplishment at a pair of successful bits of mischief. While neither the ice cream shenanigans nor today's effort exactly counted as the escapade she craved, she *had* dipped her toes back into trouble-making and enjoyed the experience. It reminded her that she'd always relished her stints at being a Menace. Growing up and becoming responsible did have its drawbacks.

Then, she recalled that look in Dair MacRae's eyes as he referenced the upcoming weekend.

Growing up had its advantages, too.

CLOUDS ROLLED IN AND OBSCURED the sun as it sank toward the western horizon. Dair flipped up the collar of his seaman's jacket as fat raindrops began to splatter against the cobblestones. He took a circuitous route to his destination, intent upon losing anyone who might attempt to follow him. By the time he paused outside the Dog and Duck Tavern, rain fell in a steady, chilling sheet, and Dair felt secure that if anyone had begun this journey with him, he finished it alone.

He sucked in a breath and tried to will away the nagging headache that plagued him almost constantly of late. He couldn't afford the distraction right now.

He opened the pub's door and stepped inside. Tobacco smoke swirled in the air, mixing with the scent of fried fish, spilled ale and unwashed bodies. Dair made his way to the table in the back where a man awaited him.

"What can I get you, luv?" a buxom barmaid asked.

"Whiskey." Dair took his seat and nodded. "Hello, Angus."

The grizzled old Scot scowled at him, his bushy eyebrows meeting in the middle. "MacRae. Tis a lousy afternoon for a meet, and I canna say I'm thrilled with the fare, either. The fish is old and the whiskey is watered. The proprietor should be shot."

Dair smothered a smile. "My apologies, old friend. I'll schedule Buckingham Palace next time."

Angus Fraser snorted. "I dinna doubt ye could do it."

Conversation halted when the barmaid brought Dair's drink and remained a moment to flirt. Once the two men were alone, Fraser said, "If this is about yer most recent request, I have little information for ye, I fear. I've had men on ye for the past three days, but they've seen no sign that you're being watched." He paused significantly, then added, "Handy, that, considering yer late-night activities."

Dair ignored the veiled reference to the Riever, his thoughts on the problem at hand. Had his apprehension of the boy resulted in the end of the surveillance? Perhaps, but he didn't trust it. Too many pieces of the puzzle remained missing to put together a proper picture. "Stay on it, if you would, Angus. It may well be a suspicious spouse, but I'd like confirmation."

"Aye." The grizzled Scot nodded. "I'll do me best. Speakin' of doing me best, I need a wee more time to dispose of yer latest delivery. Emeralds like those require a special client."

Dair considered the question. "Take another month. After that, dump them. Now, I have another task for you. I need information about a pair of Americans currently in London on a holiday. The name is McBride. Sisters, Emma and Katrina, from Fort Worth, Texas. I want a thorough report, focused especially upon the widow, Emma. Her married name is Tate." He added a few more details he'd learned from grilling Jake after his friend confessed to recognizing the sisters despite Katrina's disguise.

"Do you want financial and—"

"I want everything. I want to know the state of her investments, who her lovers are, if she owns any pets. I want you to dig deep enough that you could tell me the color of the lace on her corset if I asked."

Fraser rolled his tongue around the inside of his cheek, then spoke in a droll tone. "That's a detail yer more likely to discover than me."

Dair's lips twisted with a grin. The man did have a point.

"We've a wee bit of a problem, however. I need to leave London. I've business that requires my attention and I intend to depart as soon as possible. Would ye be trusting me man Tompkins with the work?"

"He's the man who gathered the information about the Carrington diamonds last winter, correct?"

Fraser smiled fondly. "A more beautiful diadem I have yet to see. Aye, that was Tompkins. The Highland Riever is a favorite of his ever since. Twas a nice commission ye gave him."

Dair gave him a cautionary frown. Though the Dog and Duck's status as a den of thieves made for a safe meeting location for their business, it also made it a risky place to bandy about identities best left unmentioned. "Tompkins is not to know this information is for me. Have him deliver it to Warfield House in care of Her Grace. Within three days."

The Scotsman's eyes rounded. "The duchess? I thought ye ended that liaison."

Dair shrugged. Sister Mary Margaret's decision had affected a number of his plans. "I've reconsidered the emeralds."

Avarice lit Fraser's expression. "Excellent! Excellent! I'll make it a point to return to London at the earliest possible opportunity in order to assist ye with their disposal."

Ten minutes later, with arrangements completed, Dair exited the Dog and Duck. Darkness shrouded the city. Street traffic remained sparse as the cold, unrelenting rain continued to splatter against the sidewalks and cobblestone streets. He plunged his hands into his pockets, hunched his shoulders against the chill, and headed up the street toward a main thoroughfare where he'd have better luck catching a cab back to Bankston House and the rooms Jake provided him. Half a block away, he realized he'd better detour to his rented rooms nearby.

Ordinarily Dair reserved the Whitechapel lodgings for activities related to the Riever, but tonight he sought the space simply for the proximity of a bed. The ache in his head was intensifying in such a way that Dair doubted he'd make it back to Mayfair if he tried.

Besides, better Jake didn't see him in this sorry state. He'd insist on sending for a physician or a priest or even a whore to exorcize Dair of this plaguing pain. Never mind that Dair had already tried all three treatments. Nothing helped. Not powders, not prayers, and not physical release. Only sleep granted him surcease when the headache reached proportions such as these. One day, if he were lucky, he'd go to sleep and never wake.

All in all, that was not such a bad way to go. He'd certainly flirted with harder deaths during his thirty-four years. The gunshot in Italy. The knifing in New York. The fire in Java that gave him nightmares to this day. No, he wouldn't complain about meeting his end in such a manner.

Because meeting his end, sooner rather than later, was what lay in store. Dair was dying. He had a tumor on his brain.

He'd always expected to hear a death sentence someday, though he'd anticipated receiving it in a court of law rather than a physician's office. In truth, death by hanging sounded infinitely preferable to being eaten alive from inside. He'd decided he wouldn't let it go that far. When the time came, Dair would choose the moment and manner. He couldn't control this part of his life, but he'd damn sure control his death.

The hammering in his head increased, making it more difficult for Dair to think. Making him wonder if the six-to-eight months his physician had estimated was realistic. Lord, he hoped so. He'd made little headway in finding a replacement for Sister Mary Margaret. Plus, he'd need every available minute to gather the necessary funds. After all, raising children in this day and age wasn't an inexpensive proposition.

And damned if he'd die and abandon them. Nor would he saddle Jake with responsibility for their care. His friend had his own child-related problems to manage at the moment, his own obligations. The Home was Dair's responsibility.

The pain escalated. His vision blurred and he broke out in a sweat despite the chilling cold. Only sheer determination kept him on his feet. Finally, the door to his lodgings appeared before him, and he battled his way up the three flights of stairs to his room. With a trembling hand, he fit his key in the lock. He stumbled into the room, onto the bed, managing one final coherent thought.

He'd better grab Millicent's rubies, too, while he was at it.

Strathardle Glen, Scotland

THE STONE CIRCLE RUINS ROSE like jagged teeth against a brilliant blue afternoon sky. Hamish Campbell leaned casually against the largest of the standing rocks and watched Angus Fraser huff and puff his way up the grassy mound. The fat old thief's physical condition was as weak as his character. Hamish sneered with disgust. He didn't like dealing with worms such as Fraser, men who would betray a longtime business associate for a relatively small amount of gold, but sometimes needs required.

Hamish stepped out of the stone's shadow and revealed himself to Fraser. "Hello, Angus."

"Mornin', sir."

"Lovely day isn't it?"

"Aye. Tis always nice to come home. Scotland's air breathes fresh life into a man too long in England."

"Yes, it does. You should be grateful that I required you meet me here rather than in London." Fraser shrugged halfheartedly and Hamish continued, "So, what new information do you have for me today?"

Angus scratched behind his ear and stared blindly at the cup-marks on one of the standing stones. "MacRae is headed for a wee bit of a holiday at Mr. Jake Kimball's country estate."

Interesting. "And why is that?"

Angus made a brief and succinct report about Kimball's bride hunt. "Dair requested a report on two women who are scheduled to attend—Miss Katrina McBride and Mrs. Emma Tate from Texas."

Hamish's head came up like a hound on a scent. "Texas?"

"Aye. He seemed keen for the information. Once I got

a look at the ladies meself I understood why. They're beauties. Both of them."

"Hmm..." They could be old-crone ugly for all Hamish cared. A McBride from Texas. He clasped his hands behind his back and stared out over the glen as excitement fired in his veins. A McBride from Texas with a connection to Alasdair MacRae. Had his hunch paid off, then? Was his investment in time and manpower about to bear fruit?

Was the treasure finally within his grasp?

In the months that had followed the card game, he'd begun to doubt. Alasdair MacRae's actions indicated he knew nothing of the Prize, and Hamish suspected he might be wasting his resources. Until now. A McBride and a MacRae. This MacRae. The Guardian's son.

Roslin MacRae's son.

"You have a man on duty at Chatham Park?" Hamish asked, expecting confirmation.

Fraser frowned and rubbed the back of his neck. "I had a wee bit of a problem with that."

Ice all but dripped from the word as Hamish demanded, "Clarify."

"MacRae discovered one of my watchers," Fraser replied.

He explained how Dair MacRae had spotted the boy he'd had on the job, and with every word the older man spoke, Hamish's fury grew. Now was not the time to rouse MacRae's suspicions. Nor was it the moment to leave him unobserved. In a hard, flat tone, he stated, "You've failed."

"No, no, it's all right," Fraser quickly assured Hamish. "He doesn't know it was me. I arranged for him to receive information that the person who had him followed is the husband of one of his lovers. He's quite the swordsman, ye ken."

What Hamish *kenned* was that Angus Fraser had tipped his hand and lost his quarry. That was unacceptable. Dair MacRae was an intelligent man and now he'd be suspicious and on his guard.

"As far as me not having anyone at Chatham Park," Angus continued, "I dinna believe it to be a problem. He'll not be doing any business of interest while in the country. He's there for his friend. I've put word out about town that I'm to know the moment MacRae returns to town."

If he even returned to London. Hamish's mouth settled into a grim line. "I need someone at Chatham Park. Immediately."

Scowling, Fraser shook his head. "I don't have anyone in the area. My contacts are all in cities."

"Then you are no longer of any use to me." In fact, Angus Fraser was now a liability. Fraser could lead Dair MacRae back to him and that simply wouldn't do. In light of today's information, Hamish had every intention of revealing himself to MacRae. Eventually.

At the time and place of his choosing.

He clapped the older man on the back. "I'm afraid our arrangement must come to an end."

Fraser sighed heavily, then shrugged. "Aye. All right. Tis fine enough with me. I like Dair MacRae. I haven't liked spying on him. So if you'll just pay me me final fee?"

Fool. Hamish Campbell cleared his throat. "You're a Highlander, Fraser. Do you know where it is you stand?"

Fraser looked around, then dragged his hand down his jaw, uncertain as to what his employer asked. "Ye mean, a fairy ring?"

"Aye. You see, fairies built their *sithean* before the great Flood of Noah. Locals call this one Cnoc a Chiuil, music knoll, because they often hear sprightly dance music coming from inside it. Do you hear anything, Angus?"

"Nae."

"Pity. It's said that the little folk can make themselves any size they wish, and that anyone who has the opportunity to see them dance in their underground halls can be so mesmerized that years pass with great rapidity."

Apprehension skittered across Fraser's face. "I have heard such tales of fairies. My mother said they dance and revel on moonlight nights on the moors."

"Do you know how to defend against fairies?"

The older man glanced back down the hill, but didn't respond. Hamish took his silence as denial. "You can use iron, the name of God or a horseshoe over your door."

"For good luck."

"Ah…luck." Hamish smiled. "Luck is a funny thing. It can be good or bad. Sometimes, luck can simply run out…as did yours when you allowed MacRae to discover that he was being watched."

Hamish pulled his gun and shot Angus Fraser in the chest. As Fraser let out a cry and fell to his knees, he added, "Consider it your good luck that I brought you home to die."

CHAPTER THREE

EMMA'S STOMACH CHURNED AS the carriage turned on the drive that led up to Chatham Park ten days after what she thought of as the Infamous Interview. She looked forward to the long weekend with a combination of excitement and nervousness.

She couldn't wait to see Dair MacRae once again.

A discreet pair of questions in one of London's better dress shops had confirmed the fact that he was not, in fact, married. Emma felt her cheeks warm with a blush, but it didn't stop her from thinking about the man. She'd hardly stopped thinking about him since the day of the interview. The idea that he might be her adventure wouldn't leave her alone.

Perhaps she could enjoy a temporary liaison with Mr. Alasdair MacRae.

The wicked thought had been whispering through her mind for days now, but she was trying to ignore it. She was. Really. Following through on such a scandalous notion would take more courage than she possessed, would require more mischief than she wanted to make.

Yet what better place to indulge in mischief-making than in a foreign country where no one knew her?

As the carriage took another bend in the tulip-tree-lined road, Emma studied Chatham Park. She'd never seen a building quite like it before. From its Baroque front to the Greek Revival portico, to the medieval-styled high tower, or belvedere, Chatham Park was a conglomerate of styles that would give her architect father a headache just looking at it. Emma counted four wings, three stories high, extending from the main building. Finding Kat's necklace in a place this big would take a miracle.

As the coach pulled into the circular drive, Emma spied Jake Kimball standing on a third-floor balcony. Her gaze moved past him to a figure framed in a second-story window. Alasdair MacRae.

Oh, my. Excitement sizzled through her.

Moments later, the carriage rolled to a stop. The sisters climbed a broad flight of stone steps and entered Chatham Park's great hall. Emma gazed in wonder at the painted ceiling, the paintings on the wall, the marble sculptures and rich Persian carpets. Why, this place truly was as grand as a palace.

Its king paused halfway down the stairs. "Ladies, welcome," Jake Kimball said. "I'm delighted you could join us. Alasdair MacRae, you remember Mrs. Tate and Mrs. Peters."

Emma's pulse quickened as she spied MacRae looming in the doorway of what appeared to be a library. He wore dark colors from head to toe and the intensity in his silver stare seemed at odds with his friendly smile. "I certainly do. Ladies, it's a pleasure to see you again."

Emma offered him a hesitant smile.

Kimball asked his friend to show Emma to her room, and a few minutes later, Emma followed MacRae down a long hallway. He smelled of sandalwood and spice, and he moved with silent, powerful strides. She felt as though she should attempt to make small talk. Maybe something along the lines of *Excuse me, Dair. Would you care to engage in a liaison with me?*

Emma almost tripped over her own feet at that rogue thought.

When minutes ticked by without any attempt on his part to engage in conversation, Emma grew even more unsettled. Did he plan to ignore their previous meeting, even in private? Is that what she wanted? Maybe she should bring it up. She frowned at his back and wished he wasn't such an enigma. Except, enigmas were intriguing, weren't they?

Finally, he halted outside a door almost at the end of the hallway. "Emma, your suite."

Instinct told her to remain in the hallway when he opened the door and stepped inside. Only when he glanced over his shoulder and arched a challenging brow did she manage to move. She'd never been able to ignore a dare. Taking a step forward, she caught her first glimpse of the "snow globe room" and her cautiousness faded in the face of her delight.

"It's magical," she breathed. Snow globes lined the walls and adorned the tabletops and decorated every space in the room available for display. They contained carousel horses and toy trains and village scenes. One section of shelves was devoted to bawdy globes that, upon closer look, made her blush.

She lifted a snow globe depicting a Dutch windmill off a table. "I knew Mr. Kimball was a devoted collector, but I wouldn't have guessed his interests included snow globes."

"Bernard Kimball collected everything from precious gems to toothpick sculptures."

"Toothpick sculptures?"

"I believe they're housed in a room on the third floor. I'll show them to you sometime this weekend."

"That would be nice." She smiled encouragingly. "I was hoping the weekend's entertainments included a tour of his collection. I'd love to see the toys and the precious gems."

Like stolen emerald necklaces.

"I'll arrange it." Dair MacRae folded his arms and gave her a considering look. He was obviously in no hurry to leave. Now was he going to talk ice cream? Apparently not. He asked, "Which of the globes appeals to you most?"

Emma glanced around the room. "I don't know. There are so many…it would be difficult to choose."

"Pick five."

"But why…?"

"Indulge me."

Emma decided she was in no big hurry to move him along, so she was happy to cooperate. She took her time moving around the room, studying the contents. She made sure to look at everything before making her first selection.

She chose a snow globe that contained a sewing basket with three colors of thread—red, green, and blue—and set it on the small round table he'd cleared and moved to the center of the sitting room. Next she selected a globe that contained a slingshot. Her third choice was a globe that displayed a stack of books, her fourth—prompted by mischief—a harlequin's mask.

She hesitated over her fifth selection before choosing the globe that had caught her notice the moment she walked into the room. The snow globe showed an intricately depicted four-masted barquentine in full sail with a figurehead of a woman with long, reddish-blond hair.

Emma lifted it gently, swirled the snow inside it, and smiled. Then she set it with her other four choices and turned to Dair MacRae. "Well?"

"Interesting." MacRae folded his arms and circled the table. "My challenge is to discern why you made each particular choice, what that choice reveals about you. The books are obvious, of course, considering your profession. But it was your third choice, which suggests that the first two are more important to you."

"Not necessarily." Emma took a seat in one of the rosewood chairs set before the fireplace. "Maybe I simply fancied the colors or the intricacy of the design."

"No. You carefully considered your selections." He lifted her first choice from the table. "Since you've confessed to being a pitiful seamstress, I suspect your choice of a sewing basket represents something more than a particular interest or talent. You mentioned that your mother attempted to teach you to sew. That suggests time spent together. Family time. Am I correct, Emma? Did your first choice represent family?"

Emma did so appreciate intelligence in a man. "Close, sir. But not exactly."

"It's Dair, and how was I mistaken?"

Emma stared at the snow globe and smiled. "I thought of my mother, of course, because of the subject, but the spools of thread represented me and my sisters."

"Oh? How so?"

Now it was Emma's turn to probe a bit. "The three spools of thread, the three colors. I have two sisters, and we each have a unique piece of jewelry that's quite special to us. They're alike but for the color of the stone. I've a ruby, my sister Mari has a sapphire." She watched him closely and added, "My sister Katrina's stone is emerald."

She noted only a nod, no suspicious narrowing of his eyes or flick toward her neckline to where her ruby necklace ordinarily rested. Part of Kat's plan was to keep the necklace hidden until such time that revealing it might help their search.

"You're close to your sisters." He stated it as a fact, not a question. She nodded and he asked, "Do you have other siblings?"

She smiled. "Three younger brothers."

"Ah. The slingshot."

"The boys and my father have contests at least once a week."

He studied her, his silver eyes intent. "So, the first two choices are family, the third your work. That says quite a lot about you, Emma."

The way he said her name, smooth and slow with lots of lip, she'd never heard an *m* spoken with quite so much…savor.

"Now, this…" He lifted her fourth choice, turned it up and down, and watched the snow settle over the mask. "This intrigues me. Care to explain the reason for this selection?"

Emma smoothed her skirts and offered what she hoped was an enigmatic smile. "I don't believe I do."

He looked at her for a long moment, and Emma felt a little rush of power at refusing such an intense personality as Alasdair MacRae. Then, he grinned at her, a delighted acknowledgment of her challenge. Emma found herself smiling right back at him.

"You're a fascinating woman, Emma, and that brings us to your fifth choice." He carried the ship snow globe to the window where he held it up to a beam of sunshine.

"I find this choice the most intriguing. You took great care in making your final selection. What does it say about you?"

He looked at her, then, with eyes like silver shards. "What brings you here to Chatham Park, Emma McBride?"

Startled, she blinked. Panicked. Did they know she and Kat had come to steal? How? They hadn't been here half an hour yet. What had she done wrong already? "Pardon me?"

"You're a beautiful, enchanting woman. You could garner a dozen marriage proposals with little more than a smile at a society ball. Why have you entered this humiliating marriage competition?"

Humiliating. See, Kat? I was right.

He'd distracted her with this snow globe nonsense. She'd relaxed her guard. Yet, Emma was torn between feeling annoyed and defensive and feeling flattered. When was the last time a man the likes of Alasdair MacRae called her fascinating and enchanting? And danged if he didn't have a point about the marriage contest. "Isn't that being rather judgmental when you know nothing of my circumstance, Mr. MacRae?"

"Which brings us back to my question." He idly shifted the snow globe from his right hand to his left. "What *is* your circumstance?"

Buying time, she said, "Why do you ask?"

Those broad shoulders shrugged. "I care about Jake's nieces and nephew. They've had a difficult time, what with losing their parents and the realities of having Jake as their guardian. I want what's best for them."

The comment surprised her. Dair MacRae didn't strike her as a man who'd pay attention to children, much less act as their champion. "You agree with Mr. Kimball's plan to provide them a mother so he can abandon them and travel to Tibet?"

His lips twitched. "I've known Jake for quite some time. I suspect the outcome of these events will differ from what circumstances currently suggest. I know now that family is important to you. Are you here for the children, then? Are you looking for a ready-made family?"

Persistent fellow, Emma thought. "I am not lacking in family now, sir. Both my immediate family and extended family are quite large, and we have lots of children to shower with love. I'm not here because I have maternal urges that need soothing."

Those intriguing gray eyes lit with amusement and just a hint of challenge. "So, other urges have brought you here?"

Emma's cheeks flushed. Oh, for goodness' sake. She was too old to blush. Attempting to turn the tables on him, she went on the offensive. "What brings *you* here, Mr. MacRae? Do you intend to help Mr. Kimball choose his bride? Offer a second opinion?"

Once again he held the barquentine snow globe up to the sun. Casually, he said, "Originally, I had no intentions of attending this…travesty. Emma, I'm here because of you."

She cleared her throat, then asked, "Me?"

"I've told you I find you intriguing. I want to know more about you. I want to know everything about you."

Oh, my. When she felt her hands tremble, she decided enough was enough. "Because I played pin the tail on the donkey?"

He laughed. "I find your spirit quite appealing, Emma."

"Why didn't you say anything?"

"To Jake?" When she nodded, Dair MacRae once again shrugged. "It's more interesting this way, don't you agree?

A secret between the two of us. It's..." His gaze focused on her mouth as he said, "...intimate."

Heat washed through her. She needed to fan her face. "But...but...wait a minute. I'm here trying to marry your friend."

"No, you're not."

"Oh?" She said it with some bite to her tone.

Again, he showed her that smile. He stalked across the room, took hold of her hand, and tugged her to her feet. Then, he handed her the snow globe. "Explain to me about the ship, Emma. Tell me what it represents to you."

She didn't want to tell him about the ship, not now, but when he locked eyes with her, she felt compelled to respond. Could it be that the man made his living as a mesmerist? Fighting the pull of his gaze, she said, "Not until you choose. I want you to choose five snow globes."

He paused, considered, then observed, "Ah, Emma, you are a true delight."

Dair MacRae made quick work of his first three choices. Emma halfway expected him to select from the bawdy globes, but he stayed away from that row. He placed his globes on the table with hers. A shark. An eagle. A wolf. He was an animal lover? She wondered why he'd chosen those specific animals. Because each was a predator, perhaps? Recalling the intensity of his gaze upon occasion, Emma thought it fit.

She waited for him to make his fourth choice. Instead of reaching for a grizzly bear or even one of the dinosaurs, he surprised her by selecting one of her selections. The mask.

What was the message in that?

He watched her closely as he made his fifth selection, a truly fantastical depiction of a wizard staring into his crystal ball. Emma couldn't begin to predict the reason behind that choice. "You are a most curious man," she observed.

"And you are a captivating woman. Tell me about the ship."

Bowing to what felt like the inevitable, she said, "Adventure. The ship represents adventure."

He stared at her for a long, thoughtful moment, his gaze intense, before the light in his eyes turned knowing and he murmured, "Ah."

Ah? What did he mean, ah? Annoyed, Emma folded her arms and asked him. "What do you mean, 'ah'?"

He laughed and the sound skittered across her skin like a caress. "I mean 'ah' I'm going to enjoy this weekend."

Emma didn't know whether to take that as a threat or a promise.

"Now, I'll leave you to settle in," Dair MacRae continued. "Jake has asked all his guests to congregate on the back lawn in..." MacRae checked a pocket watch "...half an hour. I trust that will be convenient for you?"

He didn't wait for her response, but turned to leave. Prodded by an emotion she didn't understand, Emma stepped forward and insisted, "I *am* here for the contest, Mr. MacRae."

At the doorway, he paused. "Dair. And there are many kinds of contests, Emma. You and I are engaged in one of infinite, intriguing possibilities. I look forward to discovering them...together."

All the energy seemed sucked from the room as he shut the door behind him. Her knees weak, her heartbeat fluttering, Emma sank into the nearest seat. Contests. Adventure. Dair MacRae.

Deep within her, the McBride Menace mischief-maker stirred.

DAIR RETREATED TO HIS OWN suite across the hall from Emma. There, courtesy of transatlantic telegraph lines and Angus Fraser's man, Tompkins, he reviewed his dossier on the eldest McBride sister once again.

So the woman dreamed of adventure, did she? He scanned the document, absently rubbing his temple. Eldest of six children. Responsible, civic-minded, former president of the Fort Worth Literary Society. A talented singer. An excellent shot. *Now, that's curious.* But then, she *was* a Texan.

And very possibly perfect for his purposes. She might be the solution to his Piney Woods problem.

Dair was a believer in fate. Was fate the reason he and Emma met in front of a shop window moments before Sister Mary Margaret changed his plans? Perhaps. He hoped so. He'd like to get this situation settled so he could get on with the business of dying.

So, was Emma Tate the answer to his troubles? Reviewing the dossier once again, he turned to the page listing her romantic entanglements. Married at age twenty to a rancher, Casey Tate. Widowed three months later. No significant extended relationship since then.

On the surface she appeared perfect. He thought of what her snow globe choices had told him. She valued family, her work. He suspected the mask might have been a symbol of this masquerade that had brought her to Chatham Park. She'd expressed a need for adventure. Physical adventure, he wondered? Or…romantic?

The woman gave all appearances of being ripe for the plucking. His mouth twisted with a wry smile. Plucking her would present no hardship on his part. A pleasant change from his recent dealings with the duchess.

Dair walked to the window and gazed down at the lawn

where the bride contestants and their chaperones had begun to congregate. The sisters had yet to put in an appearance. He'd find it interesting to see if they'd jump right into whatever mischief they'd planned, or if they'd take matters more slowly.

They were after pirate treasure, of course. Jake had relayed to Dair the story of his first meeting with Miss Katrina McBride in Galveston, Texas a few years ago when she'd attempted to purchase an altar cross from Jake's father's estate. She'd had personal reasons for wanting to buy the artifact from Jean Lafitte's booty. Jake had personal reasons for refusing her.

Now, after a bit of study and debate, Jake and Dair had concluded that the sisters' attempt to participate in Jake's bride search was their effort to gain access to Chatham Park and its famous collections. Dair wondered if attempting to steal a treasure from Jake Kimball's estate would pacify Emma's thirst for adventure. Or, would she prefer an adventure more intimate in nature?

Dair knew which choice he'd prefer.

The intensity of his own reaction surprised him. Though he'd grown accustomed to using women, as a rule he found the practice distasteful. In Emma Tate's case, he found the idea...delicious.

Admittedly, he need not use her at all. She had no grand fortune to steal, no significant jewels to rob, and Dair didn't steal from those of limited means. In all honesty, romancing her might complicate his own purposes. She might be the type of woman to fulfill his request simply from the goodness of her heart. Such people did exist. Just not in the crowd he'd been running with of late.

Nevertheless, Dair found the idea of romancing Emma

infinitely appealing. After all, considering his prognosis, it might well be his last chance.

Seducing her would answer any lingering questions he might have about her appropriateness for the job. From his experience, a woman's true character invariably emerged once she shared a bed with a man. Just because he suspected the hand of fate in this enterprise didn't mean that Emma Tate was the perfect person for the job. He wouldn't know that until he knew the woman, inside and out. The best, the quickest way to learn the information was to seduce her.

There, wasn't that tidy?

Not necessarily true, he was honest enough with himself to admit, but justifiable. Once he'd confirmed her character and secured her loyalty, her allegiance, he could spring his question upon her. If he did it right, she wouldn't refuse him.

Dair had every intention of doing it right.

So, how best to proceed? He spent a few minutes considering, then discarding various options before settling on a plan. Best to move forward with caution, he thought. First, he'd simply spend time with her, probing her wishes and desires for bits of information not to be found in the pages of any dossier. Then, armed with her likes and dislikes, he would formulate his seduction strategy.

A check of the mantel clock revealed that the time had come for the next scene in this production. Dair headed downstairs to spend the remainder of the day getting to know Emma.

She displayed a genuine affection for children and proved her claim that she enjoyed fishing during a contest with Jake's niece Caroline at Chatham Park's picturesque lake. When that was done, Dair and Caroline spent some time skipping rocks, until the girl joined Emma in picking wildflowers while he stretched out on a quilt beneath the warm afternoon sun. As Dair enjoyed the simple pleasure of watching a woman and child fill a white wicker basket with flowers of pink and blue, he mentally prioritized the other pieces of information he wished to learn.

Dair managed to lure Emma over to his quilt and he surreptitiously probed her opinions about various methods of discipline for children. Her answers to his questions suggested she was frugal, but not a skinflint; generous, but not extravagant; disciplined, but not heavy-handed. The more he learned, the more he liked. Emma Tate just might be perfect. In more ways than one.

He hadn't been lying when he said she intrigued him. Dair found her spirit delightful and her mind refreshing. Her beauty made him want. He'd love to lay her back against the ground and continue his investigation of Emma Tate in a much more intimate manner. Dair imagined tasting her, baring her breasts, running his hands and mouth over all her generous curves. He wanted her naked beneath the afternoon sun. Naked beneath him. Her legs—undoubtedly long and shapely—wrapped around his waist.

Unfortunately, the presence of little Caroline thwarted the realization of those desires. However, a kiss would not be amiss, would it?

Dair was just about ready to make his move when Emma's sister disrupted the idyllic afternoon. The two sisters moved away seeking privacy for their conversation, not knowing Dair had hearing like a hawk. He eavesdropped subtly.

Apparently, Jake had made progress because Kat knew

he'd seen through her disguise. She wanted to run. Emma...dear, darling Emma...refused.

"It's him, isn't it?" Kat declared in a shrill tone. "It's more than a simple flirtation. That man has turned your head!"

Excellent news, Dair thought.

"I don't know what it is, Kat," Emma said, her tone turning wistful. "He's...fun. I'm having fun. It's been a long time since I've had any fun. I think I need it."

While Dair digested that bit of information, the women moved a bit farther away, and he could no longer make out their words. He rolled to his feet and returned to skipping rocks, shifting closer to the sisters in time to hear Kat say, "Please, Emma. We're not children anymore. Don't you think you're too old to be talking that way?"

"Too old? Too old!"

Dair abandoned any effort at pretense and stared openly when he saw fire burn in Emma's eyes and color stain her cheeks. She looked like an avenging angel, a warrior goddess. By God, she made a man ache.

She gave her head a toss, braced her hands on her hips and declared, "Maybe I *am* too old. Maybe I'm just old and tired. Tired of always being Emma the poor widow, Emma the dutiful daughter, Emma the supportive sister. Maybe I just want to be a flesh and blood woman. Maybe I just want to be *Emma!*"

Emma the adventurer, I think.

How lucky for me.

CHAPTER FOUR

"I'M SO SORRY," EMMA said the following day as she gently wiped a smear of blood from Dair's face, the result of a minor injury that Kat—now sans disguise—had caused inadvertently. He sat at a table in the kitchen, Emma standing between his spread legs, a wet dish towel in her right hand. "My sister is, well, it's difficult to explain. Mr. Kimball sets off her temper."

His brows winged up. "That was temper?"

"Yes, or something." Emma set the dishcloth aside, then placed an ice pack against his skin. "What you don't know is how wonderful it is to see her enthused about something."

"That was enthused?"

Emma couldn't help but laugh at his incredulous tone. "That was alive. My sister hasn't been that way since her daughter died. Losing Susie just about destroyed her, but this trip has eased things, I believe. I think Kat might finally be ready."

Dair shifted the ice away. "I'm fine, Emma. It doesn't hurt. Now, what is it you think your sister might be ready for?"

Emma glanced toward the window and in her mind's eye, saw Kat's shenanigans as she'd pitched a ball to Jake Kimball. In those moments, her sister had literally glowed.

"I think she's ready to live again. When you lose someone you love, it takes time."

He nodded, then reached for her hand. Emma's heart skipped a beat as he rose and, towering above her, stared down into her eyes. He traced the curve of her cheek with the roughened pad of his thumb and spoke in an aged-whiskey voice, "And what about you, Emma?"

She licked her lips. "Me?"

"Are *you* ready to live again?"

The question hung suspended on the air like a spider's silken web. This was no simple question and she knew it. If she said yes, he'd kiss her. She could see it in his eyes.

Emma sucked in a breath, swallowed hard. "Yes, I do believe I am."

She swayed toward him, her eyelids drifting downward. But he surprised her by taking a step back. "Then come with me, Emma. Let me show you the pleasures to be found at Chatham Park."

Oh, my.

Keeping her hand in his, Dair led her from the kitchen and out of the house. She wondered where he was taking her. To the stables for a ride to an isolated part of the estate, perhaps? Or maybe back to the fish pond they'd visited yesterday? Surely not to the lawn where the rest of the visitors gathered. He'd take her somewhere private, wouldn't he?

Dair led Emma to the opening of the garden maze.

"It's beautiful," she said, eyeing the roses and honeysuckle surrounding the rectangular-shaped structure. And definitely private. Extremely private. Was she really going to do this? Step into a maze with this man? Alone?

He lifted her hand and pressed a kiss against her knuckles. Emma's knees went watery. Yes. She was really going to do this. *Oh my oh my oh my.* She swallowed her misgivings and smiled. "The maze is huge, too. I can see from my bedroom window."

"It covers almost two acres. It's easy to get lost inside, Emma. Are you certain you're up to my game?"

Game? Her blood humming, the adventurous Emma arched a brow. "Just what is your game, sir?"

He smiled, and Emma was reminded of one of his choices of snow globe: the wolf. "It's a contest, of course. If you can find your way to the Greek temple replica at the center of the northern section of the maze you will win the prize."

"What prize?"

"Hmm...how about your choice of snow globe?"

This was Jake Kimball's home, not Dair MacRae's. "Are they yours to give away?"

"In this instance, yes."

It was a curious remark, but before she could question him further, he distracted her with a caveat to his contest. "Of course, we shall need a time limit or you may be wandering this maze until dark. Shall we say...fifteen minutes?"

Emma frowned. "But it's a two-acre maze."

"I'll give you hints whenever you request. However, such hints don't come free."

"Oh?" Her gaze fastened on his mouth. "And exactly what do they cost?"

"That depends on how lost you are, my dear." She narrowed her eyes and he laughed. "My price will be a kiss."

She circled her mouth with her tongue. "That's a very bold suggestion, Mr. MacRae."

"I'm a bold man, Mrs. Tate. The question before us is how bold a woman are you?"

Emma's pulse sped up. Her mouth went dry. An idyllic

garden. He was the serpent. She was the tempted. Tempted with a capital T. If she did this, if she threw away all her good sense and embraced her inner Menace, then she couldn't later cry foul or indulge in regrets or remorse.

Remorse? The only remorse she'd have is if he didn't kiss her. Touch her. Hold her.

This was her chance. Here in England so far from home, she could indulge herself. She could do something shocking and no one need ever know. She could throw off the mantle of being Widow Tate and be a Menace again. Be Emma. The old Emma. The Emma who wasn't boring, but fun and exciting and…wicked. The Emma who wasn't about to turn thirty with no man, no babies, no life.

Emma didn't want to be selfish, but right here, right now, she couldn't help it. She was glad Mari had found her happy ending. She mourned for Kat's horrific loss. But right now, as her birthday roared toward her, she wanted to worry about herself for a change. She wanted to end the boredom. Pull a true McBride Menace prank. She wanted to rob another train or steal another horse or…

Or walk into the garden maze with a dangerous man.

"Emma?"

What was it about this man in particular? Why was she like a moth to his flame? He was nothing like Casey—lighthearted of manner and demeanor. Dair MacRae was dark and tempting and represented everything that she was not. Her father would detest him on sight. She knew next to nothing about him. Yet, there was something in his eyes. Something wild and excited. Something wicked.

Something wicked. Yes, that's what she couldn't resist.

Emma sucked in a deep breath, then said, "I'm a McBride Menace, sir. I was born bold."

A devilish twinkle lit those silver eyes. He extended his hand, gesturing for her to precede him into the maze. Emma stepped forward and excitement sizzled through her.

It was like another world. The scent of honeysuckle hung heavy on the air. A sparrow flitted from its perch atop an elaborate iron bench while a squirrel scampered along the path. "Should I follow him?" Emma asked.

"Is that a request for a hint?"

Now that she'd given herself permission to be bad, the need to play—to tease him and tantalize him and make him ache with wanting—rose within her. "Hmm…perhaps."

He took a step toward her.

She placed her hand against his chest and pushed gently. "Perhaps not."

"Hmm." He clasped his hands behind his back, the twinkle in his eyes deepening to impure amusement.

Emma lifted her chin and boldly chose the path to her left, purposely taking big steps that caused her hips to swing. A few steps later, the path dead-ended.

Dair made a show of checking his watch, and Emma's competitive nature was sparked. She wanted her kiss—oh, she truly did. However, McBride Menaces never backed down from a challenge.

She lifted her hem and retraced her steps. Her second try appeared more successful. She sent him a sly smile and sashayed forward. Dair sauntered behind her, whistling.

Then Emma hit another dead end. Hmm. Maybe now?

But when she turned, he checked his watch again.

No, not now. Emma turned around and walked past him, brushing up against him as she turned a corner, into another hedge wall. *Drat.*

"Let me help you, Emma."

He was staring at her mouth, his eyes narrowed and intense. Hot. *Now,* whispered the Menace in her. *Let him help you. You know you want it.* "Which way do I go, Dair?"

He brought her hand up to his mouth and kissed her knuckles one by one, staring deeply into her eyes as he did so. Anticipation sizzled through her. Then he turned her hand over and his lips caressed the very center of her palm. "Turn left, Texas."

Then, he dropped her hand and stepped away.

Emma's spine stiffened. *Aha. So that's his game, is it? He thinks to tease me, too. Well, he's got another think coming, doesn't he? Two of us are playing here, and I always play to win.*

She slowly licked her lips. "Well, then. Left it is."

Was that a chuckle she heard from the maddening man?

In less than a minute, she found her way blocked once again. This time she didn't hesitate. "Right or left?"

Again, he brought her hand to his lips, kissed her knuckles, then her palm. This time, though, he went a little farther. With clever fingers, he loosened the buttons at the cuff of her sleeve. Emma shivered as his lips found the sensitive skin at the inside of her wrist. She shuddered when his teeth tenderly scraped her skin. "Right."

That's more like it.

When he stepped back, she lifted the hand he'd kissed to her chest where she played with the ribbon at her collar. As expected, his eyes followed her every movement. Emma grinned with satisfaction as she took the right turn he'd indicated to continue through the maze, her awareness of the man walking a half step behind her increasing as the seconds ticked by. He moved with an animal's grace.

Apparently, she made some good choices because she

went for quite a ways before encountering another dead end. Her heartbeat racing, she turned to Dair. "Help?"

Slowly, the wolf smile stretched across his face. The wicked glint in his eyes went sharper. This time he took her left hand and repeated his previous attentions, tugging up her sleeve to expose her arm, trailing his mouth up to the inside of her elbow. His sandalwood scent enveloped her and gentle nibbles sent little strikes of lightning from her arm to her womb. "This is one of the trickier places in the maze. The price to pay is higher."

He repeated the exact same motions with the exact same speed—deliciously slow—on her left hand and arm. By the time he released her and stepped back, Emma was a puddle. "To find your way from here, you must turn right, then immediately, right again."

Wrong. She wanted so badly to go left.

She was afraid she'd reach the Greek temple too soon.

However, she knew better than to be so obvious, so she followed his directions. Moments later, she found her way blocked in a cozy little alcove adorned with a pretty iron bench and planters overflowing with a rainbow of flowers. "Foiled again," Emma declared, trying to hide her delight. She eyed the bench, then asked, "May I request you suspend the ticking clock while we rest our feet a moment?"

"Hmm." The light in his eyes turned knowing. "I guess an exception to the rules is in order."

Emma took a seat. Dair sat beside her, closer than was proper. The way he focused his attention on her without wavering wasn't exactly proper, either. But it sure was flattering. Intriguing. Stimulating.

"So." Emma cleared her throat. "How far to the goal?"

He studied her with a deliberate gaze. "Oh, we've quite a way to go yet."

"I see." She smoothed her skirt, then played with the lace trim on her bodice. "So I won't win the prize?"

"I wouldn't give up yet. Perhaps I could offer you more extensive clues."

"For a more extensive price?"

"You catch on fast, don't you?"

Emma wondered where his lips would wander next. Would he finally find her mouth and give her the kiss she craved? Or would he discover other areas to tease?

She decided she was ready to find out. "I want to win that snow globe, so I guess I should hear the more substantial clues."

Again, his predatory gaze swept over her. He reached out and smoothed an errant strand of hair away from her face, then his fingers lingered on her cheek, softly stroking her skin as he said, "Your hair reminds me of sunrise off the coast of Tahiti, a dozen different colors of gold with a subtle streak of fiery red. Tell me, Emma, is there fire inside you as well?"

Her voice would have quavered had she attempted to speak, so staring into the heated gunmetal glow of his eyes, she settled for a nod. She definitely had fire inside her. A hot one, and he'd built it.

"I suspected as much." He freed her hair from its pins and it went tumbling down her back. He buried his fist in the long, silken strands. "Beautiful. So beautiful."

Emma saw his heavy-lidded gaze drop to her mouth. She felt his fingers play at the back of her neck. Anticipation sizzled within her as his face moved toward hers. "Ask me."

"Hmm?"

His breath feathered against her skin. "You need to ask me."

Oh, the man played dirty.

Fine. That made it all the easier for her. The wanton inside Emma wanted to laugh as she decided the time had come to make her winning move.

"No. I won't beg for your kisses, Mr. MacRae. I think I'll simply take one." Then Emma closed the distance between them, and kissed him.

She sensed his startled surprise, but he quickly got over that. Dair MacRae took control of the kiss and Emma Tate let him.

It had been so long and it felt so good. It was nice to know that she could still make a man want her.

He was unexpectedly gentle with her at first, a whisper of a touch that shouldn't have sparked a fire in her blood, but did. His teeth scraped softly over her bottom lip, and Emma couldn't repress a helpless purr of pleasure.

He framed her face in his hands, tipped her head back, and deepened the kiss. Emma's world tilted. He was good at this. Very good. It had been so long since she'd allowed a man to reach past her defenses. A long time since she'd wanted one there.

Need rose within her, a hollow, grinding ache she felt through to the very core of her body. Emma lifted her hands, ran them across the breadth of his shoulders, then upward. She buried her fingers in his hair and responded to the wild, willing yearning he'd created within her by pouring all the hot, hungry need into her kiss.

His hands released her face, skimmed downward, settled at her waist, his fingers tightening in a viselike grip.

He broke the kiss, drew his head away. His breathing was heavy as his gaze locked with hers.

She'd surprised him, all right. The admiration in those heated silver eyes boring into her soul told her so.

He spoke in a low, slow rumble. "First left, second right, third left will save you."

Save her? "What do you mean?"

"A shortcut out of the maze."

Oh. Emma's stomach sank. Had she misread the signs? Oh no. Had she just made a fool of herself? "You're sending me away?"

She tried to move away from him, but his hands held her captive. "Only if you wish to be saved. I'm not a gentleman, Emma Tate, and you tempt me more than I had anticipated. If you meet me in the center of the maze, be prepared for the consequences."

She swallowed hard. "Consequences?"

"I'll not stop with a kiss."

His declaration sent a bolt of desire pulsing through her. She spoke in order to give herself time to think. "So you're a rogue with a conscience?"

His mouth tilted in a wry smile. "I'm just a man."

And she was just a woman, a woman with needs that hadn't been attended to for so long. Dair MacRae was the most exciting man she'd ever met and right now, at this moment in time, Emma wanted exciting. She wanted dashing and daring and dangerous. She wanted…him.

With that acknowledgment, any lingering insecurity disappeared. Self-confidence brought a calming sense of peace that cleared the way for her to do nothing more than feel. She was the Emma of old. Brave, courageous, and bold.

She lifted her chin, met his simmering stare with a seductive one of her own and asked, “And to the temple, MacRae? What’s the fastest path to the temple?”

His eyes went to black, and his voice sounded raspy as he said, “First right. Second right. Third right. Go, woman. Fast.”

She stood, an animal sensing danger, feeling more alive than she’d felt in years. At the entrance to the alcove, she tossed him a saucy look over her shoulder, then picked up her skirts and turned right.

She reached the replica temple in little more than a minute. Her blood was humming, her heart was singing, and she wanted to shout out with *joie de vivre.* Instead, she settled for wrapping her arms around herself and spinning around.

“My God, you’re…”

“…alive,” she breathed.

He caught her with a growl and yanked her against him, then devoured her with his kiss. His mouth was ravenous, and she sensed wildness in him, an elemental savagery barely controlled.

And Emma gloried in it. She felt womanly and desirable and…powerful. His clever fingers worked the buttons down her back and her collar loosened. When he tore his mouth from hers and nipped his way down her neck, she laughed with sheer joy.

Dair captured her lips once again, his hands fisting in her hair, his tongue plunging into her mouth, plundering even as he propelled her backwards until she came up against one of the temple columns. His hands streaked over her, ruthlessly exploring, mercilessly possessing.

He pressed his body against her, and he was as hard as the marble column at her back. She felt soft and malleable like a goose-feather pillow. The pulsing ache within her grew. She wanted to beg him. It had been so long.

He drew back. His gaze was diamond hard and lava hot. "Last chance to run, Emma."

She sucked in a quick breath. "I'm not running."

Impossibly, his gaze grew even hotter, but she sensed he drew upon a deep well of control. He took her hand and led her inside the stone structure.

It was a place made for a tryst. Emma's quick survey spied a basket of fruit, a bottle of wine, and two crystal glasses. Tall candlesticks stood at the ready beside the oversized lounging couch that dominated the space. He'd prepared for her. The man had been sure of himself, and certain of her.

"A glass of wine, Texas?" he asked, nuzzling her neck.

"No, thank you." Emma shivered.

"Strawberries?"

"I'm fine."

"I beg to differ. You are more than fine. You are fascinating. Alluring. Enticing. You've seduced me, Emma Tate, and it is quite beyond my original intentions."

The sweet sense of feminine power rushed through her as he turned her to face him. "Beautiful," he murmured. "So damned beautiful." Then his mouth captured hers once again, and Emma abandoned all effort to think as she gave herself up to the heady pleasure of simply feeling.

His practiced hands stroked her, caressed her—her face, her neck, her arms. She sensed air upon her skin as her dress fell away. His lips released her mouth and trailed lower, finding the sensitive spot where her neck and shoulder met. Emma couldn't hold back a purr as she arched away to allow him better access.

At the same time, she wanted her hands on him. She wanted to skim her hands across his bare skin, to know the sensation of corded muscle beneath her palm. To feel the rasp of his chest hair against her naked breasts.

As she lifted her hand to tug at his neck scarf, he scooped her into his arms and carried her the few short steps to the couch. Emma lay back, her eyelids heavy as she watched him shrug from his jacket and yank off his neck scarf. He knelt on one knee above her, reached for her sleeves, and bared her upper body to his heated gaze.

His gaze swept over her, lingered on the swell of her breasts rising above the lace trim of her chemise. He noted the unique front fastening corset her seamstress mother had designed with approval. "Full of surprises, aren't you, Texas?"

Moments later, he'd bared her completely to the waist. He shifted, straddled her, drawing Emma's gaze to the prominent bulge at his crotch. Her body responded with a liquid heat that readied her even as she moaned at the first touch of a man's hand on her bare breast in over a decade. She trembled. She shook, strung tighter than a bow. Oh, she'd missed this.

"Such beautiful jewels."

"It's ruby. The pendant is a ruby."

"I wasn't referring to your necklace," he said with amusement. His finger trailed across the swell of her breast. "Your skin is like silk. So soft. Creamy." His thumb brushed her taut nipple. "I'll bet you taste as beautiful as you look."

He leaned down and licked the valley between her breasts. Emma gasped and Dair murmured, "Mmm. I was right."

Then the man devoted his attentions to her breasts, kneading and squeezing, kissing. The rough surface of his tongue rasped against her nipples as he laved them, one after the other.

Emma twisted her head from side to side, arching her back, offering herself to his tender assault. When finally, he drew her slowly into his mouth and suckled, she moaned softly.

Sensation stole throughout her body. A pulse beat in her womb. Tension increased. More, she wanted more. She clutched his head to her, drowning in pleasure, glorying in the magic Dair MacRae created. She wanted it to last forever; she wanted him to take her to the next level *right now.* Urgently, Emma slid her hands down to the placket on his shirtfront and yanked at his buttons. Dair released her long enough to shrug off his shirt and yank off his undershirt. Emma sighed aloud when the weight of his bare chest came down upon her.

Then, a voice intruded. "Dair?" Jake Kimball called from somewhere beyond a hedge.

Dair appeared deaf to the interruption, blind to all but her as he took her mouth in a kiss that bordered on desperate.

Kimball called again, louder this time. "Miss McBride has come looking for her sister."

Emma wanted to scream in frustration. Kat. Leave it to Kat. She was so darn tired of Kat interfering in her life.

She placed her hand against Dair's chest and applied gentle pressure that didn't budge him a bit. "My sister…"

"Is a pain in the ass," he muttered.

The sentiment shocked a laugh out of Emma. "If you only knew."

A long, suspenseful moment passed while he waited, watching her intently, a predator over his prey. Then he rolled them onto their sides, not breaking eye contact with Emma, a finger combing her unbound hair away from her face as he called out, "I owe you one for this, Kimball."

He gave her one last hard kiss before releasing her and standing. He watched her closely, regret filling his eyes as Emma began to cover herself. He interrupted her efforts when he reached for her pendant. "This looks familiar."

Annoyed at Kat and momentarily heedless of their mission to Chatham Park, Emma said, "You've probably seen my sister's necklace. Jake Kimball has it."

Dair nodded. "It's emerald. But that stone isn't carved, yours is. It's the engraving I'm referring to."

So Kat was right. Kimball *did* have her necklace. "Engraving? I've never noticed any engraving."

He held the pendant in one hand and pointed out the carving with his finger. "It's easier to see when the stone is nestled between your breasts. I saw it best when both of us had contact with it. Perhaps body heat makes the stone glow."

Emma was amazed. She'd worn this necklace for over a decade. She couldn't believe she'd never noticed the marks on the stone before. "It's writing, but I don't recognize the language."

"It's words and a figure of sorts." His brow furrowed. "I swear I've seen something similar before."

Kat McBride's voice called, "Emmaline Suzanne!"

"I'm going to kill her," Emma muttered.

Dair chuckled, released the ruby, and stepped back. "Another time, Texas. This was interrupted. Not ended."

He had that right. Sexual frustration had her jumpy as a cat on ice. A cat with claws ready for a fight. "Damn you, Kat. Couldn't you just leave me be for a while?"

Emma did her best to put herself to rights before exiting the temple, but she knew she'd failed the moment her sister spied her. Kat's accusatory stare swept her from head to toe, then her mouth set in a grim smile. "Emma, I need to speak with you."

Emma didn't like her sister's look. How dare she! Who did she think she was? Emma's conscience? Her bodyguard? The morality sheriff? As if Kat had any room to talk. "It couldn't wait?"

"It appears to me that I've waited too long as it is," Kat fired back. "We've had a message from Monique. I'll give you one guess as to what our grandmother has done now."

Monique Day was their grandmother, their mother Jenny's outrageous mother. Knowing her grandmother's history, Emma asked, "She's remarried? Again?"

"To an earl this time! She's off on another honeymoon trip. Will you come upstairs with me, Emma? Please? We have some decisions to make."

Emma sighed heavily and muttered, "Family."

WITH A SCOWL ON HIS FACE, an ache in his loins, and the threat of a headache beginning to gnaw at his brain, Dair watched the women climb the steps and disappear inside Chatham Park. Standing beside him, Jake didn't appear any happier.

"Will Kat McBride marry you?" Dair asked his friend.

"I don't know." Jake rubbed the back of his neck. "The children are a true stumbling block. More so than I'd realized. I'm beginning to wonder if I'd be better off letting her go and choosing one of the others."

Then he leveled a frown on Dair. "You're not helping matters. What the hell are you doing with Kat's sister? You're supposed to keep her distracted, not seduce her."

"Actually, I'm not certain who seduced whom," Dair mused.

"Right. I'm supposed to believe that. You know, this is

not what I intended when I asked you to keep her away from Kat. She's not like your other women, Dair. She's…nice. She's like, hell, she reminds me of my sister."

Dair didn't see anything the least bit sisterly about Emma Tate. "You have no idea, Jake."

He'd wager a guess that her family didn't have a clue about the real Emma, either.

The two men stood scowling after the McBride sisters until finally, Jake said, "I need a drink."

"Excellent idea."

Inside the house, Jake led the way up to the second floor heading for his study. The route took the men past some of Chatham Park's collection rooms, and as they walked by the Scottish-theme drawing room, Dair sensed a pull. "Whiskey, I think, Jake."

"Yeah. Good choice."

The selection of Highland malts from which to choose was enough to make a whiskey afficionado swoon before he even opened a bottle. With his headache beginning to strengthen, Dair poured the most accessible—a twenty-year-old blend from Skye. While the liquor wouldn't make his headache go away, it did serve to numb the pain somewhat. While he refused to utilize such a crutch on a regular basis, sometimes he hadn't the will to resist. Now was one of those times. Between the ache in his head and the one in his groin, he was in desperate straits.

Dair's gaze drifted over the contents of the room. Framed battle maps. Tartans and clan maps. The nameplate beside an ivory compass claimed the item once belonged to Charles Edward Stuart. He focused on a collection of Highland brooches, upon one enameled silver piece in particular, and a memory stirred. A glowing ruby between two perfect breasts. "Like Gaelic, but different."

Still in the process of choosing his whiskey, Jake glanced over his shoulder. "What?"

Dair hesitated, strangely reluctant to talk about Emma's engraved ruby. Yet at the same time, he sensed he needed to know every possible detail about the McBride sisters' necklaces. "That emerald you carry around…where did you get it?"

Jake winced.

"It's Kat McBride's, isn't it?"

"No!"

After Dair arched a challenging brow, Jake sighed. "All right, it used to be Kat's. Now it's mine."

He relayed a wild story about hiding beneath the woman's bed while she gave birth. But it was the reason he'd gone to so much trouble that intrigued Dair the most. "You dreamed about that necklace?"

"I did. On that mountain in Tibet when Daniel disappeared. I know it's crazy, but I think…maybe…hell." He reached into his pocket and pulled out the emerald necklace. "What if this necklace can help me find my brother?"

Dair scowled at the pendant. "Emma has one just like it. A ruby necklace."

"I know. Their sister Mari's is sapphire."

Dair held out his hand, wordlessly asking to hold the jewel. He'd noted on more than one occasion the particular care Jake took with his talisman, so he wasn't overly surprised when his friend took a moment to hand the piece over.

It was the same sort of feeling he'd had when he let Emma's ruby go.

Wishing he had his jeweler's loupe with him, Dair studied the emerald closely. He'd never seen engraving on an emerald, but there was a first time for everything. The stone's surface appeared smooth, however, even after he closed his fist around the pendant and warmed the stone for a minute or two.

"What are you looking for?" Jake asked.

"I'm not sure." He handed the emerald back to Jake. "Do you know where the sisters got their necklaces?"

"A fortune-teller."

Dair's pulse accelerated. "A gypsy?"

"Actually, no. I investigated the incident when I was in Fort Worth. The McBrides claimed a Scotswoman gave them the pendants. Roslin of Strathardle."

Dair damned near dropped his whiskey. "Roslin? From Strathardle?"

"You know the woman?"

"It's a coincidence," he murmured, his mind spinning. "My mother…"

Jake pinned him with an intense look. "I thought she died when you were a child."

"I was six." Dair's mind raced. A man in his line of work knew better than to trust coincidence, but how else to explain this? "Her name was Roslin, but it's even more strange, Jake. My mother grew up in Strathardle Glen."

Jake took a moment to digest that, his thoughts mirrored in his expression. Amazement. Wariness. Confusion. Speculation. "My dream. Now this. There is something peculiar about those necklaces."

Dair nodded and took a long sip of his drink. How did this necklace development affect his plans for Emma and the orphanage? "Emma's ruby is carved with words and a symbol. They're familiar to me, but I can't place from where."

Jake rubbed the back of his neck. "If I can't convince Kat to marry me, she and Emma will leave tomorrow."

"You need to convince her."

"I don't know. If you'd have seen her...being around little ones rips her to pieces. She might not be good for the children because of it."

"Emma thinks Kat would be fine if she faced her fears and dealt with this aversion she has to children."

"That may be, but I don't know that I can risk it. The last thing I want is for the children to get attached to Kat, then her to leave them. They've had enough loss in their lives."

Dair recognized that Jake was ignoring his own place in the equation, at least for now. He knew the man well enough to feel secure that he'd work his way around to putting the children before his brother's ghost eventually. In the end, Jake always did the right thing. Sometimes it simply took him awhile.

In this instance, time worked against Dair. "I can't let Emma leave, not until I settle my questions about her necklace."

"How do you intend to do that?"

Dair considered the question. He needed to do more than simply sit around waiting for his brain to make the connection, but what? What would help? Who would help?

Angus Fraser? The Highland Riever's man in London might be able to shed some light on the mystery, but he'd left the city and Dair didn't know when he planned to return. Maybe he should travel to Strathardle himself and snoop around some, see what he could discover. Except, he wouldn't know what he was looking for. He needed a little history as background.

History. That's it. "Robbie Potter."

"Who's Robbie Potter?" Jake asked.

"He owns a bookshop in Edinburgh." Occasionally, he did some trading for the Riever, but Jake didn't need to know that. "The man is a historian, an expert on clan history. Knows something of ancient languages, too. If he doesn't have the answers I need, he'll be able to tell me where to look."

"So you'll return to Scotland?"

A little earlier than he'd planned, but...yes. "I think I should."

"With the necklace?"

Dair considered the question. A description might not be enough for Robbie, and besides, his gut was telling him not to let the jewel out of his sight. "Yes."

"Hmm..." Jake twirled the chain of Kat McBride's emerald necklace and asked in a casual tone, "So, how do you intend to do that? You gonna take Emma with you?"

Dair considered the question. He couldn't know what he'd find or where any information he learned might lead him. Having a woman tagging along would complicate matters considerably. Travel accommodations were but one example. Since the headaches sometimes left him incapacitated, he preferred to travel in private. He'd take a coach to Scotland rather than the train, and if he took Emma with him, how could he explain traveling in separate coaches?

However, leaving Chatham Park with her prized possession in his pocket meant abandoning his plan to gain her agreement to become the director of the orphanage. He hated to do that.

He visualized the stone, the carvings. Every instinct he possessed told him there was something special about them. Something important.

Something that, in the long run, might prove more useful to the orphanage than having Emma Tate as its director.

"It would be simpler just to steal it," Dair decided.

Jake nodded sagely. "Stealing worked for me, although I'll caution you against hiding under her bed during the process. Those ended up being some of the most uncomfortable hours of my life. Made me happy I was born a man. That's as close to childbirth as I ever want to get."

Dair considered his interlude with Emma in the maze, then grinned wryly. "I have no intention of hiding beneath the woman's bed. I trust I can get the job done while on top of it."

CHAPTER FIVE

"HELLO, CINDERELLA," EMMA SAID to her reflection in the mirror in the ladies' retiring room at Chatham Park. Her eyes sparkled, her cheeks glowed, and her lips simply couldn't quit smiling. She was having the time of her life.

The most dashing, handsome, exciting man in England had danced attendance on her all evening and now as the clock approached midnight, she halfway expected to find the leather slippers on her feet had turned to glass.

But no, her shoes weren't glass and she wasn't Cinderella. Tonight, she was Emma. Emma the adventuress. Be hanged if she'd run away from the ball when the clock bells tolled.

Kat could just whinny and whine all she wanted, but Emma wasn't listening. Not tonight. Tonight was *her* turn. For once, she intended to put herself first. Kat could like it or lump it.

Emma needn't feel guilty about it either. Hadn't Mari told her to quit catering to Kat so much? Hadn't she advised her to put herself first for a change, to pay attention to her own needs? Her own life? Well, tonight was her own night.

For this one night, Kat could hold her own hand, complain about Kimball to her reflection in the mirror. Emma refused to play the wallflower tonight. A handsome rake of a man was paying her attention, and she intended to bask in the glory of it.

Dair MacRae waited for her. With his dangerous air and his daring smile, he called to everything wicked and wanton that had been buried inside Emma for a decade. For a single night here at Chatham Park, far away from her family—most of them, anyway—Emma could be free. Free of her past. Free of present obligations. Free of future expectations. For one little moment in time, Emma could be free to be herself.

Dair waited for her in the hallway. He leaned with one shoulder propped against a curio cabinet, his arms crossed, the intensity in his gaze belying his casual stance. Emma glanced around. The sound of music drifted from the ballroom. Candlelight cast flickering shadows on the wall. They were alone. "Are you tired of dancing?"

He straightened away from the cabinet, those mesmerizing eyes focused totally on her, his face all angles and planes in the soft light. His gaze slowly swept over her, then fastened on her mouth. "I want to be alone with you, Emma. Will you come to my rooms with me?"

There it was, the proposition she'd been expecting ever since he'd told her in the maze that their interlude was only interrupted and not finished. Emma's stomach fluttered. Could she do this? Did she dare?

"I'll warn you that I intend to lock the door," he continued. "We shall not respond to any knocks nor heed any demands to show ourselves until we're good and ready. In other words, Emma, if your sister has need of you tonight, she'll have to wait in line behind me."

He needed her. When was the last time she'd been needed by a man? "I doubt Kat will come knocking. She only searched for me earlier to tell me about our grandmother's latest marital escapade."

Dair took her hand and brought it to his lips. The man certainly had a fondness for hand kissing. "Jake tells me your grandmother is somewhat of a scandal."

"Yes. Monique ran off with a man. Again. She's done it periodically for years. She calls it remarrying, but there's never a clergyman involved."

"You admire her. I hear it in your tone."

Emma considered it. "I do. My grandmother loves life. She *lives* life. She squeezes every bit of happiness and joy she can manage from every single minute she has. I didn't understand just how important that is when I was younger, but now I do. That's what I want—to live my life in a big way."

"Then come upstairs with me." His lips quirked as he added, "I'll give you *big*, Texas."

Oh my oh my oh my. Emma licked her lips, drew a deep breath, then tossed all caution to the wind. "Yes, Dair, I'll go upstairs with you."

His large suite was furnished in colors of green and gold with heavy, masculine furniture. Models of sailing ships graced the tables, mantels and windowsills while paintings of famous sailors decorated the walls. "Admiral Nelson," Emma observed, trying to sound casual. "Sir Francis Drake. Captain Cook. Jake's father put together the most interesting collections, didn't he? What do you collect, Dair?"

She'd have sworn he mumbled "children." "What?"

"Nothing. I'm not a collector."

"Really? Hmm...all right. If you were a collector, what sort of things would attract you? Weapons? Bird houses? Cooking utensils?"

"Why do you ask?"

Emma shrugged, uncertain herself. Now that the moment was upon her, part of her wanted to rush right into the bedroom, onto the bed. Another part of her—a larger, more wary part—wanted to slow things down. "I'd like to know more about you. It's like with you and the snow globes, I think. The things a person collects says a lot about him."

Dair took her into his arms. "Are you having second thoughts, Emma?"

"No!" she quickly declared.

"You're teasing me, then?"

"No." Well, maybe a little. The man was awfully sure of himself. She couldn't help but give him a little trouble.

Dair pulled the pins from her hair, freeing it to tumble down her back. His fingers combed her curls, stroked across her shoulder, bare above the minimal sleeve of her evening gown. "Never mind Bernard Kimball," he said, his voice a throaty growl. "He's dead and I may well follow if I don't get you into bed soon."

There was that need again, in his touch, his voice, the look in his eyes. Emma smiled.

"Dancing with you tonight, holding you." He tightened his hand around her waist. "I'm a desperate man, Emma."

Now she laughed and pulled away from him. His frank talk, intense look, and almost grim determination sent her senses soaring. To know that she, the Widow Tate, dull, boring, and bordering-on-old, could make a man the likes of Dair MacRae desperate gave her a heady sense of power. A more effective aphrodisiac she simply couldn't imagine.

"You're cruel, woman."

"No, I'm not." She lifted her hair up off her back and

whirled around. "I'm free, sir. I'm free to be me, here tonight. With you."

Boldly, she reached for his necktie, tugged at the knot until it released. "There. Isn't that better?" She whipped the necktie away and sent it sailing to the floor. "Don't you feel…freer?"

His mouth twisted in a grin and he spread his legs, his hands braced on his hips. "My neck's not the part of me feeling constrained, Texas."

Emma laughed. She couldn't help it. "I feel so…alive."

He groaned. "You're killing me."

She approached him, trailed her finger down his chest toward the part of him that so obviously yearned to be free and said, "Make love to me, Dair."

It was all the encouragement he needed. He swept her up into his arms and carried her into his bedroom. She had a vague impression of a huge mattress and midnight-blue bed hangings, but her focus remained on the heated intensity of his gaze.

He burned her. Made her burn. Emma flushed with heat as he lay her on the soft pillow of his mattress. Arousal pounded in her blood as she saw the pulse throb at his neck. He needed. Her. Her! Emma. Not Widow Tate. Not even the McBride Menace. Dair MacRae needed the Emma she'd always longed to be.

This was a dream, she thought. An illicit fantasy where everything was possible. Where anything was permitted. And Emma was committed. It would take blood or smoke or fire to chase her from his arms, from his bed. And maybe, not even that.

As he moved above her, settled against her, and captured her mouth in a desperate kiss, Emma knew that this was the excitement she'd craved. Dair MacRae was her escapade. Her adventure.

He groaned into her mouth, and his hands began to work their magic. She would take tonight, enjoy this little slice of fantasy, then return home to Texas wickedly renewed. And on the long, lonesome nights to come, she could pull out the memory of tonight and of the time she drove a dangerous man wild.

Her hands clutched his shoulders as he slowed his kisses. He played with her mouth and tongue in a way that stole her breath and tempted her in ways she'd never imagined. Reckless desire hummed through her like a song.

She whimpered, delving her fingers into the silky hair at his nape. Hers. For this night, this man was hers. Her lover. Imagine that. If Dair hadn't been nibbling on her earlobe, she might have laughed aloud.

But Emma couldn't laugh. She couldn't speak. She could barely breathe. Especially when his tongue ran over the whorl of her ear.

"Emma," he murmured. "What do you like? What do you want?"

"You. Just you." She couldn't kiss him deeply enough. She needed more. More of him. All of him. His mouth, his hands. His body. Just when she thought she'd melt into a puddle, Dair pulled back. He cupped her face with his hands. His eyes had darkened, gone nearly black. Deep. Mysterious. Beautiful.

Then something flashed in those dark depths, an emotion Emma couldn't quite place. Regret? Concern?

Oh, no. He wasn't going to stop, was he? He hadn't up and decided he was taking advantage of a lonely widow or something stupid like that. That conscience he denied hadn't raised its ugly head, had it?

Good heavens. She had to do something. Now!

Emma smiled a seductress's smile, full of promise, brimming with wickedness. "Take off your clothes, MacRae. I want to see you."

Dair's breath was backing up in his lungs. He held on to his control by a thin, frayed thread, one that grew more ragged with every brush of her finger, every whiff of her scent. When was the last time a woman had affected him this way? Had him ready to fall on her and plunder, driven by a need that pulsed in his veins like a drumbeat. He couldn't recall. But then, he could barely think at all.

He yanked at the buttons of her ball gown, tore at her laces, ripped the delicate silk of her underclothes. He wanted… no, he needed…her naked skin. Her soft, satiny skin pressed against his.

"Beautiful," he murmured, drinking in the sight of her, ivory skin against midnight-blue sheets. The ruby necklace nestled between full, coral-tipped breasts. A waist he could span with his hands. Round hips. Legs the perfect length to wrap around him and that tempting burnished-gold triangle… God. Desire balled in his stomach like a fist.

Dair struggled to slow down, to take his time and enjoy the moment. He lowered his head and kissed her again, tasting her with soft kisses, caressing her face with light fingers, all the while trying to keep the hammering need for her in check. He nipped at her full lower lip, tugging gently between his teeth. Without stopping his attentions, he slid his hands slowly from her face and traced down to her breasts.

"Perfect," he breathed against her swollen lips. "You are perfect."

He lowered his head to take one taut nipple into his mouth.

Emma arched up against Dair as he suckled, her earthy cry stoking the primal instinct burning inside him. She was his. This beautiful, spirited, most special woman was his for the taking. The knowledge pushed him over the edge.

Gripped by urgency, he stripped off his own clothing and climbed onto the bed, onto her, her sigh of pleasure at the contact a sonata to his ears. She was soft to his hard. Silk where he was rough. She was wet for him. Ready for him. Dair gave in to instinct and growled.

His hands went everywhere. Stroking, brushing, exploring. Up along her arms, across her shoulders, circling her breasts. Her creamy skin quivered and shuddered at his touch. He trailed a finger down the center of her torso past her navel toward the prize he intended to claim. Her hips moved restlessly and a needy groan escaped her throat. Her legs spread and Dair closed his eyes and sucked in a breath, summoning every ounce of his control to resist the invitation.

Too fast. Too soon. He wanted this to last.

Apparently, Emma didn't have his patience. Betraying her frustration, she reached for him, but Dair caught her wrists and pinned her to the bed as he captured her mouth in a deep, erotic kiss. He lingered there, his tongue plunging and playing until her muscles went limp. He skimmed his lips along her jaw, then paused to savor her throat.

Dair wanted to taste every inch of her, to sample and feast of her flavors. Tart. Sweet. Spicy. Arousing him beyond imagining. She smelled of roses and woman, and Dair indulged himself in her scent.

"Dair," she whimpered, her voice thready with need.

"Mmm," he murmured as he kissed his way down her body, tracing the path his hands had taken moments before.

Teasing them both, just like before, by avoiding the banquet he desired most.

Emma thrashed against the mattress. Whimpering. Dair almost echoed her as he continued the wickedly delicious torture. He gently nipped the inside of her thighs. Licked the back of her knees. Nibbled at her toes. Finally, she rose up on her elbows and begged, "Please!"

He shifted his gaze, spied the desperation in her eyes, and grinned. Her reaction caught him by surprise. Emma bared her teeth and growled at him, a sexy she-cat with fire in her eyes that mesmerized him so completely that he never saw her coming until she launched herself at him, knocking him onto his back.

He couldn't get his breath, not as a result of the force of her blow, but from her sensual assault.

Emma evidently believed in the axiom that turnabout was fair play. Her hands smoothed across his body, her clever fingers learning him, tracing the curve of his muscles beneath his skin. She tangled her fingers in the hair on his chest, scraped her nails across his sensitive nipples, then teased her way down toward his groin. He groaned when he realized her mouth was tracing the same trail.

Dair's blood was liquid fire racing through his veins. His body ached, yearning to the point of pain as his hips thrust forward instinctively. Emma shifted above him. He sensed her hovering hand, felt the warm caress of her breath on his shaft, and Dair shuddered.

Her voice came out low and raspy. "I haven't been with a man in almost ten years, MacRae." She ran the tip of her finger over his throbbing penis. "It's cruel of you to tease me."

Cruel? If he was cruel, then she was downright sadistic. "Emma, you don't have to—"

"I want to." She smiled again, that she-cat grin. "I'm going to."

Then, she gently cupped his sac, lowered her head and trailed her tongue up the length of him. When she dragged her lips over the supersensitive skin of his swollen head, she sent Dair sailing over the edge.

With a violent shout, he lifted her, rolled her onto her back and plunged into her tight, wet sheath. Emma groaned with delight and rose to meet him, taking him deep. Dair wanted to stop, to stay, to immerse himself in the pleasure of the moment, but nature had its claws in him and wouldn't be denied.

She arched against him, meeting him thrust for thrust. His hand fisted into her hair as her nails bit greedily into his back. Faster and faster they moved, driving higher. Harder. Sprinting for the crest. Dair's breath came in pants; her voice in mewling whimpers and encouraging whispers that edged him further toward their mutual need. When she lifted her legs and locked them around him, her name exploded from his lips like an oath. Dair thrust one last time, then emptied himself into her.

When he collapsed atop her, Emma let out a little sigh. Not, he realized, a necessarily satisfied sigh.

Well, hell. Dair had just enough energy to lift one corner of his mouth in a rueful grimace. For a man well-known on at least three continents for his seductive personality, his sexual techniques and his physical stamina, he'd been sadly lacking all around. The poor woman hadn't been bedded in a decade and he lasted all of what, five minutes? Eight at the outside?

Embarrassment, hell, even a bit of guilty shame slithered through him like a snake. Now, that was a new one.

Dair seldom felt shame under any circumstance and never while in bed with a woman. He didn't like the sensation one damned bit. *I'll make it up to her. As soon as I can move.*

Lying atop her, Emma's softness cradled him, her scent surrounded him, her breathing gave him comfort. He didn't really want to move—even if he could find the strength.

So, he wouldn't hurry. He'd give her a night she'd never forget. He'd devote himself to pleasing her, fulfilling her every desire, indulging her every fantasy. He'd stay with her until dawn.

That's something he never did with the women he bedded. Dair enjoyed women, enjoyed sex, but he always slept alone. Not that he'd do any sleeping with Emma McBride tonight. No, sleeping could wait until tomorrow when he was ensconced in Jake Kimball's comfortable coach headed north, her ruby necklace tucked away inside his pocket.

Such a plan would well suit his purposes, now that he considered the idea. Pleasantly exhausted, she'd undoubtedly sleep late, and by the time she awakened to discover her necklace missing, he'd be well on his way to Scotland. It tied everything up quite nicely, he decided.

Ah, the sacrifices a man must make.

Buoyed by his plan, Dair levered himself up onto his arms and smiled down at Emma. "All right, then, Texas, now that I've taken the edge off, how about we get back to business?"

"You mean…we're not finished?"

"I'm not. Were you?"

"No!" she was quick to say. "I just thought…that is…"

Heavy and hard once again, Dair made his point with a long, slow stroke. "Oh…" she breathed on another sigh.

This time, the glimmer of satisfaction was there, along with a strong note of anticipation.

Renewed and recharged, Dair applied himself to his chosen task. He touched her where he wanted, which was everywhere. Soon she was trembling beneath him, her lips full and swollen from his steady, relentless attention, her nipples pointed and wet from his tender care, her skin sleek and damp and glowing with arousal. He took her up quickly the first time, his hands and mouth greedy and unrelenting. He watched, fascinated, as her skin flushed and her eyes glazed when she shattered, screaming, the proof of her pleasure flowing over his hand like honey.

Satisfaction rolled through him as she returned to earth, sobbing, but smiling. *There you go, Texas,* he thought with a certain sense of smugness. He'd redeemed himself quite well. She'd totally lost control.

And so it began, and continued, throughout the night, lasting longer and offering more than even Dair had imagined. Her enthusiastic response, her absolute trust and her complete surrender breached his defensive barriers and destroyed them. That piece of himself he always held apart during lovemaking blended with the rest leaving Dair completely engaged, totally enthralled. He forgot he was doing this for her.

Somewhere along the way, the night became not Emma's night to remember, nor even Dair's night to recall. Somewhere along the way, it became *their* night together. They became one.

IN THE HAZY SHADE OF DAWN as Emma lay sleeping, Dair slipped from the bed and silently dressed. He reached for the ruby necklace, then hesitated as that peculiar, unusual sensation of shame came slithering back.

For a long moment, he stood frozen, uncertain and unsure, until the nagging pressure of headache he'd tried to ignore for the past hour reminded him of the reality of his future. Or rather, his lack of a future.

He thought of the orphans and his responsibilities there. He considered the mystery and coincidence surrounding Emma's necklace. If something was there…

He could find another person to run the children's home, but the promise of this necklace was unique. He knew it deep in his bones.

He reached out to touch her one last time. The soft curve of her cheek, the silken splendor of her hair. But no. He couldn't touch her again. He didn't deserve the pleasure.

Dair dropped Emma's necklace into his pocket and quit the room.

CHAPTER SIX

RAYS OF SUNSHINE BEAMED through the window glass and warmed Emma's skin, tugging her from sleep. Without opening her eyes, she stretched lazily beneath the covers, cozy as cat in a basket beside the fire. Her body felt stiff and sore in places that had forgotten they could feel stiff and sore. A smug, sated smile stretched across her lips as she finally opened her eyes. To an empty room.

Relief washed over Emma as she sat up and touched the cool sheets beside her. He'd left the bed some time ago. Good.

Call her a coward, but she didn't want to face him yet. Last night, she'd acted like a true McBride Menace, albeit a grown-up one. She'd been brazen and bold and shameless. Why, she would have made her grandmother proud!

Her father, however, would have a different outlook. "Well, Papa," she said into the silence of the room. "You aren't here."

Thank God.

Surprisingly, Emma felt no shame this morning. Well, maybe just a little. Her wantonness did go against every principle she'd been taught, every moral truth she believed in. Her mother wouldn't approve of her actions, but then, Jenny had Papa. She didn't know what it was like to sleep alone, night after night, year after year. Maybe later Emma would feel worse about her actions, but right now, she simply felt too good to feel bad.

Although, she was glad to have some time to think before she faced Dair again. She needed to understand her own emotions so she'd know how to react to him. Not that she'd have much time to do the reacting. She'd promised Kat they would leave today.

Maybe you won't even have to see him again.

That thought certainly left her with mixed emotions. The idea of sneaking off without having to face him for an awkward morning after had a real appeal. The idea of leaving Chatham Park without ever seeing him again left her feeling bereft.

"Oh, hang it all," she muttered as she threw back the bedcovers and headed for the water closet adjacent to Dair's bedroom where she found the day's first sign of his presence. He'd left her a single red rose atop a clean change of clothing. Emma smiled at his consideration and sniffed the rose. She'd save it. Press it as a memory, and take it out on rainy afternoons, thinking of the man who called her Texas.

Setting the flower aside, she washed and dressed, her thoughts in a whirl. Of course, she wouldn't leave without talking to Dair. She needed to see him one more time. She wanted one last look at those eyes, his smile. So, she'd face him and she'd thank him for a lovely night. Period. She wouldn't have to go into detail. She need not tell him how wonderful he'd been or how delicious he'd made her feel. Frankly, she'd told him all that nonverbally last night.

So, she had a plan. One that made sense. She'd speak to him, then she'd pack up her memories and her sister and she'd head home to Texas, happy to have experienced such a phenomenal man, such a marvelous adventure.

Better do it sooner rather than later. He was the type of man she could fall for if given half the chance. Fall for hard.

"Not what I need," she murmured as she picked up the hairbrush he'd left with the clothing. Dair seemed like the type of man who'd never settle for home and hearth, and as much as Emma had enjoyed her adventure, adventure is merely that. Family was real. Family was forever.

She stood in front of a mirror while she brushed her hair, debating which hairstyle would work best to cover up the love bite on the side of her neck. Although, she thought, smiling, maybe she shouldn't cover it up. Maybe she should pin up her hair and dare someone to comment.

Kat was sure to spot it right off, and she'd more than likely give Emma a piece of her mind because of it. Her sister hadn't always been so distrustful of men, but ever since she found herself with child by a scoundrel, she—

"Oh." The hairbrush slid from her hand and banged against the floor. "Oh, Holy Hannah. What was I thinking!"

They'd taken no precautions last night. She'd been prepared, had the sheaths her grandmother had given her in her evening bag. Monique always believed in being prepared. But when Dair asked her to go upstairs with him, she'd forgotten all about them! How could she have been so foolish? She was almost thirty years old, for goodness' sake. She'd witnessed that particular lesson firsthand watching Kat become an unwed mother. Kat, who'd at least had the excuse of believing herself married at the time.

What would she do if she turned up pregnant?

You'd have the baby you've always wanted. The child you didn't get to have with Casey.

Maybe she'd forgotten the sheaths on purpose.

"No!" That sort of behavior went way beyond Menacing to truly self-destructive. She'd wouldn't do that. Would she?

Maybe it didn't matter. Gnawing on her lower lip, Emma did some quick calculations in her head. No. This was the wrong time of the month. Or, the right time, considering the circumstances. While accidents could always happen, she thought she was in the clear. She wasn't the most fertile of women, anyway. She and Casey hadn't made a baby, and they'd made love every night they were married up until the day he fell sick with pneumonia.

"Don't borrow trouble," she said to her reflection. Besides, she was almost thirty, wasn't she? Often women were done having children by then. Maybe she'd be that way. Maybe she was already too old.

She ran her hand over her stomach as longing swept through her. Too old. With that depressing thought, Emma pinched some color back into her cheeks, then made quick work of finishing her hairstyle. A quick check of the clock showed her she'd slept most of the morning away. No wonder, since she'd managed only snatches of sleep during the night. Still, she was surprised that her sister hadn't come looking for her yet.

Maybe Kat had checked her bedroom and assumed she was already up and out of the house, as was her norm. That sounded like a good idea, in fact. If she could sneak outside without being seen, then she could turn around and make a grand entrance and talk about the long, lovely walk she'd taken on the estate.

Happy with the plan, she slipped into her shoes, then reached for her necklace on the bedside table. Emma frowned. The necklace wasn't there. That's strange. She distinctly remembered when Dair took it off her and set it on the table.

She checked the floor, then beneath the bed. Nothing. Where in the world could it have gone?

Emma spent the next ten minutes giving the room a thorough search. She checked the bedding, the bureaus, and even the balcony. She went down on her hands and knees and examined the wooden floor, rugs and tiles. She even stirred through the ashes in the fireplace. Still nothing. Her necklace wasn't here.

Someone had taken it. Who? A sticky-fingered maid? Hard to believe that with all the treasures in this grand house a servant would risk their livelihood for the pendant she wore around her neck. Who else, then? Her host? Maybe. Jake Kimball had already stolen one McBride necklace, had he not?

Maybe one of the children did it. They could have sneaked in and swiped it on a dare. Heaven knows the McBride Menaces had done that sort of thing all the time.

Despite those possibilities and more running through Emma's brain, another suspect came to mind. Dair. The interest he'd taken in the piece had not missed her notice. The engraving obviously intrigued him. Maybe he'd decided to do some research on it in one of Chatham Park's libraries.

Or maybe he'd stolen it like his good buddy Jake.

No. Emma dismissed the idea as soon as it occurred. He wouldn't have done that. To make love to a woman for hours, then steal from her? What a betrayal that would be! Dair had to have more honor than that.

Still, he should have left her a note explaining that he borrowed it. He should have known she'd be worried. Men. Sometimes they simply didn't think.

Emma cautiously checked the hallway for signs of life, then seeing none, slipped from Dair's bedroom. She checked the rooms she'd known him to frequent first—the library, the study, a couple of drawing rooms. She asked an upstairs maid, a cook's assistant and a gardener trimming bushes outside the music room if they'd seen MacRae that morning. They all answered no.

She joined two of Jake's bride candidates doing embroidery in the morning room and managed to ferret out the information that while Jake had been in and out of the house much of the morning, Dair MacRae had made himself scarce. Emma sipped a cup of tea and pondered where to look next. She could find Kat and ask her, but she'd just as soon not have a private conversation with her sister right now. Kat would take one look at her and know how she'd spent the night, and Emma would just as soon avoid the conversation that would undoubtedly follow if at all possible.

The stables. That's where she should check next. The stablemaster would know if Dair had gone out for a ride. She could wait for him there. And, avoid Kat in the meantime.

Emma made her excuses to the brides, then left the house by a side door. She found the stablemaster at his desk doing paperwork and muttering about the increasing price of feed. Emma pasted on her brightest smile and said, "Excuse me, Mr. Wolcott, but I'm looking for Mr. MacRae. Have you seen him, by chance?"

"Chance had nothing to do with it," the man grumbled. "I'm an early riser—have to be with my job—but I like to have my coffee before I get to work. Didn't see why he had to be in such an all-fired hurry. It's a lot of work to get a coach ready for a long journey like that."

Emma froze. "A long journey?"

"Don't know why he wouldn't wait for the train. Mr. Kimball does have fine coaches and superior teams, but he'd have saved time going by train, and I could have had my coffee!"

Emma opened her mouth and attempted to speak, but nothing came out. Her stomach took a nauseated roll. She cleared her throat and clarified. "Dair MacRae left here early this morning? Headed for where?"

"Scotland. He could have caught a train in town at noon, but no. He had to head out right that minute. Loaded up a bunch of books and a big old basket of food, and asked for a driver willing to travel hard and fast. Took my new man, Charlie. Worries me a bit as the man's only been here a few days. I haven't got a measure of his mettle yet. I hope he'll do right by Mr. MacRae."

Do right by Mr. MacRae? The idea made Emma want to giggle hysterically. Then because her knees turned to water, she grabbed the back of a chair to steady herself, and drew in a deep breath in an effort to calm her pounding heart.

She remembered Dair looking at her necklace and saying, *I swear I've seen something similar before.*

He took it. The certainty roared through her. That bastard. That no-good lying thieving rogue. Betrayal sat in her stomach like a bad piece of meat. She swallowed hard, then said, "I see. Thank you, Mr. Wolcott. I appreciate your help."

Emma exited the stables with a smile pasted on her face. Behind her upturned lips, her teeth remained clenched. She wanted to scream and shout. She wanted to kick something. Break something. Dair MacRae's head, perhaps. Right after she cut off his dingus.

She felt a sick, slow churning in her gut. He'd used her. She'd given him her body and the horrible, awful, wicked, malicious, mean villain *used* her. The betrayal was beyond anything she'd ever felt in her life. She'd never seen it coming. She, whose judgement of character had never failed her before.

Well, it sure failed you this time. He'd fooled her. Pulled the wool over her eyes. Bluffed her. Sold her a possum hide for rabbit fur. How could she have been so stupid? So naive? How could she have let him touch her? Hold her? Take possession of her body, her soul? My God, what he'd done to her last night. What she'd let him do!

"I'll kill him," she swore, fury pounding through her veins. "I swear I'll have his guts for garters."

Emma veered off to the maze where she walked without error or hesitation to the Greek temple where her downfall had begun. She gathered up a handful of rocks from the walkway before taking a seat on a stone bench. Eyeing the chaise lounge, she conjured up his image in her mind and threw a pebble hard. "You bastard." She threw another rock. "I hope your coach breaks an axle." And another. "I hope you get stranded in the middle of nowhere." She threw two pebbles at once. "I hope a robber—"

Emma broke off abruptly. A robber. She let the remaining pebbles fall to the ground. "A robber."

Rising, she began to pace the temple floor. It was a foolish idea. Really. She wasn't twelve anymore. But she couldn't actually murder him, and this would serve him right, wouldn't it?

Hmm. She couldn't be certain of his route. She might never catch up with him. Never find him.

However, this might be a good project for Kat. It might be just what she needed to do away with the doldrums for good. Look at how much she'd enjoyed impersonating Wilhemina Peters. She'd get a real kick out of this. During the McBride Menace days, her sister loved this sort of mischief.

"Why not?" Emma murmured. "What can it hurt to try?"

Nothing. Not a darn thing. She gave a pebble she'd dropped a swift kick. As it bounced off the chaise, she left the temple and retraced her steps out of the maze. With a goal now in mind, she knew the urge to hurry, so she picked up her skirts and rushed toward the house. She'd try Kat's room first.

Upstairs, she gave a cursory knock, then walked inside saying, "Kat? I think it's time the McBride Menaces rode again."

But the room was empty, the only sign of her sister a half-written letter lying atop the desk. Thinking it might offer a clue to her sister's whereabouts, Emma snooped.

Dear Mari,

I held a baby yesterday. A beautiful little boy. Reminded me a lot of your little Drew. Holding him broke my heart.

I owe you an apology, Mari. I've been a terrible aunt to Drew and Madeline. I'm weak and sorry for it.

Kat went on to talk about Jake Kimball's nieces and her reaction to them. The last lines she wrote struck a chord in Emma's heart.

I'm trying very hard to get past losing Susie. I think had I a little more time, I might overcome the pain. However, Emma and I will be leaving Chatham Park today. Perhaps by the time I reach Texas I'll

There, the letter ended. "Oh, Kat."

Emma returned the page to the desktop and drummed her fingers on the surface. If what her sister had written was true, then Kat couldn't leave. For her sake, for Mari's sake, for Mari's children's sake, Kat needed to put this fear she'd developed after Susie's death behind her. If being around Jake Kimball's dependents a little longer would do the trick, then that's what Kat needed to do. Emma would give up on her idea.

Unless...I went alone. Emma's pulse jumped. She drew a deep breath, stepped away from the desk, and paced the room, her thoughts spinning. Alone. Hmm. Could she? Dare she? After last night, she figured she could dare just about anything.

Actually, going alone would be better. Kat wasn't as good a rider as Emma. She'd slow her down. Not to mention lecture her ears off. Ever since Rory Callahan did Kat wrong, she considered herself an expert on scoundrels. Because she'd tried to warn Emma about Dair, the I-warned-yous and I-told-you-sos would last all the way to Scotland. Besides, Emma didn't really want her family to know about her lapse in judgement—her night with a thief. That would only compound her feeling of stupidity.

What a fool I was. Thinking about it...recalling the boldness of her actions...her reaction to him. Her response to him. Emma closed her eyes. Humiliation flowed over her in waves. Fool! Fool! Fool! So she finally had an orgasm. Was it worth it? Was it worth losing her most prized possession? Not to mention her pride. And her self-respect.

How he must be laughing at her. The poor widow, so

desperate for a man that she'd let a thief into her bed. Into her heart.

"No!" Emma's spine snapped straight. Not her heart. Never that. She'd by God make sure the bastard knew it, too. She'd wrestle both her necklace and her self-respect back from the sorry scalawag, and her family—Kat—need never know.

Yes, going alone was looking better all the time.

I'll do it. Emma took a fresh sheet of stationery from the writing desk drawer and penned a note for her sister. Placing it in an envelope, she wrote Kat's name on the front and propped it atop the desk where her sister would see it. Then, hurrying to her own suite of rooms, she quickly packed a bag.

Emma made one more stop before leaving the house. She spent a good ten minutes in the armament room, choosing her weapons. Last night Dair MacRae had showed her his talent with a sword.

Soon he'd see what a McBride Menace could do with a gun and a Bowie knife. She'd never let him know that he'd broken her heart.

CHURCH BELLS CHIMED THREE in the afternoon throughout Edinburgh as Hamish Campbell stood on the front steps of his town house and accepted delivery of the telegram. He tipped the messenger generously, then opened the envelope, read the contents, and smiled.

Well, well, well. Wasn't this a surprise? He'd best get ready to welcome the boy home.

TEN HOURS AFTER DEPARTING Chatham Park, Emma stood in the shadows of a stand of trees keeping watch on the entrance to the Sleeping Dog Inn. An apt name, she decided, since this was where Jake Kimball's stablemaster claimed Dair would spend the night.

After confirming his route to Edinburgh, she'd taken the train north to get ahead of him. The ride passed in a blur, partly because her mind had been occupied with plans and problems and regrets, but also because she had difficulty seeing through the excess of tears in her eyes.

Emma never actually cried. She was too proud to do that. No, the wetness in her eyes was due to wind rushing through the open windows of the rail car, or perhaps from an allergic reaction to a plant in bloom. Be damned if she'd cry over the likes of Dair MacRae.

She drew a deep, calming breath and noted the scent of rain upon the air. Great. That's just what she needed to top off a simply horrid day.

She dared not leave her watch post. Though Jake Kimball's employee had been certain of the coachman's plans, Emma wanted visual confirmation before taking the next step in the scheme as it was rather labor intensive.

A raindrop smacked against her cheek and she stifled a groan, then moved beneath a leafier branch of the oak tree just as a coach pulled up into the yard. Awareness of any discomfort disappeared as her pulse sped up. Was it…? No. An elderly gentleman descended from the coach and tottered into the inn just as the skies opened up.

Lovely. Just lovely.

As rain seeped into her clothing, she reminded herself that she'd endured worse conditions during some of her McBride Menace escapades. A little rain wouldn't hurt her. She wasn't sugar. She wouldn't melt. After all, true adventure often required a bit of discomfort, did it not? And she wanted adventure. Didn't she? It was an itch in her blood. A need deep in her bones. Wasn't it?

Or had this morning's revelations in the wake of last night's...activity...cured her of the desire?

"No," she murmured. Her lust for life had been reborn and be hanged if she'd let Dair MacRae take that away from her.

In fact, she intended to have a good time dealing with the necklace thief. She'd indulge the remnants of her Menace-hood while achieving an adult's victory. An adult's revenge.

By God, she'd make the bastard pay.

Her spirits restored, Emma smiled as the rain continued to fall. When a second coach pulled up in front of the inn, she sensed that her prey had finally arrived. The door swung open and Dair MacRae stepped down...into a puddle of mud.

Emma allowed herself a little chuckle.

For a brief moment she was tempted to go after him here and now. She envisioned herself storming forward, treating him to a roundhouse punch, knocking him flat on his behind in the muddy yard. But that wouldn't have the drama she'd been looking for, the humiliation factor she craved, so she resisted, watched him enter the inn, and planned.

"Until tomorrow, thief."

Secure in the knowledge that Kimball's stablemaster had indeed known Dair's route, Emma retreated to the tidy cottage near the train depot and the room she'd rented earlier in the day. There she bathed, dressed in her nightgown, and crawled into a warm, dry, comfortable bed. She slept, and dreamed of retribution.

EMMA AWOKE BEFORE DAWN. As she pulled on her uniform for the day—a young man's shirt, trousers and boots—excitement sang in Emma's veins. It was really too bad that her sisters weren't here with her. She so much would have enjoyed sharing the adventure with them.

Outside, she retrieved her rented horse and headed out. Dawn broke in a beautiful palate of mauve, purple and pink, and Emma laughed aloud with sheer joy, filled with the sense of her own power. She, Emma McBride Tate, was back. She'd teach that thieving scalawag to mess with a McBride Menace. Sometime within the next hour, she figured.

Taking up position on a hill some eight miles from town at the spot she'd prepared the previous day, she watched the countryside below. When she spied his coach climbing the winding road, she'd rolled the hired wagon into the middle of the road and destroyed its axle.

Dair's coach had stopped exactly where she'd intended, and as she drew her weapon, again, Emma grinned.

DAIR LAY SPRAWLED ACROSS THE coach's leather seats lost in a sea of pain. A herd of horses thundered across his brain, their steel shoes pounding his tender head mercilessly. He seriously considered instructing the driver to turn the coach around and return to the inn they'd left a short time ago.

He'd awakened with a headache this morning, but that was nothing new. It had eased after breakfast, and he'd felt fine as he boarded the coach and resumed his reading of the research books he'd brought from Chatham Park. Then, while reading about the history of the Kandabhar Ruby, pain struck with a speed and intensity beyond anything he'd previously experienced.

Was this it, then? Had his time run out? At the moment, he'd almost welcome death. How pitiful was that? He'd die a weakling curled up like an infant in a borrowed coach. He never thought he'd live to an old age, but he'd expected to meet his end in an honorably violent manner. Shot by a jealous husband or brought down by a lawman's gun. Not killed by a damnable disease devouring him from within.

Dair heard the gunshot, and at first he thought his mind was playing tricks on him by conjuring up the violent end he'd anticipated. But when another shot sounded and the coach slowed, then stopped, he realized they were in reality under attack.

Despite the agony in his head, Dair smiled. Here was his chance, his opportunity to meet death on his own terms rather than wait for it to take him.

He thought of the orphanage with regret. He'd failed in his mission, but he'd put his faith in the letters he'd sent yesterday. He knew that the others—the three Texans who'd been like brothers to him—would step in to take up the slack.

He had a longer memory of his night with Emma. In his mind's eye, he saw her lying in his bed, sated and sleeping. Now there was an image to take to one's grave. The smile on his face widened as he reached for his gun.

As the coach rolled to a halt a voice rang out, "Stand and deliver."

Stand and deliver? Dair snorted at the dated line. Who was out there, a century-old highwayman? More likely a fifteen-year-old boy, judging from the lack of depth to his voice. Probably lads on a dare. Foolish boys, he thought. With mischief like this, someone could end up dead.

From outside the coach, he heard horses neighing. The driver began cursing.

"Drop the gun!" cautioned a voice.

A familiar voice.

No. Surely not. The pain must be affecting his hearing.

"Driver, climb down. No, not this side. The other. Away from me." Then, "You, in the coach. Throw out your weapons."

It *was* her. Dair lurched forward, shoved open the door, and stuck his head and shoulders out of the coach.

She sat astride an animal more nag than horse. She wore a boy's trousers and shirt, and she carried a Colt revolver in one hand and a Bowie knife in the other. In his pained fog, he recalled she was an excellent shot. Maybe she'd put him out of his misery. "Emma?"

Even as he spoke her name, his speed of forward motion caused the pressure in his head to explode into debilitating agony. Nausea swirled in Dair's stomach. His eyes rolled back in his head, and his legs lost the ability to support him. He tumbled from the coach onto the ground.

The last thing he heard before losing himself in the pain was Emma Tate's sigh of disgust. "Get up, MacRae. I haven't shot you yet."

THAT'S WHEN THINGS WENT wrong. Climbing down from the sorry excuse of a horse she'd rented, she stared down at the man sprawled on the ground and nudged him with her boot. At least he was still breathing. "You weren't supposed to fall down before I so much as touched you."

Then she shot a glare toward the driver. "What's wrong with him, Charlie?"

The cowering driver dragged his gaze off her Colt long enough to lower his hands and asked, "You know my name?"

"Yes." She sighed in frustration, then lied, "Jake Kimball sent me."

"To rob his own coach?"

"It's a joke. What's wrong with Mr. MacRae?"

"I don't know, ma'am." Charlie-the-driver shrugged. "He didn't say much when he came out to meet me this morning. I did notice he was rubbing his head, though."

Was he drunk? Emma leaned over him and sniffed. She smelled no sign of alcohol mixed in with his usual sandalwood scent. The appealing fragrance triggered a memory of the man rising naked above her, but Emma quickly shoved it away.

He groaned as she squatted down beside him and felt his forehead with the back of her hand. No fever. She tested the pulse in his neck. Steady and strong. "Was he ill yesterday?"

The driver shrugged. "He didn't have much to say, ma'am. I can't say I noticed anything peculiar."

Emma frowned down at Dair for a moment, then touched his shoulder and tried to shake a response from him. He did let out another little groan which she found reassuring. She'd been around a lot of sickness over the years, but she'd never seen anything like this. She didn't want him to die. Not until she had the chance to kill him, anyway.

"Well, first things first," she murmured. Reaching out, she began to search his pockets. When her fingers brushed against a familiar gold chain, she smiled with satisfaction.

Emma pulled her necklace from Dair MacRae's pocket, then slipped it over her head and around her neck, back where it belonged. Rising, she braced her hands on her hips, stared down at the prone man, and pondered her options.

She had her necklace back. She could just wash her hands of the sorry bounder and head back to Chatham Park. Back to Texas, for that matter. It's what she should do, probably. He deserved no more. She should just climb back on her horse and ride on. Never mind that she'd be leaving him lying helpless and vulnerable in the middle of the road. He'd left her lying helpless and vulnerable, hadn't he? Was the middle of the road a worse place for that to happen than his bed? Not from her point of view, it wasn't.

And yet, Emma couldn't quite find it in herself to kick the man when he was down. Either literally or figuratively. Exhaling a heavy sigh, she said, "Help me get him into the coach."

The driver hemmed and hawed and backed away. "I don't know, ma'am. What if he's sick? I don't wanna catch nothin'."

Calmly, Emma reached for her gun belt and drew the Colt once again. Taking aim at the driver, she said, "Pick him up."

"I thought this was just a joke."

"Not anymore."

Dair was deadweight as Emma and a visibly disgruntled Charlie struggled to lift him back into the coach. Emma wished she could direct the driver to take MacRae to the nearest physician while she went on about her business, but she didn't dare trust the man at this point. She couldn't trust any man, for that matter. Well, except for her father, her uncle. Mari's Luke. Maybe her younger brothers. And they were all on the other side of the ocean. *Thank goodness.*

Most infuriating of all, Emma realized she was worried to death about the blackguard. "Don't you dare die on me, Dair MacRae. I want the pleasure of killing you myself."

When she caught Charlie eyeing her rented horse speculatively, she snapped, "Don't even think about it. You're going to drive us back to the village to the physician's office."

"But that town doesn't have a doctor. I've a lady friend

who lives there, so that's how I know. If you want a doctor, you'll have to go all the way to the next town."

"How far is that?"

"From here? Probably a two hour drive by coach."

So far. Emma's teeth tugged at her bottom lip as she gazed at Dair worriedly. As she watched, his brow creased and his face stretched in a grimace. "Dair?"

Nothing.

"Tie my horse to the back, then drive us as fast as you can to the doctor." Emma didn't know what else to do.

Once the coach was on the move, she tried to spend her time looking out the window. She'd never traveled this particular road before. She might see some unique and unusual sights if she kept a close watch. At the very least, she'd be able to give her students a thorough description of the area during their geography lesson.

Instead her gaze kept drifting back to the man slumped against the seat across from her. She hated him. She did. She truly did. Nonetheless, he looked so pitiful she couldn't stand it, and she switched seats, sat beside him, and lifted his head into her lap. Almost against her will, her fingers stroked his thick, silky hair and smoothed away the creases at his temples.

He appeared to be in pain. She wished he'd open his eyes. She wished they weren't out in the middle of nowhere far away from a doctor's help. "What's wrong with you, Dair?" she murmured. "How can I help you?"

"Don't stop," he mumbled into her lap.

Her hand froze midstroke, her thigh muscles beneath his head went tense.

"Please, don't stop."

Her fingers curled into his hair all ready to pull. But

something in his voice—a note of pleading pain—caused her to hesitate. "What's wrong with you, Dair?"

"Head. Hurts."

Emma continued to pet him. She'd do that much for a dog, she decided, making the excuse her pride demanded. This was basic human kindness. She'd do this much for anybody. That's the way she'd been raised.

It's not like she was enjoying having his head in her lap or anything, because she wasn't. Truly. It was difficult to be near him. Hard to touch him. Each time she did, she was reminded of what a fool she'd been. She'd loved touching him. Thrilled at being touched by him. She burned with embarrassment at the memory of it. "You'd better get better so I can hurt you, MacRae."

"Mmmm," he responded.

The coach continued to move forward, Emma continued to stroke, and Dair continued to lie quietly in her lap as both minutes and miles rolled by. From time to time she checked his pulse, his body temperature, her watch. Time crawled in circumstances like this. The half hour they traveled seemed more like an hour and a half.

The change occurred slowly, so slowly that Emma almost missed it. It was more a difference in the air than in the way he rested, and it took Emma a moment to figure out what it was.

"You're better." She shoved him off her lap, then scrambled into the opposite seat.

Dair grimaced as he sat up. "So I wasn't dreaming. You really are here. And you're wearing pants?" He paused a moment, winced, then added, "Emma, did you hold up my coach?"

"Yes I did," she snapped. "I got what I came for, too."

Dair frowned, then reached into his pocket. "Well, hell."

"Are you sick, MacRae? What happened to you?"

"You stole the necklace."

"Excuse me? *I* stole the necklace?" Rage, hot and volatile, bubbled up inside her like lava. Drawing her gun, she demanded, "Are you recovered, MacRae? Tell me now so that I can get on with killing you."

Dair eyed the gun, then the light in her eyes. "My thinking is slow right now, so you'll forgive me if I'm confused."

"I'm not forgiving you anything."

"All right, then. Just let me see if I have this straight. You followed me in order to reclaim your necklace and shoot me."

"Stabbing you is an option, too. After I cut off various appendages, that is."

Dair grimaced and rested his hands over his lap. "I never realized you were so vicious."

"And I didn't realize you were such a villain."

Dair leaned his head against the seat back and closed his eyes. "Should I be grateful I still have all my body parts?"

"Definitely." He still looked pale, Emma thought. Concern battled with anger inside her. She appeased both by asking in a snotty tone of voice, "So, are you going to die or what?"

It took him awhile to respond, and Emma's stomach clenched. His mouth quirked. "Eventually. We all do. Although, my demise is evidently not at this particular moment unless you have a hand in the process. While you've been quite convincing with your threats, I doubt you'll actually follow through—"

"Oh, I wouldn't be so certain if—"

"—once I explain why I stole the necklace."

"—I were...what?"

"Aren't you curious about why I stole your beloved jewel and left you lying naked in my bed following the most thrilling night of my life?"

The most *thrilling?* A shiver danced up her spine.

Emma almost fell for it, but then she remembered that he was a liar, a thief, a rogue, a blackguard, a cad, and undoubtedly another dozen similar monikers not presently popping to mind. She cocked the gun. "Whether I'm curious or not doesn't really matter. I can't trust anything that comes out of your mouth."

She could see in his eyes that he didn't like that. When speculation replaced irritation and his gaze dropped to focus on her mouth, she shook her head. "Don't even think about it."

"I haven't stopped thinking about it, Texas."

"Don't call me that."

"Do you believe in fate, Emma Tate?"

She shrugged, unwilling to engage him in any more conversation. Doing so would only encourage him, make him think he'd stirred her curiosity. Never mind that he'd succeeded. Pride wouldn't allow her to let him know it.

"I do," he continued. "I believe fate brought you and me together. Fate and perhaps the mystical power of a mysterious engraved ruby."

Mystical power? Emma about chewed her tongue in order to prevent herself from asking him to elaborate.

And he didn't, the bounder. He just sat there with his eyes closed, relaxed as a cat sleeping in sunshine, totally ignoring both her and the fact that she still had a gun trained on him.

Emma decided she'd never met another human being as annoying as Alasdair MacRae.

After a five minute or longer silence during which she fantasized about taking her knife to him, toe by toe, he finally spoke. "So, where are we going? Back to Chatham Park?"

"No. To the nearest physician. I thought you were dying. It's unsanitary to leave corpses beside the road, and it's my understanding that in small towns, physicians also often serve as morticians."

Dair, the bastard, started laughing. "Definitely a vicious streak. I'll have to remember that."

The sound of his laughter grated on Emma's nerves, and in that moment, she wanted away from the man. Far away. She rapped on the window and called to the driver. "Stop. Let me out."

"Is he dead?" came the reply.

"Not yet," Dair called back.

"Might not be long, though," she added. "Stop the horses, Charlie. I'm leaving."

The coach began to slow and Dair casually propped his feet on the seat across from him. Next to her. Blocking her exit. "That won't stop me."

"I never thought it would. I'm simply stretching my legs, getting comfortable while I tell you the story of Roslin of Strathardle."

Roslin of Strathardle? How did he know about her? Emma shot him a look. He studied his fingertips as if he hadn't a worry in the world.

He knew he had her, of course. The villain. He didn't say a word when the coach rolled to a stop and Charlie climbed down from his perch and opened the door. "Ma'am?"

It hurt, but Emma grumbled, "I've changed my mind."

Charlie opened his mouth, but apparently thought better

of complaining when Emma shifted her gun. He nodded, shut the door, and moments later, their journey resumed.

The bastard had the good sense not to make her wait this time. After rolling his tongue around in his mouth, he said, "I believe I told you that I was born in Texas. I never knew my father, but I'd like to tell you about my mother. She was a Scot. Her name was Roslin and she grew up in Strathardle Glen."

Emma reached to hold her pendant. "You think your mother gave us our necklaces?"

"That's a tough one." Dair rubbed the back of his neck. "While I do believe in fate, I'm not so certain about ghosts. My mother died when I was a child."

Emma leaned away from him. "No. I don't believe…"

"I don't know what I think about that. What I do know is that I recognize the engraving on your ruby. It has something to do with my family."

She stared at him long and hard before giving her head a shake. "You're lying. You're a liar."

"Yes, it's a fair accusation. However, I'm not lying about this. I've seen a similar carving before, and I know that it's something important. Think about it, Emma. You and your sisters received your necklaces from a woman named Roslin of Strathardle."

"How do you know that?"

"We had you investigated." Ignoring Emma's outraged gasp, he continued, "It's too coincidental not to mean something. Jake with his interest in the emerald and—"

"Why did he steal Kat's necklace?"

"That's his story to tell, not mine. I will say this, however. After meeting Kat, I believe she's destined to become his wife."

"You think she'll marry him?" she asked, thinking of the bride hunt.

"I do. And the two of them will make a family with the children left to his care."

Emma's thoughts drifted back to the night when she and her sisters were given their necklaces. It was shortly before Emma married Casey, and the three McBride sisters had decided to act like McBride Menaces one last time by visiting Fort Worth's red light district, Hell's Half Acre, and having their palms read. Instead of Fort Worth's own Madam Valentina, they were met by a beautiful, ethereal woman who called herself Roslin of Strathardle. She read their palms, declared they had a Bad Luck Love Line, and announced that as a circle of three in the thirty-third generation, they had the opportunity to end the bad luck curse for all time. Roslin told them they could break the curse if they each found a love that was powerful, vigilant and true, and accomplished a mysterious task.

Emma's pulse began to race. Love that is powerful, vigilant and true. What if Dair was right? "Is he a good man, Jake Kimball?" she demanded. "A worthy man?"

"Worthy of what?"

My sister's love. Emma could use a little reassurance. The ramifications of what he was proposing were daunting. "All I know about him is that he's a thief and a treasure hunter. Kat's already been put through hell by a scoundrel once, and she doesn't need to go through a similar trauma again."

"Jake doesn't give his word often. He doesn't commit himself very easily. Once he does, he's fierce about it. If he marries your sister, he'll be loyal to her. He'll be faithful."

But will he love her? Would Jake Kimball be the one who finally helped Kat heal? Would he be the love who helped Kat meet the requirements to fulfill her part in breaking the curse? If so, what did that mean for Emma?

Mari had found a powerful, vigilant and true love and accomplished her task. If not for her sapphire necklace, that might not have happened. If Kat found similar success with Jake Kimball, her emerald pendant would have played a significant role in the process. Logic then suggested that the ruby might play a similar role for Emma. Oh, my. Did that mean…could it be… surely it's not. *He's* not.

"What is it, Emma?" Dair asked. "Why such a sour look?"

Emma swallowed hard. No, she couldn't believe it. She wouldn't believe it. He'd lied to her. Stolen from her. After he'd slept with her!

Dair MacRae could not be her destiny.

CHAPTER SEVEN

"WHY THE SOUR LOOK?" Dair repeated, wanting to know what he'd said to cause such a strong negative reaction. He'd be sure to avoid a similar mistake in the future.

"I just…I don't…oh, my."

She drummed her fingers on her pants leg and Dair was momentarily distracted by the intriguing sight of a woman wearing male clothing. Tight-fitting male clothing. His fingers itched to touch her.

Instead, he cleared his throat and searched his mind for something to distract them both. "Jake will be good for your sister. Rest assured."

"This isn't about my sister!" The words exploded from her mouth. "Why does everyone always think the world revolves around Kat. What about me? If your theory is correct, where do I fit into the equation? If you're trying to tell me that since my necklace is somehow connected to your family that means I'm fated to be tied to…to…to you, then I have to tell you, MacRae, you're crazy."

"What? I don't think I ever said that." Fate was tying him to the grave, not a beautiful woman. He opened his mouth to reassure her that he wasn't crazy, but dying instead, when instinct stilled his tongue.

He didn't want her to know he was dying. Be damned

if he'd open himself up that way, to her or to anyone. He didn't want pity. Didn't want anyone feeling sorry for him. He'd rather Emma think he'd lost his mind.

Dair reached for her hand and kissed her knuckles. "That's exactly what I think, Texas. I think you and I are destined—" he bit back a grin as she snatched her hand away "—to be lovers."

"My God. You *are* crazy."

Warming to the game, he continued, "We've exciting times ahead of us. It will be a real adventure to—"

"Stop it!" she demanded. "I won't listen to this. Not only do I not believe a word you say, it's asinine for you to think I'd even consider the possibility of a relationship with you."

"Why? We were great together in bed."

She blinked hard twice. Aha. That struck a blow, didn't it? She might not admit it, but he'd curled her toes.

Now, color crawled up her skin. If a cartoonist were portraying the moment, he'd draw her with steam shooting from her ears. Maybe the top of her head blowing off. It was all Dair could do not to chortle, to guffaw, to laugh out loud. She was so damned beautiful when she was angry.

Dair settled back into his seat and idly took her measure. Obviously, he had a lot of ground to make up. Emma felt betrayed, and he couldn't blame her. He didn't like how events had played out, himself. Emma Tate was a good and decent woman, and he'd treated her poorly.

Yet, he didn't know what he'd change. If he had to do it over again, would he pass up the night spent in her bed? No. Absolutely not. He could live with a little guilt in the time he had left. One more sin. And this one he'd gladly burn for. He might regret hurting her—but he'd never regret bedding her.

Since he wasn't letting her walk off with the ruby, it only made sense to convince her to accompany him to Scotland. In fact, this might work out for the best, after all. Maybe he'd solve the puzzle of the ruby *and* convince her to take the position at the children's home. And if he soothed her ruffled feathers enough to lure her back into his bed, could it get any better than that?

Besides, she'd already seen him at his worst. Once the pain faded to where he could think again and he realized where he was and who he was with, he'd been torn between anger and gratitude. He'd been embarrassed, his pride battered at having been observed in vulnerable circumstances. He hadn't experienced those emotions in years. He'd found it humiliating.

Yet, the sensation of lying on her luscious lap, her fingers stroking his head with gentleness, comfort and care had appealed to something within him long neglected, long forgotten. If he'd died right then, it would have been all right. Instead she'd caught him playing possum as he'd tried to string thoughts together that made sense to his sluggish, pain-muddled mind.

He'd recovered well enough, he assured himself. Now he needed to set aside his lingering embarrassment and go on the offensive. Her appearance—surprising though it was—offered an opportunity. Dair simply needed to take advantage of it. Take advantage of her.

Judging by the furious look on her face, he faced an uphill climb gaining what he wanted, but Dair never shied away from difficult tasks. In fact, he enjoyed a challenge now and again, and it had been quite some time since a woman offered any. If he tired of the effort, he could always fall back on force.

Calling on his vast experience with women, he leaned forward, braced his arms on his knees and went to work. "Come with me to Edinburgh, Emma. I want to take the necklace to an acquaintance of mine who is an expert on clan history. I suspect he'll know what those words and symbol on the ruby mean."

Temptation sparked briefly in her eyes, then she shook her head. Hard. "No. Absolutely not. I'm not going anywhere with you. You're certainly not taking my necklace anywhere."

His voice ringing with an honesty that even he found surprising, Dair continued, "Leaving you the way I did was one of the most difficult things I've ever done. I'm sorry if it hurt you. I thought I was doing what was best for you."

She'd gone totally still. Though she obviously tried to hide it, she was listening hard.

"Now, after reliving those wondrous hours and analyzing my own reaction, I realize just how wrong I was. I should have been honest with you from the beginning. I should have given you the choice to come along with me, to pursue this quest. In my effort to protect you, I hurt you, and for that I apologize."

"You amaze me." She shook her head in wonderment. "That speech was as shy of the truth as a pig is of feathers."

Dair sat back, unaccountably pleased. This wouldn't be as easy as it usually was. He'd find it a pleasure to match wits with an intelligent woman for a change. "Obviously, trust is a problem I must overcome. What do you need from me, Emma?"

She folded her arms. "Your head on a platter, for starters."

"Vicious, Texas. Vicious."

He allowed silence to fall, giving her a chance to think matters through. Giving himself a chance to do the same.

Emma Tate invariably managed to surprise him. The woman was unpredictable. Exciting. Stimulating. He had spoken nothing but the truth when he'd talked of their night together. He couldn't wait for a repeat performance.

"I borrowed some books from Jake's library, and I learned some interesting things about rubies. Do you know it's a common belief that when one dreams of rubies, it means coming success in matters of love? Have you dreamed about your ruby as of late?"

"Last night I dreamed of wrapping my chain around your neck and using it to strangle you."

He let out a laugh at her petulant tone. "In China, rubies were carved with images of dragons and snakes to increase their owners' power and wealth. It's thought that a ruby grows darker when its owner is in danger, and that rubies can be used for protection from evildoers, enemies and thieves."

"Well, my ruby must be broken in that case."

"Ah, Emma, I'm crushed."

He stretched out his legs, propping one boot on top of the other. He intended to continue his ruby soliloquy, but she attempted to take the conversation in a different direction. "So what was wrong with you, MacRae? What made you so ill?"

Dair gave a nonchalant shrug. "Bad kidney pie at breakfast, I expect."

Emma's eyes narrowed with doubt. "That didn't look like a case of bad food to me."

"Well, I'm fine now," he replied, waving her concern away. "No need to go to the doctor, after all."

She did that drumming thing with her fingers again. Dair could all but see the wheels turning in her head. "No. It's better if a doctor examines you. We'll continue as planned."

Dair dragged a hand down his jaw and considered his options. Judging by what he knew of Emma, she'd be suspicious if he refused. Hmm…it'd probably be more expedient in the end to go ahead and humor her. He'd lie to the doctor, hand him the food poisoning diagnosis on a platter and few pound notes for his cooperation, and they could be on their way. "It's a waste of the man's fee, but I'll talk with him if it will reassure you."

She lifted her chin. "I don't care what you do. It doesn't matter to me. I'll be leaving at the first opportunity."

No, Texas, you won't. Dair continued his subtle campaign. "The ruby in the King of England's coronation ring is engraved with the figure of St. George's cross. Aren't you curious to understand the engraving on your ruby?"

"If I am, I can find out on my own. I don't need you."

"So you know an expert in ancient languages to consult? Someone in Fort Worth, perhaps?" he added, knowing the scant likelihood of that.

Emma narrowed her eyes. "I thought your expert was a historian, not a linguist."

"He's a man of many talents with extensive contacts in the academic world. One way or another, he'll be able to solve the mystery of your ruby."

Emma looked away, staring out the window. Sensing he'd made a bit of progress, Dair waited, allowing time for his words to simmer and stew. He watched her carefully, reading her response in the tilt of her head, the firmness of her chin. When a slight squaring of her shoulders clued that she was shoring up her defenses, he casually added, "I would have thought that the mystery of the ruby would have fired your imagination. I expected that a woman with such a strong streak of adventure in her character would leap at the opportunity to track down answers about the necklaces playing such a large part in her life."

Her head turned slowly, regally. Her voice dripped with disdain. "I won't be manipulated."

"I'll say it again, Emma." Dair reached out, but she shied away from his touch. "I'm sorry if I hurt you. That's honesty, not manipulation."

Her eyes flashed with anger, then glimmered with pain and humiliation. "I was easy plucking for you, wasn't I?" she said, bitterness heavy in her voice. "The lonely widow, desperate for a romp between the sheets. And I just happened to have something you wanted. A mysterious ruby. How lucky for you."

Seeing that look on her face, hearing the ugly words made his stomach churn. "It wasn't like that. It wasn't just about the necklace. I wanted you, too."

She flinched away in disbelief. "You know, it doesn't matter. No matter what you say at this point, it won't change the past. That's the past. We've only the present to deal with. I'll see what the physician says, then I'll make my decision."

"But I said—"

"What you say doesn't matter. My eyes are opened to you, Dair MacRae. You might as well keep your lying mouth shut. You have no influence over me whatsoever."

Frustrated, Dair set his teeth. How could he make her listen? How could he make her want to stay? That, Dair realized, was imperative. He didn't want her to leave, not his mind and not his presence. In a moment of selfish self-honesty, he admitted that, mysterious rubies and needy orphans aside, he wanted her with him for himself.

He faced a fierce battle to get back into her good graces.

He'd need better weapons than his usual charm and wicked grin. She wasn't like other women whose defenses he could breach with a suggestive wink. The memory of Emma's telling him she hadn't had sex in a decade flashed in his mind.

Weapons, hell. He might need a miracle to win this fight.

Dair braced himself for battle when the coach rolled to a stop in front of a small building and Charlie opened the door saying out, "This is the doctor's place."

"Very well," Dair replied, his gaze locked on Emma. When he made no move toward the door, the flash of temper in her eyes betrayed her frustration.

Finally, she let out a sigh. "Oh, for goodness' sake. Go in and be examined. Have him look into your ear. He's likely to be able to look straight through to the other side."

"Will you be here when I return?"

"I'm going with you." She placed her hand in the driver's and allowed him to assist her to the ground. "The doctor might have questions I can answer since I witnessed the event."

Hmm. Dair followed her from the coach, mentally preparing a classic description of food poisoning symptoms to present to the doctor for Emma's benefit.

Then another thought occurred. If he managed to get her to come along with him, she'd likely witness another headache. Food poisoning would be a tough sell twice.

Once inside the office, Dair allowed Emma to do the talking while he pondered a solution to his problem, eventually deciding that an exotic illness was his best bet. It took the portly, gray-haired physician a few minutes to get past the scandalous sight of a woman dressed in men's pants, but once he started listening, he began to ask questions. He played right into Dair's hands when he asked Emma to adjourn to the waiting room while he conducted a physical examination.

When the door shut behind her, Dair reached into his pocket and withdrew a wallet. Setting a handful of banknotes on the doctor's desk, he said, "You'll tell her I have a rare disease similar to malaria—call it Malaysian Yellow River Syndrome—that can strike at odd times."

"What?" The physician's eyes widened at the sight of the cash. "But…but…I've never heard of such a syndrome."

Of course not. Dair had just made it up. He added another bill to the stack saying, "Is that a problem for you?"

Avarice gleamed in the physicians's eyes. "No. No. Not at all."

"I didn't expect it would be. Now, listen well. You are to tell Mrs. Tate to take her caretaking cues from me. When I tell her to leave me alone, she must do that. Tell her it's very important I not be disturbed in any way."

Now that he thought about it, Dair could see other ways such a diagnosis could come in handy. "On the other hand, tell her that if I request her presence, ask for her touch, then it's imperative that she accommodate me. This syndrome is a tricky thing. Tell her she may well have saved my life this morning."

Hell, for all he knew it could be true. This morning's headache had been horrible, and her touch had soothed him.

The doctor's brow furrowed as he accused, "You intend to take advantage of that poor woman!"

What he intended was to win the battle. While he didn't want her to pity him because of his mortal condition, he wasn't above accepting any comfort she might be inclined to provide. As long as she offered it as a result of his lie, rather than the truth. Perverse of him, Dair realized, but a man had his pride.

Arching an inquisitive brow toward the doctor, Dair scooped up the cash. "I'll take my business elsewhere if you've trouble—"

"No. No." The physician waved both hands as he watched Dair start to put the money away. "Malaysian Yellow River Syndrome is a serious illness, and as your physician, I want you to have the treatment you need."

"Sensible thinking." Dair deposited the money into the desk drawer before taking a seat on the examination table where he shrugged from his coat and unbuttoned his shirt. "Make it good."

"Oh, I will. I spent a summer with a theater troupe in my younger days, and I played an excellent King Lear." He opened the door. Dair could see Emma seated in the waiting area thumbing through a book. "Ma'am, would you care to join us now?"

Dair was gratified by the worry she tried, but failed to hide. "Well, is he going to live?" she asked, just the slightest bit grudgingly.

"That depends." The physician's tone was solemn, his expression serious. "He's a very sick man."

Emma's concerned gaze darted toward Dair as the doctor launched into a theatric description of Malaysian Yellow River Syndrome. He overacted a bit, Dair thought, and when he saw the first flicker of doubt in Emma's eyes, he stepped in.

"I still think it was bad food," he said as he buttoned his shirt, then pulled on his jacket. "Don't pay any attention to the man, Emma. It's simply coincidence that I've had these spells from time to time since visiting Malaysia. I've had a finicky stomach all my life."

"I watched you eat eels at Chatham Park. Mr. Kimball's cook fixed haggis for breakfast specifically for you." She turned to the doctor. "What treatment do you recommend?"

Noting Dair's cautioning stare, the man kept the directions simple, repeating Dair's instructions almost to the word. Emma's brow furrowed as she considered what she'd just heard, and Dair thought it best to ease on out the door before she took it in her head to ask for more details. He handed the physician one final bill saying, "Your fee, sir. Thank you for your assistance." He then took Emma's arm and ushered her outside.

"But wait a minute," she began.

No, he didn't want her to have time to think. Emma was too intelligent. Better to close the deal now. "So, Emma. What will it be?" He reached out, fingered the ruby pendant. "Will you join me in the coach, or shall we ready your horse for a ride?"

She slapped his hand away from her necklace. At the show of spirit, Dair felt a surge of lust and he halfway hoped she'd refuse him. Look at her, dressed like a man, those britches showcasing her curves. He wanted his hands on her. He could easily visualize scooping her up and tossing her into the coach. He'd hold her tightly to restrain her, and he'd be forced to muffle her angry screams with his kiss. Either way, Dair came out a winner.

"I'm not a fool," she said, crossing her arms, her right foot beginning to tap. "I don't entirely trust that doctor and I certainly don't trust you. I recognized your attempts to prick my curiosity. I suspect that if I tried to climb on my horse right now, you would attempt to prevent me from leaving. You wouldn't succeed, MacRae. I've taken precautions."

"Oh?" He bit back a smile. Damn, she was something.

"I despise men who lie. That's one reason why I find the idea of traveling with you so disturbing."

"So, you'll come with me," Dair said, sensing victory, if not in the battle, at least in this initial skirmish.

"It's expedient," she said, shrugging. "However, we'll do this on my terms. You keep to yourself. I don't want you talking to me any more than necessary or touching me at all. We'll travel together, but separately."

She's scared of me. Good. I can work that to my advantage. He studied his fingernails and said, "If that's what you want…"

"It is. Now, a few other details. We'll need to hire someone to return my horse and arrange to have my things sent…where?"

"I own a town house. Number three Bennington Place in Edinburgh."

She looked up, then down the street. "In the meantime, I need to find a dress shop. My highwayman's adventure is over and I need more appropriate clothing."

"A pity. You look fetching in pants."

She offered him a droll smile. "I suggest you begin the no talking part now, MacRae. In fact, I can use a bit of a break from your company. Why don't you see to my horse and baggage while I make my necessary purchases. We can meet back here in say—" she thought for a moment and her hand reached up to hold the pendant "—three-quarters of an hour."

It was a test. Of that, Dair had no doubt. In an effort to show his cooperation, he kept his mouth shut and answered her with a nod. Turning to Charlie, he said, "If you'll see to Mrs. Tate's horse, I'll take care of the baggage arrangements."

He checked his pocket watch, gave Emma a two-fingered salute, and walked away whistling. She'd be waiting at the coach forty-five minutes from now. Emma Tate's word was gold.

So, then what? How best to accomplish his goals? Ride all the way to Edinburgh without talking to her? Sounded boring as hell. And no touching? That would be sheer torture. But it appeared to be important to her, and he guessed it'd be a good way to start earning back her trust. As he entered the telegraph office, Dair decided that particular task needed to be top of his list. To win the battle, he'd need Emma to trust him. Smart, intelligent Emma Tate.

"Can I help you, sir?" asked a man behind the counter.

"Know where I can find a miracle?"

THE TRIP TO EDINBURGH proved to be a nightmare. The coach broke down twice. Charlie took a wrong road three times, and Dair had another spell of sickness that had him holed up in a village inn and left her twiddling her thumbs and wondering if she'd made the biggest mistake of her life by tagging along. Her doubts increased the following day when he again claimed illness and asked for what he'd termed the "touch treatment."

Emma smelled something fishy about that whole Malaysian Syndrome business, but she couldn't deny his suffering. Though he hadn't been pale and shivering like the first time, no one could fake the glassy sheen of pain in his eyes. Could they?

So as he lay with his head in her lap, her fingers stroking

the furrows from his brow, threading through the thick, silky locks of his raven hair, sliding over the hard bulge of muscle in his arm, she'd reminded herself that she'd chosen to pursue the mystery of the ruby because that's what she wanted to do, not because it meant prolonging her contact with the lying thief. She'd made her decision in spite of that fact, in fact. Being around Dair MacRae all day every day was pure torment.

The man was a veritable sneak. When not incapacitated by his illness, he played by the letter of the law she'd laid down, never touching her, speaking to her only when necessary. And yet, he…hovered. He surrounded. He intruded. Without saying a word, he made her think and remember and feel. The sound of his breathing as he dozed reminded her of their night spent together. The scent of sandalwood that clung to him called to her. The lazy stretch of his leg as he propped a boot on the seat beside her drew her gaze and made her fingers itch to touch.

And then there was the way he watched her. She'd made a huge mistake by not including staring in her list of the forbidden. Time and time again she'd felt the weight of his gaze, and she'd look up and discover him watching her, his gray eyes intent. Sometimes smoldering. Sometimes downright hot. He'd look her over slowly and despite her effort to prevent it, her body would respond. Her nipples would tighten, her pulse increase. An aching heat would pool in her womb and she'd have to force herself not to squirm in her seat. It was maddening. Humiliating. She despised him. Abhorred him. He was a liar, a thief and a rogue.

A liar, thief and rogue whom she'd allowed past her defenses, allowed into her bed. A mental image of his hard, naked body rising above her flashed in her mind until she quickly quashed it.

He'd done as she'd required; she couldn't fault him for that. And yet, she sensed he went along with her demands because doing so fell in with his own plans. He was a predator stalking his prey. Biding his time and waiting for the right moment to pounce.

They finally arrived in Edinburgh in the middle of a rainy night, a full week later than she'd expected. They retired to a town house Dair claimed to have won in a card game the previous year. Dair immediately made himself scarce, and a maid showed Emma to her room. She welcomed the privacy of bed and adjoining bath with relief. If she'd had to spend another day shut up inside a carriage with Dair MacRae she'd have lost her…objectivity.

Emma wore her necklace to bed and locked her bedroom door.

Little did she know that the man would go missing.

When Dair failed to put in an appearance the next day, Emma had supposed he'd suffered a spell. She attempted to be patient. The second day when he again failed to show himself she'd quizzed the suspiciously tight-lipped servants. Whether clueless or loyal to their employer she couldn't have said, but it wasn't until she threatened to bring in a lawman to make sure the man didn't lie dead in his bed that they produced a key and let her into his suite. His empty suite.

Emma's hand slapped against her chest as she made sure the pendant hadn't somehow disappeared.

Furious and frustrated, she pondered her options. She could catch a train to London, a ship home. She could take a seat in the entry hall with a shotgun in her lap ready to blast the blackguard when he walked through the door. While both of those options offered some appeal, neither would have solved the ruby's mystery. So Emma had decided to work on the effort herself.

She spent her third day in Edinburgh tracking down Robbie Potter only to learn he was away on holiday. The fourth, fifth, and sixth days she spent haunting bookshops and circulating libraries for information about Clan MacRae. To please herself, she spent some time playing tourist. She observed the Black Watch on the Castle Esplanade, explored the Princess Gardens and toured the open exhibition of the Edinburgh Photographic Society where she purchased a photograph of Donald's Hospital. The architecture reminded her of the Texas Spring Palace before the awful fire that destroyed it.

It was late on the afternoon of the seventh day that she first ran across the name Roslin of Strathardle in a bookshop on Princess Street. In the time of Kenneth McAlpin, Roslin had been a healer who'd saved a village from an outbreak of a deadly, never-before-seen disease. Excitement sizzled through Emma as she purchased the book and headed back to Dair's house. She read late into the night and fell asleep to dreams about magic-makers, secret spells and potions.

She awoke to find a rose on her pillow.

Dair. Panicked, she grabbed for her necklace and breathed a sigh of relief to find it still around her neck where it belonged. "The cad." She stalked to the balcony doors and flung them open, prepared to fling the flower into the street.

He was down there on the sidewalk in his shirtsleeves playing marbles with a trio of neighborhood boys. Upon hearing the window open he looked up, shot her a carefree grin, and gave her that jaunty salute he favored. Emma stopped herself from smiling back. Just barely.

Instead, she worked up a scowl and made a show of tossing the rose away. Dair's grin widened as it floated downward, and graceful and powerful as a panther, he moved to catch it. He sniffed the blossom, then offered her a courtier's bow and tucked the rose inside his shirt. Against his heart. Then he winked at her, and Emma let out a frustrated groan and slammed the door so hard that it bounced right back open.

His laughter echoed on the morning air.

A knock sounded against the door, a feminine voice calling, "Ma'am?" Emma bade her to come in, and the door opened to reveal a maid with a breakfast tray. "Mr. MacRae thought you might like breakfast abed this morning, ma'am. Would you like it served there or at the table?"

It took Emma a moment to get past her surprise at hearing three whole sentences come out of the normally taciturn maid's mouth to register just what she'd said. "The table is fine, thank you."

"I've other good news to share. The railroad office finally located your baggage and it arrived here first thing this morning. We'll bring it up as soon as everything is pressed."

"Excellent," Emma said in a dry tone. She didn't believe that pack of lies for a minute. She'd bet her favorite hairbrush that Dair MacRae had held her things hostage up til now.

Nevertheless, she'd be glad to get her own possessions back. Emma had purchased one dress during the trip to Edinburgh and another upon her arrival. Neither fit her particularly well and she'd been tempted more than once to return to the comfort of her highwayman's costume.

"Mr. MacRae says you're to have anything you request,"

the maid continued. "I'll be honest and tell you that we're all a little out of practice around here when it comes to caring for women. We've been a bachelor abode for many years now. Mr. Campbell—he's the man who owned this home before Mr. MacRae—he seldom entertained overnight guests. We never have any ladies like yourself for an extended stay, so from now on if service is lacking, it's because we're new at it."

Ladies like myself? What sort of "ladies" did he ordinarily entertain? She could guess. "So as a rule, Mr. MacRae's guests stay only overnight?"

The maid smiled sheepishly. "Oh...I see...no, ma'am. You misunderstood. Mr. MacRae doesn't have guests at all. He seldom spends the night here himself."

Oh. Now she really did see. "Well, then. I'm sure your service will be fine. The bacon and warm biscuits smell delicious. I do have one request, however. Please relay a message to Mr. MacRae that I wish to see him downstairs in half an hour."

"Certainly, ma'am. Enjoy your breakfast, ma'am." The servant made a little half bow then left Emma alone.

Emma took a seat at her breakfast table, then set the newspaper aside to read later. She'd been following the exploits of the Highland Riever with interest since her arrival in Edinburgh. After an extended period of inactivity, the jewel thief had struck in a flurry of activity in recent days. Newspaper interviews with both the authorities and victims proved quite entertaining. The man was a veritable legend.

The news, however, could wait. She planned what she'd say to Dair as she ate, working up a good mad while she was about it. Her temper gained steam while she bathed, but it wasn't until she reached for her towel that the most disturbing thought occurred.

During her visits to bookshops and circulating libraries over the past week, she'd searched for information about Malaysian Yellow River Syndrome. She'd found nothing. What if he'd lied in order to hide his true sickness? A sickness he'd contracted through his dissolute lifestyle.

What if Dair MacRae had the clap?

He could have given it to her.

Oh, no. Emma's hand trembled as she reached for a fluffy white towel. What did she remember about the symptoms of Venus's Curse? She'd spent a good chunk of her childhood growing up in a saloon befriended by whores. What had the women of Rachel Warden's Social Emporium had to say about such things? She recalled that syphilis made people crazy. Gonorrhea hurt. She didn't remember anything about causing severe headaches.

Emma simply didn't know enough. As a schoolteacher, she should be more knowledgeable, but the fact was she'd had no reason to concern herself with sexual diseases. She taught young children, for one thing. For another, sexual things simply weren't a part of her life!

Emma gave her body a close examination as she dried off. How long did it take for disease to take hold? Would a woman's symptoms be different from a man's? She didn't see anything unusual on the outside, and she hadn't noted anything peculiar happening inside her since that night at Chatham Park. She had suffered one mild headache earlier in the week. And, thank the dear Lord, she'd had her monthly right on schedule.

But…the clap? "I'll kill him," she murmured. "I really will."

Sounds from her bedroom indicated that the maid had returned with her baggage. "Leave my yellow silk out for me, please," she called, picking up her brush from atop a cabinet. "That's all I'll need."

That and her gun. Or, maybe her knife instead. Knives were handy for cutting off appendages, after all. Maybe it's time she quit making empty threats. She'd definitely take her knife.

Emma wrapped the towel around herself, and while tugging a brush through her hair, walked back into her bedroom where she stopped short. Her dress wasn't the only thing lying on her bed.

She clutched her towel tightly against her breast. The rose was back on her pillow—as was the man who'd delivered it. "MacRae!"

Dair whistled soft and slow as he levered himself to a seated position. "Texas, you're a sight for sore eyes."

"You think your eyes are sore now, wait until I scratch them out," she threatened, her voice flat and serious. "I have to tell you, MacRae, I can't say that I'm impressed by your Scots hospitality. Leave my room now."

The cad smiled, then shook his head. "I'd really rather not. We've talked about fate before, but do you believe in evil, Emma? Do you feel it in this house the way I do? Maybe it's my Celtic blood, but every time I walk in the door I feel a real sense of loathing. It's spooky. I feel shaky. Nauseated, even. I know it sounds crazy, but last night when I peeked in on you, I realized that your room is different. This is the only room in this house that isn't...dark." He twirled the rose by the end of its long stem. "I've put the place up for sale."

"The only evil I sense is you," she snapped. "Be gone,

MacRae. If you don't want to meet me downstairs we can talk in the back garden. We can talk in the street for all I care."

"I don't mind talking here, Texas. The scenery is much nicer here than in the garden." He ignored her sputtering and continued, "I have a lot to tell you, but before we get started, I want to point out that I did as you asked. I stayed away and I stayed quiet. However, that sort of approach won't work from here on out. I'm not trying to break faith with you. I'm being up front with you because I'm trying to earn back your trust. Now, the man we've come to see is back in town today. We need to—"

"Stop!" she demanded. "Stop right there. I'm not about to hold this conversation with you in my bedroom while I'm next to naked and you're fully clothed and lying on my bed."

"I certainly don't mind, but if that's the way you feel…" Dair rolled off the bed, then started unbuttoning his shirt.

"What are you doing?"

"Getting half-naked to equalize things. I'll even strip completely if that'll make you more comfortable."

Emma's mouth opened and closed like a fish out of water as he shrugged out of his shirt. The man robbed her of speech. "That's not…I didn't…for heaven's sake, Dair!"

He laughed, his gray eyes going warm with affection as he watched her. "Ah, Emma, I've missed you. The women I've been around during the past week pale in comparison to you."

That comment cleared the fog from her mind in a snap. Her gaze raked over him, searching for sores or some other sign of disease. "The women?"

"For clarity's sake, you should know it was work, and I didn't bed any of them." Moving quick and graceful as a mountain cat, he sprang off the bed, grabbed her hand, then pulled her back onto the bed. On top of him. Emma's pulse throbbed and reckless energy kindled, then sizzled along her veins. His voice rumbled a dark, erotic purr. "The very idea of it left me cold."

He rolled them and she found herself on her back. "You're in my blood, Texas. I only want you."

Then he lowered his head and kissed her. Dair's mouth was soft and persuasive. He nibbled at her lips, slid his tongue over and around, coaxing them to open for him. When she surrendered to the tender seduction, he slipped his tongue inside, deepened the kiss, and clouded her senses.

Passion hummed inside Emma. She reveled in the weight of him atop her, and the hard press of his body made everything inside her go soft. When his clever hands made the towel float open and flesh touched flesh, breast rubbed against chest, a wild, reckless yearning surged through her. Emma wanted.

As, undoubtedly, had legions before her.

Breathing hard, she tore her mouth away from his. Her hands pressed against his chest attempting to shove him away. "Get off of me! I swear if you've passed along Venus's Curse to me I'll make your life hell on earth."

Dair propped himself up on his elbows and stared down at her in shock. "What?"

"There's no such thing as Malaysian Yellow River Syndrome."

He rolled back on his haunches. "Wait a minute. Wait one damn minute. You think I gave you the clap?"

She grabbed for the towel to cover herself. "Did you?"

His silver eyes flashed. "Where would you get a ridiculous idea like that?"

"What's wrong with you, MacRae? Why the headaches? Why the loss of consciousness? What have you exposed me to?"

He spat a filthy curse and rolled off the bed. Emma scrambled to fasten the towel around her once again as Dair prowled the room like an angry mountain cat. "I do not have the goddamned clap. That is the most insulting...what sort of man do you take me for?"

Emma climbed from the bed. "Just tell me the truth. Don't try to fool me with some illness you pulled out of the air. It was you, wasn't it? Not the doctor? What did you do, bribe him?"

Guilt flashed so briefly across his face that she'd have missed it had she not been watching for it. Emma's stomach sank. "You did."

"I didn't want to tell you." Dair raked his fingers through his hair, then braced his hands on his hips. "It's private, Emma. I swear to you it's not a venereal disease, and it's certainly not contagious. Can't you just take my word that it has nothing to do with you? There's no danger to you from me?"

"No."

He growled low in his throat, then dropped his head. Emma's bare foot tapped against the hardwood floor. When he finally looked up, he stared her right in the eyes. "It's alcohol. I have a drinking problem."

She almost laughed at his poor performance. What a liar. Emma had grown up in a frontier town. Back before he went respectable, Emma's father had owned a saloon. She might not know the signs of syphilis, but she darned sure knew what a drunk looked like.

Dair MacRae didn't have broken capillaries in his face

or trembling hands or a raspy voice. His skin tone wasn't yellow. And, recalling a tidbit she'd overheard from a discussion between her father and her brothers, neither had Dair MacRae lost size in his testicles due to overconsumption of alcohol. Therefore, the man was a liar. She'd told him how she felt about liars.

Emma pursed her lips. "A drinking problem. I see."

"I try to control myself," he explained. "Sometimes I slip."

"Yes. I understand that a dependence on spirits can do that to a person." Wait until he saw what an angry woman can accomplish.

"I'm ashamed, Emma, but I'm not contagious. You need not concern yourself over that."

Now that had a ring of truth to it. Either his acting was improving or he was telling the truth.

Had to be better acting. The cad. "Well, then. That is a relief. I admit I was quite frightened at the thought."

He scowled and hooked his thumbs at the waistband of his pants. "It's insulting that you'd think so little of me, Emma. The clap." His scowl deepened to a glare.

You think that's insulting? Wait until you see what I have up my sleeve, MacRae. Or, to be more precise, beneath my towel. "Well, we can just put that behind us now, can't we?" she said, smiling seductively and taking a step toward him. "In fact, I think we should move forward, don't you?"

His gaze dropped to the finger she ran along the swell of her breast rising above the shielding towel. "Forward is good."

"If the bookseller is back and the time has come to move forward in the quest to solve the mystery of my ruby, then I think we should put *all* the unpleasantness behind us."

"I'm perfectly agreeable to that." He never looked above her shoulders.

Got you, you predictable idiot.

"Shall we seal the deal? With a..." Emma braced herself to follow through, then boldly dropped her towel "...kiss?"

"Emma." He said it like a growl and took two steps toward her.

She shifted sideways, held up her hand. "No, we'll be on equal footing this time." Deliberately, she dropped her gaze to where the evidence of his desire was very much in evidence.

He stripped in seconds, then naked as she, again stepped toward her.

Emma's laugh was honest. The man was predictable and easily swayed with a little show of skin. She shook her head slowly, shook her finger no. "Allow me to set the rules for this...compact, Alasdair. Allow me my fantasy. Follow my lead?"

He nodded. "For as long as I can bear, Emma."

It was, she thought, as good as she was likely to get. She stepped into his arms and lifted her face for his kiss. "You must think of me and only of me, MacRae."

"That won't be a problem," he replied in a raspy tone.

Even as his mouth touched hers, she wrapped her arms around him and started to move, to twirl. Kissing him, moaning into his mouth, fitting her body against his, she demanded his focus, captured his complete attention. Pouring every ounce of passion she could summon into the moment, she backed him up to the french doors' threshold. Then, Emma kneed him in the groin, not viciously, but hard enough to make him gasp and release her. She set her hands against his chest and gave him a hard shove before darting inside, slamming and locking the French doors.

As the catcalls began to rise from the street and fury flooded Dair's eyes, she smiled. "Lie to me again, boyo, and next time I'll use my knife."

CHAPTER EIGHT

AS FAR AS DAIR WAS concerned, all bets were off. She wanted to fight dirty? Fine. He was an expert at dirty fights. Emma could use some lessons. She'd only knocked his jewels up into his stomach.

Doubled over, he worked to regulate his breath. Fury burned in his blood like raw whisky. Emma Tate might not know it, but she had more than met her match.

When the pain finally eased, he straightened and stared into the room. He'd expected her to have run off. Hit and run. That's what women did, wasn't it?

Instead, he discovered that she'd tugged on a robe and now stood on the other side of the doors, her arms folded, her chin up, watching him with fire in her eyes. God, she was gorgeous. All flame and fury. A dusky nipple peeked through the V in her robe and despite his lingering discomfort, arousal stirred. *Glutton for punishment,* his good sense whispered.

Dair could have gone right back through the French doors—he could have used wire from the hanging basket of flowers to pick the lock in seconds flat. He could have her on her back on the bed before she could draw a breath to scream. The tease. The termagant. Knee him, would she?

Instead, cognizant of the truth of the old saying that revenge was a dish best served cold, he decided to take a more subtle approach. So to speak.

From the building across the street, he heard his elderly neighbor call for her sister. "Hurry! You can't miss this."

"Heaven," came the sister's voice. "I saw some prime meat in my day, but never so fine a sight as Mr. MacRae's bare behind."

From down below, came the sound of a younger female voice, a startled gasp, then a man crying out, "She's fainted. Quick. Get her out of the street before—stop! You there in the wagon!"

Crash. Squeals. Shouts. Dair didn't turn to look. He didn't take his gaze off Emma.

"Silly twit," came the neighbor's voice. "Fainting in the street. It wasn't the wagon driver's fault he swerved into the orange cart. She should have to pay for all the fruit."

Dair ignored all the commotion—along with that perky nipple—as the anger flowing through his veins spiked his desire. He braced his hands on his hips and helped matters along by recalling the moment Emma Tate dropped the towel. He pictured the fullness of her rose-tipped breasts, the slimness of her waist, the curve of her naked hip. The allure of the delta between her legs. Stimulated by such an erotic vision, his pride rose to the occasion, issuing the promise he'd intended.

On the other side of the glass, Emma's eyes widened and she took an inadvertent step back. Dair winked at her, then with long-practiced ease and grace, he swung his arms and leaped up, grabbing hold of a water pipe and using it to crawl like a cat up to the balcony one floor above. As he turned to raid a flower basket for wire to pick the lock, he gave his wide-eyed neighbors a jaunty salute.

"I can die a happy woman now, sister," he heard the woman say as the lock clicked open. He blew her a kiss before disappearing indoors.

In the privacy of his suite as the rush of anger faded, Dair allowed himself a few minutes to brood. Blast the woman. She'd led him around by the spigot and caused him to bare his ass to Edinburgh. Literally. It was humiliating. Embarrassing. When was the last time he'd allowed a woman to get the best of him?

Never, that's when. Emma Tate was a first.

Almost against his will, his mouth lifted in a rueful grin. Damn, but she was a spitfire. Spirited. Saucy. Smart. She'd found his weak spot and capitalized on it. A man had to admire that. As much as he appreciated beauty, Dair had always found intelligence in a woman equally alluring. Emma Tate packed a double punch.

The more he thought about the situation, the better he felt. Once he could get past the embarrassment of flashing his backside to the neighbors, he realized he could now let go of any lingering guilt about his departure from Chatham Park. He and Mrs. Tate were even on the humiliation point. Also, by using sex as a weapon, she'd made it fair for him to draw his own gun, so to speak. Seduction was now back on the table. Thank God.

Of course, before he got around to that he'd better disabuse her of the notion that his illness had anything to do with his sexual health. The clap, for God's sake. Where had she come up with that idea? And how could he make her believe him? What excuse for the headaches could he use now that Malaysian Yellow River Syndrome was no longer an option?

He'd chosen poorly with the alcohol excuse, and he had

no one to blame but himself. He'd underestimated her. He should have had a backup sickness at the ready.

"I didn't lie well enough," he muttered. He was truly losing his touch. Lying to Emma Tate was work. It didn't come naturally. Didn't sit well when he did it. Who would have ever thought?

Dair put that concern aside and pondered the likelihoods and possibilities as he dressed. He'd suffered a headache every damned day since arriving in Edinburgh. Either the thing in his head was growing faster than predicted or something about this town made his symptoms worse.

Perhaps he should consider offering her a version of the truth. Now *there* would be a novel approach. Emma was an intelligent woman. He'd need to be extra careful about just what he said and how he said it. The absolute truth was his enemy. He'd rather die here and now than have her gaze at him with pity.

He continued to mull over the situation as he knocked on Emma's door a few moments later. "I'm off to visit with Robbie Potter. If you wish to come along, be downstairs in ten minutes."

He expected her to play games and make him wait because of course, he couldn't go without her. Robbie needed to see the necklace. But again, the lady surprised him, joining him almost immediately. She flounced downstairs, her head held high, her shoulders squared, a woman ready for battle.

"You look beautiful, Emma," he told her, sucking some of the wind from her sails.

She narrowed her eyes in suspicion. "Thank you."

He opened the front door. "It's a lovely day and the bookshop isn't far. I thought we'd walk."

He needed to see if he'd picked up another tail. The fact he hadn't left that problem behind in England bothered him more than he cared to admit, and he'd spent part of the past week investigating the situation. The possibility that this was Riever related was becoming stronger all the time. While he'd gained no hard evidence, instincts told him he needed to leave Scotland—for that matter, leave Great Britain—as quickly as possible. While he'd originally planned to return to Scotland to die, he wasn't quite ready for that yet.

He wasn't quite finished with Emma Tate.

"Hmm," the lady said as she swept past him. "A walk suits me fine, although I've a stop I wish to make on the way. I'd like to pay a quick visit to a brothel."

Dair tripped over the welcome mat. "Pardon me?"

"Take me to a whorehouse, MacRae. I'm sure you know where to find one or twelve."

For a long moment he simply stared at her. Damn it, she still thought he had the blue balls. His temper flared. "Fine. Any particular peccadillo you're interested in? Bondage, perhaps? I must say I find the idea quite appealing in your case."

She wrinkled her nose with disdain. "Do we need transportation or is a brothel within walking distance?"

He shoved his hands into his pockets and took off at a brisk pace, not bothering to narrow his strides or calm his temper. If she wanted to keep up, she could damn well run. Then he stopped short and whirled on her. "Aren't you the least bit concerned about your reputation, Mrs. Tate?"

She beamed a brilliant smile his way. "Not at all. I'm a stranger in town. I'm anonymous. It offers a certain freedom."

She was insane, that's what she was.

"That's a poor argument, anyway, MacRae. After all, I'm living in your house. I traveled with you from England. If I worried about my reputation, do you think I'd have done that?"

"I don't know what to think. First this morning's peep show, now a brothel visit. Are you running out of funds, Mrs. Tate? Are you hoping to secure a job?"

She gasped. Wounded eyes revealed her hurt. "That was uncalled for."

Yes, it was. Guilt poked at Dair which only added to his frustration. At wits' end, he demanded, "Why do you want to visit a whorehouse?"

"Because prostitutes will have the information I need, and I can trust them to tell me the truth!"

Aha! His brain might be rotting, but he hadn't lost all his faculties. Dair braced his hands on his lips and leaned over her. "I. Don't. Have. The. Clap."

"Then what's wrong with you?" she demanded, throwing both arms wide. Her voice was tight, her eyes brimming with emotion, with concern. "Something is wrong with you, and I'm not going to stop hounding you until you tell me what it is!"

She cared. Not for herself and for her own health concerns, but for him. She was worried about him. The realization knocked Dair back a step. *Oh, Emma. Don't let me break your heart.*

He wasn't ready for this. He wasn't ready to let her go. He sure as hell wasn't ready to— "I'm dying…to tell you, Emma. But not on a public street."

She twisted her head, looking up and down the street, then she grabbed his hand and tugged him half a block to a shop bearing the sign Beal's Women's Wear. "What th—?" he began.

"Wait," Emma snapped. She dragged him past a startled customer and a scandalized clerk saying, "Your dressing rooms?"

"I'm sorry, ma'am. You can't—"

But then Emma saw them, and she did. Heedless of feminine squeaks and squeals from a second dressing room, she shoved him into the first. Flinging the curtain closed, she whirled on him. "Now. We're private. Talk to me, Dair."

Dair's notice snagged on a filmy nightgown in transparent, garnet-colored silk. For a moment, he had trouble thinking.

"Now, MacRae!"

His stomach rolled. He didn't want to do this. He searched his mind for another way…any other way…to no avail. Hell. Pitching his voice low, barely above a whisper, he said, "I have a…swelling…in my head. It causes me headaches that can be quite severe, as you have seen. My doctor has prescribed these…" He reached into his pocket and pulled out a small brown bottle containing small white pills "…to reduce the swelling. It will take some months, but I will be fine."

From the other side of the curtain, the clerk's shrill voice exclaimed, "Sir! Sir! Excuse me. You're not allowed in here."

Dair and Emma both ignored the interruption. "What causes this swelling?" she asked.

He shrugged. "My physician believes it is the result of a blow to the head I recently received."

"Then why the Malaysian foolishness? Why would you lie?"

"It's…embarrassing."

Emma snorted. "Being stranded naked on a balcony is embarrassing. Having an illness is not."

"Sir!" called the clerk. "I must insist!"

"We need a moment of privacy," Dair snapped back. Turning to Emma, he spoke with an honesty he hadn't anticipated or intended. "I'm a man who prefers to be in control. When the headaches begin…I'm not. You've seen me. It isn't pretty, and it's not something I wanted to subject you to."

It was as close to the truth as he was going to give her. Being an invalid, being dependent on someone else appalled him. Having her see him as such disgusted him. He wanted to give in to the urge to give the dressing-room chair a good hard kick.

"Men and their sacred pride." She folded her arms, tapped her foot and studied him for a long tense minute. "So rather than subject me to your illness, you'd prefer that I—your lover—believe you've a case of Venus's Curse instead of knowing that the headaches result from an injury?"

"I don't know why you—" He pinned her with an intense stare. "So you still consider yourself my lover?"

"Don't try to change the subject, MacRae."

"I didn't want you to know, all right?" He raked his fingers through his hair. "I haven't told anyone. Not even Jake. You're the only one. I don't want people knowing!"

"Why not?" When he didn't answer, she answered for him. "Pride, right? Foolish male pride."

Her toe continued to tap, her stare continued to measure. Finally, she nodded. "My father would be just the same way. I can't believe I'm saying this, but I think I believe you."

He started to touch her, but ended up shoving his hands in his pockets. "I didn't give you a disease, Texas. I swear on my mother's grave."

She nodded.

"Speaking of giving…I wondered…well…" He stared pointedly at her stomach. "That night at Chatham Park I was careless."

"Oh. No, Dair, you didn't give me a baby, either."

"Good. That's good." He felt a twist, a sharp pang of regret, but he firmly shut the door on that. He studied Emma's expression, trying to read it. Was that regret in her eyes, too? Damn. "So then, do you still wish to visit Madame LaRue's or are you ready to continue on to the bookshop?"

"I guess I can skip Madame LaRue's. Just don't lie to me again, MacRae. I deserve better than that."

True, lass. But we don't always get what we deserve.

Dair shoved back the dressing room curtain to discover one clerk wringing her hands and the other holding the broom as if it were a club. Ever so much the gentleman, he put his hand against the small of Emma's back and escorted her out. To placate the clerks and please himself, he snagged the red nightgown and said, "We'll take this."

Emma observed the purchase without comment, her thoughts obviously somewhere other than the dress shop. Taking advantage of her inattention, Dair added a couple more provocative items to his transaction, then quickly ushered her from the store. They were halfway to the bookshop before she spoke again.

"MacRae? Just what are the symptoms of Venus's Curse?"

Dair scowled, his mouth opening, then closing like a fish out of water. Amazingly, what being caught on a balcony naked as a babe couldn't accomplish, the prospect of answering that particular question did. The back of his neck went warm with an embarrassed flush. "Emma…I…how about we stop by Madame LaRue's on the way back home?"

BELLS JANGLED AS DAIR OPENED the door of Robbie Potter's bookshop and motioned for Emma to precede him inside. The expected musty smell of old books greeted her along with the more surprising fragrance of bayberry and jasmine. "Robbie's latest hobby is perfumes," Dair explained.

Emma nodded and glanced around the shop at the intriguing items hanging on the walls and stacked atop bookshelves. Outside of Bernard Kimball's collections at Chatham Park, she'd never seen such an eclectic assembly of items. A Comanche war bonnet, a pair of wooden shoes. One leg to a suit of armor.

"Interesting place," she observed, watching dust motes dance in a beam of sunlight shining through the plate glass window.

"Robbie is an interesting man." Dair led her toward the back of the shop through a labyrinth of narrow passages framed by tall bookshelves that all but blocked out the light.

Emma took pride in the fact she managed to swallow her scream when she turned a corner to face a human skeleton hanging from an iron pole.

"Welcome home, Robbie," Dair greeted the burly, bespectacled man seated behind the counter.

Robbie Potter glanced up from the book he was studying and delight lit his brilliant blue eyes. "MacRae! I suspected you might be back in town when I caught up on my newspapers last night. Sounds like you've enjoyed a profitable couple of weeks."

Emma shot her companion a curious look. What was that about?

Dair gave her no opportunity to enquire. "Has anyone been by asking for me since I left Edinburgh last winter?"

Potter scratched behind his ear and frowned. "Anyone?"

"Anyone out of the ordinary."

"Hmm...nae. I dinna think so. Just Mrs. Holl—"

"May I introduce Mrs. Emma Tate," Dair interrupted. "Emma, Robbie Potter, scholar, perfumer, and displaced Highlander."

"A terrible fate we share, MacRae." Potter winked at Emma. "Pleased to meet ye, pretty lass. The boy here has left out some of me more interesting pursuits, but we'll leave that be until I get to know ye better."

"Excellent choice," Dair drawled. "Mrs. Tate and I are in need of some information, Robbie. Put on your scholar's hat and see what you can tell us about this. Emma? The ruby?"

Emma's heart began to pound as she reached to pull the pendant from her bodice. She was probably being silly, but this felt like such a...moment of import. It was as if she stood at a crossroads about to take a step that would change her life.

Clasping the ruby in her hand, she slipped the chain from around her neck. She placed the back of her hand against the counter, drew a deep breath, then slowly opened her fist. The necklace spilled out onto the counter and Robbie Potter's eyes went wide. "Quite a stone ye have there."

"It's big," Dair agreed. "But that's not all. Look." He switched on the lamp on the counter and pointed out the engraving.

Robbie Potter stared at it for a long moment, then his eyes went round with shock. "I knew it," Dair murmured with satisfaction. "Tell us what you know about this stone."

"I dinna...I think...oh bide awee." The Scotsman dragged a hand down his whiskered jaw and he started mumbling to himself. "Lost...legend...never existed. Treasure. Hmm."

Abruptly, he moved from behind the counter, clucking his

tongue as he began searching the stacks. "A woman. Women. Tis it. A journal. Aye. Still have it. Leather bound. Hmm…"

Emma glanced at Dair to see him staring out into space, his own thoughts obviously churning. "Dair? Are you following this?"

"Actually, I think…there's something. It's just beyond my reach. He said a…journal. That's—" He broke off, grimaced fiercely. Emma saw his hand make a fist, his knuckles turn white.

It took her a moment to recognize the problem, then she touched his arm. "Headache? Do they always come on this fast?"

He spat a particularly foul expletive beneath his breath. "Can't do this now…"

"Where are your pills?" She felt his jacket pocket.

"Pants. Don't…hell…forget the pills." He closed his eyes, swayed on his feet, and Emma feared he'd fall.

"Mr. Potter?" Emma dug in Dair's pants pocket for the brown bottle. "Dair is ill. Do you have somewhere he could lie down?"

The bookseller didn't respond, and when a faint moan escaped Dair's lips, Emma lost patience. "Potter!" she screamed.

Still, he didn't answer.

"For goodness' sake," she muttered. She hurried behind the counter and grabbed Potter's chair, then set it beside Dair. She pushed on his shoulders, trying to get him to sit down but the stubborn man kept his knees locked.

"Sit down before you fall down!" She shoved again, and this time he sank into the seat. She forced a pill into his mouth, then went looking for Robbie Potter.

It took Emma every bit of two minutes to track the bookseller down in a narrow alcove, his head buried in a book. Emma let out a frustrated growl and whacked him over the head. "Potter! Dair is sick. Where can he lie down?"

"What? Oh. Sick, ye say?"

"Do you have a couch in the store?"

"There's a bed upstairs."

"I don't know if he could make it upstairs," Emma muttered. She recalled the other headaches she'd witnessed and compared the severity of the onset of this one with those. "I think we should try, though. Help me."

It was a struggle, and once Emma feared all three of them would tumble down the stairs. By the time Dair collapsed onto the narrow bed, not a drop of color remained in his complexion.

"Ye want me to send for the doctor?" Potter asked.

Emma chewed her bottom lip in indecision until Dair reached out and grabbed her hand in a viselike grip. "No."

"Let's give him a little time," she said, sitting beside him on the bed.

"I have a potion my sister sent me right afore she died. A great cure-all. A bit of a witch, she was. Me only relative."

"Thanks, Mr. Potter. Maybe later." Robbie couldn't leave the small room fast enough and once she and Dair were alone, Emma gently massaged his temples, his forehead, the back of his neck. Acting instinctively, she leaned down and kissed his brow. He stirred restlessly and she shushed him. For the next half hour, she watched him suffer and her heart simply broke.

Now she understood. Now that she knew him better, she could see why he went to such lengths to keep his illness secret. To see such a strong man laid low…to witness his total vulnerability…Emma shook her head. How he must hate it.

When he began to stir and she sensed his recovery was at hand, Emma took heart in the fact that despite the obvious severity of the pain, he'd recovered more quickly than she had expected. The medicine his doctor prescribed must be working. This headache had appeared just as bad if not worse than the one he'd suffered the day she robbed the coach, but he came to in half as much time. Faster, but grumpier, she thought as he sat up and growled at her like a wounded bear.

"This is lovely. Did Potter see this disgrace? Of course he did. He helped drag me up the stairs." He finished with a string of curses mean enough to make a Hell's Half Acre cowboy proud.

"Excuse me," she drawled in a dry tone. "Are you feeling better? I can't quite tell."

He rubbed the back of his neck. "Sorry. I just…forget it. Let's go see what Robbie's turned up."

They found him seated at a table near the skeleton, a stack of books beside him. He busily scribbled on a tablet already half-filled with notes. Hearing them approach, he looked up. "There ye are. Glad yer better. I have something for ye."

"Oh?"

The older man laid down his pen. "I have…" he paused theatrically before adding, "…treasure. It's called the Sisters'—"

"—Prize," Dair finished.

Just the words made Emma's heart beat faster. Potter looked up at Dair in surprise. "You know of it?"

"That's it? That's what it's called?" Dair dragged his hand down his jaw.

"Yes." Potter pushed to his feet. "Where did you learn of it? Your clan? Is it still whispered about?"

Dair stared off into nothing for a long minute before shaking his head. "I don't know how I knew the name."

"What is it?" Emma asked softly. "What is the Sisters' Prize?"

Potter blew out a heavy breath. "It's a lost treasure of Clan MacRae. Its value is said to be beyond measure, though any who share in its wealth are guaranteed great happiness."

Emma clasped her pendant. "You think my ruby is the treasure?"

"If it's the Sisters' Prize ruby, it's part of the treasure, one of its cornerstones," Robbie explained. "An engraved ruby the size of a hen's egg."

Dair's brow had furrowed. "When was the treasure lost?"

Robbie pursed his lips. "That is uncertain. History holds that the Prize aided the clan at significant points in history—sieges, battles and the like. I have found no reference to it after Duncan MacRae's successful defense of Eilean Donan in 1539, although I've not yet had the opportunity to make an extensive search."

Emma thought it all a little too far-fetched. "My ruby is not the only large engraved ruby in existence. There might be no connection between it and your legend at all."

Besides, if Dair MacRae thought he could claim ownership of her necklace based on an old family legend, he had another think coming.

He reached for the pendant, held it in his hand. He rubbed his thumb over the engraving. "It's these words, this symbol. I don't know *how* I know it, Texas, but your ruby is the key."

She smoothly repossessed the necklace and slipped it over her head. Where it belonged.

"It's not just the ruby, but the necklace itself," Potter

added. He tugged a handwritten manuscript from his pile of materials and flipped through the pages until he found what he sought. He pointed to a paragraph. "Look."

Emma moved to stand beside Dair and she leaned over the page to read. The script was faint and flowing, smudged in places, totally illegible in others. It took a moment of study to comprehend. Once she adjusted to the rhythm of it, she was able to make it out.

> *...riches beyond comprehension. The Sisters' Prize grew throughout the centuries...smudge smudge smudge...began with the three treasures nestled inside a small chest made of silver. Three smudge smudge on long chains of finest gold. Three stones—sapphire, emerald and ruby—set in filigree pendants are of value beyond measure bring to their smudge smudge...*

Emma grabbed Dair's arm. "Our necklaces."

"I was right. I knew it." Dair drummed his fingers on the table. "What about the engraving? Have you found anything about the words or the symbol? Can you identify the language?"

"Nae, though something plagues me, a memory I canna quite place. Although, if you believe in the fanciful, I never will find the key. Look." Robbie Potter pulled a book from the middle of his stack. He opened it to a marked page, then sat back in his seat and gestured for them to read.

Emma viewed the fanciful drawing of mythical characters on the opposite page before focusing on the words he'd indicated.

It is told that in days long ago, a fairy prince fell in love with a mortal woman, the fair Ariel. As fate would have it, she gave her love to another man, a mere mortal.

Emma's knees went weak and she placed both hands on the table to support herself. She'd heard a version of this story before.

The prince was mightily displeased, and in an effort to prove the mortal unworthy of the maiden's love, he put the man to a series of fearsome tests. To the prince's dismay, the mortal withstood every challenge, though at great physical cost. Finally, fearful of her beloved's safety and at substantial risk to herself, the fair Ariel called upon the prince and demanded that he recognize that the love she and the mortal shared was powerful, vigilant and true, and that no trial or challenge would change it.

Ungracious in defeat, the prince acquiesced to her demand with a caveat. Since the fair lady claimed her mortal love would outlast a union with a fairy prince, it must be proved. Her children and her children's children and their children, down through the ages, would be called upon to enforce her claim.

Lady Ariel elicited a promise from the prince. When, in any one generation, three sisters, three daughters marked with the sign of Ariel find love to prove the claim of Ariel and accomplish a task of great personal import, the curse will be broken for all time.

After all his trials, the mortal warrior placed no trust in the word of a fairy prince, so he appealed to a higher authority, the prince's mother, and asked for a physical symbol of the pledge between immortal and man. The fairy queen gave him three stones—blue, green and red—to be presented with the claim that conditions had been met for the ending of the curse.

For many long years, Ariel and her mortal lived in peace and harmony and happiness. She bore him a child, a daughter they named for the fairy queen—Roslin.

"A Clan MacRae fairy tale?" Dair said scornfully. "Surely you've something else, Potter. Something based in reality."

"I thought you believed in fate," Emma said, her mind spinning.

"Fate, yes. Fairies, no."

She opened her mouth to challenge him, but second thoughts stopped her. She needed to think about this, to reason it all through. Yes, this story was known to her.

Roslin of Strathardle had repeated it the night she gave necklaces to Emma, Mari and Kat McBride. Emma looked down at her left palm and retraced the line Roslin had traced a decade ago. The mark of Ariel, she'd called it. Kat considered it more appropriately referred to as The Bad Luck Love Line.

Emma had neither believed nor disbelieved the tale. She'd been about to marry Casey—a love she believed met the strong, true and vigilant qualifications—and the prospect of a tragically short end to her marriage never entered her mind.

Things had changed since that night in Hell's Half Acre. Both Emma and Kat had learned the lesson of being unlucky in love.

Emma glanced at Dair who'd propped a hip on the table and now thumbed through another of the bookseller's tomes. Fate, not fairies, hmm? How would he react when she relayed the news that the story in the book wasn't news to her? What would he say when he learned that the tale Roslin told that night differed in two key details from the one they'd just read?

That night in Fort Worth, Roslin had named the mortal Ariel loved—a McBride. Thus, the tale became the Curse of Clan McBride.

However, Roslin had neglected to mention Ariel's surname—MacRae.

MacRae and McBride. A treasure and a curse. And three unique necklaces. "I need to sit down," she murmured.

Potter scrambled to his feet. "I'm sorry, lass. I completely forget my manners when I get involved in a mystery."

She offered him a wobbly smile. "No, I…actually, I think I want to walk."

Turning abruptly, she headed for the door. She wanted to flee. The bookshop. The stories. Mr. Alasdair MacRae.

She heard him ask the historian to continue his research into the Sisters' Prize to which Potter responded that he knew of another expert to consult. The bell jingled as she pushed the door open, then she was out on the street in the sunshine breathing in great gulps of fresh air.

She struck out walking blindly, heedless of her direction, barely aware that Dair trailed right on her heels. Memories crowded her thoughts. Roslin of Strathardle handing her the necklace, reading her "mark of Ariel" and telling her it revealed her to be a nurturer. Her sister Mari running into her bedroom at Willow Hill using a description of Kat's necklace to prove their younger sister hadn't died in the Texas Spring Palace fire. Luke Garrett sitting in the back room at Mari's candy shop giving Emma's necklace credit for helping him to rescue Mari from certain death at the bottom of a cavern. Kat's grief-dulled eyes lighting with delight upon learning that Jake Kimball had her necklace. The look on Dair MacRae's face as he pointed out the engraving on her ruby that she'd never noticed before.

Oh my oh my oh my.

Mari and Luke had already proved to share a love that was powerful, vigilant and true. Now the necklaces had led Kat to Kimball. Led her to Dair MacRae.

Destiny. Fate. Fairy queens and princes. Did she believe in any of it? The first two she could accept with little effort. The last? *Oh my oh my oh my.*

"Emma, slow down," Dair said, taking her by the arm and holding her in place.

She shot him a glare. "Just because you're stronger than me doesn't give you leave to use that strength against me."

"Just because you have wings on your feet doesn't mean I should have to run down the street after you, either. Haven't you already caused me enough public humiliation today, Texas?"

She sucked in an audible breath, then blew out a heavy sigh. "I need some time to myself. Please. All this…this…" She waved a hand back in the general direction of the bookshop. "I need time and peace and quiet to digest it."

He shoved his hands into his pockets and studied her. "You've a rather wild look in your eyes. Are you all right?"

The gentle breeze sent an errant strand of hair dancing around her head, and Emma impatiently tucked it behind her ear. "It's too much to soak in."

"It's a treasure hunt, Emma. Don't make it more than that."

"But the story..."

"Is just that. A story." He gently touched her cheek. "The treasure...now that, I believe, is something more. The Sisters' Prize is out there somewhere and I'm going to find it. I hope you'll join me in the hunt. I think it will be a true adventure."

Emma closed her eyes. The lure of adventure—her greatest temptation—until the lure of Dair MacRae had usurped its place.

"I don't know, Dair. I think..."

"Don't think." His smile was teasing. "When a woman starts thinking, it's nothing but trouble."

"Well!"

"Look, I have other business that needs tending to today unrelated to our treasure quest. Why don't you come along with me? I think you'd enjoy meeting the person I need to see."

"Who is that?"

"Hmm...how to describe Bess Dowd?" He paused, stared off into the distance. "I recall little of the time before my mother died. But I have vivid memories of the stories she used to tell about her dear friend Bess. I looked her up when I first came to Scotland. We've been friends ever since. I'd like you to meet her, Emma. She's important to me."

Emma grabbed hold of the distraction like a lifeline. "In that case, Dair, I'd love to meet her."

DAIR SECOND-GUESSED HIMSELF all the way to the park where he expected to find Bess. Maybe it wasn't a good idea for the two women to meet. Bess knew a lot about him. She might pass along information he'd just as soon Emma not have.

They found her on her usual park bench feeding the pigeons. Dair sensed Emma's surprise as they approached. Bess was…different. This morning she wore a green satin ball gown and a black lace scarf over her snow-white hair. Approaching sixty, she remained an attractive woman—as long as one looked past her stage makeup. When she spied Dair approaching, her entire expression lit up. "Alasdair! I didn't expect to see you today."

"Hello, Bess." He leaned down and pressed a kiss to her wrinkled cheek. "I've brought someone to meet you."

"Oh?" Bright blue eyes turned toward Emma. "Why, aren't you a pretty girl."

"This is Emma Tate, Bess. She's a friend of mine from Texas. Emma, this is Mrs. Elizabeth Dowd, friend both to me and to every pigeon in Scotland."

The older woman giggled, then smiled up at Emma. "Texas? Is that near Dornoch?"

Dair sighed inwardly. "No, darling. It's in America. Remember? Texas is where my mother went to live. It's where I was born."

"Do I know your mother?"

"The two of you grew up together. Her name was Roslin MacRae."

Her eyes clouded and her bottom lip trembled ever so slightly. "I don't remember."

"That's all right." Dair's heart ached as he took hold of her hand and took a seat beside her. "It's not important."

"It's happening again, isn't it?"

While Dair fumbled for words, he offered a comforting kiss on her hand. Emma, thank goodness, stepped into the void. "I'm very pleased to meet you, Mrs. Dowd. May I say that's a lovely dress you're wearing?"

"Why thank you, dear." Bess's smile chased the shadows from her eyes. "I wear it to annoy Mr. McFarland. He's up there, you see. Watching. Look across the street at the house with the white shutters. Second floor, last window on the left. He's always watching me. Not like Margaret, of course, who Dair has hired to watch me and who I truly adore." She finger waved toward the heavily pregnant young woman seated on a stool at a flower cart. "Mr. McFarland sits up there and stares at me and broods. I'm the one who got away, you see."

"Oh?" Emma asked, her eyes lighting with amusement. "Tell me."

Bess did just that. She rambled on about her grand romance with McFarland which led into a discourse on her relationship with a man named Barstow which soon had Bess and Emma laughing together like schoolgirls. When she went on to discuss a liaison with a baker and his talent with tarts, Dair excused himself. He walked over to the flower cart to see if Margaret had anything of import to tell him.

He chose roses for Bess and a bright bouquet of daisies for Emma. "Any more episodes?" he asked the flower seller.

"Yes, I'm afraid so. Shortly after you left yesterday, she wandered over to the fountain and started removing her clothes. She thought she was at the beach. She intended to go swimming. I was able to stop her, but when she came back to her senses… she cried, Dair. She truly breaks my heart."

"I know. Mine too." He grimaced at the mental picture her words had painted. Bess's mental deterioration continued at a faster pace than he'd anticipated. Seeing it disturbed him for a number of reasons—he truly loved the woman—but considering the state of his own brain…well…give him headaches any day over what Bess Dowd was going through. "The good news is I've found a place for her."

"You have? Where? What's it like?"

He explained about the house in a lovely little village not far from Nairn where Bess had lived with her third husband for almost a decade. It was managed by a physician's widow and her daughter and son-in-law. "They've room for four women and six men."

"Extra men? Bess will love that."

"That's what I thought." He blew out a heavy breath, then added, "I told them to expect her next week."

"Oh, I'm so glad. My husband's mother thinks the babe will come early, and I've been worried. I just don't think I could properly care for Bess in addition to a new baby and a sickly mother-in-law."

They discussed the arrangements he'd made and he reassured her that the cost was all covered—the Riever had done extremely well these past few nights. "All that's left is to get her agreement. That's the part that worries me most. She does love this park."

"I think she'll be relieved," Margaret suggested. "She's aware of the troubles with her mind. I think knowing arrangements have been made will make it easier for her."

Dair hoped so. He was counting on something similar in his own situation. He thanked Margaret for her help, then returned to the park bench where he interrupted a story about Emma's father's reaction to one of her and her sisters' pranks. He presented the ladies their bouquets, and the older woman said, "Oh, aren't you just a dear. This reminds me of when your father brought your mother and me flowers. He called them practice bouquets since it was a week before the wedding. The accident happened later that day. Such a tragedy. The man died way too young. Poor Roslin, I worried the loss made her crazy. It wasn't a week after his funeral that she just went quiet. Didn't speak to anyone for two weeks, and when she did talk again, it was to announce that she was moving to America to live with her aunt and uncle. She never got over losing Ryan, but I know it was a blessing to her to find out she was expecting his child." Then she gasped and brought her hand up to her mouth. "Oh, my. Now I remember your mother. Oh, dear. I'm losing my mind, aren't I?"

Dair closed his eyes against the dull throb that suddenly flared up in his head. "Bess, I have a surprise for you."

"Another present?"

The pressure built steadily and came in waves. Dair suspected he didn't have much time until it burst into a killing headache. As quickly as possible, yet taking care with his words, he outlined his arrangements for his mother's old friend. Bess grew quiet while he spoke. Emma reached over and took his hand.

When he finished, he waited for Bess's reaction. The dull throb was growing sharper. He needed to get somewhere where he could be alone fast.

The older woman's eyes filled with tears and his stomach sank. Then, she said, "Thank you, Dair. You're a good, good man. Your parents would be proud."

Turning to Emma, she said, "Roslin once told me that if a McBride and MacRae ever came to me, I was to pass along this message: the fairy ring holds the key."

It was a curious comment, but Dair couldn't think about that then. The headache hit with a vengeance, and it was all he could do to stay conscious. He kissed Bess goodbye, then escorted Emma from the park.

Dair was thankful Emma was preoccupied with her own thoughts and didn't try to converse with him as they made their way along the city streets. He could hardly manage to put one foot in front of the other, much less string sentences together. At the town house, he asked her to join him for dinner, then headed upstairs to his suite.

He fell into bed and gave himself up to the agony. His last conscious thought was, *I don't want to die here. Please, God. Don't let me die here.*

IN HER BEDROOM AT DAIR'S TOWN house, Emma gave her thoughts free rein. Almost immediately, her knees went watery and she sank onto the thick Persian carpet.

Destiny. Fate. Fairies. Oh my.

Alasdair MacRae. Oh my oh my oh my.

Her head spinning, she asked herself what she believed. Where, once and for all, did she stand on the Curse of Clan McBride? Did she consider it to be nothing more than a story? An interesting bit of fantasy that had entertained her and her sisters' thoughts over the years? Or did she believe in it? Did she accept the idea that she, Mari and Kat had been given the necklaces for a reason, that they had opportunity to end her family's bad luck in love for all time?

Emma was an educated woman. A teacher. She shouldn't be sucked into nonsense of fairy tales and treasure hunts. She was almost thirty years old, for goodness' sake, and here she was actually considering....

She thought of Casey. Dear sweet Casey. She'd married him and loved him and he'd died three months later. If that wasn't bad luck, she didn't know what was.

She remembered Rory Callahan, Kat's disaster. She thought about Jenny and her father and the Bad Luck Wedding Dress. She thought of Aunt Claire and Uncle Tye and the Bad Luck Wedding Cake. She thought about her dear sweet niece Susie, gone before she had much of a chance to live. Bad luck followed her family like a cloud. Of that there was little doubt.

Emma wrapped her arms around herself and rocked back and forth, thinking hard, looking deep within herself for the truth. Arguing with herself because an answer was so uncertain.

Destiny. Fate. Did she have to believe in the fairies to accept the curse?

Well, curses don't just happen. Somebody had to make the curse to begin with, didn't they? But fairies?

The Roslin she'd met had been a bit strange. Beautiful. Ethereal. She could pass for a fairy queen at a costume ball.

Destiny. Fate. Fairies.

Emma blew out a heavy breath. Maybe she was looking at this all wrong. Maybe she didn't have to know for a certainty all the way down to her bones. Say she chose not to believe, not to follow through. What was the worst thing that could happen?

She could be wrong. She could doom her family to having to fight the ominous black cloud of bad luck and love forever.

What was the best thing that could happen? Well, she could be right. The curse could be like Dair had said, nothing but a story. She'd be protecting herself from being a fool.

She'd also be protecting her heart, a heart already broken by fate, by bad luck. Did she dare risk it again?

What if she did? What if she lost her heart to Dair Mac-

Rae? Would that be so terrible? He was a thief and a liar and probably lots of other bad things she didn't know about. But, he was a good man, too. Today was a perfect example of that. Look at the trouble he'd gone to for his mother's old friend. Dair MacRae had a good heart—even if he kept it hidden much of the time.

Also, if she was his destiny, then wasn't he her destiny, too? Wouldn't he lose his heart to her in return?

It was a heady thought. She could see herself married to the man. Making a home with him. Having his children. Would he be willing to settle in Texas? She hoped so. The idea of leaving her family left her bereft.

And if Jake Kimball was Kat's destiny, he and Dair were already friends. Wouldn't that be nice? And Luke would like Dair. They both were men's men. They'd surely find a lot in common.

Emma drummed her fingers against her knee. If she believed, if fate had a hand in these events, then it stood to reason that she had a chance. That they had a chance. With Dair, Emma could find a love that was powerful, vigilant and true.

Oh my oh my oh my.

It made a curious sort of sense. Wasn't she halfway in love with him already? Heaven knows she was attracted to him. He made her laugh. He roused all her passions. Didn't he in some ways—the good ways—remind her of her father? Trace McBride was far from perfect, but no man had a better heart. Dair was like that, too. She saw past his outer…unsavoriness…to the good man inside.

Yes, she was already halfway in love with him. It wouldn't take much to fall the rest of the way. If she let herself. If she accepted the risk.

Emma made her choice. Destiny, fate, and maybe fairies. That's as far as she had to go. Down to the bones didn't really matter. Where the curse came from didn't matter. The breaking of it did. "I'll do it."

From here on out, Emma believed in the Curse of Clan McBride. She believed she had the opportunity to put an end to it for all time. From here on out, by thought, word, and deed, she'd hold to that belief.

It wasn't until she'd stood and brushed the dust off her skirts before starting inside the house that another thought occurred. Now that she'd accepted Dair MacRae as her destiny, now that she'd admitted to herself that she had feelings for him that ran deeper than a wish to share adventure, she could see no reason not to join him in his bed. Tonight.

HAMISH CAMPBELL STRUCK A match and held the flame to one corner of the note. The paper caught fire, and Hamish blew out the match with a short puff of air. He dropped the burning note onto a silver tray and watched as the paper curled and disintegrated to fine gray ash.

Excitement hummed in his blood. MacRae had paid a call to Robbie Potter and now Potter had turned to him for information. Turned to him for the book. Hamish crossed the room to the bookshelf that held the antique tome. Removing the book from the shelf, he traced the image on the cover with his fingertip.

Finally, progress. He'd dreamed of this moment for so long.

Half an hour later, he stepped into Robbie Potter's shop, the book tucked beneath his arm. He locked the door behind him. "Robert Potter?"

"Aye. Aye. Back here."

Campbell followed the narrow path between bookshelves toward the back of the store until he came upon the bookseller, seated behind a counter, a bowl of mutton stew set before him. Surprise flashed across the bookseller's face, then he hastily dabbed his mouth with a dingy white napkin. "Mr. Campbell, sir. I dinna expect…oh, goodness."

"I've brought the book, Potter."

Potter's mouth dropped open and his gaze flashed to the item in Hamish's hands. "Ye brought the book here? By yerself? Without any guards?"

Shaking his head, Campbell laughed. "I do not worry about being robbed of a book. The ordinary Scotsman on the street wouldn't recognize the value of such treasures as do you and I."

He set it on a nearby table, then motioned for the scholar to take a seat. "At your pleasure, Mr. Potter."

Potter abandoned his meal in a heartbeat. He cleaned his hands before approaching the table with reverence. The book was bound in animal skin with the words on the pages handwritten in Gaelic. What had caught Hamish's notice at a small shop in Perthshire so many years ago was the painting of a dirk on its cover.

Hamish had seen that dagger before. He recognized the intricate engravings on the blade and the sapphires, emeralds and rubies on the hilt because Roslin MacRae had stabbed him with it. Hamish had purchased the book, then brought it to Potter to translate.

"The Guardian's blade," Robbie Potter murmured as he traced the dirk's image on the book's cover. "Me memory isnae what it once was, but it plagued me all afternoon. I knew I'd seen the symbol before. I finally recalled the work I did for you. T'was the first time I ever heard of the Sisters' Prize."

He flipped through the pages as he spoke. Hamish watched him carefully, slipping in questions in such a way that Potter never realized how much he'd revealed with his answers.

So, he hadn't needed the surveillance after all. Alasdair MacRae had come to him. What peculiar quirk of Fate was that?

"There! I knew it!" Potter pointed to a marking on a page. "That's the symbol on Mrs. Tate's ruby?"

"Aye. Aye. It is. And it says…" Potter's voice trailed off as he read. "Glory be." The bookseller looked up from the page, wonderment in his eyes. "The symbol marks the prize."

"Like a pirate's X? There's a map?"

"Nae…nae. It's the old language. Hmm…" The bookseller jumped up, rushed around the bookshelves in his store gathering an armful of books then setting them on his worktable. He muttered as he flipped through the books, jotting down notes. "'Tis a journey of three, though the ruby leads the way. The Prize goes to the fleet. It's the phrase I'm missing, Mr. Campbell. Words on the ruby beneath the symbol. I should have copied them, but I didn't. I'm not certain I'm remembering exactly. I'll need to see the ruby again."

"Mrs. Tate kept the necklace?"

"Aye. But they're returning tomorrow to see what else I've discovered. I'm sure she'll have it with her and I can finish the translation then."

This time, Hamish Campbell was the one who said, "Hmm…"

Fate had led him to Roslin MacRae on the moor that

night. Fate took him to a card game almost thirty years later. Now, fate had dropped this opportunity into his lap.

He smiled at the bookseller. "Actually, Potter, I have a better idea. Wait here. I'll be right back."

CHAPTER NINE

DAIR ARRANGED FOR DINNER to be served on the rooftop garden. It was a pleasant setting, a little Eden in the midst of the city with potted orange trees set around the perimeter to provide privacy and hanging baskets of wildly blooming flowers that perfumed the temperate evening air. Most important, it didn't give him the cringes like most other parts of his house.

As he made his way upstairs, Dair looked forward to the meal. He'd spent much of the afternoon dealing with Highland Riever business with his fence and his banker, and a quick visit to a land agent had yielded an interesting piece of information he was anxious to share with Emma.

He stepped out onto the rooftop to discover she'd already arrived. His first glance at her took his breath away. The lady had been busy this afternoon, too. She'd dressed for dinner.

She wore a low-cut gown of shimmering silk in a rich, deep ruby shot with threads of gold, a perfect complement to the necklace she wore. Dair hardly spared the gem a glance, so enthralled was he with the swell of breasts pillowing the ruby.

When he finally dragged his gaze upward, he saw that she'd piled her hair in tousled golden curls atop her head.

Simple gold hoops hung from her ears. Her blue eyes gleamed with an intriguing light and a secretive smile hovered on her full red lips. Dair wanted her like he needed his next breath. "Now I understand why Harvey laid out my good suit for me to wear," he said, forcing a casual tone. "You're a vision, Emma."

"Thank you. You're looking rather dapper yourself."

"New dress?"

"No. It's my mother's design. A Christmas gift. My sisters and I each received special gowns to match our necklaces."

His gaze made a slow, careful study from head to toe. "Your mother is a talented woman."

"That she is." Her smile widened, warmed. "So, how was your afternoon, Mr. MacRae?"

Not as interesting as hers, by the looks of it. This was a different Emma Tate from the one he'd left swaying on the front stoop. That Emma had been pale and nervous and shaken. This Emma was all color and confidence.

Immediately, he went wary. Drawing on past experience with women, he concluded, "You've made a decision."

"Clairvoyant, MacRae?"

Unnerved, Tate. "Observant."

She slipped a rose from the vase at the center of the table set for two and twirled its long stem. "I like that in a man."

Dair had the sudden feeling that this would be a very long night. He signaled for their meal to be served and they strolled around the rooftop garden engaging in small talk until the servants departed, leaving them alone.

Emma picked up her wineglass, then said, "I thought about what you said, Dair, about fate. I've decided not to fight it. The night Roslin gave my sisters and I our necklaces, she said we must each accomplish a task of great personal import. Maybe finding the treasure is my task. Wouldn't that be exciting?"

Not as exciting as you. He forced himself to pay attention to her words rather than her lips. "So you intend to stay the course? You are not ready to take your ruby and run?"

She played with the neck chain teasingly. "Why tempt fate?"

"Indeed." Dair lifted his own wineglass and sipped it sparingly. Instinct cautioned him to keep his wits about him.

The woman was in a mood, and he didn't know that it was any different from the one this morning that had left him bare-ass naked on his own front balcony. "I've given some thought to our next move. I spoke with a man today who imparted a piece of information I find curious. It seems that in the Strathardle Valley, many families name their firstborn daughter Roslin."

"Why?"

"My acquaintance didn't know, but I believe that's a good line of questioning to pursue. I sent a note to Potter requesting any information he might have in that respect. Depending on what he has for us when we call upon him again tomorrow, I suspect we might find it helpful to travel to Strathardle ourselves."

"The Highlands?" Pleasure lit her expression. "I love the Highlands. I've cousins there, you know."

While they ate, she shared stories about her family, beginning with the Scots branch, then moving west to the McBrides of Fort Worth. She told silly, entertaining tales that thoroughly distracted and enchanted him. Until dessert was served, that is.

The way the woman ate lemon custard was downright sinful.

She licked and sucked and purred and savored. Watching Emma Tate savor her dessert was as erotic as observing fire dances on South Pacific islands. When her tongue dragged slowly, lusciously over her spoon, then she let out that little hum of pleasure, closed her eyes and shuddered with delight, it was like watching someone have sex at the supper table.

Dair wanted to play, too. But not with lemon custard. Hell, he wanted to be the lemon custard.

He was rock-hard beneath the napkin in his lap, and as he reached for his water glass, he debated tipping it and dousing the fire. With a strangled chuckle he imagined steam rising from his lap into the night air.

Then it occurred to him what this was about. Payback. This was payback for his…display…on the balcony. She was teasing him. She probably had plans to work him into a froth then pour ice water on his passion by word or deed or some scheme she'd spent the afternoon concocting. It was just like the woman.

Well, Texas. Surely you've heard the old saying about girls who play with fire getting burned. I'm of a mood to scorch you.

She'd caught him by surprise with this. After the events of the morning he'd expected her to be full of questions about the treasure—either that or saying her goodbyes prior to rejoining her sister or heading home to Texas. Instead, she barely mentioned the treasure and declared her intention to remain with him. It was curious. He'd take a moment to think about it when he had blood in his brain again.

Dair took another slow slip of wine and studied his dinner partner over the crystal glass. Was she at all aware of how dangerous it was to tease a man like him?

Emma finished her dessert by boldly licking the spoon. Then she licked her lips with a slow circle of her tongue that had Dair gripping his wineglass so hard he expected the stem to shatter. "Delicious," she purred. "Simply delicious."

"Yes," Dair agreed, his gaze fastened on her mouth. *Go ahead, seduce her,* whispered a voice inside his head. *She has it coming. You know she does. Remember this morning.*

He should put an end to this game of hers right here and now. He should sweep the dessert dishes off the table, rip up her skirt, and take her on the table. He set his wineglass on the table, then stood and called her bluff. "Delicious. I didn't get enough." He tugged her to her feet. "I want more."

So he kissed her. Dair ravished her mouth with his lips and tongue, unleashing the passion that had burned inside him for hours, days, from the moment he first laid eyes on the woman in his arms, now clutching his shoulders and kissing him back with an eagerness that aroused him to new heights. He yanked pins from her hair and it tumbled, a golden waterfall, as she opened to the erotic stroke of his tongue. She whimpered his name against his mouth as his hand slid up to cup her breast through the silk of her gown.

He took it as permission and his practiced hands went to work, soon freeing her breast to the cool evening air. She moaned as his thumb rubbed across her sensitive skin and she arched into his hand. He gave a deep hum of satisfaction, then lowered his head. His lips closed on her nipple and greedily tasted heaven.

Desire was a hard, pounding force inside him and Dair knew that this time would be no gentle seduction. When she dragged at his jacket then tore at his shirt until her hands found his bare skin and stroked over his ribs, he growled his pleasure. She was as impatient as he. He released her breast and returned to her mouth, feasting there a moment before burying his face in her neck. He sucked hard, drawing heat to the surface while she panted and whimpered and helped his hands deal with laces and tapes and hooks-and-eyes.

Finally, she stood naked before him, a pagan goddess bathed in moonlight, her lids heavy with passion, her lips swollen from his kisses, her full breasts rising and falling with her rapid breaths. Devouring her with his hot, hungry gaze, he murmured, "Emma."

"Just so you know, MacRae, if you're thinking about leaving me stranded up here in retribution for this morning, I'll cut your heart out and feed it to the dogs."

"What?" He started to protest in his own defense, but he lost his train of thought when she reached for his belt buckle. Then she rubbed her breasts against his naked chest as her inquisitive fingers found him, fondled him, and freed him and he quit trying to think at all. He lifted her off her feet and captured her mouth with his. He steeped himself in the sweet taste of her, the scent of her—old roses and ripe woman. When she wrapped her legs around his hips, Dair resisted no longer. He backed her against the chimney and took her standing up.

It was furious and raw and rough. Need clawed through him as her nails raked his back. His blood roared in his veins. His breaths came in labored pants. She was wet for him, hot and tight and he pumped into her feverishly. He heard her whimper and moan and gasp. Felt her nails dig into his skin, her teeth nip his shoulder. "More…" he demanded, thrusting faster. Harder.

"Yes," she moaned, gasping for air. "More."

He plunged into her, deep and desperate, blinded by the

red haze of desire. He felt the orgasm building at the base of his spine, and he tried to hold it back. But when she screamed a wild, primal sound of release and her feminine muscles gripped him like a vise, he could stand no more. Groaning and swearing, Dair drove into her once more, then erupted. A tidal wave of pleasure crashed over him, sucked him down into the heated vortex of a climax stronger and more powerful than any he'd ever known.

When he finally surfaced minutes—or maybe days—later, he realized she'd gone limp in his arms. His heart stuttered and remorse washed over him. "Oh God. I hurt you. Emma, I'm sorry—"

She lifted her head off his shoulder and smiled with smug satisfaction. "I drove you crazy."

Regret melted away to amusement. "Since the day I met you."

"I'm not through with you yet, MacRae."

"Dear Lord in heaven I hope not."

She laughed and her delight rang like wind chimes on the night air. Then she brushed a tender kiss across his lips. "Take me to bed, MacRae. The sex was delightful, but now I want to make love with you."

Dair tried to ignore the apprehension her words sent shuddering down his spine. He wanted to shut his mind to everything but steeping himself in the heat of Emma's passion.

Amazingly, he couldn't do it. Any other woman, any other time, he wouldn't have a problem putting his own needs first. For some strange reason, right now, with her it wasn't working that way. He couldn't forget that core of goodness she constantly revealed. Couldn't dismiss that streak of innocence she occasionally betrayed. "Emma, wait. What's going on here?"

"Isn't it obvious?"

"Sex is obvious. Making love, on the other hand, is open to many interpretations. I think it's important we make sure we're both singing from the same hymnal."

Her smile flashed. "I know I was good, MacRae, but a religious experience?"

He literally trembled with need. *Good Lord, I'm cutting off my nose to spite my face.* "Look, I want to make certain that you understand where I stand. I don't want to be accused of leading you on at some later date. This…liaison… of ours is only temporary. Don't look to me with thoughts of marriage or family or home. It will never happen."

"Are you sure about that?"

See, he'd been right. That innocence of hers was undeniable. She was just the type to think that a sexual relationship inevitably ended up at the altar.

Hell, even if he wasn't dying, that would never happen. Dair shuddered at the thought of marriage. The notion of fatherhood scared him to death. He'd never known his own father. He grew up in a orphanage. He barely remembered his mother's love. What did he know about family ties? Nothing. Not a damned thing.

Emma, on the other hand, was all about family ties. She was marriage and babies and picket fences. Even if he had a future, there would be no future for the two of them. He allowed his certainty to ring in his voice. "I'm positive, Emma."

She gave him a long, searching look, and Dair thought for sure that his little speech had meant the end of the evening's pleasure. He feared it might even affect her decision regarding the treasure hunt. See what trying to be noble got a man?

Trouble. Trouble and frustration.

Finally, she nodded. "I heard what you said, Alasdair MacRae. I give you my word that I'll never accuse you of leading me on. Take me to bed, MacRae. Make love to me."

He all but keeled over in shock. Emma Tate had surprised him yet again. Thank God. He cleared his throat. "That sounds like a fine idea, Texas. I can't think of anything I'd like better."

For once, Alasdair MacRae spoke the God's honest truth.

EMMA SLIPPED INTO HER bathroom to don the nightgown he'd purchased at the dress shop. The red silk clung to her curves, showcased more than concealed. It tied at the shoulders and as she formed the bows, she pictured his fingers tugging the knot free and she shivered with anticipation.

She brushed out her hair and dabbed an exotic scent of bergamot and spice on her wrists, behind her ears, and between her breasts. She felt wicked and wonderful and gloriously alive, and the night was just beginning. A new life was just beginning.

Emma might have doubts about the existence of fairies, but when it came to her feelings for Dair, she now suffered no such indecision. Emma recognized that this was meant to be. *They* were meant to be.

She stepped out into the bedroom. He'd left a single lamp burning and lit a half dozen candles which bathed the room in a soft golden glow. He lay stretched out on the bed, naked, powerful and sleek. His smoky eyes watched her with an intensity that brought shivers to her skin.

He again reminded her of a jungle cat, she decided. Primed and ready to pounce upon his prey. Then he rolled off the bed and stood. His sex jutted out, huge and ready.

Tension coiled inside her. Emma forced herself to stand her ground.

He crossed the room to her, towering above her, the heat of his body rolling off him in waves. He reached out and curled a lock of her hair around his finger. "I don't know when my money was so well spent. You look like a pagan goddess in that gown."

Then he bent his head and brushed his lips across hers. "The first time I saw you, I wanted you. You made me hungry."

"You bought ice cream."

"And thought about licking you. Same thing happened the day you walked into Jake Kimball's study hoping, I thought, to convince him to marry you, I pictured you like this." With one finger, he traced the swell of her breast just above the gown's neckline and Emma quivered beneath his touch.

"While your sister sold my friend on your skills, I mentally stripped away that pretty yellow dress and put you in red. Briefly, I'll admit. I got you naked very fast." With two quick tugs, the gown slipped to the floor. "I couldn't take my eyes off you."

"I noticed you staring." She drew a sharp breath when his fingertip began to trace feathery circles around her nipples.

A mocking smile played upon his lips. "It was rude of me."

"You're a rude man." Her breasts ached for the touch of his hands.

"I don't mean to be rude," he said, his voice rough with arousal. His finger trailed between her breasts and down her belly to her navel. Her muscles clenched. "My intentions are to torment."

"I've observed that you seldom fail in your endeavors."

"That's true." In a movement that surprised her, he

turned her around. He stood close, pulling her back against him. His sex was hot against her bottom. "I almost always get what I want."

Emma's mouth went dry when she realized that he'd maneuvered them in front of a full-length mirror. She watched, her breathing quick and shallow, as his large, tanned hands covered her breasts. Her body arched, an instinctive offering, as he circled and kneaded and stimulated. In her reflection, she saw her erect nipples peeking through his fingers as he played with them, pinching and tugging and rubbing. Pleasure arrowed through her straight to her woman's core and her legs trembled. "This is wicked," she breathed.

"I like wicked," he replied, his voice husky and raw. In the mirror, their gazes met and held. "I like watching you. I like watching what I do to you. Look."

Emma watched their reflection, transfixed, as one of his hands swept lower, across her flat belly. Anticipation built within her. She wanted to groan when his hand paused just above her reddish curls.

"There. See how your thighs parted, how you instinctively opened for me?" He bent to nibble at her earlobe, then nip gently at her neck. "Now watch my fingers find you, Texas. See how they explore your soft, feminine folds."

As he spoke, his hand moved between her legs. Watching him, hearing him, and feeling him all at the same time—it was the most erotic experience of Emma's life.

"You're so wet. Swollen and hot." The hand on her breast tightened as he slipped a finger into her sheath. His breath hissed between his teeth. "Tight."

He stroked her with his finger. Stretched her. His thumb flicked over her most sensitive skin and Emma whimpered, then moaned with protest when he took his hand away.

He brought his hand up to his face, closed his eyes, and inhaled the scent of her on his finger. "Mmm…" Then he opened his eyes, stared deep into hers, and licked her wetness from his hand. "Sweet."

Oh, my.

"And not enough. I simply must taste more of you."

Oh my oh my.

"Watch me drink from you, Emma." He moved in front of her, sank to his knees. He dipped his head and licked her.

Emma's heart hammered, her knees turned to water. His hands grasped her waist and supported her weight, lifted her, gave him better access. She threaded her fingers into his hair to steady herself as he attended to her with the most intimate of kisses. Her head lolled back and her eyes threatened to close, but she couldn't drag her gaze from the reflection in the mirror.

Tension inside her built. His breath was hot against her, his tongue bold. When he fitted his mouth against her and sucked, she cried out. "No. No more. I can't bear it."

Dair glanced up at her and smiled. "I fear you'll have to bear it, Texas. I haven't drunk my fill. Now, watch how your skin flushes and your eyes glaze over when I make you come. I find the sight incredibly arousing."

He proved his point within seconds and when the spasms of pleasure racked her, Emma melted, her legs no longer able to support her. He made a masculine growl of satisfaction as he lowered her gently onto the floor.

Still, he didn't stop. With his hot mouth and busy tongue, he brought her up again, over again, until, writhing beneath him, she begged him to stop. "Please. It's too much. Dair, it's…oh-h-h…" She ended on a sigh as he gave her one last sweetly tender intimate kiss then rolled up onto his knees.

"Delicious," he repeated. "The perfect appetizer."

She lay exhausted against the Persian rug. It took a moment for his words to penetrate. She lifted her head. "Appetizer?"

"I intend a full course meal. I've been hungry for you for a long time, Emma. It will take some time to sate my appetite."

"You'll kill me," she said as he lifted her into his arms, carried her to the bed, and gently laid her down.

"You're a strong woman." Dair climbed onto the bed and stretched out beside her, propping himself up on his elbow. "You can handle me."

Emma wanted to handle him. She wanted to drive him wild, to create within him the same desperation, the same urgent passion that he'd stoked to life within her. So she took control of the moment by rolling him onto his back and lifting herself over him.

She kissed his chest as he'd kissed hers, nipping at his small round nipples, sucking him, coaxing a groan from his throat. Then she licked her way down his body, savoring the salty male taste of him. Lust sizzled through her, itchy and achy and immediate. Her tongue circled his navel, then she lifted her head, allowing long strands of her hair to stroke across his sex. It twitched when she paused, her mouth mere inches away.

"God, Emma."

Power roared through her, an aphrodisiac more potent than any other. Her pulse pounded in an age-old rhythm. She smiled, purred, then licked the velvet length of him. He muttered a curse. She laughed, blowing her warm breath across his swollen tip, then tasting. "Salty," she murmured. "Musky."

His hands grabbed the sheets and his expression went taut with arousal bordering on pain. When she took him in her mouth he bore it but a moment before crying out and losing control.

The jungle cat pounced. Triumph flashed through Emma as he flipped her onto her back, positioned himself, and thrust deep. He was hard and hot inside her and Emma reveled in it.

Supporting himself by his arms, his head thrown back, the cords in his neck and the grimace on his face betrayed the intensity of his need. Dair pulled out, then pushed back in, pounding her hips into the soft mattress, stroking her own arousal back to a fevered pitch. She rose to meet him, again and again. Was that his voice or hers whispering, "Faster… harder…more?"

Dair's rhythm matched the words, his thrusts urgent. Savage in intensity. Emma sensed it coming. Tension building… stretching tight…tighter…

She shattered. Waves of pleasure surged through her and she surrendered to sensation. Through the haze of her own fulfillment, she saw him look down at her, look into her eyes, into her soul. "Emma." He thrust hard once more and emptied his hot seed inside her.

Their gazes locked, Emma said his name. Then silently, completely, she gave him her heart.

CHAPTER TEN

DAIR DRIFTED TOWARD WAKEFULNESS a contented man. He'd spent the night under his own roof in a comfortable bed snuggled up to the most exciting, sensual, sensuous woman he'd ever known. How many times had he wakened her through the night? Three or was it four? She'd awakened him twice. God, it was good to be alive.

All right, MacRae. That's not a direction you want to take your thoughts. Not today. He frowned into his pillow, then reached for the woman with whom he shared the bed.

He found empty space. His frown deepened and he wrenched open his eyes. The sudden hot weight in his belly eased when he spied Emma Tate back in her nightgown and down on her hands and knees beside the bed.

He rolled and sat up. "I hesitate to ask, but…"

Worry dotted her expression. "I can't find my necklace."

The hot weight settled back into his belly. "Emma, I didn't steal it. I didn't leave the bed all night. I wouldn't do that to you again. Not even before last night, but especially—"

"I know, Dair. I know you didn't take it."

"You do?" He rubbed his hands over his face. "I'm confused."

"I know you wouldn't steal the necklace from me again." She rose to her feet, then added, "Nevertheless, it's missing."

Thinking aloud, he said, "You wore it with the nightgown. When did you take it off? Did I take it off?"

"I did." She took one more survey of the floor beneath the bed, then stood. "I took it off after the first time we made love. You collapsed on top of me when you were done and it was pressing into my chest."

"Oh, that's right," he said, remembering.

"I set it on the bedside table. I know I did. It's disappeared, just like Kat's did." She frowned, her eyes narrowing. "Jake Kimball hasn't come to visit, has he?"

Dair shot her a scowl, then rolled out of bed and grabbed his pants from the chair where he'd left them. As he pulled them on, he made a quick scan of the room. Silver candlesticks remained on the mantel. An ivory trinket box sat on the desk. A Flemish landscape hung on the wall. Nothing but the necklace was missing. A Highland Riever type hadn't paid a call.

"This makes no sense," he said. "Someone would have had to get into this room while we were asleep. Through a door that squeaks every time it's opened. That simply couldn't have happened. I sleep lightly. I would have awakened. It has to be here, Emma. You're just not looking in the right place."

"Then you find it," she snapped. She flounced to her wardrobe and removed a clean set of clothing, then paraded into the bathroom and slammed the door behind her.

He winced at the noise, then muttered a foul word and made a quick, but thorough search of the room. When that failed to turn up the missing piece of jewelry, he did it again. The hot weight of dread settled into his stomach like an extended-stay guest.

He tested the door. The hinges squeaked each time he

opened it. He repeated the action with the French doors leading out onto the balcony. Their hinges were even noisier. Dair might not like this home he owned, but he valued his possessions. Squeaky hinges served a purpose—one of the little lessons the Highland Riever had learned long ago.

What happened to the damned necklace? Was it in any way possible for a thief to have sneaked into the room without waking him? To have found the necklace in the dark, then made off with it and only it without detection? Who in the city's underworld but himself had the ability to pull off such a feat? No one.

Had someone been in there the whole time he and Emma had been making love? How did he get in? And out? Anger pumped through Dair's veins. He'd kill the son of a bitch when he found him. Standing in the middle of the room, his hands braced on his hips, he murmured, "This is damned strange."

The bathroom door opened and a freshened, fully dressed Emma stepped out. He could all but see the words *I told you so* hovering on her tongue, but she wisely held them back. "Are you confident in the characters of your household staff, Dair?"

"They weren't in residence last night. I gave instructions for everyone to be dismissed after our supper was served." He rubbed the back of his neck, then shot her a puzzled look. "This is in no way a criticism, Emma, but it occurs to me that you're taking this rather well. Considering everything that's happened, I'd expect you to be...well...you're not ordinarily a ranter, but I find this calmness of yours curious."

"I'm not exactly calm," she told him. "I'm entertaining explanations other than the obvious."

"What do you mean by that?"

"It occurs to me that three possible explanations for the necklace's disappearance exist." She ticked them off on her fingers. "One, a thief sneaked in while we were asleep and stole it. You've assured me that's not possible, which brings us to two. A thief might have stolen it while we were making love."

Dair muttered an expletive beneath his breath.

"I think that's a legitimate possibility. I suspect that at various times during last night a bomb could have gone off at our feet and we wouldn't have noticed. We were quite involved."

Dair couldn't argue, but he didn't have to like it. "What's the third explanation?"

"Magic."

His mouth gaped. "Magic?"

"I've never really believed, but after reading Ariel's story yesterday...well...Roslin of Strathardle called us the Chosen, a circle of three in the thirty-third generation. She said we have the chance to end the curse."

"That fairy tale?" he scoffed. "You've decided you believe in magic because of some silly story you read in a book?"

Her chin came up. "You believe in fate."

"Yes, but it's a big step from fate to fairies."

"I thought so, too, until yesterday, and honestly, I'm still not entirely certain about the fairies. It could be that's just a way to explain a concept...well...that's beside the point. Dair, I'd heard that story before. That night when Roslin gave my sisters and me our necklaces? She told us the same tale."

He gave an exasperated shrug. "So what? It's a MacRae legend told by some rogue clan member who robbed from the Sisters' Prize. It doesn't have anything to do with your necklace disappearing. Or with a goddamned voyeur possibly creeping about while we were naked and…occupied."

"We don't know that." Emma folded her arms. "Look, MacRae, you obviously believe in the treasure. What makes your legend any more legitimate than mine?"

"It's a treasure. Treasures exist. Besides, why are you laying claim to a MacRae legend? If you think I might challenge your right to the necklace since it's part of the Prize, then—"

"No, Dair. That's not it at all. Remember the part of the story that talked about Ariel's children and her children's children having to prove the strength of their love? That's the Curse of Clan McBride. You're missing a detail. A rather important one. The mortal man who Ariel chose over the fairy prince? Well, listen to this. He was a McBride."

He went still. "That wasn't in the story."

"It was in the version Roslin told us in Fort Worth. You said you investigated us. Didn't you learn about the bad luck curse? My family has seen it played out over and over. My father, my Uncle Tye. They were forced to overcome great trials before they achieved luck in love. Even my own love for Casey—"

"No." Dair waved a hand, dismissing the entire idea.

She drew a deep breath as if summoning patience. "Nevertheless, Dair, the reality before us is that my necklace has gone missing under a peculiar circumstance."

"So you're ready to believe in magic? Good Lord. Maybe you really should have competed for Jake Kimball's hand in marriage. You two would make a pair. He thinks Kat's necklace will lead him to his brother who disappeared in a Tibetan storm years ago."

"Does he really? Why?"

"Apparently, he's dreamed about her necklace ever since his brother disappeared."

"Oh, my." Her eyes widened. She fell back a couple of steps until she sank down onto a chair. "It's true, then. See, this further proves my point. Call it fate or destiny or magic, or voodoo, for that matter, some force is at work here. And my necklace has disappeared."

"Look. As distasteful as I find the idea, someone managed to steal it from beneath our noses while we were otherwise involved. I knew you were dangerous, Texas. I didn't realize being with you would wipe a man's senses from his head. I'll have to remember that in the future."

"You're not ready to believe, are you?"

"Believe what?"

"Believe in destiny. In a love that is powerful, vigilant and true, and in a task of great personal import. Dair, my sisters and I are the circle of three. We're the Chosen. We have a chance. It began with a McBride and MacRae. It's logical that it should end in similar fashion."

In that moment, the blinders lifted from Dair's eyes. This morning, her calm reaction to the ruby's disappearance. Last night, the vixen in his bed. Her response when he told her point blank they didn't have a future. She didn't believe him. She flat out didn't believe him! She believed in fairy tales instead.

I knew it was too good to be true.

Anger roared through him. Hardheaded, stubborn woman. What was he supposed to do? He'd tried, hadn't he? He'd told her the truth. Most of it, anyway. This wasn't right. She had no right to drag him along into her fantasies. Not her fairy-tale fantasies, anyway. She'd given herself to him last night under false pretenses. Well, that was her responsibility. Not his. He was by God not responsible for her silliness.

Dair dragged his fingers through his hair in frustration as he realized that now he'd inevitably hurt her. Wonderful. Just wonderful. He didn't want to hurt Emma. She deserved better.

One more time. He'd try one more time to get her to listen to reason. "Emma, I'll admit there are some curious things happening here. I agree that fate has brought you and me together. But you need to put your feet back on the ground here. What we're dealing with isn't some supernatural phenomenon."

"But what if…?"

"Honey, reality is that someone, at some time, robbed the Sisters' Prize of the three necklaces. We know that for some unknown reason a decade ago, a woman who likely had ties to Clan MacRae gave those necklaces to you and your sisters. I suspect your Roslin was somehow connected to mine because I had such a strong reaction to the engravings on the stone. Maybe my mother was the one who took the necklaces."

"Would she have done that?"

"Who knows? Maybe your Roslin was a friend or even a cousin of my mother's. Hell, maybe she believed the fairy tale too and when she ran across three McBride daughters, she decided you should have the treasure. That's all guesswork, though. Who knows what the truth is? But it doesn't really matter. The fact is that your necklaces prove the treasure exists. That's what's real in this whole thing, Emma. The treasure. It's out there and I intend to find it."

"I want to find the treasure, too," she agreed, nodding.

"Why? Because you think it's your 'task'? Because you think your fairy godmother has declared us a couple? Emma, you need to listen to me this time. Happy-ever-after isn't going to happen for us. I cannot be your strong, vigilant, true love. Last night was wonderful. Making love with you was special. More special than it's ever been for me. But there are things you don't know about me. Private things I'm not inclined to share."

Her spine snapped straight. "Oh, my God. You're married."

"No I'm not married! I may be a thief, but I'm not a cad. Neither am I your destiny, Emma. You have to accept that. And you should recognize that it's a *good* thing. I'm not much of a prize, Emma Tate. You deserve a whole lot better than me.

"Now. I think you must be correct in your assumption that somebody spied on our lovemaking last night and took advantage of our distraction to steal your necklace. Whoever took it might well try to sell it today, so it's best we move quickly. I'll quiz the staff. Also, I know every fence in Edinburgh so I'll check with them, too. While I'm doing that, would you check with Robbie and see if he's discovered any more information for us? We'll meet back here at noon. With any luck, we'll have the necklace back, and we can still leave for Strathardle today."

He strode toward the door headed for his own rooms and a change of clothes. Her voice stopped him as he reached for the doorknob. "Alasdair MacRae? I think under the circumstances it's important I tell you something I've recently discovered."

Something in her voice warned him. Warily, he asked, "What's that?"

"I've fallen in love with you."

He jerked. She might as well have thrown a knife in his back. He wrenched open the door and stalked into the hallway. "Stubborn, hardheaded female."

If deep within him, happiness warmed his heart, he did his best to ignore it. He almost succeeded.

But not quite.

EMMA DAWDLED OVER HER breakfast, leaving the way clear for Dair to interrogate his staff before departing for his dealings with the Edinburgh criminal element. She'd finished her bacon, eggs and toast and was savoring a second cup of coffee when the pounding on the front door began.

"Open up! Open the door immediately!"

Apparently, "immediately" didn't happen soon enough. Emma dotted her lips with her napkin and prepared to stand as the door opened and what appeared to be a dozen men in blue uniforms and badges rushed inside. Policemen? This couldn't be good.

"Stop," called Dair's man, Harvey, as the policemen trailed past him like ants in search of food.

"Where is he?" demanded the lead official, a barrel-bellied man with thick red brows and a handlebar mustache.

"Where is who?" Harvey asked.

"The damned Riever!"

"I think there has been a misunderstanding, sir," Emma interrupted in a placating tone. "The robber isn't here. The robbery was here. My necklace was stolen."

"Who are you?"

"I'm Emma Tate. I'm a friend of Mr. MacRae."

"Oh? Then perhaps I should arrest you, too."

Her smile died. "What?"

"Have ye been helping him, lass?" Captain Ketchen demanded. He braced his hands on his wide hips and scowled at her fiercely. "Have ye assisted the Highland Riever with his nefarious deeds?"

"The Highland Riever? What are you talking about? I don't know the Highland Riever." *Do I?* She tried to ignore the sinking sensation in the pit of her stomach. "I'm the victim. My necklace was stolen."

"No surprise, that, if you are staying here," offered one of the other officers.

Emma turned her attention back to the police captain. "Are you suggesting that the Highland Riever works for Mr. MacRae?"

"Nae." The big man's face went red. "The Highland Riever is MacRae!"

Emma's mouth gaped. Shock widened her eyes, even though deep down inside, she wasn't all that surprised. "No."

"Aye. We obtained proof of it just this morning."

The soldier ants began streaming downstairs and from out of the back rooms. "He's not here, sir," one man said. "Servants all deny any knowledge of his whereabouts."

Captain Ketchen instructed one man to remain inside, and four men to position themselves at the front and rear of the town house. Then he turned to Emma and the interrogation began. What was her relationship with MacRae? How long had she known him? What was her business in Scotland? What about this necklace she claimed to have lost?

Emma's mind spun as she tried to mentally process this new information. First, did she believe it? Yes, she feared she did. The man she loved was more than a simple robber. He was a master thief. Wouldn't her father be thrilled about that?

Second, how should she respond? Should she share her

knowledge of Dair's plans with the police? No. Absolutely not. In that case, should she deliberately mislead them? Heaven knows it wouldn't be the first time she lied to the law. She was a McBride Menace, after all.

She answered the man's questions in such a way as to alleviate his suspicions about her, yet cause Dair no further harm. Deciding she should gather as much information as possible to pass along to Dair when she saw him, she began asking questions of her own. "What proof? Where did it come from? Why do you believe something so preposterous?"

"It's not preposterous at all. We've an eyewitness. He's an acquaintance of MacRae's, a coachman named Charlie Baldwin. He saw MacRae acting suspiciously, so he followed him and observed his criminal acts. Then he reported it like any good citizen would do."

Charlie Baldwin? A coachman? Was he the Charlie from Chatham Park? Jake Kimball's man? Emma thought hard, then nodded. Yes, she did believe she'd heard the surname Baldwin. Why would Jake Kimball's man report Dair to the police? Did Jake want Dair in jail for some reason? It made no sense. "I don't believe that. This man must be lying."

"He's not lying. We've authenticated his information."

"That can't be. Where is this Charlie? I want to talk to him."

"You'll talk to no one, ma'am. I'm not at all certain you are innocent in the matter."

Emma let out the well-practiced gasp of an innocent, wrongly accused.

The captain gave instructions for Emma not to leave the house, then departed, continuing his search for the fugitive.

Emma stood in the dining room rubbing her brow, thinking the situation through. She had to find Dair. She couldn't allow him to walk into this ambush. "I have to get out of here."

"There's a way, Miss," the worried Harvey said. "A side door that leads to the neighbors' house. It's quite discreet. I've a key. The housekeeper and I…." A blush stained his cheeks.

"I see. Good. That's good." How would she find him? Where should she go? Would he come here before meeting her at the bookstore? Where could she head him off? "I have to warn him."

"We've a signal, Mrs. Tate," Harvey shared. "You need not worry that he'll walk into a trap here."

"So it is true, then? What Captain Ketchen claimed? Dair is the Highland Riever?"

Pride shone in the man's weathered face. "Aye. He's the best that ever was."

Emma grimaced. "I don't suppose he's secretly working for the authorities?" That's what Mari's husband, Luke Garrett had done. Mari had thought Luke was an outlaw when she went to him for help, but it turned out that he was actually a Texas Ranger.

"No, ma'am. If the authorities were ever to catch the Riever, he'd certainly hang."

He wouldn't come back here, so she needed to meet him somewhere else. She'd go to the bookstore. Await him there as planned. Surely he'd realize that's what she'd do. He was a master thief, after all. He had to be smart.

She made a quick trip up to her room where she gathered the barest of necessities into a single bag. At the writing desk she hesitated. The envelope addressed to her parents lay ready and waiting to be posted. She'd written the letter yesterday afternoon, filling the missive with news that sometimes leaned more toward fiction than fact. It was the fifth such letter she'd written. She wanted to do everything she could to alleviate as much of their certain worry over her adventure as possible.

Trace and Jenny McBride had suffered grievously during the months they believed Kat had died in the Spring Palace fire. Emma knew they'd worry about her trip to Scotland no matter what, but she hoped the news she sent in her letters might hold the worst of that worry at bay.

She wrote chatty little notes that made Dair sound more like a brother than a lover. Not that she expected her father to actually believe it, but she imagined he might pretend it was so from time to time. Yesterday's letter had been especially cheery. Dare she send it now in the wake of her discoveries about her lover? The idea felt particularly deceptive.

Emma picked the letter up, tapped it against the desk, then slipped it into her handbag. She'd send this one, then stop. In her next letter, she'd tell her parents the truth—about the engraving on the necklace, the Sisters' Prize, and falling in love with MacRae. Mama would understand. She'd make Papa understand, too. Eventually.

Emma turned to leave, then stopped, reconsidered, and retrieved the garnet nightgown. Downstairs, she followed Dair's employee into the kitchen and across a narrow alley to the house next door. There, with the help of his lady love, he offered her a servant's apron and bonnet and a large basket in which to conceal her bag.

She made her escape without detection and made her way toward the bookshop, her thoughts a jumble. *Am I in love with an outlaw? Who's now a fugitive? What will we do about the treasure hunt? I wonder if he's found my necklace? I can't believe I've fallen in love with an outlaw.*

Well, you wanted adventure. I'd say you got it.

She breathed a sigh of relief when she spied the bookshop sign half a block ahead. She'd quiz Robbie Potter while she waited for Dair. Maybe his expertise included good escape routes from the city.

The familiar jangle of the doorbell settled her nerves a bit because it signaled she'd no longer be alone. Though Emma was long accustomed to trouble, she ordinarily had company while being involved in it.

She retraced yesterday's path through the labyrinth, and at about halfway toward the counter she noted a new, troubling addition to the familiar musty-bookstore scent. It was…coppery. Disturbingly familiar.

Emma smelled blood.

Her stomach clenched. "Mr. Potter? Robbie?"

No response.

Her knees went weak. Emma dragged her feet forward, dread weighting every step.

He lay on his stomach behind the counter in a pool of drying blood, his head turned to the right, his eyes open and fixed. A knife hilt protruded from his back. *Oh my oh my oh my.* "Robbie."

The poor, poor man. Tears stung her eyes as she fell back a step, her besieged brain trying to make sense of a nonsensical day. First the disappearance of her necklace, then the revelation about Dair, and now this. If this was fate or fairies at work, she wished they'd take a holiday.

"Oh, Robbie," she repeated. She wanted to close his eyes, to cover him. To somehow make it better. But she knew from hearing her sheriff brother-in-law talk about his work that it was best she didn't touch a thing. The police would want to see everything just as it was.

The police. The same police who'd told her to remain at Dair's town house. "Holy Hannah," she muttered. "I'm in trouble."

Actually, Emma only thought she was in trouble then. She knew she was in trouble seconds later when the doorbell jangled and she heard a man's voice say, "At first I didn't notice it because of all the blood and the knife sticking out of his chest. Then I looked at his hand and saw his finger and I realized he must have written the name of his killer."

Emma's gaze shifted to Robbie Potter's hand and she gasped. There, written in blood on the wooden floor, were two words: *Emma Tate.*

She heard footsteps approaching. She didn't have time to think. Acting instinctively and moving as quietly as possible, she darted up the staircase she'd used the day before. In the room where Dair had recovered from his headache, she eased open the window, then stepped out onto the roof.

A strong summer wind whipped her skirt around her and paper trash from the street below swirled up and over the chimney as Emma made a quick survey around. Luckily, the bookshop's roof butted up against the butcher shop's roof next door which in turn was connected to a law office. She scrambled from one rooftop to the next until she decided she'd traveled far enough to descend to the street. Locating a fire escape, she made her way down.

When her feet touched the ground, she paused. She drew a deep breath, then exhaled on a shaky sigh. Emma looked from one side to the other, in front of her, then behind her. She was alone, in a foreign country, being pursued by the police.

She hadn't a clue what to do next.

CHAPTER ELEVEN

"HOW COULD SHE just disappear?" Dair threw a Meissen pitcher against the bedroom wall in the master suite of his Edinburgh town house and watched it smash to bits. "She has little money. Little knowledge of the area. She's wanted for murder and yet she's managed to evade the authorities for weeks."

"It's a puzzle," his man Harvey agreed, wincing at the destruction now scattered on the master suite's hardwood floor. "I expected the Highland Riever would evade capture, but the fact that the hunt for the 'Black Widow' has met with no success is certainly surprising."

"Surprising? It's damned unbelievable!" And it was scaring Dair to death. He'd looked everywhere for her. He scoured the city—not an easy task for a man at the top of the police's most-wanted list. He'd traveled to Rowenclere Castle in the hopes that she'd fled to her distant cousins. He'd made a quick trip through Strathardle Glen in case she'd decided to continue the treasure hunt without him. He'd even gone to England only to learn that Jake and Kat had married and departed Chatham Park. Without Emma.

The days since Emma's disappearance had been one nightmare after another. Shortly after leaving the town house that fateful morning, he'd been felled by a headache—by far the worst he'd suffered so far. As a result, he'd been out of his senses during those first hours of the hunt for the Riever—lying in an alley and taken for a drunk by any who might have noticed. By the time the pain cleared enough to let him think and he went to meet Emma, the bookstore was filled with lawmen and she had vanished.

He was concerned the first day when he couldn't find her, worried the second, and frantic by the third. That emotion had only escalated in the days since when none of his efforts to find her proved fruitful. And now, a quarter of an hour after sneaking back into his town house, he could feel another damned headache coming on. *I hate this house.* "What have you been able to learn about the murder, Harvey?"

"They've circulated a drawing of Mrs. Tate. She made quite an impression upon the fellow who works the desk at the lending library, and he provided a fair description. The most disturbing piece of news I have to impart is the appearance of a witness."

"Oh?" Dair pinned him with a stare. "A witness should be good news."

"It's not. He claims to have seen a woman fleeing the bookshop shortly before the body was discovered. His description matches Mrs. Tate."

"That's preposterous. Who is this witness? He's lying."

"Reverend Harold Markhum from Dublin Street Presbyterian Church."

"Well, hell." Dair rubbed his brow and tried to will away the pain. It wasn't going to work. The blackness was coming on fast. "I need to rest and it's probably better I not do it here."

"They searched the house an hour before you arrived, sir. I doubt they'll be back. They've never searched twice in one day."

"All right, then." Not here, though, in the master suite. He'd go to Emma's room, Emma's bed where the scent of her would linger on the sheets. Guilt rode him as hard as the headache. She was in this trouble because of him. He'd brought her to Scotland. He'd gotten her tangled up in the Sisters' Prize. If not for him, she undoubtedly would have returned to Texas with her sister. She'd be safe and sound at home instead of lost and alone and pursued by police here.

He stumbled onto her bed just as the pain overtook him. "Emma, I'm sorry," he murmured, his face buried in her pillow. "Emma, where are you?"

Hours later when the pain receded and his ability to think returned, he put together a plan. Removing a sheet of paper and a pen from the desk drawer, he sketched out an advertising flier, which Harvey delivered to a printer along with a large monetary incentive to do the work immediately.

The following morning, the man took delivery of boxes of fliers reading: *Do You Have Bad Luck In Love?* The seminar about improving one's romantic relationships would be hosted by Mr. Trace McBride one week from tonight. Interested parties should contact Mr. McBride for more information by way of a postal box. Return contact information should be included.

Through Harvey, Dair had hired help to plaster Edinburgh with the advertisements. If Emma was still in town, she'd see it. If she saw it, she'd decipher the message. With any luck tomorrow he'd find directions to her whereabouts in the mailbox rented in her father's name.

Because he couldn't bear waiting around and doing nothing, he'd saved a stack of his own fliers to disperse. Donning an old man's disguise, he retraced the route Emma would have taken the morning she disappeared. Eventually, that led him to the bookstore. He was surprised to see an Open sign in the window. Potter had bemoaned the fact that he had no heir to run the shop after he was gone.

Dair ducked his head as he entered the bookshop, listening carefully for any sign of authorities. Though he believed his disguise would hold up under most circumstances, it was reasonable to assume they'd look hard at anyone arriving at the scene of a murder. Hearing no conversation, he moved toward the sales counter at the back of the shop.

The large, gray-haired woman seated at the study table surrounded by books looked vaguely familiar at first glance. She looked up briefly from her reading, and as soon as she went still, Dair made the connection to the "companion" who accompanied Emma to Jake Kimball's bride interview. "Emma?"

"Dair?" she asked simultaneously.

"Emma!" Relief crashed over him like a tidal wave.

She stood, braced her hands on unnaturally wide hips and snapped, "Well. It's about time you got here."

Dair couldn't help it. He burst out into a loud, strong laugh.

"Oh, hush," she scolded. "You totally betray your disguise. Old men don't laugh with such gusto."

"True." He marched toward her, grabbed her arm, and tugged her into his embrace. "They don't do this with such gusto, either."

Then he kissed her, pouring all his anger and frustrations, worry and relief, joy and jubilation into the act. He let her know in no uncertain terms how he felt about losing her, then finding her again.

When he finally released her, Emma's makeup was smudged and both her wig and bosom were askew. When she caught her breath enough to speak, she said, "I…uh…you…oh."

Dair marched to the front of the store, turned the lock and flipped the Open sign to Closed. Without saying a word, he took her hand and tugged her along behind him upstairs where he tossed her onto the bed, then fell on top of her.

He made love to her fast and furiously, with a desperation that surprised them both. When they were done, he rolled off of her panting. He flung an arm over his face. "I swear I feel as old as I look."

It took her a minute, but Emma started laughing. "Look at us. My bosom is lopsided and I have cotton in my ears. Your beard is hanging by one side and your belly has shifted around to your back."

Dair cocked open one eye. "It's impolite to laugh at a man's deformity."

She sniggered and a warmth spread throughout his chest. "Oh God, Texas. Have you been here all this time?"

Now she frowned at him. "It's where we agreed to meet."

He groaned and shut both eyes once again. "I came as soon as I heard about Robbie, but the place was swarming with police. I didn't go inside, but I searched the area. Where were you then?"

Emma told him about her race across the rooftops. "When I realized I had nowhere to go, I got scared. I just started walking. After a while—hours, actually—my brain thawed out and I started to plan. I couldn't get near your town house or even the one next door to contact Harvey. I remembered Mr. Potter mentioned his sister recently passed on and that he had no relatives. I decided that pretending to be Miss Potter and taking up residence here until you came for me would be the safest thing to do. I traded my clothes for these." Her lips flashed a quick grin. "Besides, it was my turn to play Wilhemina Peters."

"The character Katrina played when you came to Jake's bride interviews."

"Yes." Emma propped herself up on her elbow. "It's tedious, though, being in disguise. You must do it quite a lot as the Highland Riever. You're quite good at it. I almost didn't recognize you."

Dair knew he'd have to explain about the Riever, but he wasn't ready to leave the subject at hand yet. "When I couldn't find you here in town, I went to Rowanclere, then to Strathardle, then to Chatham Park."

"You saw Kat?"

"No. But I do have news. She married Jake, Emma, and she's taken the children and returned to Texas."

She heard what he didn't say. "Where's Jake?"

"He apparently went through with his plans."

"To sail to Tibet? That scoundrel." She sat up and began righting her clothes, stuffing her stuffing back into place as she thought aloud. "Maybe the children have something to do with her task. She must have made progress on her problem with little ones. That's good. It's wonderful. And who's to know what Jake will find in Tibet or how fast he'll find it. Why, he might change course and head for Texas for all we know."

"I suspect at some point, he will. He's on a wild goose chase." Something in his voice alerted her because she stopped and looked questioningly at Dair. "Another bit of information I picked up at Chatham Park. Remember Miss Starnes? One of Jake's bride prospects?"

"I do," Emma said, nodding. "I thought he might choose her."

"Apparently so did she, and when he didn't, she found a way to get back at him. She stole an old letter of his brother

Daniel's from a file Bernard Kimball kept and had a forger copy the handwriting. Jake received a letter from his "brother" which led him to think Daniel was alive and waiting to be found. That's why he left your sister and the children."

Emma winced. "How cruel. How did you discover this?"

"Miss Starnes's father discovered her perfidy and he arrived at Chatham Park to beg Jake's forgiveness while I was there. With Jake already gone, he confessed all to me."

"So Daniel isn't alive. Jake won't find his family. That's so sad. And poor Kat. His leaving would have hurt her. She didn't deserve that."

"Life isn't fair more often than not." He pressed a quick kiss against her lips, then said, "Look Emma, Edinburgh isn't safe for either of us at the moment. I need to decide our next move, but I'm not certain where we should go."

"I am." Excitement lit Emma's eyes and she hurried to put herself to rights. "Get dressed, MacRae, and come downstairs. I've something to show you."

Dair frowned at her leg, distracted by a truly ugly garter and stocking. "I hope we can be done with Wilhemina Peters soon."

She sniffed. "I've never liked facial hair on men, myself."

Dair's disguise took longer to repair than Emma's—it was important for his beard and mustache to appear natural—so when he finally descended the staircase, he found her back at the reading table with a leather-bound book and a box full of correspondence in front of her. "What's this?" he asked, reaching for one of the letters.

"Read this first." She handed him a receipt for one box of personal correspondence from the private library of a Duncan MacRae. "Look at the date and time. Mr. Potter borrowed this box after we visited him and showed him the necklace."

"It's information about the treasure," Dair surmised, glancing back at the box.

"Yes. He'd hidden the letters well. It took me almost a week to find the box. Dair, the letters were written by a woman named Roslin MacRae."

"Another one."

"Yes. She emigrated to Australia with her husband in 1840."

"Australia?" he repeated, putting the pieces together. "She took the Sisters' Prize to Australia?"

"I think so. For a time. But then in one of the later letters, she mentions another Roslin, a cousin to whom the burden was soon to pass. Dair, I think the cousin was your mother."

Dair thought that through. "You think she took the treasure to Texas."

"It's possible. And if my necklace was originally part of the treasure, maybe that's why it was familiar to you. Maybe you'd seen it before."

He considered it, then shook his head. "It doesn't feel right. It's not the necklace that felt familiar, but the engraving."

"All right, then. Maybe the box holding the treasure is engraved with the same symbol, the same words. You were just a boy. Your mother could have showed it to you, but you don't remember it well."

While he was still trying to digest that idea, she hit him with another blow. "I've thought about this every day we've been apart. Dair, I think someone else knows about the treasure. I think it's possible that someone has had you followed to see if you'd lead them to The Sisters' Prize."

He rubbed the back of his neck as he considered it. "He

could have found out about the Riever that way. Found out about you."

"And used the information when he considered it to be most valuable." She paused significantly, then added, "After Robbie was able to put together the clues."

"You think this mysterious someone killed Potter."

"I do. We know Mr. Potter spoke to someone after we left this shop that day because of this box from Duncan MacRae's library."

"I know Duncan MacRae," Dair said. "He's a good man. He didn't do this."

"All right. If not MacRae, then maybe Potter borrowed another source of information from someone else, too."

"The killer."

"I think Mr. Potter told the killer about my necklace, about the treasure, and what he'd discovered in those letters."

"The killer stole the ruby," Dair said, a shudder running down his spine as he pictured a murderer standing beside the bed where Emma lay sleeping.

"Or had it stolen," Emma agreed.

Dair paced the bookshop aisle. "If Robbie discovered a piece of information that offered up a clue to the treasure's whereabouts, then the killer didn't need us anymore."

"He gave up the Riever and framed me for the murder he committed to get us out of the way." Emma nodded her agreement.

"What was the clue, Emma? What did Robbie discover and how did the killer know I'd get involved with the Sisters' Prize before I did?"

"Magic?" she offered.

He scowled at her. "I need something more solid than that."

"What if the killer knew your mother? What if he thought she told you the secret?"

Dair's blood ran cold. He lifted his finger to trace the faint scar beside his eye that he'd carried most of his life. "What if he's the one who killed her?"

"Your mother was murdered?" Emma's eyes widened at that. "You never told me that. What happened, Dair?"

"I don't know. I've never known. I don't remember anything about it. I barely recall living with my mother in our cabin."

She fired off a dozen questions about his past, but Dair shook his head. "I don't know, Emma. A man delivering some lumber she'd ordered found her lying on the floor of the cabin. I was hiding under the bed. Nevertheless, it's not relevant to this. Let's not get distracted."

"All right," she agreed, although the look in her eyes told him she'd revisit the subject again. Then her expression turned pensive as they both took time to think the matter through.

"It fits," she said a few moments later, excitement lighting her eyes. "The killer knew about the Sisters' Prize. Maybe he wanted your mother to give it to him, and she wouldn't so he killed her. Then, sometime, somewhere, he saw you and recognized you. He thought you might lead him to the treasure and sure enough, you did. You led him to Mr. Potter and my necklace."

She shuffled through a stack of papers on the desk, then pulled out a single sheet. "I found this the other day. Look. Mr. Potter copied the engravings. See, the words are partially translated. It's 'The Land of….' You said it was familiar. Can you remember now, Dair. 'The Land of—'"

"Beginning Again," he murmured, the words popping into his mind.

"That's it?" The paper slipped from Emma's fingers and floated to the floor. "That's what it says? The Land of Beginning Again?"

Silently, Dair nodded.

"You know, don't you?" she asked. "That's what they call—"

"Texas." Dair sucked in a deep breath, then blew it out in a rush. "Texas is the land of beginning again. I think you're right, Emma. It all makes a horrible sort of sense. Some villain knows about The Sisters' Prize and now has a good idea where to find it. He killed Potter and put the police on our trails so that we wouldn't put it all together and follow him."

"To Texas," Emma stated.

"Yes, Emma. To Texas."

CHAPTER TWELVE

Texarkana, Arkansas-Texas

EMMA STOOD ON THE depot platform staring up at the chalkboard which announced the imminent departure of a train to Dallas, then Fort Worth. A wave of homesickness rolled over her. She missed her mother, her father and the boys. She wanted desperately to talk to Mari who would have had her baby—or babies—by now. Did she have a new niece or nephew or both? And what of Kat? Emma wanted to know that Kat was all right and learn how she was managing motherhood.

"You're not having second thoughts, are you?" Dair came up behind her and placed his hand at the small of her back.

She leaned into him, happy for the contact. Though he appeared confident that she wasn't about to bolt, Emma thought she detected a slight hint of worry in his tone. She gave him a reassuring smile. "No. I intend to see this through. I am anxious to see my family, though."

"With any luck, you'll be on your way to Fort Worth before the month is out."

Noting he'd said "you'll" rather than "we'll," Emma worked to keep the smile on her face. She didn't know what to make of Dair's behavior since leaving Scotland. She had expected their close physical proximity, along with the threat hanging over their heads, to draw them closer during the trip. Instead, just the opposite had happened.

Emma wasn't sure just what had caused the breach. She'd tried to bring up the subject a dozen times, but the mule-headed man refused to cooperate, skillfully changing the subject or successfully distracting her with kisses and more.

At least he hadn't shut her out in that area. In fact, as the closeness of their relationship outside of the bedroom waned, the intimacy of their lovemaking intensified. Almost every night, Dair made love to her with an emotional energy that soothed the little wounds his distance during the day created. Of the two, Emma believed his behavior in bed was more truthful.

She suspected the headaches were a big part of it. They'd increased in frequency during the trip, and as a result, she and Dair had fallen into a hurtful little pattern. Invariably, he'd try to isolate himself when the pain began. At first, aware of the embarrassment and vulnerability he felt at her witnessing his incapacitation, Emma had allowed it. But it didn't pass her notice that he appeared to suffer less and recover faster when she sat with him, stroked his poor head and whispered soothing words. She couldn't bear to see him suffer, so she'd wait until the pain was such that he couldn't stop her, and she'd invade his privacy and care for him. His reaction upon coming around was seldom pleasant.

Emma felt uneasy about the headaches. She questioned his assurances that he was getting better. She'd decided that the first order of business upon reaching Fort Worth was for Dair to see a doctor she trusted.

That's if the man didn't desert her beforehand. *Not* I'll

be on my way to Fort Worth, MacRae. We'll *be on our way. And if necessary, I'll pull out all my old McBride Menace tricks to make it happen.*

"We have an hour before departure," Dair said. He gestured toward a café across the street. "We need to grab an early lunch. We should have a good meal while we can. The place where we'll have supper tonight isn't known for its fine cuisine."

Emma perked up. "What is this mysterious destination? Are you finally ready to tell me why we're not going straight to the farmhouse where you lived with your mother?"

He grimaced, rubbed the back of his neck, then glanced up at the departure board. "Over dessert. I'll tell you over dessert."

Observing the path of his gaze, Emma wondered if he wanted to wait until after the Fort Worth–bound train left the station. Maybe he didn't want her to have an opportunity to leave him after telling her where he was taking her. The idea wasn't exactly comforting.

Emma had expected the hunt for the treasure and Robbie Potter's killer to take precedence over everything, so she'd been shocked earlier this morning when Dair told her he had other business to see to in Texas, first. Her subsequent demands for more details had been met with stubborn silence.

The café, however, proved to be a delightful distraction from her pique. On the Texas side of State Avenue, the restaurant offered a menu that told Emma she was home. "Beef barbecue. Yum. Corn bread. Peach cobbler. Look, they even have calf fries."

Dair winced. "You know, I've eaten a lot of…unusual…things in my travels. Gazelle in Africa. Bugs in the far East. I've eaten rattlesnake here in Texas. But just the idea of calf fries...that's a little too personal for me."

He sounded so much like Emma's father that she almost dropped her water glass. Trace McBride was just about the bravest man she knew, and he wouldn't go near a calf fry. She could hear the echo of his affronted voice in her mind. *It's unnatural for a man to eat a bull's balls.*

At that point, she could do little else but smile sweetly up at the waitress and order, "I'll have the calf fries, please."

Dair narrowed his eyes and frowned at her.

She batted her lashes. "Chicken."

"What!" Obviously affronted, he reared back.

She had to purse her lips to keep from laughing as she gave a casual shrug. "They taste just like chicken."

Dair ordered a steak, then when the waitress left, folded his arms and observed, "You have an evil streak, don't you?"

Now she did laugh. "It's the Menace in me." Then she rose from her chair, leaned across the table, and kissed him right on the mouth. "It's so good to be home!"

Dair gave her a reluctant grin, then almost as an afterthought mentioned, "You're so beautiful when you're happy."

It was the most intimate thing he'd said to her outside of bed in weeks, and Emma's heart and hopes lifted.

He must have had second thoughts about his slip because he hastened to say, "What will you do when our adventure is over?"

Heart and hopes immediately crashed.

He smiled up at the waitress as she brought a basket of corn bread. "Will you return to your teaching position? You enjoy the children, don't you? They're certainly an adventure, and we know how much you like dangerous undertakings."

She refused his offer of a muffin, having completely lost her appetite. "I do enjoy children," she said quietly. Then, tired of the hot and cold nature of his attitude as of late, she decided the time had come for some plain speaking. "I enjoy children very much. In fact, I hope to have my own someday soon."

Dair went still. Carefully, he set down the butter knife. "Emma, you're not…?"

"No." And her heart twisted a bit at the reality. She'd been glad when he'd taken steps to prevent pregnancy, but at this moment in time, she'd have been happy to answer affirmatively. "My birthday is tomorrow. I'll be thirty years old, Dair. Thirty. I want children. A home. A husband. Most women my age already have them."

He devoted his attention to his steak. A few bites later, he said, "Being married doesn't preclude a woman from having an outside occupation in this day and age."

Now that was a strange response to her statement. "Yes."

"Your sister kept her chocolate shop after she married, didn't she? After she had children?"

Cautiously, Emma answered, "Mari put a lot of time and effort into making Indulgences a success. She's not working as many hours now. She's not neglecting her children."

"Of course she's not. Your mother was a businesswoman, too, wasn't she? And your aunt?"

"What point are you trying to make, MacRae, and why?"

"No point." He squeezed a dollop of honey onto the last bite of his corn bread, then popped it into his mouth. "I'm just reminding you that women aren't limited to being only a wife and mother."

Emma didn't believe him. Something was cooking in that brain of his, and it had to do with her. Whatever it was, she suspected she wouldn't like it. Dair might want her, but he didn't want her love. He'd made that perfectly clear.

Her heart twisted and for a moment, she thought of the other man she'd loved. Casey Tate had treasured the gift of her heart. The first time she told him she loved him, he'd declared it his personal miracle. He'd loved her just as much in return.

That's what she deserved, by God. Not this wishy-washy I'll-treat-you-like-the-love-of-my-life-in-bed-and-my-sister-out-of-it attitude. Why, if it weren't for the legend and her necklace, she'd put a stop to it here and now.

But she had to believe they had a future. She had to believe that her patience would pay off, that she and Dair would eventually share a love that was powerful, vigilant and true. She had to believe it for her and for all of the McBrides.

Of course, that didn't mean she couldn't gig him a little. "I don't need reminding about anything. I haven't forgotten the dreams I shared with Casey, the dreams that died with him. I was content to be a rancher's wife. I *loved* being a rancher's wife."

"That was a waste of your talents," he scoffed. "You've a lot to share with children who deserve a good teacher. Talk about an adventure…"

"My life with Casey offered all the adventure I needed. Casey was an exciting man."

Dair sawed at his steak and scowled. Emma bit back a smile and gave the knife a bit of a twist. "I never see a rain barrel that I don't think of him. He'd ride in all dusty and dirty from a day on the range, and he'd stop to wash at the rain barrel in the yard. He'd strip right down to the skin, then he'd look at me with that twinkle in his eyes and he'd—"

"I'm skipping dessert." Dair shoved back his chair and stood. He grabbed three dollars from his wallet and tossed them onto the table. "I sent some telegrams a few days back. I'm expecting replies to be waiting for me here. I'll meet you back at the depot."

"All right." *Score one for the lady.* Emma allowed her grin free rein as he stalked out the door. Her appetite restored, she finished her calf fries. With relish.

DAIR'S BLOOD CHURNED WITH anger. He was angry and frustrated with Emma. Resentful of her dead husband. He wished he were in a barroom so he could start a brawl. Instead he was trapped on a train, headed for heartbreak. Wasn't that just a kick in the groin?

Guilt ate at Dair just like the tumor in his head. He found it almost impossible to look Emma in the face. The life he'd led was enough to condemn him, but his actions where she was concerned surely assigned him to the lowest levels of hell.

When he imagined a killer standing above her bed, when he recalled those weeks she'd spent on her own pursued by police without a penny to her name, waves of fear rolled through him. The killer wasn't the only villain in this story. Dair, himself, had dragged her into danger, put her life and liberty at risk. Even worse, he'd lured her into a liaison that had no future. She'd given him her heart, her love, when he had only heartache to give her in return. What a sorry bastard that made him.

He'd known before they left Scotland that he'd need to put some distance between them. He'd tried, too. During the daytime, he managed the task all right. Any time he found himself weakening, he'd conjure up the memory of her declaration of love, and his sense of shame would add another layer of brick to the wall he'd built between them.

Nighttime proved to be his downfall. Once darkness fell, his frail sense of honor couldn't withstand Emma's innocent assault. All it took was a whiff of her scent, a brush of her hand, or the sound of her sleepy sigh for the walls to come tumbling down. Dair wasn't accustomed to failure, but he'd damned sure failed at staying away from the woman. She was an addiction he didn't have the strength to quit. He was a sorry-ass bastard.

Still, he'd done what he could to make it up to her, though sending those three telegrams from New York had just about killed him. It was the right thing to do, however. He would die knowing he'd tried to right the wrong he'd done her. All he had to do was keep from shooting Logan Grey, Cade Hollister and Holt Driscoll on sight.

The train began to slow, and Dair glanced out the window to see a flat rock bigger than a man standing on end at the edge of a thick pine forest. He, Holt, Cade and Logan had placed the marker there over twenty years ago. "This is our stop, Emma."

"Oh?" It was the first word she'd spoken to him since leaving Texarkana five hours earlier. "Where's the town?"

Dair swung out of his seat. "There isn't a town. It's not even a real stop. I asked the engineer to let us out here because it's closest to our destination."

"The destination you've avoided mentioning? That one?"

He ignored that. The woman certainly wielded a sarcastic tongue when she was in the mood.

Dair gathered their bags and by the time the train rolled to a halt, he'd escorted her to the vestibule where they waited to disembark. As he stepped onto the rail bed, a warm summer breeze swept away the stink of coal floating on the air and brought that unique scent of pine forest and honeysuckle that would always remind him of home.

Some of the tension eased from his shoulders and a faint smile played upon his lips. He'd lived away from East Texas a lot longer than he'd lived here and he didn't consider himself Texan, but damned if he didn't feel comfortable here. If he'd ever wanted a home, he just might have picked here. But that was all water under the proverbial bridge. A home was not in his fast-fading future.

As the train pulled away, Emma took a long look around. "All I see are pine trees. I trust that we've yet to arrive at our final destination?"

"It's not a bad walk. I'll carry the bags."

"To where, Dair? Why are you being so darned secretive? What out here in the middle of a forest is more important than finding the man who killed your friend? Finding the Sisters' Prize?"

"This isn't about the treasure, damn it!" he exclaimed, rounding on her. "It's about children."

She blew out a breath as if she'd been punched in the stomach. "Your children?"

"Yes! No. Not like that." He set down his bag and rubbed the back of his neck. Hell. He'd known this wouldn't be easy, but he didn't expect it to hit him quite so hard. The time had come to tell Emma the truth. "There's a lot I need to explain. Follow me, Emma. I'm taking you to Piney Woods Children's Home."

"An orphanage?"

"Yes. I grew up here. It's just through the trees."

He led her into the pine forest along a well-worn, sun-dappled path. The musty scent of forest decay raised a memory of games of hide-and-go-seek. The mocking-bird chattering in the tree branches above them reminded him of lazy summer afternoons coaxing crawdads out of their holes along the creek bed. "It's a nice place, Emma. A good place for a child to grow up. It was a small-scale cotton plantation back before the war. There's a big main house, and the slave cabins were converted to dormitories. The creek that runs through it is spring fed, so there's a great swimming hole, and the fishing's so good they all but jump onto a fellow's line."

He felt the weight of Emma's curious gaze as she said, "It sounds lovely."

"A minister and his wife ran it. Reverend and Mrs. Jennings. He died a few years after I arrived, but she kept the place running. She passed on about a year ago now."

"It's still operational?"

"She placed as many children as possible in the final year, but a few youngsters are still there. I've had a difficult time keeping a headmistress."

"You?"

"I...um...send money now and then."

Emma mulled that over a few moments before asking, "Is this the puzzle piece I've been missing? Is this why you become the Highland Riever? Are *you* supporting these children, Dair?"

He ignored the question and marched on through the trees. Emma didn't speak after that, and he knew she must be thinking the matter through. Moments later, he broke through the forest at the crest of a small rise and the fallow cotton fields stretched out before them.

His gaze went to the main house where he noted signs of wear. The place needed paint badly. Looked like some shingles needed replacing, too. Rails were missing from the fence around the vegetable garden—the deer must be having a heyday.

Standing beside him now, Emma asked, "How long has it been since you visited?"

"Sixteen years."

"How long have you been sending them money?"

"A while." Dair hitched up the bags and started down the hill.

Emma spied the disaster in the making first. She grabbed Dair's arm, saying, "Oh no. Look. The roof."

A little girl—she couldn't be more than seven years old—had climbed out an upstairs window and was crawling up the drainpipe toward the roof.

Dair dropped the bags and took off at a run. When he saw her slip down a few feet his heart leapt into his throat. He ran harder and faster than he'd ever run before, planning his route up on the way as he put his Highland Riever skills to work.

He breathed a tiny bit easier when the girl made it safely up onto the roof. What was it about little girls and roofs, anyway? Jake had a devil of a time keeping his nieces off the roof. Weren't boys supposed to be the adventuresome ones?

He thought of Emma and muttered, "I guess not."

A dog started barking as he approached the house and he heard a young boy shout, "Hey! Who are you? What the hell do you think you're doing?"

Dair ignored both the boy and the dog that came nipping at his heels as he started up the side of the house. When his head rose above the shingles, he scanned the rooftop looking for the girl. What he saw shocked him so much that he almost lost his grip and fell.

Four little girls sat atop a large quilt, a china tea set and a plate holding two raw carrots at its center. "A tea party? You're having a blessed tea party? On the roof?"

The little monkey who he'd hastened to save shot to her feet, braced her fists on her hips and declared, "Go away! No boys allowed!"

"He's a stranger," another girl said. "We shouldn't talk to him."

A third child stuck her thumb in her mouth while a fourth one scrambled to her feet. "I'm going to go get Johnny."

Johnny, however, was already on the mark. By the time Dair pulled himself up onto the roof, a teenaged boy came up the other side. With a gun. "Stop right there," the kid said. "You take one step toward the girls and I'll shoot you dead as a fly in molasses."

Dair held up his hands. "I saw her go up the waterspout. I thought she'd fall. This was a rescue attempt."

"Who the hell are you?"

"MacRae. I'm Alasdair MacRae."

The oldest of the girls gasped. The boy's jaw dropped. "MacRae?" he said, his blue eyes round with hope. "Money MacRae?"

The little curly-blond climbing spitfire asked, "You're Nana Nellie's Dair?"

Nana Nellie. The name invoked memories of warm cookies, hugs, and a wellspring of love. Smiling, he nodded. "Yes. I'm Nana Nellie's Dair."

Squealing, the girls all scrambled to their feet and rushed him, grabbing him around the legs and holding tight. Dair braced a hand against the red brick chimney to keep from falling over.

"Finally," cried the spitfire.

"We've been praying you'd come. Every night."

The boy lowered his Colt and scratched the back of his head, grinning with satisfaction as the burden of responsibility rolled off his shoulders. "I really didn't want to have to rob that bank."

The smallest girl took her thumb from her mouth and lifted her arms. "Pick me up, Mr. Dair."

He didn't think of denying her.

"My name is Genevieve Roberta Elizabeth Marks, but you can call me Genny." She wrapped his neck in a strangle-hold, then kissed him right on the lips. "I love you, Mr. Dair!"

As Dair fumbled for a response, a voice behind him spoke in a tender, amused tone, "That's easy for a girl to do."

"Dammit, Emma!" Leave it to Emma Tate to follow him up on the roof.

Genny put her fingers against his mouth. "Shush, Mr. Dair. Bad words aren't allowed at Sherwood."

"Sherwood?" he repeated.

The boy nodded. "Nana Nellie renamed it right before she died. She said our Robin Hood needed to have a home."

AN HOUR AFTER DESCENDING FROM the Sherwood House rooftop, Emma stood stirring one of two stew pots on the stove. The children were starving. All ten of them.

She and Dair had both been appalled at the conditions they'd found at the orphanage. Apparently, there had been no adult supervision in over a month. Foodstuff supplies were terribly low. Dair had taken one look at the larder, loaded up a wagon and the boy named Johnny, and headed out bound for the nearest town. In some ways, Emma regretted his departure. She had lots of questions, and she really wanted answers. But in other ways, she was glad for the break. Children, she knew, were excellent sources of information.

And Dair MacRae was a legend around the place.

"Nana Nellie liked to talk about her babies," twelve-year-old Annabelle said. "That's what she called us. Her babies. No matter our age. She especially liked to talk about the first ones—Dair and Holt and Cade and Logan. She said she always hoped Elton would turn out like them."

"Who is Elton?" Emma asked.

"He's Reverend and Nana Nellie's good-for-nothing liar son," piped up a boy, Andrew, who Emma had put to work washing dishes with Annabelle. "He promised Nana Nellie that he'd keep Sherwood House running, but then at her funeral he said he was going to close us down and ship us all off and grow tobacco in the fields. That's so stupid. Our dirt is plumb wore out. That's what Nana Nellie always said."

"What happened to Elton's plan?"

Annabelle and Andrew shared a look, then they both shrugged. "Don't know," the boy said. "We never saw him after Nana Nellie's funeral."

Annabelle made a gallant effort to change the subject. "Can you teach me how to make biscuits, Miss Emma? Mine are always heavy as a rock."

"Sure, honey. Not to be boastful, but I make wonderful biscuits. My Aunt Claire is a baker and she taught me all her tricks." Emma tasted the stew, then added a pinch more salt. "So, what else did your Nana Nellie have to say about Mr. MacRae?"

"She said how sorry she was that he had to leave Texas. That made her feel really bad."

"Why did Dair have to leave Texas?"

"Because of the bank robberies."

Emma dropped her spoon. "The what?"

"Do you want to see her collection of wanted posters?"

"Anna!" The boy gave her a shove. "You're not supposed to tell!"

Wanted posters. Her lover was an outlaw on two continents! "Yes, please." When Andrew started to protest, Emma added, "Don't worry. I won't turn him in."

"It's a lot of reward money," the boy said glumly. Annabelle stuck her tongue out at him as she dried her hands on a dish towel, then exited the kitchen saying, "I'll go get the book. I'll be right back."

Emma added more seasoning to the other stew pot, then took a seat at the long kitchen table. Annabelle returned quickly with a scrapbook bound with leather ties. Emma opened it and caught her breath at the drawing of a young Alasdair MacRae. "He couldn't have been fifteen years old."

"He was thirteen. Nana said he was tall for his age."

Emma shook her head as she flipped through the posters. "Goodness gracious. He's another Billy the Kid."

"Dair never killed nobody," Andrew corrected. "And Nana Nellie said he quit stealing as soon as he started earning money legitimately. He just couldn't come back home 'cause he was a wanted man."

"Hmm," Emma said, wondering if that were true. If so, why the Highland Riever? Why had he started stealing again? "Does Elton still own Sherwood?"

The children shrugged. "We don't know."

Emma bet she knew. She'd bet her most comfortable pair of shoes that Dair MacRae had either purchased Sherwood or was in the process of purchasing it. So why the secrecy? His support of an orphanage was to be admired, not hidden.

What reason would he have for keeping it secret? Was there a law in Texas that criminals couldn't own property or something? She didn't think so. "It makes no sense."

But then, quite a few things here didn't make sense. True, it would be difficult to supervise the orphanage from an ocean away, but she couldn't see Dair allowing them to starve. "How long have you been without a director?"

The boy Andrew muttered a particularly ugly curse beneath his breath. Annabelle scolded him with a scowl, then said, "About six weeks. Mr. and Mrs. Teasdale replaced Miss Halloran who followed Mr. Moffett. The Teasdales weren't here a week before they stole our money and disappeared in the middle of the night."

That explained current conditions, Emma thought. "How have you managed since then? What have you been eating?"

"Too much squirrel stew, that's for sure," Andrew said. "We go hunting every day hoping for something different, but somebody must be warning the rabbits and the deer."

Annabelle added, "You got us a wild hog...what...two weeks ago, Andrew? That was nice."

"Didn't last long," he said with a sigh. "What I wouldn't give for a big old beefsteak."

Emma decided one way or another, she'd see that these children dined on beef before the week was out.

She mulled over all she'd learned while teaching Annabelle to make biscuits, using the last of the flour and sugar. She'd wondered from time to time just why he was so anxious to find the treasure, why he'd invented the Highland Riever. It had seemed incongruous to her, considering that she'd never seen signs in him that he coveted material things. Well, except for her necklace, that is.

But he obviously wanted the treasure for the orphans.

Dair MacRae was a thief with a heart of gold. If she weren't already in love with him, today's revelations would have done the trick.

Once the meal was ready, Emma stepped aside and allowed the children to implement the system in place for feeding such a crowd. It was a boisterous event, the prospect of full stomachs putting everyone in a good mood. Oh, there were the normal mealtime squabbles and a few battles over biscuits, but those only served to remind Emma of supper at Willow Hill. Just a little bigger.

They'd made a family, she discovered. A family of orphans who'd been orphaned twice. First from their birth families, and then with the loss of their beloved Reverend and Nana Nellie.

It broke one's heart to think about.

Dair returned with a wagon overflowing with supplies while the supper dishes were being tended to. Though he laughed and joked with the children while unloading the foodstuffs, Emma could tell he was furious. After passing out fried pies and peppermints to every child, he looked at Emma. "I need to make a tour of the place. Care to come with me?"

"Sure."

"Take me, too!" little Genny said.

"Not this time, doodlebug." Dair gave her nose an affectionate pinch. "I have an important job for you and the other children."

"More work!" she whined.

"Yep. Tomorrow is Miss Emma's birthday and I need y'all to plan the party."

Emma's heart warmed at his gesture. The little girl's eyes rounded. "A birthday party? Are we gonna have cake?"

"Yep. I bought two chocolate cakes and one white one. You think that will be enough?"

"Cake and fried pies in the same week." Genny clapped her hands together, hopped up and down, and squealed. The other youngsters chimed in with party questions and suggestions, and Dair told them to organize their thoughts and requests and write them down.

He held a hand out to Emma. "Coming?"

Emma took his hand, grabbed her hat, and followed him out into the warm evening air. He didn't speak as he led her toward the forest and Emma was content to allow the silence to hold. A birthday party. Months ago, her mother had suggested the McBrides throw a big party to celebrate her thirtieth. Unable to see any reason to celebrate the occasion, Emma had flatly refused.

Now, she was excited by the idea. She felt as giddy as little Genny, all because the notion had come from Dair. Bank robber, jewel thief and birthday party planner. She wondered if he bought her a present.

The sun hung just above the treetops as he led her into the forest. Despite the aging of the day, the heat remained brutal, the humidity so high one could almost drink the pine-scented air. During her travels she'd encountered all kinds of weather, but none quite so uncomfortable as summertime in Texas. Still, it was great to be home.

Somewhere above her hidden by the branches of a hickory, a dove cooed. Chattering squirrels scampered from loblolly to the shortleaf to longleaf pines, and off to her right, she caught sight of a white-tailed doe just before she sprang away.

A dozen different questions hovered on Emma's tongue, but she decided to wait until Dair broke the silence between them. The man obviously had a lot on his mind, and judging by the set of his jaw, not all of it was pleasant.

They walked through the forest for at least five minutes before he spoke. "I was the first orphan the Reverend and Nellie took in, but within six months three other boys had come to stay. They were all a couple years younger than me, but despite the age difference, we bonded like brothers. We'd been here a year when Nellie announced a surprise pregnancy—she and the reverend had been married a dozen years—they thought she was barren. We spoiled Elton when he was small. All of us did. Then his daddy died when he was just a squirt and without a father around to guide him…well…that's when things started going downhill. He was jealous of us. Me and my brothers. Hated us, in fact. Didn't like it that the reverend and Nana Nellie had shared their love with mongrel whelps. He didn't like it that we'd had his daddy's love longer than he had. He especially didn't like it that money was tight because his parents had continued to take in children. He hid his meanness from his mama, but the rest of us knew it." He paused, reflected. "He made sure we knew it."

"The children told me he inherited Sherwood House."

"Yeah. Lying bastard. But I…um…kept a long-distance eye on things around here, and I made a deal with him. He sold the place to me at an inflated price with ridiculous terms." He gave a pinecone lying on the path a violent kick. "Lot of good it did the kids, though. I damned near starved them to death."

"It wasn't your fault, Dair. They told me their caretakers robbed and deserted them. I am curious, though. Is this all on your shoulders? Is there no one else to help? What about these brothers of yours?" Had she not been watching him closely, she wouldn't have seen the way he momentarily stiffened.

"They're busy men. Important men. Holt Driscoll is a Texas Ranger. Cade Hollister is a former Pinkerton man who's gone out on his own. He hunts missing children. Logan Grey is a range detective for Waggoner Land and Cattle Company. They're busy men. Important men with important jobs. They're damn fine men, Emma. I thought the Teasdales—the interim caretakers I hired—would be here until September, so I didn't want to involve the others." He let out a sigh. "Poor judgement on my part. I knew better than to hire sight unseen."

"What's happening in September?"

This time when he stiffened, he didn't relax. "I need to talk to you about that, Emma."

She waited expectantly, but he didn't elaborate.

Moments later, she heard the burble of running water and the forest path broke onto the bank of a creek just where it widened to form a placid pool. Dair immediately began shucking his clothes. "It's hot. Let's go swimming. Johnny said he'd keep the kids away from here. I gave him a big bag of licorice to pass out."

"They'll all have stomachaches," Emma said absently as she watched the dappled sunlight play across his muscular chest.

When he'd stripped naked, he turned to her. "Swim with me, Texas."

"I thought we were going to talk."

"We will. Later." He tugged the ties on her bonnet. "Much later. We need to cool off first."

"I certainly am…hot."

Seeing that he had her cooperation, Dair stepped away

from her and made a flat dive into the water. She watched him as she undressed, his strong strokes cutting through the water, swimming hard, as if some unseen predator chased him through the water nipping at his heels.

Emma didn't really mind a few moments to herself. He'd given her a lot to think about. Stripping down to nothing but her chemise, she stepped into the cool, inviting water. As memories of frolicking at the "swim hole" with her sisters fluttered through her mind, she again experienced the lovely sensation of coming home. Emma smiled.

They swam until the fireflies appeared, twinkling in the deepening evening light. Dair exited the water first, then walked over to a large wooden trunk she hadn't noticed before. There, he removed towels and big fluffy quilt which he spread beneath the spreading boughs of an old oak tree.

He used the towel, then sat on the quilt, his back against the tree trunk. He watched her with steady eyes that glittered in the night, a lean, sleek, strong animal. "Emma, come to me."

Emma considered staying put to tease him, but no, the time for that was past. She rose from the water, stripping off her chemise and tossing it aside. Wet, naked and highly aroused, she approached him. Wordlessly, he tossed her a towel.

Emma dried herself, her movements slow, sensuous and provocative. Heat leapt in his eyes. She kept her gaze locked with his as raw need gleamed in those silver depths along with another emotion she could not put a name to.

"You need me," she said as she straddled his legs.

"Oh, yeah."

He meant physically, she knew, whereas she referred to emotions. *He's vulnerable. That's what I see. He's afraid to believe in miracles. He's afraid to need me beyond the physical....*

That tiny crack in Dair's facade made Emma love him all the more. It felt so good to be needed in ways only a man could provide. So right. So overdue. For so long, Emma had believed that dream was lost to her.

"I still believe in dreams, Dair."

"Me, too. You're a dream. My dream."

Emma couldn't help but smile as Dair's lips teased the sensitive skin beneath her ear. "I believe in dreams, in fate, and in fairy tales. Every woman does, deep down. Every woman wants a prince to come riding up on a white horse to save them."

"That's silly."

"No, it's not. It's real for me, Dair. You're my prince. You saved me, not from an evil queen or a dastardly villain, but simply from myself."

"Ah, Emma. You didn't need saving. You're the strongest woman I know."

She placed a finger on his lips. "You broke through the melancholy encasing my heart, and in doing so, gave me back life's greatest joy. I can love again."

He stared deeply into her eyes as he kissed her fingertip, and Emma knew that she could give herself to this man. She could give him not only her body, but her soul, her mind. Her heart. This was what dreams were made of.

Allowing the emotions to pull her into the moment, Emma pulled her hand away, then covered his lips with her own.

Dair murmured something appreciative against her mouth and cradled her face with his hands as they kissed for what seemed like an eternity. Breaking away, he grazed his lips over Emma's flushed cheeks, chin and eyelids.

"I believe," she whispered.

"In?" Dair kissed the tip of her nose.

"Dreams. Miracles. Us."

He lifted his head and searched her face in the dull evening light. Emma saw the uncertainty there, the brief shadow of vulnerability she found so incredibly endearing. She smiled at him, hoping to put him at ease. "Meeting you was like my own private miracle." The confession choked her up a bit, and Emma blinked back the sudden sting. "I love you, Dair MacRae."

Before she could say any more, he groaned and kissed her again, and again. And again. He took his time and Emma gloried in his passion.

Her body tingled while her soul danced. She could imagine doing this for the rest of her life, and the idea filled her with complete and utter joy. Absorbing the mingled sounds of their breathing blended with nature's harmony, her heart pounded in tandem with Dair's.

Something about tonight was different. Dair's kisses were gentle, seeking, almost inspiring. Gentler than he'd ever been, he touched and stroked, caressed and worshipped. Blissful, Emma let her body melt against him as he whispered mindless praise and taunting promises of what was to come.

"You are perfect, you know." He licked the whorl of her ear as his hands sought her naked breasts.

"You're the one who's perfect, MacRae."

"I'm trying to go slow. Trying to make this good for you."

"It's always good." Emma arched her back as his thumbs brushed across her nipples, slowly. He bent his head and kissed the top swell of her breast, then the side, pointedly ignoring the straining tip. He nibbled and nuzzled, teased and tempted. With the barest of movements, he drove Emma into a frenzy.

"Please," she whispered.

"Hmm?" He tasted the heavy underside of one breast. "Did you say something, Texas?"

Her breathing quickened, then burst out in a sharp hiss when his lips finally closed over the tight crest.

He kept to his word and continued his loving slowly—much to Emma's chagrin. He suckled her sweetly, and the absorbing sensation swirled a path to her toes. Heat pooled in her womb, and her legs shifted apart in anticipation.

Sitting back, Dair's gleaming gaze met hers, and his smile went positively wicked. His eyes admired her nakedness as he fondled the aroused peaks of her breasts.

Her hips jerked. "Oh, please…please!"

"Not yet, my impatient beauty."

His hands trailed a path down over her belly, seeking her center. Finding what he sought, Dair parted the wet folds with his thumbs and proceeded to drive her insane with erotic demands. His exploring fingers took full liberty, until her body quaked and shivered. Gripping his shoulders for purchase, Emma thought she'd surely die from the pleasure he gave her. When he lightly stroked the aching nub that strained for release, Emma was dying from anticipation. "Dair, I'm almost…"

"Take me, Emma." His hands cupping her bottom, he positioned her quickly. With a groan, he thrust upward, hard and fast.

Gasping at the intimate contact, Emma exploded, her cries echoing through the evening air as he drove her higher into bliss. Without waiting for her to recover, Dair rocked her forward with an insistent push.

Keeping his thrusts easy and deep, he nudged her back into the sensual waves. Perfection, Emma thought mindlessly. Every tender movement touched her very core. Pleasure blazed from the depths of her body.

Gripping her hips tighter, Dair held her firmly. "Now you'll come with me, Texas."

"I can't. Not again."

"You will." He tilted her hips while angling his body to drive even deeper inside her. He probed, stroked and pleasured her…wringing moan after moan from her throat.

Leaning forward, he suckled her breasts again with more urgency, latching on to one nipple until she caught his hair and dragged him upward to meet her kiss. He kissed her then, moving his tongue in and out to match the insistent movements of his body. Instinctively, Emma matched his ardor as she found her own rhythm.

Labored, he coaxed roughly, "Just let yourself go, Emma. Feel me. Feel yourself. Just a little further. Reach for it."

He could have asked her anything, done anything, said anything, and Emma would have complied. She was clay in his hands, soft and boneless. Dair could shape her within his palms into anything he wanted. She belonged to him. Heart, soul and mind.

Throwing back her head, Emma rode him until she shattered a second time. Her body clenched around his shaft in agonizing contractions until she milked the hot rush from him. With a hoarse shout of completion, Dair followed her over the edge as his pleasure pumped through her.

IF HE DIED AT THIS VERY moment, Dair would face his judgment a content and happy man. He kissed Emma deeply, hoping that he could show her that they shared far more than a physical connection. Something he'd never had before, something he'd always wanted but never dared hope would happen. She was right, their love was a miracle. He didn't deserve it, but he wanted it anyway. Needed it. Needed her. For as long as he had left.

"I can't help myself," he murmured against her lips in a brief moment of weakness mixed with bittersweet realization. "I just can't help it."

"What can't you help, MacRae?" She broke away from his searching mouth and looked up at him, the gray twilight shadowing her expression. Her blue eyes glistened with love and hope against dark lashes, scorching Dair's soul. Suddenly, it didn't matter that it was a mistake. He needed to say the words. He needed for her to hear them.

Lost in her eyes, he bared his heart. "I love you, Emma."

She stilled for a brief and shining moment. Then her slow, perfect smile had him smiling back. "I know."

"You do?"

"Mmm-hmm." She laid her head upon his shoulder and sighed with obvious happiness. "I've known you loved me for a while, now. You just had to come around to the idea yourself. Took you long enough."

"How can you know me so well?" he asked, kissing her hair and closing his eyes against the pain welling within them.

"Loving you is the easy part," she said with a laugh. "Knowing you is quite another story. Sometimes I think you're hiding a deep, dark secret and the rest of the time I think I know you better than you know yourself. That's all part of the great mystery of being in love, MacRae. You'll have to promise to get used to it."

"I promise that I'll always love you." At least that was a vow he could keep. He would love her until his last breath.

Too bad he couldn't promise her the moon and the stars, promise to cherish, honor and protect her all the days of her life. Too bad they were going to be cheated out of happily ever after. But as Emma nibbled on his earlobe, Dair decided that he'd worry about lost love and broken promises in the morning.

Fighting the despair renting his chest, he rolled her beneath him and wrapped himself in the wonder of Emma. All he wanted was to lose himself further into her safekeeping and ignore the impending demons. They would claim their due in time. Talking could wait until tomorrow. For right now, for tonight, she was his.

And he was hers.

CHAPTER THIRTEEN

JUST AFTER DAWN ON THE morning of her thirtieth birthday, Emma awoke to the sound of a party horn blowing in her ear. Loudly.

"Get up, Miss Emma," Genny shouted. "It's your birthday and Annabelle and Johnny have made pancakes for breakfast and we need to eat fast so we can do our chores and you can give us the lessons you promised because Mr. Dair says the party can't start until all the work is done but Annabelle says we can't eat breakfast without you because that would be rude. Nana Nellie didn't like us to be rude."

Emma grabbed hold of the horn just before the little girl stuck it back in her mouth. "Thank you, Genny. Why don't you run back downstairs and tell Annabelle I said not to wait on me. I'll be right down."

"All right. Hurry, Miss Emma."

"I will, dear."

Emma rolled from the bed and stretched her stiff muscles. She'd slept four to the bed last night—herself, two wiggle worms, and a lump of a log that wouldn't move. Despite the lack of rest that resulted from sleeping with three girls, Emma hadn't minded. After weeks on the road in all sorts of conveyances, it was nice to sleep in a bed that didn't move. Also, the children were so thrilled to have her around that they made her feel like a princess. Last night, a princess with three little peas in her bed. An impish smile stretched her lips as she mentally added, *Instead of a prince. Or a prince disguised as an outlaw.*

It was a surprisingly pleasant beginning to a day she'd long expected to be anything but, and when she made her way downstairs, she did so with a smile on her face. In the kitchen she found organized chaos that reminded her of home, though on a larger scale. The kitchen boasted two stoves, two iceboxes and two long tables each with chairs for fourteen. Annabelle flipped flapjacks at one stove while at the other, Dair fried bacon in a pair of cast iron skillets. "Think five pounds will be enough?" he asked a redheaded boy around eight years of age.

"Yes, sir." Then, he grinned. "For me, anyway."

One of the older girls spied Emma in the doorway and called, "Happy birthday, Miss Emma."

The greeting led to a whole chorus of good mornings and happy birthdays. Dair glanced over her and winked. That, along with the memory of the previous evening's lovemaking, brought a flush of warmth to her skin.

Upon finishing her meal, Emma rose to help with the dishes but a pair of bossy ten-year-olds shooed her outside instead. The sun was a bright yellow ball in a clear blue sky. Dew sparkled like diamonds on the grass and roses perfumed the air. Emma drew a deep breath and sighed on a smile. Turning thirty wasn't so bad after all. Happy, she twirled around and laughed.

"Well, now. Isn't that a right fine sight on a summer morning."

Emma turned to see a stranger—actually three strangers—approach the house from the direction of the barn.

She took an instinctive step back. They were big men, each of them standing well over six feet. They wore broad-brimmed, high-crowned straw hats, bandanas around their necks and gun belts around their hips. They all wore their trousers tucked into knee-high boots.

"I say 'right fine' doesn't do her justice. She's a real beauty, Lucky." The man in the center whipped his hat off his head. "Mornin', ma'am."

The man on the left stepped in front of the man in the center. "Beauty isn't good enough. She's a goddess. Howdy, miss." He tipped his hat and winked.

The man on the right—who by elimination must be Lucky—shook his head sadly. "Boys, y'all are pitiful. The lady is not only pretty as a field of bluebonnets, she's also too smart to fall for such blatant flirtation. Don't waste your time on them, honey. These windbellies blow harder than a middlin' hurricane." He thumbed his hat back on his head and folded his arms across a broad chest. "I'm the man here with the follow-through."

"You'll be following-through all the way to Hades." The screen door banged shut behind Dair. "Johnny, you better get me a gun. Looks like we have varmints in the peanut patch."

In that moment, Emma lost the men's attention. She might have felt slighted had she not paid attention to the four pairs of eyes. In the three strangers, she saw identical emotion—joy. In Dair's eyes the emotion she saw was more difficult to pinpoint. Joy, yes, but she saw more than that. It was the same kind of look Kat sometimes got when she looked at Mari's children. Sadness, almost grief. But it was gone in an instant, replaced by a gleam of pleasure and the twitch of a grin on his lips.

The one called Lucky said, "Sonofabitch, MacRae. I didn't think we'd ever see you again."

Then he was striding toward Dair, his friends right on his heels. Dair took three steps forward, then the four men met with handshakes and back slaps and punches to the shoulders. Cade Hollister, Logan Grey and Holt Driscoll, of course. And Alasdair MacRae.

They were, Emma thought, breathtaking examples of the male of the species. And she was staring. Unabashedly appreciative. Why, she was acting just like her grandmother Monique. Is that what happens when one gets old? You lose your sense of shame?

Recalling her interlude with Dair yesterday, she grinned. Yep. Not an ounce of shame. Too bad it took her until thirty to be shameless.

Children hung out windows upstairs and down, gathered in doorways and eased out onto the porch, watching the quartet with wide eyes. Emma could only imagine how they felt, going so long without an adult presence at the home now overflowing with grown-ups. And not just any grown-ups, but the first four, the legends of the Piney Woods Children's Home.

"So what's the emergency?" one of the newcomers asked. "Not that I wasn't happy to make the trip, but your telegram sounded serious."

Dair nodded, then cut his gaze toward Emma. "We do have business, but it can wait until after the party. Today is the lady's birthday, and y'all arrived just in time to help us kick off the festivities. Now, find your manners, boys, and I'll introduce you. Maybe a miracle will happen and you can fix her first impression of you so that you don't seem so stupid."

He paused, appeared to draw a bracing breath, then smiled at her. "Emma Tate, I'd like to introduce you to Mr. Holt Driscoll."

The man who'd called her a beauty stepped forward. Like the other two, he was tall and muscular, his features chiseled, his grin ready. His eyes were a deep sapphire blue that reminded Emma of Luke Garrett's. He reminded her of Luke in a lot of ways which probably wasn't all that surprising since Dair had said Holt Driscoll was a Texas Ranger, too.

"It's a pleasure to meet you, ma'am. I hope my comments didn't offend you. It's just that you made such a pretty picture and I had to speak from my heart." His eyes gleamed and he offered up a boyish grin as he added, "Happy birthday, ma'am."

Oh, my. He certainly is a charmer. "Emma. Please call me Emma. All of you."

Dair's eyes certainly didn't twinkle as he gestured toward the man who'd called her a goddess. "Cade Hollister."

Mr. Hollister was probably the most classically handsome of the three with dark hair, brown eyes and shoulders almost as broad as Dair's. She could picture him as an investigator. Dair had said he hunted missing children and she wondered how being raised in an orphanage might have affected his choice of profession.

He moved toward her with a leonine grace, took her hand, and brought it to his mouth for a courtier's kiss. "It's a pleasure to meet you, Emma. I, too, apologize if I gave offense with my entirely truthful comments. I hope your birthday offers nothing but pleasure."

Oh my oh my.

Dair looked positively grim as he said, "Finally, Emma, meet Logan Grey."

The range detective, she recalled. Now those men were often real characters. Basically hired guns, they had a lawman's authority, but often a criminal's heart. She wondered why his friends called him Lucky.

Probably his luck with women, she decided. He was one of those men who oozed with sexual appeal. He had a loose-hipped walk, a lazy smile, and intelligent green eyes that spoke volumes when they focused on a woman.

He winked at her. Slowly.

Oh my oh my oh my. This was a dangerous man.

"Happy birthday, beautiful."

No apology from him. No pretty words. Just a blatant male saying hello. Definitely a dangerous man. Her gaze flew to Dair and she waited for him to stake his claim.

And waited.

And waited.

He had a strange look on his face—sort of sickly, but stoic—and when he finally spoke, they weren't the words she expected to hear. "Emma is a teacher from Fort Worth. Her family is prominent—the McBrides. Holt, you might know her brother-in-law. A former Ranger named Garrett."

"Luke Garrett." Holt nodded, his smile going wide. "You're Mari's sister? Why, isn't it a small world. I visited with her just last week when Luke dragged me by their house to meet the new—"

"The baby!" Emma gasped excitedly. "I haven't heard. Was it a boy or a girl, or did she have twins, after all? Is everyone healthy? When did she deliver? What about names?"

The ranger laughed. "Your sister did have twins. They came a little early, but everyone is in fine fettle. Cute little things. Named them Jenna and Travis."

"Twins." Emma steepled her hands in front of her

mouth. That made four little ones for Mari. She tried to smother a twinge of jealousy as her gaze flew to Dair's sympathetic expression. He knew. He understood. *It's all right. He loves me. Our babies will come.*

She blinked back happy tears. "That's wonderful. Just wonderful. My father is a twin. We've always wondered if one of us would continue the tradition."

"The Garretts are thrilled. Luke is so swelled up with pride he keeps busting his buttons."

"A new niece and nephew," Emma mused. "I'm anxious to meet them."

"We'll get you there as soon as possible," Dair told her. To his friends, he explained, "Emma ran into a little trouble in Scotland. We need to make sure she's safe before she goes home."

Again, she waited for him to claim her, and when it didn't happen, she felt a twinge of insecurity. *If he loves me, why isn't he hinting at our relationship with his friends?*

Cade Hollister twirled his hat on a finger. "Is her trouble the same as whatever trouble you're in?"

Dair glanced at Emma, then rubbed the back of his neck. "Let me get the children lined out on their chores, then we'll take a walk. Things have been a mess around here."

He told them about the caretaker who'd stolen the operating funds and left the children on their own. The language that emerged from his friends' mouths at that wasn't appropriate for children, so Emma shooed them all back inside.

Dair joined them a few minutes later, his friends remaining outside. He mustered his troops like a general. "Now that you have food in your bellies, it's time to put your muscles to work to keep this place from falling down around you. I made some lists. There's something for all of you to do—youngest to oldest. Now, since today is a special day being Miss Emma's birthday, you get a reprieve. The chore list for today is short." He looked toward Emma. "I didn't know if you'd want to tend to school lessons or not."

"I would enjoy that. Once I know where the children stand lesson-wise, I can suggest a curriculum for their next teacher."

Dair nodded. "All right, then. Let's get started."

"But what about my list, sir?" Annabelle piped up. "The one you asked me to make?"

"I'm sorry." Dair snapped his fingers. "Yes, Annabelle, I think we'd all like to hear your list."

She beamed up at him, then pulled a piece of paper from her skirt pocket. "I thought we could begin with Blind Man's Bluff. Everyone enjoys that game, even the littlest ones."

"She means me," Genny called out.

"After that, we could play baseball. That's our favorite game here at Sherwood. Mary Ann is an excellent pitcher."

Johnny nodded sadly. "She strikes me out at least half the time."

"Next would be lunch," Annabelle continued. "I think we should have a picnic at the swimming hole. We can make ham sandwiches and have fruit and dill pickles. Then we can swim and have Miss Emma's birthday cake to finish out the party. Would that be all right with you, Miss Emma?"

"I think that sounds lovely," Emma replied honestly. "One of the best birthdays I ever had was when I turned twelve and my papa took me, my sisters and the woman we wanted him to marry to a swimming hole. He was Mr. Throw-Fish and we had so much fun. Maybe we can talk Dair into being Mr. Throw-Fish today."

"Why not," Dair agreed. "So, snap to it, everyone. The sooner we finish our work, the sooner the party can start." He passed out his chore lists and the kitchen soon emptied. Dair motioned toward the door, saying, "I need to explain..."

"I'm not happy with you."

"Emma, I—"

"You've made secretiveness an art form, Alasdair MacRae, and it insults me."

"Now wait a minute."

"Are you denying you sent for them?"

"No."

"And you kept the information to yourself, just like you kept Sherwood House to yourself because...why? I'll tell you why. Telling me meant sharing with me, and the only thing you like sharing is my bed!"

"Now hold it right there. That's neither right nor fair."

"I don't really care. I'm also not going to fight that fight here and now. Let's talk about the treasure. Do you think we'll need their help finding the Sisters' Prize?"

He stuck his hands in his pockets. She could see him wavering over whether or not to continue the squabble. Finally, he said, "I want you safe, Emma. That's my number one goal."

"So they're here to provide protection?"

After a moment's hesitation, he nodded. "That's definitely part of it. We've followed a killer to Texas who wanted you blamed for his misdeeds. The more guns I have watching out for you, the better I'll feel."

Emma wanted to quiz him about protection being "part of it," but his friends were waiting on him, and frankly, she'd lost her head of steam. Right now, she wanted him gone so she could lick her wounds in private. "Annabelle told me they used the cabin at the end of the row as a schoolroom. I think I'll walk down there and see what supplies they have."

"Good idea." Dair appeared relieved as he held the door open for her to proceed him outside. "When I was in town yesterday, I ordered a few more things to be delivered today. Make a list of whatever they need in the schoolroom, and I'll send the order back with the deliveryman."

As Emma walked toward the schoolhouse, she surreptitiously kept an eye on Dair and his buddies. They began with more grins and back slaps and even a loud guffaw or two. Dair motioned toward the forest, and they headed that way. As Emma reached the schoolroom, just before the men disappeared into the trees, she saw Dair say something that wiped the smiles off the men's faces.

Hmm. She didn't like the looks of that.

DAIR SUGGESTED THE OLD CAMPFIRE site as the location for their talk. He expected the spot to be overgrown, but the boulders wouldn't have moved. They'd all have a place to sit where they could see one another. He wanted to see everyone's expression as he told his story.

Apparently, the campfires had continued because he found the spot little different from the last time he'd been here. The trees surrounding the fire ring were bigger, the pile of ash deeper. You could still see the initials they'd carved in the sweetgum tree going on twenty years ago. Dozens of other sets of initials had joined them, but his still led the list. He couldn't help but smile.

Without speaking, they all took their usual seats. Holt

led the questioning. "You ready to explain that remark you made a few minutes ago, MacRae?"

"Yeah." Cade propped one boot up atop the boulder, then draped his arm casually around his knee. "It's not like you to dip into melodrama. Life and death, MacRae?"

"Exactly. Emma's life and my death. Let me start with Emma, if I may." Dair gave them a rundown of his acquaintance with Emma and of his plan to ask her to be the new caretaker at the orphanage. He talked about her character and her intelligence. He didn't need to sell them on her beauty. They could see that for themselves. While neglecting to detail the circumstances, he admitted to stealing her necklace. They laughed when he described her stint as highwayman, but grew serious when he mentioned Robbie Potter's revelations.

"Buried treasure?" Logan murmured. "Hell, there are dozens of stories about lost Spanish gold and buried pirate treasure in this neck of the Texas woods. Do you honestly believe there's anything to it?"

"I do," Dair replied. "And I'm not the only one." He relayed the story of Robbie's murder and their theory about the killer.

Holt's mouth set in a grim smile. "You think the villain is after Emma? You need us to be bodyguards as well as investigators?"

This was it. This was the moment Dair had dreaded ever since the need for it occurred during the train ride between New York and St. Louis. "Yes, but I have something else in mind for the three of you, too. Something just as important. More important, in a way."

Cade, Logan, and Holt shared a quick, curious look.

Dair swallowed hard. His stomach rolled. "I would consider it a great favor if one of you would consider courting Emma with the intention of marriage."

"Excuse me?" Logan said.

Holt gave his head a shake. "What did you say?"

"What the hell!" Cade exclaimed. "You're sleeping with her! I thought you were fixing to tell us you were getting hitched, and now you're trying to pass the woman off on us? What the hell is wrong with you? She seems like a real lady. Not some painted-up saloon pass-around. It's you who should be doing the right thing. I oughta kick your sorry ass."

"I oughta help," Holt declared.

Frustration and guilt rolled in Dair's stomach like soured milk. "I didn't say I was sleeping with her."

All three men grimaced. "For God's sake," Logan scoffed. "Do you think we're stupid? It's obvious, MacRae. You had her last night. And judging by the way you looked at her, it wasn't the first time. Hell, she's in love with you. It shows. You'd have to be blind not to see that."

Dair couldn't deny it. Hell, he didn't want to deny it. He wanted everyone in Texas—hell, the world—to know that Emma Tate loved him and he loved her in return. But he couldn't, damn it all, and the time had come to explain why. If not to her, then to the men he hoped would take care of her in his absence.

"Emma is a wonderful woman," he explained. "She's loving and caring and witty and strong—everything you could ever want in a mate. But the poor woman has had a sad run of bad luck when it comes to men. Ten years ago, she married her childhood sweetheart, but he died a few months later. It took her a long time to recover from his loss, but finally, she was ready to look for love again. It was her bad luck to lay eyes on me at a time when she was vulnerable. She thinks she loves me, true, but she hasn't known me all that long. Not like her Casey. She'll get over me."

Deep in his heart, Dair wondered if he really believed all that. Was he trying to convince them or himself?

Logan folded his arms, his eyes flashing with anger. "You don't want her? So you were just using her? This wonderful, caring, witty woman you just described? Sorry, Dair, I don't buy it. That's not you. So why don't you tell us what the hell is really going on?"

"Yes, I want her!" Dair drew back his leg and kicked a small rock, sending it flying off into the trees. "I can't have her, goddammit! I'm dying!"

His friends looked at him in disbelief. Cade said, "What do you mean?"

Frustrated, Dair all but bared his teeth. "It's pretty simple, boys. Dying as in dead. Croaking. Kicking the bucket. Fixing to promenade home. Pushing up bluebonnets. You get it now?"

There was a long pause, then Logan said, "Shit, MacRae. That's crazy. Are you sick? You don't look sick."

Good Lord, he'd have to spell it out. "I have a growth on my brain. It's killing me. There's no cure, no medicine, no hope. Does that spell it out for you? I'm not passing off Emma because I don't want her. Believe me, I want her. I'm just trying to make sure someone is here for her when I'm gone. She's going to need..." His throat closed. He couldn't talk anymore. Couldn't think about her being with anyone other than him.

Yet, he needed to take care of her. To do the right thing for her. "Whichever of you..." He paused, cleared his throat. "You'll be the luckiest damned man in Texas."

"No," Cade snapped. "This is bullshit. You're not dying." He started to pace, shoving his fingers through his thick dark hair. "You're not dying, goddammit. Have you been to a doctor?"

"Yes."

"Then you need a better one. This is just goddamned bullshit. You're gone forever and now come back just to tell us you're croaking? Well, fuck that."

Holt reached out, put a calming hand on Cade's arm. "Dair, what can we do? There must be something we can do for you."

"Emma…"

"Not her, you."

Dair grimaced, dropped his gaze to the ground. He didn't want to do this. Didn't want to tell them or anyone else. Talking about it just made it all the more real. He wanted to be like an old dog, to go off by himself somewhere private to die. Somewhere alone. He didn't want to see pity in anyone's eyes. But he couldn't, he couldn't do it to these men, his brothers. Or, to Emma. God, telling them was bad. Telling her would rip his heart out.

"How long do you have, MacRae?" Logan asked quietly.

"I'm not certain. I was supposed to have another couple of months, but the way it seems to be progressing…I just don't know."

"Shit!" Cade shook off Holt's arm, grabbed the knife from the sheath at his hip and sent it sailing, end over end, into a helpless tree. "I can't believe this shit. You're just giving up? You're just gonna roll over and die?"

"What choice do I have?" Dair shot back. He stalked across to the tree, grabbed the knife hilt and yanked the blade from the wood. He mimicked Cade's action, sending the knife flying at another tree. "It's not like I woke up one day and said I think I'll grow a brain tumor."

Holt closed his eyes. Cade sat back down and gripped his knee until his knuckles turned white. Logan spat an ugly epithet, then said, "Hell, Dair. I don't know what to say."

"Just tell me you'll think about Emma."

Logan cleared his throat. "Does she know you're asking us to do this?"

"I haven't told her that I'm…sick."

"Good Lord," Holt muttered.

"That's downright cruel." Cade shook his head.

"You're bein' a real shit leading her on like you are," Logan added.

"Look. I'm going to tell her, just not today because I don't want to spoil her birthday. I'll tell her tomorrow. I'll sit her down and ask her to oversee the children's home. I'll tell her I've put all the bank accounts in her name. My plan is to leave two of you here with her to watch over the children and over her. The other one I'll ask to go with me to my mother's place. I expect to find the killer there. If he's already found the Sisters' Prize, we'll see signs of it, I'm certain. If he hasn't found it, he'll be there looking."

"Any idea who he could be?"

"I've wracked my brains, and the only thing I'm certain about is that it has to be someone I know."

Logan folded his arms. "So it'll be shoot on sight, more than likely. You'd better take me with you, Dair. I'm the fastest gun amongst us. I'm not having anyone cheat you out of any time you have left."

Dair nodded. Time was his biggest enemy right now. That and his own cowardice, perhaps. He'd almost rather meet his maker right now than tell Emma the truth. He cleared his throat. "So, what do you think?

Cade shook his head. "A man would have to be a fool not to think about your Emma, Dair, but the fact of the matter is, she *is* your Emma. If she's as special a person as you say she is, then she's not going to change men like a new bonnet."

"Not right away, she won't. I know that. It'll take her some time to be ready again. But I think she'll be ready faster if one of you has been watching over her, waiting in the wings, as it were."

"Why us?"

"Because you're good men. Honorable men. Look, I'm not saying you're good enough for her—no one is—but one of you will be exactly what she needs."

"Again, why?"

"It's the Bad Luck tradition. Emma and her sisters are sometimes called the Bad Luck Brides. Emma's first husband died. The next man she gets close to does the same thing. The whole family is steeped in bad luck, to be truthful. Emma will need to feel very secure to risk dipping her toe back in the bridal pond."

"For good reason."

"Not if she's dipping that toe with one of you. Face it, if the McBride sisters are the Bad Luck Brides, then the three of you can damn well be called the Good Luck Grooms."

All three men groaned, but Dair pressed ahead. "It's true. Holt, look at you. You're Mr. Nine Lives yourself. How many gun battles, knife fights and barroom brawls have you broken up? Hundreds? Maybe even a thousand? And how many times have you been wounded? None. Not a single time. Cade sent me that article from the *San An-*

tonio Times where the reporter wrote that bullets all but bounce off you."

"That's just talk," Holt protested.

Dair turned to Cade. "And what about you? You admit to having a sixth sense when it comes to finding missing people. You admit to being lucky. How often have I heard you say that the reason you were successful first as a Pinkerton agent and now on your own is because you're lucky?"

"I've never been lucky in love," Cade pointed out.

"Have you ever tried?" Dair snapped back.

"He has you there," Logan commented.

Dair turned on him. "And you. How many people other than me still use your proper first name? You're Lucky Logan. The man who never loses at cards. Never bets on the wrong horse. If Lucky Logan tells you to do something, the smart man takes his word. If the three of you aren't the luckiest men in Texas, then I'm not a train robber."

"Ah, hell, Dair," said Texas Ranger Holt Driscoll. "Are you still doing that stuff? Never mind. Don't tell me. I don't want to know."

Dair waved that away. "Look, I'm not asking for a commitment. I'm asking for the possibility of a commitment. For her sake and for yours. I've watched out for you boys for most of my life and for some strange reason I like you. I want you to be happy. The next man who wins Emma's heart…he'll be the luckiest man in the world. I just want her to have a chance. She deserves a husband, a family. I'm about to put her through a second wave of hell, and I'm not proud of it. But if one of you is willing to help me, at least I can die knowing she'll be taken care of. That's why I'm betting on one of you—as long as you give her half a chance. Hell, consider it my last request." A sad smile played on his lips as he added, "I'd ask Nana Nellie to make me fried chicken if I could, but…."

His words trailed off into silence as the men sat each lost in his own thoughts. Dair was reminded of the last time the four of them had assembled in this spot. It was the night before he'd fled Texas, two steps ahead of the law. Mid-winter, the night had been bitter cold, and with lawmen waiting back at the Home, a fire had been too much to risk. Little more than boys, they'd spoken of their dreams, their hopes for the future. The one thing they'd all had in common was the desire to have a home. A real home.

Over the years, Dair had all but given up on that dream. Now it was within reach, only he wouldn't be around to enjoy it. What a load of bad luck that was.

Bad luck. *Ah, hell, Emma. I wish your fairy tale was more than fantasy.*

"So," he said, figuring they'd had enough time to chew on his news. "Can I count on you? All of you?"

The sour expressions told him none of them liked the idea, but to a man, they owed him. They might resist for a while. Might fight it. But unless they had other commitments elsewhere, other women no one had bothered to mention, they'd come round. And once they agreed, once they gave him their word, it was gold. Emma's future would be one worry off his mind.

"She isn't going to like it," Logan observed.

"She doesn't have to know. Not about this. This is something we all need to keep to ourselves. Otherwise, she'll throw you out on your ears just out of spite."

Cade, Logan and Holt all shared an unhappy look. Holt asked, "Do you have a…uh…favorite? Do you want her with one of us more than another?"

He didn't want Emma with any of them. "You are all good men. I figure that part will work itself out."

"It's a stupid idea, Dair," Logan snapped.

"Nevertheless…"

"Hell. Yeah, I'll do it. I'll look out for her, anyway. Anything more than that, well, it has to be her choice."

"Fair enough." Dair looked at Cade.

Wincing, he agreed. "Yeah, me, too."

Holt nodded. "Oh, all right. For you, MacRae. Only for you."

A weight rolled off Dair's shoulders and he tried his best to ignore the pain that plagued his heart. It was the best he could do for her. Someday, he hoped, she'd appreciate it. Maybe after she'd been married to one of these yahoos for ten, fifteen, twenty-five years.

The men returned to the house and pitched in with chores. Though they tried to hide it, their moods remained somber. The morning passed quickly and when the children were on the verge of mutiny, Dair declared it time for the party to begin.

The youngsters bickered over which game to play first—Blind Man's Bluff or baseball. They called upon Emma to settle the matter. She made a show of considering the question, then shot Dair a gleeful look. "Baseball sounds perfect. I call dibs on pitching."

"Well, hell," Dair muttered. He bet his bank account that she was recalling the bloody nose he'd received the last time he'd played baseball with women and children.

Emma exaggerated the swing of her hips as she walked toward the cotton field where the children indicated the game would be played. The men trailed behind her. "Something tells me this game is gonna be fun," Logan observed.

It was torture.

It was payback. Impure and far from simple.

Dair suffered through three innings of a pitching performance that made Kat McBride's shenanigans at Chatham Park look innocent. He saw Holt nearly swallow his tongue the first time he witnessed her fast pitch wind up.

Dair agonized through a game of Blind Man's Bluff where he knew damn well she somehow peeked through the blindfold. What else could explain her "accidental" exploration of Cade's chest, Holt's shoulders, and dammittohell, Logan's ass. That bit of boldness she'd practiced by the lake last night obviously had taken.

Even the picnic lunch was a trial. Batted lashes and wiggling hips were bad enough. Did she have to keep licking her fingers that way? When she made such a show savoring her birthday cake, it was all he could do not to put her over his knee and spank her. The little witch.

Dair knew it would only get worse. He'd confessed his love at night, then failed to mention it in the light of day. She was mad as hell at him, and he couldn't blame her. Just wait until she found out about the rest of his plans.

Good thing he'd bought her the birthday present. Might be the only thing that kept her from killing him herself.

He waited until after supper to approach her and ask her to take a walk with him. The scathing look she gave him told him she thought he was wanting sex. Well, he did. Of course he did. What red-blooded man wouldn't, especially after last night?

But he had no intention of pursuing it. He'd said his goodbyes last night and they'd ended with perfection. It was a good way to go out.

So why did it hurt like hell? Being close to her, smelling

the sunshine scent of her hair. Hearing the giggles she shared with the children. The intimate memories of last night. He should just shoot himself and be done with it. Love hurt worse than any damned brain tumor.

"Just a walk, Emma. I'm not blind to your feelings."

Her reluctance to go was obvious, so he held out his hand and said, "Please? I need to walk with you, Texas."

With an ungracious sigh, she removed her apron and sailed toward the door, her chin up, her shoulders back. "A short one."

Dair grinned at her back, waiting until she'd turned toward the path to the swimming hole to call, "Not that way, Texas. We need to go by the barn first."

She rolled her eyes, sighed again, and altered her route. Dair lengthened his stride to catch up with her, and without speaking, they walked side-by-side toward the barn. Upon reaching it, rather than leading her inside, Dair steered her around back. In addition to being a beautiful scene—three fine horses in a corral set against a backdrop of a thick forest and the vermillion and gold of a Texas sunset—it was a private spot out of sight of the house and the dormitory cabins.

"Wait here a moment, Emma. I have a birthday gift for you."

Suspicion lurked in her beautiful blue eyes. "Honestly? If it involves nakedness, you can forget it. I'm not interested. You treated me like…why are you ashamed of me, Dair? Ashamed of us?"

"Ashamed!" The hurt in her eyes twisted his heart in two. "Emma, I'm not ashamed of you."

"Then what do you call your performance this morning? You gave your friends no indication of our relationship. Not one word. My friend, Emma Tate, schoolteacher extraordinaire. You might as well have said I can cook and have a good sense of humor. Isn't that what men say about woman they don't want romantically?"

Dair closed his eyes against the pain in hers. "I want you. You'll never know how much."

"Then why treat me like a secret?"

"Can I just give you your gift? It's your birthday." Weariness bled into his tone as he added, "I don't want to argue."

"There is only one thing I want, Dair. You know what it is. I want you. Us. I want a life with you. A future—"

Unable to bear any more, he put his finger to her lips. "I wanted to give you something special, Emma. Since you only gave me a day's notice, my choices were limited, but I want you to know, this gift truly comes from my heart."

"Oh, Dair." She wrapped her arms around herself. He could tell she was trying to stay mad at him, but was weakening. Because she loved him. "Sometimes I simply don't understand you."

That's because she didn't know he planned to destroy her love, destroy her hopes, in the morning. Dair had a lump in his throat the size of her ruby necklace. This was so damned hard. Gruffly, he said, "You don't have to understand me. Just…let me give you your birthday present?"

She shrugged and turned her attention to the horses, leaning up against the corral's wooden railing. Dair wanted so badly to kiss her. He almost reached for her. He almost took her in his arms and crushed her to him. Instead, he disappeared inside the barn.

A crate sat inside a long unused horse stall. Inside the crate, her gift lay sleeping. The puppy was a chubby ball of white fluff no bigger than a rabbit with a little yip of a bark and a tail that never stopped wagging when he was awake. Sure enough, when Dair reached inside and picked the puppy up, the tail started swinging even before his eyes opened.

Dair shook his head at his own foolishness. Considering their circumstances, giving her a dog was probably one of the stupidest things he'd ever done. But when he'd walked into the mercantile yesterday looking for a gift and he'd heard the merchant trying to give the last of a four-pup litter away, he'd acted on instinct.

Emma would love this dog. She'd have something to play with, something to care for, to mother. She'd love this pup long after Dair was gone.

Dair paused just inside the barn door. Outside, Emma gently stroked Holt's palomino's muzzle as the sinking sun turned the sky above a brilliant orange-scarlet. Nearby, mourning doves cooed and at the other side of the corral, Logan's roan gelding strolled in a majestic oval. This, Dair thought, was life. When the palomino did something to bring a giggle to Emma's lips, the sound physically hurt. He hadn't made Emma giggle in weeks.

Scratching the puppy behind its ears, he said, "Love her for me, Fluffball. Love her for me."

When the dog licked his chin, Dair grinned and tucked it beneath his shirt. It snuggled up against him as he approached the corral fence. The puppy's razor claws dug into his chest as Dair winced, readjusted the pup, then stood beside Emma. "Did you enjoy your party?"

She shrugged, didn't meet his eyes. "For the most part, it was very nice."

Dair's fingers itched to touch her. Instead, he slipped his hand beneath his shirt. "I hope you think this is one of the nice parts."

Her blue eyes lit like sparklers when he pulled the dog from beneath his shirt. Dair handed her the puppy, saying, "Happy birthday, Texas."

She forgot to be angry with him as she exclaimed, "Oh! Look at him! He's darling! Oh, Dair. You got him for me? He's so cute. No bigger than a minute. Hello, you precious thing." She nuzzled the puppy's neck. "Does he have a name?"

The word "no" sat on the tip of his tongue, but what came out was different. "Riever. His name is Riever."

God, MacRae, you are such a sap.

Emma laughed and for the first time since he'd introduced the others that morning, the hurt was gone from her gaze. "That is quite a coincidence, MacRae. However, I like it."

The puppy licked her on the nose and she laughed again. "He's so sweet. So friendly. Hello, my precious." She inspected him closely, then carried him away from the corral toward a hay bale where she took a seat, setting the puppy at her feet. The first thing he did was try to crawl beneath her skirts. "Definitely your namesake," she declared, laughing. Then when he took a seat beside her, she gazed at him with soft eyes. "Thank you, Dair. Riever is the best birthday present I've received in years."

"He'll make a good lapdog," he responded gruffly. "I saw his sire and dam. He shouldn't get much bigger."

Emma played with the dog until the sun went down and the puppy crawled into her lap, curled up, and fell asleep. Dair knew he should say good-night, return to the house, and go to sleep early. Tomorrow would be a killer of a day.

Instead, he stayed where he was, listening to the crickets chirp and the cicadas buzz. He was loath to end the moment. As the last bit of sunlight slipped away, he murmured, "I wish this day would never end."

He felt rather than saw Emma's smile. "I can't believe I spent so much time wishing it would never get here. I dreaded my birthday with every fiber of my being. Had I known then how happy I'd be today—despite being mad at you—I'd have counted the minutes for it to arrive."

"I wanted you to have a happy day."

She stroked the puppy's head. "It would have been perfect if not for the secrecy. Dair, I understand the concept of privacy, but you told me that these men were like brothers to you. Why would you keep our relationship a secret from them? It hurt me."

"I don't want to hurt you, Emma. God knows, that's the last thing I want. It's just..."

"Just what?"

Dair propped his elbows on his knees and leaned forward, his head down. His eyes shut. "Let's not do this now. It's your birthday."

"The sun is down. My birthday's over. Talk to me, Dair. Explain to me why you've been so distant to me during the day and so desperate for me at night. Explain why you claim to love me, but at the same time shut yourself off. Shut me out."

"It's not like that."

"Yes, it is. I love you, Dair. You love me. I know you do. I knew it even before you finally got around to telling me last night. I've wondered if the problem might be the difference in the way the two of us grew up, especially after seeing Sherwood. I grew up in a house where my parents frequently and flagrantly expressed their love for one another. If your reverend and Nana Nellie weren't so demonstrative, I can understand that you would approach a relationship with different sensibilities than I. But Dair, we need to reach an understanding about this. I don't want to live this way."

He laughed without humor. "I just want to live."

"What you mean is you want to call all the shots. You want to have all the control in this relationship. Well, that's stupid, Dair. Didn't I prove that much to you last night?"

Hell, he hadn't intended to do this today, but maybe this was best. They were out here alone. It was dark. He wouldn't have to look at her. She had the pup to cuddle. Maybe it was meant to be this way. He still believed in fate, didn't he? Still, he thought about it long and hard before saying, "You're wrong, Emma. I meant exactly what I said. I want to live."

She waited, then said, "I don't understand."

"I lied to you, Emma," he told her, his voice raw and gruff. "About the headaches. They're not getting better."

He shoved to his feet and paced back and forth in front of her. Emma's voice quavered. "Dair?"

He clenched his teeth, dropped his head back, and let the pain of what he was about to do wash through him. It hurt so bad that for a moment, he considered lying to her again.

Then he looked at her and saw the woman he loved beyond reason. Ah, Emma. Beautiful, perfect, wonderful Emma. She didn't deserve this. Didn't deserve having another man to bury. Better for her sake if they'd never met. Easier for him, too, to go to the grave not knowing what it was like to love and be loved in return by a woman like Emma.

But life had seldom been easy for Dair and death wasn't shaping up to be a breeze, either. He couldn't lie to her. Not now. He had to tell her the truth. "I'm sorry, Texas," he said, his voice low and gruff. "I'm so damned sorry. I never meant to..."

She stood and clutched his sleeve. "Dair, you're scaring me. What are you saying?"

He drew a deep, bracing breath, then said, "I'm dying, Emma. I'm dying."

CHAPTER FOURTEEN

EMMA HEARD A roaring in her ears. "Excuse me? What did you say?"

He repeated the God-awful words. Then he continued, his voice low and strong and honest, with a tale of physicians and tumors and a prognosis that left her numb and shaking. *I'm dying.*

She couldn't think clearly. Her mind was mush; thoughts had to fight to get through. She knew she should work up a protest, tell him it had to be a lie, but her tongue wouldn't move and her throat was too tight to get out a sound.

His expression was somber, his demeanor serious. He was telling the truth.

I'm dying.

Oh, God. Emma shut her eyes. She believed him. It explained so much. The signs had all been there. The increase in the frequency of the headaches. The intensity. His response to her. The distance he put between them.

The desperation she sometimes sensed in his lovemaking.

I'm dying.

Dair started talking about the orphans. She heard his voice saying something about nuns and investigative reports and how he wanted the treasure to endow the children's home. She heard the words, but she couldn't process them.

Couldn't listen. All she'd heard clearly and for certain was that he was dying.

He's dying.

Oh, God.

She should comfort him. How frightened he must be. She should be strong for him.

Emma couldn't be strong. The man she loved was dying. Again. Leaving her alone. Again.

"Oh, God." With Riever still cradled in her arms, she shoved to her feet. Nausea rolled in her stomach. Bile rose in her throat. "I can't…I've got to…"

He reached for her, but she pulled away. "Don't. Don't touch me. Please."

"Honey…"

"No!" She dashed away from the barn, away from Dair, away from the sound of his voice calling her name. At the edge of the inky dark forest, she stopped. Her stomach revolted and she leaned over and was sick. The puppy whimpered when her hold on him tightened. Horrified, she relaxed. *Sorry. I'm sorry.*

She pulled the handkerchief from her pocket and wiped her mouth. Her breaths came in harsh, labored pants. She couldn't do this again. She couldn't go through this again.

Dear Lord, I'm selfish. He's dying and I'm worrying about myself? Shameful. How shameful am I.

But she loved him. Oh, God, she loved him with every fiber of her being. Losing him would be like losing part of herself. He was part of her, the other half of her. For the first time in forever she felt whole.

Losing Casey had almost killed her. The pain sharp and brutal and agonizing. The loneliness had settled into her bones, into her soul. Until Dair. He'd brought life back into her existence. He'd made her sky a brilliant blue and her music an arpeggio of joy and her air smell like fresh apple pie.

Now, just when she'd awakened, the darkness hovered poised to descend once again. How can life be so cruel? So unfair? This was more than bad luck. This was a curse. A wicked, evil curse.

Emma stumbled along the tree line, walking blindly in the night until a three-quarter moon rose above the forest and illuminated her way with a silvered, ghostly light. Despite the improved visibility, her foot snagged on a branch and she tripped, though didn't fall. She heard him calling out to her, but she didn't answer. She couldn't face him. She didn't have the strength. *I can't. I can't I can't I can't.*

She picked up her pace, pushing ahead, breaking into a run. But no matter how hard she tried, she couldn't leave reality behind. Finally, exhausted, she sank to the ground. Riever scrambled to be free and she let him go, then wrapped her arms around herself and rocked back and forth. She hurt too badly to cry.

As if from far away, she sensed when Dair joined her, when he lifted her into his arms. Emma turned her head into his chest and vaguely heard him whistle for the puppy. She was aware that he carried her somewhere.

A block of ice encased her. She was cold, bone-deep, bitter cold. Her only source of warmth was Dair.

Through muffled senses, she noted door hinges creak. Boots scraped against a wooden floor. Something bumped, fell to the floor and Dair muttered something. A curse?

Emma pried open her eyes, but pitch blackness proved it wasted effort. He set her down on something soft. Left her. She shivered with chill.

She heard fumbling, the rattle of glass and the scratch of a match. Lamplight flickered and burned, its yellow glow chasing away the darkness. Emma turned away, curled in a ball on a lumpy mattress. She rocked herself until Dair rejoined her, spooned against her, and pulled a quilt over them.

"Emma," he murmured against her ear. "It's all right."

No, it wasn't all right. It would never be right again.

She sank against him, drew in his body heat. They lay without speaking for the longest time. At some point, Emma slept.

She dreamed of a pirate chest filled with golden horseshoes, of a winged fairy with kind eyes and a gentle smile who watched over three little babies crawling on a quilt and cooing with contentment. Then a dark shadow blackened the sky. A dragon swooped in, breathed his fire, and her dream melted away, leaving a nightmare behind.

Dair's lifeless body lay spread-eagle on a bloodred plain, arms and legs shackled to iron stakes sunk into granite boulders.

Emma awoke screaming.

"Shush, now. Calm down. Everything's all right."

But it wasn't. Reality came rushing back and she gasped at the pain of it. "No," she moaned softly. "Tell me it was all a dream. Tell me it isn't true."

"I'd give anything if I could, sweetheart. I don't want to lie to you any more."

She wanted to tell him not to worry, to keep on lying, but she wasn't quite that far gone. "It isn't fair. It just isn't fair!"

"I know, darling. I know."

He held her, shushed her, warmed her until she stirred enough to ask, "Where are we?"

"One of the old slave cabins. Johnny's been sleeping here, but I chased him out, claimed it for myself last night."

"Are the children all right?"

"They're fine. Don't worry about them."

Emma didn't have the energy to argue. At least she was warmer now. She wasn't trying to think her way through a brain filled with cold molasses.

"You should have told me, Dair. You shouldn't have let me fall in love with you." It hurt too much. She wouldn't survive the pain of losing him.

He was silent for a long minute. "Maybe. But by the time I realized where we were going, we were already there. Plus, I'm a selfish man, Emma. I couldn't make myself give you up."

"Until now. Why tell me now, Dair? Why not keep it to yourself until…"

"I'll be honest. The coward in me considered it a fine idea. But I love you, Emma, and that means I owe you the truth."

"It'd be easier if you lied."

He laughed without amusement. "I don't think you and I get to do 'easy.' Emma…" he raised up on his elbow and gazed down at her. "Will you agree to oversee the home? I'm not asking you to live here, but to do the hiring of staff, to oversee them and manage the funds I've established for them. The accounts are healthy as they are. If we find the treasure, well, you'll be able to make this the nicest children's home in Texas."

"Dair, I…"

"You're their best hope, Emma. Please?"

Emotion was a strangling noose around her neck. He was dying—leaving her to pick up the pieces. It was admirable that he worried about the children, but…dammit...what about her? He's leaving her. Once again, she'd be poor old Emma withered and abandoned and alone.

She bit her tongue against the self-pitying thoughts and tried to be unselfish when in truth, her heart was breaking. "Yes. Of course. I won't let them down, Dair. Don't worry about that."

"I wasn't actually worried. I know the kind of woman you are. Now that you've met them, you'd have watched over them whether I asked you to or not."

"You place a lot of faith in me. I'm afraid that's a mistake."

"Now why do you say that?"

She looked away from him. "You say you're selfish, but I'm the selfish one. You tell me you're facing the ultimate test, and all I can think about is how awful that is for me."

"It is awful for you. I have to tell you, Emma, if our situations were reversed, I'd be...well...it wouldn't be pretty. Being the one left behind takes more courage than being the one going."

"I'm ashamed." She couldn't help it. She didn't want to think about the children, the home, anything. That was all in the future. Her cold, empty future.

"You absolutely shouldn't be ashamed. You're human. A dear, wonderful human with a heart as big as Texas. I'm a lucky man to have known you. A lucky man to have loved you, and especially, to be loved by you."

"Luck, hah," she scoffed. "Better for you that you'd never met me. After all, I'm the Bad Luck bride."

He stroked his thumb down her arm. "Don't be that way, Texas. I had this lump in my head long before I met you. Look, I'm still a believer in fate. I think we were meant to meet and be important to one another, but we were never destined for happy-ever-after. I feel lucky we had happy-for-a-time. These months with you, they've been more than I ever could have imagined. I never dreamed I'd have a woman like you in my life."

He paused a moment, took her hand. "But I don't want you to think that happy-ever-after can't happen for you. Someday, you'll meet a man who can give you that. That happy-ever-after person is still out there waiting for you."

"No," she said flatly. Angrily. "I will not listen to this. How dare you say that to me!"

Dair placed his finger against her lips. "Listen to me, Emma. Open your mind for just a little bit. Every step on our life path prepares us for the next one. Whether you can see it now or not, I'm a step on the path that's leading you to your fate, to your true destiny."

She closed her eyes and sighed, snuggling close against him. She understood what Dair was trying to do, but the man didn't have a clue. The only destiny she had was to bring bad luck…

Emma's eyes flew open. Bad luck.

Her pulse sped up. Bad luck. Destiny. Fate.

Fairies.

Oh my oh my oh my.

She sat up. "Dair, who gave you this diagnosis?"

"I went to a doctor. Two of them, in fact."

"Where?"

"London. They both were reputable men, Emma. I know what you are thinking, but they didn't make a mistake."

"But—"

"You've seen me have the headaches. You know they're getting worse. One physician told me I might see Thanksgiving, but at the rate they've been increasing, I doubt I'll last that long."

Destiny. Fate. And fairies.

Magic. Miracles.

She drew a deep breath, then said, "A few minutes ago you asked me to keep an open mind. Now I'm asking you to return the favor. Dair, you said that you believe in fate and that you think we were meant to meet and be important to one another, and I agree with that. But maybe it has to do with more than our love life. Maybe it has to do with life itself."

"What do you mean?"

"Dair, I'm not ready to write you off as a dead man. Maybe there is a cure out there that the London doctors didn't know about. I know a doctor in Fort Worth...he's young and smart and he studied medicine back east. Maybe fate brought us together so that I could tell you about him. So that I could save your life. Maybe that's my task."

"Your task? What do you...oh. That fairy tale." Pity and heartbreak softened Dair's expression. "Texas, don't do this to yourself."

Anger flared like a match. "Don't you dismiss me."

"I'm not dismissing you. I can't let you get your hopes up. I've already caused you enough pain. I don't want to cause you any more."

"Then come with me to Fort Worth. Let's go tomorrow."

Dair shook his head. "I don't have time to waste, Emma. You probably won't like hearing this either, but I may as well get it all over with. Tomorrow Logan and I are going after the Sisters' Prize. Holt and Cade will remain here to watch over you."

The anger within her intensified to fury. How dare he. Did he honestly believe that after everything they'd been through, she'd let him ride off into the sunset? She opened her mouth to rail at him before experiencing second thoughts. She was tired, physically spent and emotionally exhausted. And he was a stubborn, pigheaded man. Why go through the effort of an argument when better ways to solve the problem existed?

"If you think that's best..." *You're stupid.* "I'm tired, Dair. Hold me while I sleep?"

His hesitation showed he didn't quite trust her. Maybe he wasn't entirely stupid after all. "Of course I'll hold you."

"Good. You can keep me warm." She thought better when she was warm and she had plenty of thinking to do.

First, I need to find a gun.

DAIR SLEPT LIKE A DEAD MAN and when he awoke well-rested and refreshed long past his normal awakening time, he credited his newly clean conscience for the good night's sleep. They say confession is good for the soul. It seemed to be worth something for the soulless, too.

The sheets beside him were cold, Emma long gone. Good. He could use a little time to shore up his defenses before facing her. Leaving her today would be the hardest thing he'd ever have done.

He expected she might argue a bit before he left, too. It wasn't like Emma not to complain when he made decisions for her, but last night she'd been exhausted. He doubted he'd be so lucky this morning. That's if he could trust her to stay behind. He halfway expected her to try and follow him.

Dair sat up and took a quick inventory of his physical condition. That heavy sensation that often preceded his headaches wasn't in evidence. Good. He didn't need that on top of everything else, though he knew he was due another bout. He'd had a nice break from them since arriving at the children's home, but he couldn't expect that to continue.

Dair dressed and left the cabin in search of breakfast and Emma. It looked as if a nice day were in the making. Hot, of course, but it was summer in Texas. His mind was on the journey ahead as he made his way up to the main house. His mother's old place was a half day's ride from here. While he couldn't formulate a definitive plan of action until he determined who and what awaited him, he expected that by suppertime tonight, he'd know who had pinned the murder on Emma. Dair looked forward to making the bastard pay.

"Mr. Dair. Mr. Dair. *There* you are," little Genny said as she and two other girls skipped down the path to meet him. "We've been waiting for you forever. We need your help."

"Oh? For what?"

"It's a trick the boys are playing on us, Mr. Dair," one of the other girls explained. "We need to figure out how they do it. Will you help us, please? It won't take long."

"Sure, honey. What would you like me to do?"

Genny's smile was angelic. "First, you lace your fingers behind your back like this." She twirled around to demonstrate.

"All right." Dair did as requested.

"Can you hold your arms out away from your back a little further, Mr. Dair?" the third girl, Lila, asked from behind him.

Dair extended his arms and heard Sarah count, "One. Two. Three."

Cold metal touched his wrists. *Snap. Jangle.* They'd cuffed him. Not a pleasant sensation for a thief. "Girls? I don't know what sort of trick the boys are playing on you, but it needs to end. Unlock the handcuffs and I'll see that they—"

"We were lying to you, Mr. Dair," Genny confessed, her smile unapologetic. "Miss Emma asked us to do it."

"What?"

"She has the key."

Anger pumped through Dair's veins. Of course she had the key. Dammit. He should have known she surrendered too easily last night. He shouted, "Emma!"

She sashayed out the front door of the main house, her expression both challenging and set, dark circles under her eyes. Johnny followed at her heels carrying her satchel and wearing a sheepish grin. Dair pinned her with a furious glare. "Emma, this isn't funny. I want these cuffs off now."

"I'm sorry, Dair. I can't do that. Not until we're on the train, and I have your word that you'll cooperate with my plans."

He squeezed a word past the cords in his throat. "Plans?"

"After discussing train schedules with Logan, Holt and Cade, it appears we can be in Fort Worth by suppertime. We'll see Dr. Daggett first thing tomorrow morning."

Logan, Holt and Cade? Those bastards. "Grey! Driscoll! Hollister! Get your butts out here!"

The reply came from the cabin his friends had claimed as theirs. "That's not a good idea, MacRae," Holt called.

"Now!"

After a moment, the door to their cabin opened and the men stepped outside. Wearing bed sheets. "She stole our clothes," Cade explained.

Dair whipped his head around to stare at Emma. She looked him right in the eyes. "You thought I'd simply lie there next to you and wait for you to die? You should know me better than that, MacRae."

Admiration rang in Logan's voice as he said, "Woke us in the middle of the night, she did. She waltzed in and demanded all our things. Said it was wash day. Said she'd found fleas and lice on the kids and everything we had owned needed to be deloused. Hell, I was still half asleep and her voice reminded me of Nana Nellie. I didn't think twice." Scratching his bare chest he added, "I'm still itching from the very idea."

"Not until morning came and we went looking for something to wear," Cade agreed. "That's when she told us she was holding our britches hostage."

"I think you should go on peaceably," Holt added. "She makes a convincing argument. I don't see what it'd hurt to see one more doctor, under the circumstances."

Dair's jaw was clenched so tight he had to concentrate to open it to speak. They weren't going to help him. That was obvious. They wanted him to see another doctor. They wanted him to be poked and prodded only to get the same death sentence. And, they were willing to allow Emma to watch it happen.

Bastards. Betrayal washed through him. In a tone low and deadly calm, he said, "Emma, unlock these handcuffs."

She lifted her chin. "No."

Frustration flowed like hot lava. "There's a killer out there—"

"Who can wait a few more days for justice. Now, walk over to the wagon, Dair. Our train leaves from town in little more than an hour."

Without taking his gaze off Emma, he said, "Boys. Y'all need to deal with this."

"I'm not going anywhere dressed in a sheet," Logan declared. "Besides, I agree with the lovely lady. Go to Fort Worth. See the doctor."

"Have you forgotten I'm a wanted man? I'd just as soon not die in a jailhouse or at the end of a rope before my time."

"Emma's brother-in-law is a lawman," Holt said. "He won't let that happen."

"Besides, those wanted posters are old. You've changed a lot since your last bank robbery," Johnny offered helpfully.

The last time Dair felt ganged up against this way he'd been running from the police in Edinburgh. "With friends like you…"

"Oh, quit whining," Emma snapped. "They're not enemies. They want what's best for you. They care about you, Alasdair. You need to be gracious."

"Gracious? You want me to be gracious?"

"I want you to live. More than anything else in the world, I want you to live. So, get in the wagon before I shoot you."

Coming from Emma McBride Tate, that actually made sense.

Dair knew he could put a stop to this. He could refuse to cooperate and wait her out. The woman was stubborn, but he'd developed a near infinite store of patience during his days as a thief. But she looked so brittle…as if she were on the verge of breaking…that he felt compelled to deal with her.

"Tell you what, Em. Let me go deal with the killer, then I'll go to Fort Worth with you. I give you my word."

She started shaking her head before he finished speaking. "We're going today. You owe me, Dair. I could spend an hour explaining why, but that would be a waste of time for both of us. You know you owe me, so here's my deal.

You do this for me, and I'll consider us even. After that, you can do whatever you want."

It wasn't the words she spoke that had Dair reconsidering his position, but the sheen in her eyes. Emma looked like she was about to cry. He realized that never once, through everything they'd been through, had he seen her shed a tear.

That was one sight he'd gladly go to his grave without witnessing. *God, please don't cry over me, Texas. I couldn't bear it.*

In that moment, he couldn't refuse her anything. "Two days. I'll give you two days. That, and I'll have your word that you will stay home in Fort Worth where it's safe while I go look for the killer."

Her lips pursed in a begrudging pout, Emma nodded. Dair demanded, "Say it aloud."

"All right, you have my word."

Dair didn't believe it for a minute, but at least he'd have ammunition in his pocket for the argument sure to come. He turned around and presented his wrists. "The key, please?"

"Not until we're on the train."

"Oh, for God's sake, Emma." He dropped his chin to his chest and shook his head in frustration. "Fine. Be that way."

He glanced over at Logan. "I'd like you to come with us. We'll go straight to my mother's old place from Fort Worth."

Logan nodded. "Miss Emma, can I please have my pants back? I think we'd all be more comfortable if I was wearing more than a toga on this trip."

Emma called, "Annabelle, give Mr. Grey back his clothes, please."

"What about us?" Cade protested.

"The children have instructions. You'll have your clothes back by lunchtime."

Holt rubbed the back of his neck. "You're tough, Emma." To Dair, he added, "I'm gonna hope real hard this doc of hers has a cure. After this morning, the idea of keeping my promise scares me half to death."

Dair just shook his head and sighed and climbed into the wagon. Though he and Emma had little to say to one another on the trip into town, Logan and Johnny kept the conversation flowing until they arrived a little less than an hour later. Only upon their arrival at the train depot did Emma relent and release him from the handcuffs. Dair rubbed his wrists and posed a question that had occurred to him halfway into town. "Emma, are you certain this trip to Fort Worth won't backfire on you?"

"What do you mean?"

"Your hope is to prolong my life, correct?"

"It is."

"Recall that I had you and your family investigated before you arrived at Chatham Park. In light of those discoveries, one must wonder if presenting myself at Willow Hill might not be the final act of my misbegotten life."

"Why do you…oh." She grimaced. "Papa."

"Trace McBride will surely want to kill me."

"Yes, but he won't do it." She hesitated, chewed on her lower lip. "Maybe I won't send that telegram, after all. I think it's better if we simply surprise them. Papa will be so happy to see me, he won't think about killing you. Not right away."

"Wait a minute," Logan interjected. "Am I understanding that Trace McBride is Emma's father? You ran off with Trace McBride's daughter?"

"Technically, she ran off after me."

"Trace McBride." Logan shook his head, then laughed.

"And you're gonna waltz into his house with his daughter on your arm with no ring on her finger? Damn, MacRae. I don't know if I want to be party to this. Dying is one thing. Suicide is something else."

Dair pursed his lips. His friend did have a point. "Emma, would it make things easier for you if we stopped somewhere and got married before reaching Fort Worth?"

"Was that a marriage proposal?" Irritation snapped in her eyes.

"If you'd like it to be." He would be fine with marrying her if that's what she wanted. Although, he couldn't imagine she'd want to be a two-time widow. He truly didn't know what was best. He simply wanted to make this as easy on her as possible.

"The romance of the moment overwhelms me," she dryly replied. She smiled then, but it didn't reach her eyes. "Thanks, MacRae, but who said I'd marry you anyway?"

After that, there didn't seem much more to say.

"She sure is something, Dair," Logan murmured in his ear as they followed Emma onto the train. "If you beat this death sentence, then I'd say you're the luckiest man on earth. And if you don't, well, I reckon you'll understand when I say I hope like hell I live up to my nickname."

"Shut up, Lucky." Dair didn't want to think about his Emma in the arms of Logan Grey or any other man. He didn't want to think about the upcoming meeting with Trace McBride, either. That's why, for the first time ever, when he felt the first telltale signs of an oncoming headache, he smiled.

Some kinds of pain were easier to deal with than others.

CHAPTER FIFTEEN

Fort Worth

TRACE MCBRIDE'S BACK HURT like a sonofabitch. "Ah, hell, treasure," he said to his wife, Jenny. "Not another trunk. We're not moving to Scotland you know."

"Quit whining. I'm taking gifts for the Rosses. I'm not arriving at Rowanclere castle empty-handed."

"Is this all of it, then?" Trace eyed the pile of luggage at the bottom of the stairs and scowled. "Where are the boys? They need to be helping me load the wagon. That's the reason I had boys to begin with."

"Don't give me that. The boys did load the wagon, all but these last few pieces." Jenny walked out of the dining room shuffling through the pile of mail she'd stayed up half the night preparing. "I sent them over to Kat's and Mari's to help Jake and Luke. We were about done and they'll need the help with all the children."

Trace shut his eyes and shook his head. "If they bring half the amount of stuff you've packed, Jenny, we might as well hire our own ship to take us across the Atlantic. I should have left yesterday by myself. Traveled fast and light."

Jenny looked up from her pile of mail and her eyes softened with compassion. "Darling, I know you're worried. I'm worried, too. But think about what Jake has told us about this Dair MacRae. He'll take care of Emma. We have to believe that or else we'll worry ourselves sick long before we ever reach Scotland."

Trace set his teeth and raked his fingers through his thick salt-and-pepper hair. "I'm scared, treasure."

Jenny set down her mail and wrapped her arms around her husband. Laying her cheek against his chest, she murmured, "I know. Me, too."

How quickly life can change, Trace thought as he stood in the foyer of his Fort Worth home, Willow Hill. Yesterday, life had been pretty damned good. They'd celebrated the christening of Maribeth's new additions to the family and Kat's marriage to a reformed scoundrel who—though he wasn't good enough for Kat—made her happy. Then, during the barbecue reception Trace and Jenny were hosting on the back lawn at Willow Hill, a messenger arrived with news that shook the McBride family to its collective soul. A murder warrant had been issued in Scotland for Emma and she was on the run.

Now, the entire family was leaving on the evening train. While Trace didn't like the idea of taking the womenfolk along, he knew he could use the help of his sons-in-law. Jake Kimball knew the man Emma had run off with. Luke Garrett had a lawman's badge that might come in handy if professional courtesy came into play. Since neither man would leave their families behind—not that Kat or Maribeth would let them do it anyway—and his own Jenny sure as hell wouldn't remain in Fort Worth with Emma in trouble overseas, Trace hadn't fought the idea of taking the family too hard. They'd make the Highland home of the

Rosses their base of operations, and if all went well, they'd be back in Fort Worth in time for the Harvest Ball.

How's that for positive thinking?

Trace gave Jenny one more squeeze, then stepped away. "I'd better get the rest of the luggage loaded. But let this be the last of it, all right? I'm worried I'll throw out my back. The only good thing about an ocean crossing is having all those hours with nothing to do but make love to you, and if a trunk full of geegaws prevents that from happening, I won't be a happy man."

"And I won't be a happy woman. This trunk holds our pillows. If that's too much for you, wait, and I'll help as soon as I finish my paperwork."

Trace smiled for the first time that day. "I do like a woman with a sarcastic tongue."

Jenny snorted a laugh. "What you like is a woman who knows how to use her tongue."

He waggled his brows. "Often."

She slapped him on the butt. "Go load the wagon, McBride. Don't forget to lift with your knees."

Trace placed a satchel atop the lightweight trunk on his shoulder, then sauntered down the sidewalk, his mood temporarily lightened by the byplay with his wife. Jenny had that touch, the ability to make even the darkest days brighter. He wouldn't have survived those black months when they thought Kat was dead or the awful time after sweet Susie was killed without Jenny. No, the day Jenny Fortune decided to move her dressmaking business into the building where he'd lived with his Menaces was beyond a doubt the luckiest day of his life.

Setting the trunk on the ground behind the wagon, Trace frowned. He'd need to do some rearranging. He climbed up into the wagon bed and using his legs, not his back, shifted the baggage around, his thoughts drifting between past and present.

Luck. Good luck and bad luck and the Curse of Clan McBride. Mari and Kat were all excited about the news out of Scotland. Crazy girls. They were certain Emma was about to break the infamous Bad Luck curse.

Trace didn't know how he felt about the whole idea. There was no denying that the McBride family had a tough time when it came to love. He and his brother, now Mari and Kat, all had to overcome great trials before finding happiness in marriage. And poor Emma, losing Casey like she had…no one would accuse her of being lucky in love. Now she was running around Scotland with a man who Luke had found out this morning had his name listed on a dozen different wanted posters.

Why is it my girls go after men who live their lives on the wild side of trouble? When he'd asked that question last night while lying sleepless in bed with his wife, Jenny had responded that young women often look to marry men like their father. He hadn't had a good response to that one.

Trace gave a suitcase a shove. Unlucky in love, he could buy, but a fairy curse? That stretched superstition to a whole new level. Could Trace actually make that leap? He wouldn't even consider it, except…those pendants weren't paste.

Say there was something to this legend. Would Emma be safer or in more danger if she were about to break the fairy prince's curse? Chances are, the guy wouldn't like it. What sort of nasty tricks could a fairy prince pull on his little girl? *Good God, I can't believe I'm even thinking such nonsense.*

"I've lost my mind," Trace grumbled beneath his breath. "I've finally cracked from the stress."

He jumped down from the wagon and shoved a trunk off to one side, leaving the perfect amount of space for Jenny's carpetbag. His mind occupied with the geometry of fitting the rest of the luggage into the wagon bed, Trace glanced over his shoulder when he sensed someone behind him. "Hand me your mother's bag there, would you please, Emma?"

She did as he asked and the bag slid right in. Good. They might just make this in one trip after all. Trace started up the front walk toward the house where the last pile of bags waited. Halfway there, his mind registered what had just happened. "Emmaline?" he said, whirling around. His heart stuttered.

There she stood, his eldest, his sweet beautiful darling Emma. Safe. Sound. And not, thank God, in Scotland.

"Baby." He held his arms wide and rushed toward her even as she flew at him. Once he held his little girl in his arms, Trace felt the axis of his world shift. All was right again. "Ah, Em. You had me so scared."

"I'm sorry, Papa."

"I was coming to get you."

"You were? Why? Didn't you get my letters telling you everything was fine?"

"Uh-huh." He loosened his hold on her, took a step back. She looked tired. Weary. Sad, even. "You don't look like a murderer."

"Murderer!" She winced. "Oh."

"You want to tell me about it?"

"Not necessarily, but something tells me I don't have a choice." Her voice trembled slightly as she said, "Papa, I—"

"Emma!" Jenny let out a squeal of delight that echoed through the city streets.

Then Emma was out of his arms and into her mother's, and Trace folded his arms and watched the reunion with a wide grin on his face until he belatedly realized somebody else observed the scene, too.

The man stood by the wagon. He was tall with broad shoulders and large hands. Hard, silver-colored eyes glowed with a possessive light as they watched Trace's daughter.

The goddamned Scot. Had to be. Stupid sonofabitch actually came with her? Trace drew his gun. "MacRae, tell me why I shouldn't shoot you where you stand."

Damned if the man didn't laugh. "Like father, like daughter," he murmured before his expression went serious. "You can't shoot me, Mr. McBride, because your daughter is in love with me."

"Hell. That's never stopped me before." Trace's finger flexed. The gun exploded. Emma shouted, "Papa!

Outlaw MacRae took the hat from his head and fingered the bullet hole in the crown, his confident gray eyes gone wary.

Trace McBride smiled.

DAIR WONDERED JUST HOW GOOD a shot Trace McBride was. Had he hit the target he aimed for or had he missed?

"Papa! Stop it." Emma pulled from her mother's arms and faced her father. "Put the gun down."

"Why? Give me one good reason why I should."

"You can't kill him."

"Are you married?"

"No."

"Then I can kill him."

Emma rubbed her temples with her fingertips. "He did ask me to marry him, Papa. I refused."

"Oh for crying out loud." Trace sent his wife an aggrieved look. "We have to go through this again?"

Jenny gave Emma's hand a squeeze, then moved to her husband's side. "She's home, Trace. He brought her home."

It took a moment, but eventually Trace McBride lowered the gun.

"Let's go inside, shall we?" Jenny continued. "It's too unbearable to be standing out here in the afternoon heat. Besides, I'll need to call Kat and Mari and tell them the news. Claire and Tye, too."

Scowling, Trace nodded, then a sly look entered his eyes. He acknowledged Logan Grey's presence for the first time by saying, "Emma? Did you bring this other fella with you, too?"

"Yes, Papa. I'd like you to meet Mr. Logan Grey. He's a friend of Dair's."

"That's handy for you, MacRae," Trace said. "You'll have help unloading the wagon. Bring everything inside and leave it at the foot of the stairs."

Then, with his wife on one side and Emma on the other, Trace disappeared inside his home. Dair breathed a little sigh of relief.

"Well, that was quite an interesting welcome," Logan observed, eyeing the bullet hole in Dair's hat. Then, frowning at the baggage piled high in the wagon, he added, "Helluva way to treat a dying guest, though."

"I'm not their guest," Dair snapped. He intended to take a room in one of the hotels downtown. Neither was he dying—at least, not that the McBrides would know. That was one hard-won promise he'd extracted from Emma during the train trip, one difficultly negotiated deal. He'd be honest and forthright with her precious doctor as long as she kept her mouth shut about it.

He had not left his pride behind in Scotland. He'd told Logan and the others because circumstances required it. He'd told Emma because the tiny bit of conscience he still possessed required he do so. Other than that, the fact he had a tumor growing in his brain was nobody's business.

"C'mon, Lucky. Give me a hand with the bags. As much as I'd like to walk away right now, for Emma's sake I'd rather the old man not suffer a heart attack while toting this small amount of luggage."

Logan arched a brow. "Small amount?"

The two men started grabbing trunks and bags and hauling them inside Willow Hill. Hearing sounds of conversation coming from a room toward the back of the house, Dair set down the trunk and took a moment to look around the house where Emma grew up.

It was nice. Comfortable. Warm and homey. In a room off the entry hall, he spied portraits hanging on the wall and curiosity drew him near. His gaze went first to Emma, of course, and he smiled. She wore a burgundy gown that complemented the necklace around her neck. The artist had captured her perfectly. Her mischievousness, her confidence. Her wholesome beauty. A smile that held just a little bit of sadness. The portrait must have been painted after her husband's death.

Next Dair glanced at Kat's portrait, a vision in emerald, before focusing on the third sister dressed in blue, the one he hadn't met. Maribeth, whose sparkling eyes were the color of the sapphire hanging around her neck. She had golden hair that sparkled with shimmers of red just like her sisters. She was beautiful, just like her sisters.

"Whoa," Logan said from behind him. "The last time I saw that many pictures of gorgeous women on a wall I was in a high-dollar whorehouse trying to choose my evening's entertainment."

"Shut up, Grey."

"Now, I know you probably don't approve of buying affection, but don't forget, my work takes me places where the West is still wild. Sometimes professionals are the only option available."

"There are more bags in the wagon."

"I'm resting my muscles and indulging in a bit of fantasy. Are either of the other two single? If you manage to ruin my chances with Emma by staying alive, maybe I could—*humph.*"

Dair removed his elbow from his friend's stomach. "Maribeth is married to a lawman. Remember? Holt knows her husband."

"Oh, yeah. What about the other one?"

"Kat is—"

"Mine," snapped a voice from behind them. "She's my wife."

Dair turned to see Jake Kimball glaring at Logan Grey from the doorway. Dair's lips lifted in a grin. "That was a fast trip to Tibet."

Shooting Logan one last warning glance, Jake advanced and turned his attention to Dair. They shook hands and slapped each other's shoulders. Jake said, "Well, MacRae. You sure managed to cause a stir."

"Your father-in-law took a shot at me."

Jake's mouth twisted with a grin. "Yeah? He had me thrown in jail. I suggest you do some fast talking, yourself, to avoid a similar fate. I'm afraid my brother-in-law discovered some outstanding arrest warrants for you, and Luke can be a real law-and-order fellow."

"I was afraid of that," Dair said with a grimace. Turning to Logan, he asked, "Can I count on you to have my back?"

"Of course," Logan said, a faint sneer on his face as he looked at Jake. "I protect my friends."

Not liking the way the two men were sizing one another up, Dair stepped between them. "If you two could refrain from fisticuffs for a moment, I'd like to get caught up on what I've missed. Jake Kimball, meet Logan Grey. Don't be an ass about the fact that Logan admired your wife. With a woman like Katrina, that's a reality you'll have to learn to live with. And Logan, don't be an ass about Jake needing to get along with his brother-in-law. The lawman is his family, just like you are mine."

Jake arched a brow. "I didn't know you had a sibling."

"There's quite a lot about Dair you don't know, Jake," Emma said from the hallway just outside the room. Her gaze fastened on him as she said, "My parents are asking for explanations, and I'd appreciate it if you'd join us. It'll be easier to tell the story once to everyone than to have to repeat it over and over."

"I'll be right there. First, though, let me tell Jake about the news I learned at Chatham Park."

Emma nodded. "Logan, you want to come with me? I'd like to introduce you to my family. Everyone is here now."

Out of orneriness, Logan grinned big. "Excellent. I'm excited to meet your sisters, Emma."

Once Jake and Dair were alone in the room, Dair rubbed the back of his neck and said, "I could use a drink."

"I understand. Here." Jake walked toward a cabinet where he pulled out two glasses and a decanter filled with amber liquid. "We'll raid the old man's bourbon. I figure he owes you a drink for shooting at you."

"He ruined my hat." Dair accepted the glass, clicked it against Jake's in a wordless toast, then sipped the drink. As it burned a smooth path down his throat, he decided how to approach the problem at hand. "You look happy, Kimball."

"I am. Though Kat and I officially married in England, yesterday we had a wedding. Today I don't have to spend my second honeymoon with my in-laws, after all. Life is good."

"You love her."

"I do. Very much. I was a little slow about realizing it, so she made me pay, but in the end, well, I found my family, Dair."

He couldn't ask for a more perfect lead-in. "About that. Jake, I have some hard news for you. It's about Daniel."

Jake closed his eyes and blew out a long sigh. He tossed back a bracing gulp of whiskey, then his mouth settled in a grim line. "What is it?"

Dair told him about his trip to Chatham Park looking for Emma, and the visit by Miss Starnes's family while he was there.

While Dair spoke, Jake turned away, moving to stand in front of the window. Dair finished his story, then waited for Jake's reaction. When it came, its direction surprised him.

"Do you believe in ghosts, MacRae?"

Ghosts were easier to accept than fairies. "I don't not believe in them."

Jake nodded. "I think that maybe he's been dead all along. I think maybe time runs a bit differently on the other side than it does here, and that my dream was Daniel's goodbye gift to me. It worked, too. 'Find the necklace, find your family.' I was just too blind to see it for awhile."

"You loved him." Dair took his own bracing sip of liquor and added, "It's hard as hell to let go of those we love."

Jake exhaled a heavy breath, then turned to face Dair. "Daniel is dead. I can finally accept it. Thanks, though, MacRae, for tying up that loose end for me." He shook his head. "To think I almost settled for a woman who would pull a stunt like that."

"You wouldn't have gone through with it." Kat McBride Kimball swept into the room. "You were already crazy in love with me. Hello, Dair."

He nodded. "Mrs. Kimball."

She grinned, but spared him little attention as she directed her focus toward her husband and walked into his arms. "I eavesdropped, Jake. What that horrible Miss Starnes did is awful. I'm so sorry. I'm so sorry about Daniel."

Jake dipped his head and rested his forehead against hers. "Thanks, sweetheart."

Such was the intimacy and emotion of the moment that Dair felt like a voyeur. Now there was a couple who'd been lucky in love. *Poor Emma. She'll have a hard time being around those two. Even worse if her other sister's marriage is so blatantly joyful.*

Dair was relieved when Kat stepped away from her husband, braced her hands on her hips, and turned a challenging look toward him. "Mr. MacRae. I swear I don't know whether to slug you or hug you. Thank you for bringing my sister home."

Though that wasn't exactly the way it had happened, Dair saw no reason to correct her. "You're very welcome."

"Now I think it's time to join the others. My father is about to bust a gut to find out the details of this murder you got Emma involved in, and if that's not enough, I'm afraid your friend Mr. Grey and Mari's Luke are about to come to blows. Mr. Grey is quite the flirtatious fellow, isn't he?"

"Who is that sonofabitch, Dair?" Jake demanded.

Quite possibly, your future brother-in-law. "Logan and I grew up together."

Jake groused, "Well, he doesn't have very good manners."

"That's funny coming from you."

"Funny? I'll tell you what's funny. Me watching you at the McBride Inquisition." Jake glanced at his wife. "Honey? You think Jenny has any peanuts in her pantry? I like having something to munch on while I'm watching a show."

In the doorway into the kitchen, Dair paused. The large room was crowded with people and the vast majority of them were giving him the Evil Eye. He wasn't so sure about ghosts, and he didn't believe in fairies. He did, however, believe in the power of family. He wondered if he'd survive this with his skin intact.

Only for you, Emma. Only for you.

CHAPTER SIXTEEN

IN HER OLD BEDROOM AT Willow Hill, Emma held her breath as she eased open the door to one of the "secret passageways" her architect father had built into his design of their home. Modeled after the hidden staircases of the house where Trace McBride grew up, the space had provided the McBride children hours upon hours of fun in their childhood make-believe games.

This morning, they served another purpose. Stepping carefully and quietly, Emma made her way down a hidden staircase to a second-floor window. She slid up the window, then reached for a vine-covered trellis which she climbed down until her feet touched the ground.

Now came the tricky part—making her way off Willow Hill property without being seen. She'd given her word to keep quiet about the morning's mission, and she preferred sneaking away to telling an out-and-out lie. She'd done enough of that last night.

Lying to her father, to her mother, was exhausting. She'd found it so much easier to give them the facts about Robbie Potter's death and the hunt for the Sisters' Prize than to gloss over the details of why she'd left Chatham Park and traveled along with a "sorry-low-down-no-good-sack-of-b.s.-outlaw."

As difficult as it was to lie to her parents and Uncle Tye

and Aunt Claire, looking her sisters in the eyes and fudging the truth was twice as hard. Mari and Kat knew Emma. They knew she wasn't telling them the whole story, and when the two of them ganged up on her in the privacy of the nursery while Emma played with the twins, the words had bubbled on her tongue like a lemon fizz. But Emma had given Dair her word and she wouldn't break it. Not about something as important to him as his privacy.

Luck was with her, however, and she made her escape without detection and headed downtown to Dair's hotel. Thank goodness she didn't have to break him out of jail this morning. She'd worried about that a time or two last night. Luke took his job as sheriff seriously, and it went against his grain to turn his back on a train robber. It wasn't until Mari pointed out that she'd robbed a train before, too, and that if her husband arrested Dair she'd insist he arrest her also did Luke agree to Dair's offer to turn himself in once Robbie Potter's killer was found. Emma suspected that everyone in the room at the time had believed Dair was lying, but this made it easier for Luke to turn his back. Kat had declared it a minor miracle when Dair and Logan finally left Willow Hill last night without any blood being shed. Emma had to agree.

"I'll make it up to them," she murmured as she approached the hotel. Once she was able to tell them everything, they'd understand. If her hopes proved true and she was able to end the curse, then all certainly would be forgiven. Billy and Tommy and Bobby wouldn't need to worry about the Bad Luck curse. Not even her father could argue with her in that case.

Dair waited for her in the lobby. Spying him, she offered up a shaky smile. This was their first private moment together since he met her family, and she wasn't exactly sure what reception to expect from him.

He didn't exactly look happy. In fact, he appeared downright grim. Without offering so much as a good morning, she asked, "Does your head hurt?"

"No. Let's go get this over with."

They were halfway to the door when a shrill voice called, "Emma? Emma Tate is that you?"

"Oh, no."

Glancing over his shoulder, Dair's steps faltered. "Don't tell me. That's the original—"

"Wilhemina Peters." Emma continued her march outside without slowing down.

"The woman Kat impersonated the day of the bride interviews," Dair said as they joined a bustling early-morning crowd on the sidewalk. "Kat caught her perfectly. I'm impressed."

Emma didn't want to talk about Wilhemina Peters, but at least her appearance had distracted Dair from his bad mood. Or so she thought. When she attempted to make ordinary walking-along-the-sidewalk small talk, he shot her a scowl and said, "Honestly, Emma, I don't give a damn about the weather."

She kept quiet until they arrived at Dr. Peter Daggett's office in a block of professional buildings just west of downtown. "Peter…Dr. Daggett…studied medicine at Massachusetts General. He's developed quite a reputation in town for being on the leading edge of science."

Dair's only comment was a *humph.*

Inside, they found the physician in the office reception room. Upon seeing Emma, his face lit up. "Emma! How lovely you look. Obviously your trip agreed with you. I was so pleased to get your note last night. Fort Worth has been a pale and boring place without you to brighten the days."

Dair leaned toward her and murmured, "A suitor? You brought me to a suitor of yours?"

Emma smiled weakly. Wonderful. Just wonderful. Weren't they off to a great start? She made the introductions and thanked Peter for agreeing to see Dair on such short notice.

"Anything for you, Emma, dear," Peter replied. He motioned toward a doorway. "If you'll follow me to the examination room, Mr. MacRae?"

When Emma moved to join them, the doctor smiled and shook his head. "You'll need to wait out here, my dear."

"No," Dair piped up. "I need her with me."

Peter Daggett glanced between them, frowning. "That's not the usual…"

"Emma and I have a…special…relationship, Doctor. I hope we can trust in your discretion?"

"Oh, I see." He gave Emma a quick look of regret before formalizing his manner into one of complete professionalism. "However, I still prefer to perform my examinations in private."

Dair shook his head. "She has to be there, doc. She'll need to see and hear for herself. The last time she took me to a doctor I lied to her about his diagnosis."

With that, Emma reached the end of her patience. "Physicians in England have told him he has a brain tumor. They've told him he's dying, Peter. I'm not ready to accept that inevitability, and I trust you to give him the best medical care available."

Peter nodded and led them into the examining room where he asked Dair to describe his symptoms, prodding for more details when Dair responded in general terms. Then he studied Dair's eyes and used a tuning fork to test his hearing. He tested Dair's reflexes, balance and coordination. He pricked his patient with a pin to test his sense of touch, doused cotton balls with different liquids to examine his sense of smell, then instructed him to smile, grimace and stick out his tongue.

The wink Dair gave Emma was all his own idea.

Peter had Dair move his head this way then that. He asked him the current time and date. He asked him to perform some simple arithmetic, then posed questions obviously designed to test his memory.

When that was done, he folded his arms and furrowed his brow, thinking deeply. "Any nausea, Mr. MacRae?"

"Sometimes," Dair responded, shrugging. "When the pain is particularly bad."

"Vomiting?"

Dair nodded.

"Tremors?"

"Yes, at times."

"Have you noticed a change in your vision?"

"No. Well, nothing permanent. A bit of fuzziness from time to time."

"Ringing or buzzing in your ears?"

"No."

"Excessive drowsiness? Any trouble speaking? Writing? Changes in your personality?"

"No."

Again, the doctor spent some time in thought. "When you saw the doctors in England, were you experiencing any symptoms at that time that do not present themselves now?"

"Not that occur to me. The first doctor witnessed one of the headaches. He suspected the tumor so he sent me to someone else for another opinion."

"I see."

Emma couldn't wait any longer. "What do you think, Peter? It doesn't have to be a tumor, right? Some other thing could be causing these headaches."

Turning to Dair, he said, "You wish me to speak freely?"

"You may as well. She needs to hear it."

"While it's impossible to prove the existence of a tumor on the basis of a basic neurological examination, certain responses do suggest the presence of one."

He went through his reasoning step by step, his every word pounding in Emma's head like a death knell, until he ended with a statement that offered a lone ray of hope. "I had a colleague at Massachusetts General who is now at Johns Hopkins, a brilliant man by the name of Harvey Cushing. He started the first laboratory in this country dedicated to investigating neuroscientific issues. Dr. Cushing has successfully removed tumors from living brains."

"Oh, no." Dair shook his head. "One of the fellows in England told me about that. There's a doctor over there who cuts open people's skulls. Two-thirds of his patients die. Half of those that live can do little more than drool afterwards. No, thank you. I'd rather be dead."

"But Dair…!"

"No, Emma."

"Dr. Cushing's mortality rate is not as high as—"

"No!" Dair glared at her, then shot an angry look at Peter. "Have you seen enough here?"

"I'm through with my examination, but I'd like to discuss—"

"Too bad. I'm done." Dair yanked open the door, tore out of the office, then out of the building.

Emma closed her eyes. She was shaking. Trembling. Frightened beyond measure. She steepled her hands in front of her mouth and cast a pleading look at her physician friend. "Peter, couldn't it be something else?"

"You're in love with him, aren't you?"

"Yes!"

"Oh, Emma. You don't catch any breaks, do you?" He reached for her hand, gave it a squeeze. "Our medical knowledge is limited in circumstances like this, but I tend to agree with the previous physicians. I suspect your Mr. MacRae does indeed have a tumor of the brain."

"And he will die from this?"

"Not all such growths cause death. If it doesn't grow, if the disease isn't established in other areas of his body, it's possible he could survive."

"How big are those 'ifs'?"

Again, he gave her that pitying smile that scratched her nerves like fingernails on a slate. "Those are substantial ifs. Emma, you should try to convince Mr. MacRae to reconsider surgery. I know the procedure is still new, still experimental in many ways, but it may well be his only chance."

His only chance.

"But at least it's a chance." Sounds from the front of the office indicated that the day's first scheduled patients had begun to arrive. Emma gave her head a shake. "Thank you, Peter. Thank you very much."

"I'm sorry I had no better news."

Outside, she looked up and down the street searching for any sign of Dair. Would he have gone back to the hotel? Surely not straight to the train station. He wouldn't run out on her, would he? There. At the corner two blocks away, she saw Logan Grey waving at her. Emma picked up her skirts and ran toward him. "Dair?"

"He's on a tear. What the hell happened in there?"

"Where is he? Which way did he go?"

Logan pointed toward Main Street. "That way. I don't know where he's headed unless it's looking for trouble. He looked dangerous. What did the sawbones tell him?"

Emma just waved a hand. She couldn't say it. Wouldn't say it. Then she saw him a block away, standing in front of the Fort Worth National Bank, his hands shoved in his pockets as he stared up at the sign.

"What the hell is he doing?" Logan muttered, then, "Good Lord, he's not gonna try and rob the place in broad daylight, is he? Is he trying to get himself killed?"

"No! Dair Macrae is neither stupid nor suicidal." Nevertheless, Emma increased her speed. She watched him take one step back, then watched him sway and stagger.

She cried out when he dropped to his knees.

She screamed when he pitched forward and lay still.

THE PAIN CLAWED MERCILESSLY. Stabbed through him. Yanked him down…down…down. Tearing. Agony. Torture.

Make it stop. Let me die. I want to die.

Emma. I want Emma.

I want to die.

DAIR AWOKE IN A LAVENDER-SCENTED bedroom filled with sunshine and the sound of Riever's snuffling snores. The puppy lay curled on the blue-gingham-padded seat of a bentwood rocker. Jenny McBride stood at the window smiling at a bluejay perched on the sill.

Dair knew she wasn't blood related to Emma and her sisters, that their widowed father had married Jenny when the girls were young, yet he saw something of this woman in each of them. In their inner character. Their strength. Their humor. The depths of their love. She must be a remarkable woman, he decided.

She had to be a saint to have put up with that husband of hers all these years.

He must have made a sound because she turned and looked at him. Her smile widened. "Oh, you're awake. Emma will be so relieved. She about wore the rug out pacing from worry. She's so much like her father that way. How are you feeling?"

"All right." He sat up, trying not to grimace. "Bit of a hangover. Where's Emma?"

"Her sisters finally convinced her to take a walk. She's a basket of nerves, so I hope the exercise will help. Dr. Daggett left a curative for you. There, beside the bed. He suspected you'd be achy upon awakening."

He saw two pills and a glass of water.

When he hesitated, she said, "Take the pills. Braving your way through pain when it's unnecessary doesn't make you courageous. It makes you foolish. You should save your strength for more important battles. Such as the one you face with Emma."

Dair's head came up. He met Jenny McBride's solemn gaze and silently asked her to elaborate. She glanced pointedly at the medicine, then waited until Dair had tossed down the curative. "She wasn't able to hold to her promise to you in light of the circumstances. She told us about your illness."

Dair wasn't surprised or upset. After the public humiliation on the city street, what did it matter?

"You have my sympathies, Dair. It must be a frightening time for you."

"I'm not frightened," he quickly corrected. "I just want—need—to get everything settled before…" He shrugged.

"You carry quite a burden, it seems." Seeing that Riever, too, had awakened, Jenny scooped the puppy into her arms. She scratched him behind the ears, saying, "Orphans and Emma—I think they'll be good for one another."

"I agree." Then, because she appeared to offer a sympathetic ear and because he didn't think it'd hurt to have someone on Emma's side aware of the rest of his plans, he added, "I have three friends. Three good men. Logan is one of them. They've all promised to look out for the children. To be there for Emma."

"To *be there?*"

Gruffly, he said, "She shouldn't be alone. She should have children of her own to care for."

Jenny clicked her tongue. "She said you need to be in control, but I doubt she realizes you're hoping to do it from the grave."

Dair rubbed the back of his neck. "It'd probably work better if you kept it to yourself."

"Hmm…" The dog started squirming and Jenny set him down. He padded to the not-quite-closed door, nosed it farther open, and slipped out into the hallway. "Emma says you love her."

"I do."

"Then why won't you fight for her?"

Dair scoffed. "Who am I supposed to fight, Mrs. McBride? The Devil? Fate? God?"

"How about yourself? How about you fight your own fears?"

"I told you I'm not afraid to die."

"I can see that." Her smile was tender, yet filled with pity. "I think, however, that you are afraid to live."

Dair set his teeth. He didn't know what she was talking about, and frankly at this moment he didn't care. His mind was too fuzzy to think clearly and he wanted to see Emma. He needed to…what? Apologize? Take her in his arms?

He needed to tell her goodbye.

After today's event—the worst yet—Dair sensed time ticking away at an accelerated pace. What happened in front of that bank building was different from any other episodes. He'd glanced at the bank while walking past it, and something had stopped him. Some elusive thought had hovered at the edge of his mind—until the pain struck. Vicious and fast. No nagging ache that slowly intensified. One minute he was fine, the next he was flat on his face.

That doctor had asked about change. He'd certainly encountered change this morning, and judging by the clock on the mantel, he'd been out of it much longer than ever before. He wondered if next time, he'd simply never wake up.

"Here come the girls," Jenny said, nodding toward the window. "Let's meet them downstairs, shall we?"

Dair reached for the boots someone had set neatly beside the bed and pulled them on. He followed Jenny and was halfway down the central staircase when Emma and her sisters entered Willow Hill through the front door.

At a glance, Dair saw that Jenny McBride was right. Stress stretched Emma's features tight. She looked brittle and anxious and edgy. Kat and Maribeth looked worried.

When Emma saw him on his feet and moving, relief flashed in her eyes. The tension, however, didn't leave her. "You're better?"

He descended the rest of the steps. He'd have opened his arms for her to run into, but the audience stopped him. Instead, he simply said, "I'm fine."

She nodded, then turned and walked into Willow Hill's drawing room. Dair didn't quite know what to do. Did she want him to follow her? Judging from the expression on her family members' faces, Dair guessed so.

Lovely. No chance for privacy in the family manse.

At the doorway, he stopped and tried. "Emma, wouldn't you like to go for a walk?"

"I just went on a walk."

From the corner of his eyes, Dair saw Trace McBride approach from the direction of his office. Wonderful. Just wonderful. Frustrated, he tried again. "How about we go sit outside in the gazebo? Your mother's roses are a pretty sight."

"It's hot outside."

Yeah, well, it was getting hot under Dair's collar, too.

He stepped into the drawing room, then turned and shut the doors. In Emma's sisters' faces. "Well!" Kat exclaimed.

"I like him," Mari murmured as the catch snicked shut.

Dair turned back to Emma and folded his arms across his chest. "Emma, can we avoid the temper tantrum and get to what's important here? I did as you asked and heard the results I expected. It's time to move forward and stop wrestling with things that can't be changed. I need to be on the next eastbound train and—"

"Stop!" She whirled on him, her eyes wild. "They can be changed! Peter gave you an alternative, Dair."

"I'm not letting some witch doctor cut open my head so just stop it. Hell, that's worse than dying."

"You fell on the sidewalk. You scraped your fingers raw trying to claw into the bricks. You made horrible little mewling noises like an animal caught in a trap. I thought you were dying in front of my eyes!"

"I wanted to die!" he snapped. "Can you possibly understand that? I'm so damned tired of having a ticking clock sitting on my shoulder. So damned tired of watching the pain this situation is bringing you."

"Well, I can't bear watching you squander the only chance you have!" she screeched. "You fool. You pig-headed, stubborn, prideful fool! Fate is giving you a chance and you toss it into the wind."

"Better a fool than a drooling idiot invalid," he thundered back. "Better your father shoots me than that. I won't be trapped in a body that won't function. I won't do that to myself and I won't do it to you. I want you to have a life. Children. All the things you said you wanted."

She brought her hands up to her head, threaded her fingers through her hair. "I. Can't. I can't live through this again."

Dair took a step toward her, but she waved him off. "No. No no no. Don't come near me. I can't have you near me. It's not fair. Not fair."

She drew a deep, shuddering breath and Dair was shocked to see tears pool in her eyes, then spill over. He'd never seen her cry, never once, and the sight paralyzed him. Because Emma didn't simply cry, she sobbed. Uncontrollably.

Dair's own throat closed, his eyes stung. Watching her fall apart caused his heart to break. "Oh, God. Emma, don't. Please don't do this."

"This is why I stayed away from men all these years. They bring nothing but trouble. Nothing but heartache. Why did I let my guard down? Why did I act so stupid? I knew better. I knew deep down it wouldn't last. Couldn't.

Forever doesn't exist for me. Happily-ever-after is for everyone else. For Mari, for Kat. For my parents. I'm glad for them. Truly, I am. I just wish...but you'd think I'd have learned by now. Why in God's name did I let myself fall in love again?"

"Emma," he tried, his tone conciliatory.

"Shut up!" She grabbed a delicate porcelain flower vase off a table and sent it sailing at his head. Dair ducked and the vase smashed against the wall, then fell to the floor in shattered pieces. "Don't you dare patronize me! This is all your fault."

"Emma, I—"

"You made me believe, Dair. I started believing again. In dreams and miracles and fairy tales. In happy ever after. Now you won't even try. You're giving up on us. You won't even consider trying to make my dreams come true."

"Texas, don't do this," he begged. "I can't let them cut open my head. I won't risk being a burden to you."

"So you'll just roll over and die?" Tears streamed down Emma's face. "Well, you can manage that without me."

Fear clawed at the pieces of his heart. "What are you saying?"

"I can't do this, Dair. I barely survived Casey. I won't survive you."

Dair was at a loss. He didn't know what to say, how to act. Finally relying on his instincts, he went to her and attempted to take her into his arms, but she wrenched herself away. "Don't *touch* me. Don't speak to me. Don't even look at me. Oh, God, I can't bear to look at you."

She buried her head in her hands and wept from the depths of her soul.

Dair stood still as a statue, though inside, his pulse

pounded and his heart twisted. He'd done this to her. He'd taken this beautiful, vivacious, adventure-loving woman and left her raw and bleeding. The final tiny spark of hope he'd harbored for the salvation of his soul flickered out.

"Go," she sobbed. "Get out. Leave here. Leave me."

She lifted her head, met his gaze with blue eyes gone red with tears. "You have to go, Dair MacRae. I cannot, I will not, watch you die."

CHAPTER SEVENTEEN

DAIR TURNED WITHOUT A word to her, opened the drawing room doors, and stepped out into the entry hall. Emma watched him walk silently past her sisters, her parents, and even her brother, Billy. Slumped against the opposite wall, Logan straightened, nodded toward Emma, then followed his friend outside.

Emma turned away. She wouldn't watch him walk away from Willow Hill, walk away from her. She had to protect herself.

That particular job got more difficult when Kat and Maribeth marched into the room. "Emma!" Kat glared at her. "You can't do this. He loves you."

"Not enough," came her flat reply.

Mari, by nature more patient than her younger sister, handed Emma a handkerchief. "Dry your eyes, Em. You're looking rather wilted."

Wilted. Wrung out. Down-to-the-soul weary. Tears welled up inside her again and she made a valiant, though ultimately unsuccessful, effort to hold them back. She sank onto the sofa and let go. She cried out her heartache, sobbed out her pain, wept for all her hopes and dreams and desires now dashed by the cruel mistress fate and the intractable stubbornness of a man.

She sensed her sisters taking seats on either side of her. She felt the comfort of their embrace. Emma cried hard, as hard as she'd cried when Susie was killed. Finally though, the waterworks dried up leaving her exhausted, sad and hopeless.

Mari gave her sister a hard hug, then asked, "So, are you done? Ready to talk?"

"What is there to talk about?"

"Quite a lot," Kat replied. "Beginning with how phenomenally foolish you're being."

Temper flared. "I'm foolish because the man I love is dying and I find that upsetting?"

"Foolish because you believe he's dying."

"He has a tumor in his brain!"

"Alasdair MacRae is not going to die. He's the final piece. He's the last person we needed to break the Curse of Clan McBride. The two of you are already in love. All you have to do is prove that it is powerful, vigilant and true and accomplish your task, and the bad luck will be done. Forever."

"Oh, Kat, just let it go." Emma grimaced with disgust. "I was there. I heard Dr. Daggett. This isn't a fairy tale, it is real life. Dair has made up his mind and I can't change it."

"Why not? You love him, don't you?" Kat folded her arms. "I made Jake realize what was important to him, what really mattered. Me. And the children. Why can't you do that? Make yourself matter."

"It's not that easy."

"Well, it should be. You should fight for him. Convince him. You can do it. You *have* to do it. Otherwise, you'll be letting down not just yourself, but all of us. Billy and Bobby and Tommy. Mari's little Drew and Madeline and the twins. Now, I'm not sure if the curse carries to adoptive children, so I don't know if the children I already have will pay, but the one I'm carrying now certainly will."

"You're pregnant?" Emma and Maribeth asked simultaneously.

"Yes." Kat's smile was smug, though the look in her eyes was bittersweet and perhaps a bit fearful as they all spent a moment remembering the child Kat lost, sweet little angel Susie.

"That's wonderful," Mari said, giving her sister a hug.

"I'm so happy for you," Emma told Kat, echoing Mari's sentiments. It was true. She was happy for Kat and if her heart twisted a bit in envy, well, she'd simply ignore it.

"Then be a good aunt and don't ruin my child's future happiness."

"Stop it. Just stop it," Emma demanded. Anger bristled in her tone. "I won't listen to that for the next twenty-five years, Kat Kimball. Nothing in this family ever changes. Does no one in this family ever consider my happiness? Doesn't anyone ever think that maybe I'd give anything if you were right, if happiness was there for my taking?"

"Emma…"

"No! But I have to be realistic. The man I love is going to die soon. I have to recognize that fate has dealt me another cruel blow and do my best to live with it. That is the only task I have before me."

"You're wrong, Emma," Mari said, reaching out and taking Emma's hands in hers. "Living through grief is not your task. Your task is letting go of it."

"That's what I'm trying to do! I'm letting go of my dreams and my desires. I'm letting go of Dair."

"Dair isn't the problem, honey. Casey is."

Emma jerked away from Mari, turned away and rubbed

her temples. "I've let go of Casey. I've fallen in love with another man, for goodness' sake."

"Listen to me." Never one to give up, Mari took her hand again. "Do you remember what Roslin of Strathardle said about our tasks?"

"She said we had to accomplish a task of great personal import."

"Yes, and she also said our tasks would be revealed at the proper time. After the Spring Palace fire when I discovered Kat might still be alive, I thought my task was to find her."

"I remember that," Emma said.

"Do you remember my wedding?"

Kat sniffed and interrupted. "How could anyone forget your wedding, Mari? I still have nightmares about quacking ducks."

Mari ignored Kat, focusing on Emma. "You stood next to me. You heard Luke and me take our vows. Do you remember what he said?"

"I recall him saying he was the luckiest man alive." Tears stung Emma's eyes and she tried to blink them away.

Mari smiled tenderly at the memory, then continued, "He told me he was proud to be marrying a McBride Menace, that Menaces are strong, loyal, courageous, and that when we love, we do it with every fiber of our being."

Kat nodded. "I always knew Luke was smart."

"It made me want to cry," Mari continued. "To see myself through his eyes that way. I told him that when it came to being a Menace, I saw only the mischief, the troublemaking, and the bad reputation."

"You always were too worried about your reputation."

"With scandalous sisters like you two, somebody needed to worry." Mari took a seat on the sofa and tugged Emma down beside her. "Nevertheless, as I stood at the altar and made my wedding vows, my task was revealed to me by the man I was marrying. Luke said, 'You just had to find yourself, sugar. That's a difficult task for all of us.' That's when I saw it, Emma. I had to accept who I was to be able to give myself wholly to the man I loved. That was my task—to find myself. Once I did that, I was able to give myself to a love that was powerful, vigilant and true."

"I was wrong about my task, too," Kat confessed, finding a seat on the other side of Emma. "Though I only figured it out a couple of days ago. I wasn't free to love Jake wholly and completely until I forgave myself. I had to forgive myself for Rory, for Susie, for the pain and anguish I put our family through when they thought I was dead. I had to forgive myself in order to trust in my own emotions, to trust in the strength of the love Jake and I share, and not be afraid. That was my task, Emma, though I was blind to it for so long. Once I forgave myself for my past, I was able to embrace the future—Jake, and our family, and a love that is strong enough to prove the claim of Ariel."

"I'm glad you figured it out," Emma said. "I'm happy for both of you. Honestly, I am. But the fact you found your powerful and true loves and accomplished your tasks has nothing to do with me. The man I love is dying."

Mari squeezed her sister's hand. "Does that mean you can't love him? That he can't love you? That you can't share a love that is powerful, vigilant and true if only for a little while? Em, I can't help but believe that you're making a mistake. Instead of driving Dair away, you should be holding him close and making the most of the time you have."

"You make it sound so easy."

"I's not easy. It's terrible. It's unfair and horrible and I hate it for you." Tears pooled in Mari's eyes and she blinked them back. "But as God is my witness, if Luke Garrett told me that he had a brain tumor, I damn sure wouldn't send him away because of my own selfishness."

"I'm not being selfish! He is. But you wouldn't understand that, would you, Mari? Because Luke would have the operation. He wouldn't wait around to die."

"Oh, you think so?" Mari scoffed. "Honey, Luke Garrett would be shaking in his boots at the idea for the same reasons Dair is. Getting him to do it would be a battle from beginning to end."

"Jake would put up a fuss, too," Kat added. "Think about it, Emma. Try to see his point of view. He doesn't want to end up a burden—"

"Shut up! If I hear that word one more time I swear I'm going to blow like a whiskey still."

Mari hardened her tone. "He's alive now. Savor that, Emma. For however long it lasts. You know, it might just be enough to break the curse. I don't recall Roslin saying anything about the longevity of our loves."

Emma reared back. "But we always…none of us…when Casey died we all thought that was the end of the whole curse business. If it doesn't matter how long a love lasts, then my marriage to Casey fulfilled the requirements and the curse is already broken."

Maribeth shrugged. "Emma, I loved Casey. Kat did, too. You know that. He was a wonderful man and he left this earth way too early. But the fact is we don't know that your love was powerful, vigilant and true. Your love was never tested. You never had obstacles to overcome."

"Death is a rather difficult obstacle to overcome."

"Maybe you'll manage it this time. Maybe God will

grant Dair a miracle. Maybe the miracle is you being in his life to convince him that he has a reason to live. If you give up on him now, you'll never know, will you?"

"You don't understand, Mari."

"I understand, Emma," Kat said. "I understand grief. The loss of a child, the loss of a spouse—what could possibly be worse? You know how horribly it hurts and how you want to avoid the pain at all costs. But we're not cowards, by God. We are strong women. Courageous women. We are the McBride Menaces. Grief is a heavy burden to bear, Emma, but you can do it if you have to. Take that lesson from your past and use it to free yourself of your fear."

"That's your task, Emma." Mari gave her sister a quick, hard hug, then stared her straight in the eyes. "You have to conquer your fears by risking the pain of your past. I found myself. Kat forgave herself, and now, Emma, it's time for you to free yourself."

"How? If I can somehow summon up the strength to try, how do I go about it? He's dying. He's leaving me. How do I find the strength to just stand by and watch?"

"You won't be doing it alone, that's for sure. We'll be there for you, sister." Now it was Kat's turn for a hug. "We'll be there *with* you."

She smiled mischievously and added, "What do you say, sisters? How about we all go treasure hunting?"

LATER, DAIR COULDN'T REMEMBER leaving Willow Hill. Logan told him he walked right out the door and kept on walking—along sidewalks, up and down streets, right into traffic. Logan said he had to yank him out of the way of a freight wagon barreling down toward him on Throckmorton Street. After that, Logan took charge of the direction they headed and as a result, they ended up at a saloon in Fort Worth's Hell's Half Acre.

"Trace McBride used to own this place," Logan told him as they pushed through the saloon's swinging doors. "Unlike a lot of joints in the Acre, this saloon never watered its whiskey."

Moments later, Dair lifted his glass in salute and spoke his first words since leaving Willow Hill. "Selling good whiskey was the least Trace McBride could do considering that his daughters surely drove half the town to drink."

"I can drink to that," Jake Kimball said as he sauntered into the bar.

"Me, too," Luke Garrett agreed, waving to some old friends before snagging a bottle and glasses to join Dair and Logan at their table.

"I hope you're drinking a toast to your good luck in brides," Trace McBride groused as he straddled a chair next to Logan. "Not a one of you are good enough for my girls, you know."

"Yessir, we do." Luke winked at Jake. "In case we were inclined to forget, you remind us of it regular enough."

Dair banged his head on the table. "Just leave me alone."

"I can't do that," Trace said. "You made my Emma cry. Emma never cries."

Dair slowly lifted his head and met the older man's gaze head on. "So shoot me."

Logan shifted in his chair. "Now wait a minute."

Jake topped off his drink and murmured, "Don't worry. Leave it be, Grey."

Trace continued, "I oughta shoot you, that's for sure. Gallivanting all over the world with my daughter in tow, making her party to your schemes and scams. Accused of murder! My Emma. And don't think I don't know that the two of you have had supper before you said Grace."

Logan choked on his whiskey at that.

Trace didn't even pause. "Then you don't bother to tell her you're about to kick the bucket until she's gone and fallen in love with you. Nope, a bullet is too good for such a selfish bastard." He glanced over at Luke. "Does Texas still castrate criminals?"

"Can't say we ever did."

"Hmm. We could start. At the very least you need to be locked away in Huntsville." Trace looked at his lawman son-in-law. "Why haven't you arrested him?"

"Jake wants to buy him a pardon from the governor."

"No one is buying me anything." Dair banged his fist on the table. "You know what, old man? You're right, and nothing you can say will make me feel any worse than I already do. You said your piece, so leave me the hell alone. All of you."

"Fuck that," Jake said. "I'm your friend."

"And I'm the law in this town," Luke added. "You're a wanted man, and for Emma's sake I'm not going to arrest you, but I'm not letting you ride off into the sunset, either."

"You should have the surgery, Dair," Jake stated.

"Easy for you to say," Dair exploded. He whirled on Logan. "Tell him, Grey. Tell him about Jimbo."

Logan winced. "Dair..."

"Boy at the orphanage with us. His father dumped him on Nana Nellie one day. Horse had kicked him in the head. He couldn't talk, couldn't walk, couldn't eat. Nana had to do everything for him. He was fourteen years old and she changed his goddamned diapers. She worked herself to the bone. Damn near killed herself. Even Nana Nellie was glad the day poor Jimbo caught the croup and died, and she suffered with guilt for it for years afterward. I will *not,* by God, put Emma in that position."

Trace pursed his lips and nodded. "Have to say I respect you for that. Can't say I blame you for not wanting to get your head cut open, either. That's awful personal. It'd take a lot of guts for a man to literally put his life in a stranger's hands that way and you apparently don't have the balls for it."

"Goddammit!" Dair snapped.

"Of course, it's not like you have much control the way things are," Trace continued. "I mean, you have something growing in your head right now, and it could turn you into droolin' fool without a surgeon's knife ever gettin' near you."

Dair betrayed the slightest of shudders at that. It was his biggest fear, one he never verbalized and rarely acknowledged to himself.

Trace drummed his fingers on the table, his brow furrowed in thought. "I'm confused though. My Emma is one smart woman. She probably has more sense than anyone I know and better instincts than anyone, save my Jenny. Why the hell she would pick you to love is beyond me. But she did and there it is. And as much as I hate to admit it, you seem to care about her, too. You just need to wake up and realize it before it's too late."

"What the hell is that supposed to mean?"

"It means you had better figure out a way to make it right with her. Have the surgery or not. That's your choice and it's one I don't envy. But if you really love her, you'd best make the most of the time you have left."

"Enough, McBride. Hate me all you want, but you have no right to question my love for her."

"I have every right. I was there when she was born. I walked her down the aisle to marry Casey. I stood beside her the day she buried him. Do you think I relish the thought of going through that kind of hell again? But I'll have to, won't I? Because she'll be left alone again with no more than a memory. As much as it pains me to admit it, I'm not sure Emma will recover this time." He paused, sipped his drink, then said harshly, "She'll never risk her heart a third time. She'll just bury it with you."

Dair closed his eyes and shuddered. "I have to hope you're wrong. If you'd seen Nana Nellie with Jimbo…better a broken heart than a broken back."

"Broken hearts can kill a person, too," Luke observed. "Seems to me you're missing something when you go to chewing on this. What if the surgery cured you, MacRae? It doesn't have to end badly, you know."

"He has a point," Jake agreed. "Dammit, Dair. Can't you just think about it? Let Daggett contact the surgeon he knows. Find out more about it before you dismiss it entirely."

Dair shot a look at Logan. "What about you? Aren't you going to chastise me, too?"

"I can tell that you've already made up your mind. Stubborn as always. No sense trying to change what's carved in rock."

Disgust laced Jake's voice. "Now, there's a good friend."

"Would you do it?" Logan fired back.

Jake was silent for a moment. "I don't know. But I wouldn't just throw a chance into the discard pile without a second thought. Think about it, Dair. Mull the idea over. That won't hurt anything, will it?"

Dair had had enough. "Can't a man drink in peace in this town?"

"Not in this family," Luke observed dryly.

"I'm not family."

"You're my family," Jake declared. "You've been my brother for a lot of years already, MacRae, and now we up and fall in love with sisters. If that doesn't make us family, I don't know what does. Since we're being honest here, I have to tell you I'm pissed as hell that you didn't confide in me. That's no way to treat family."

"I'm sorry. I didn't want...this."

Jake arched a brow. "This?"

Pity. Pressure. Dair just shook his head and stared into his drink. *Emma, I'm so damned sorry.*

Trace drained his drink, then poured another. "So, it's decided. He'll mull it over. In the meantime, how about you tell us where we're headed?"

"Pardon me?" Dair set down his glass.

"Where do we start the treasure hunt?" At Dair's blank look, he added, "You didn't think we'd let you go without us, did you? The good news is we hadn't finished unpacking from the aborted Scotland trip yet, so it's a simple thing to load up and go."

"This isn't your concern."

"Sure it is. Like I told your knuckleheaded friend who is now my knuckleheaded son-in-law a few weeks back, I've battled this bad luck business off and on for a good part of my life, and though it took a bit of convincing, I believe in the Curse of Clan McBride. Bottom line is that a decade ago some spooky gal gave my girls their necklaces and my family has been riding the bad luck merry-go-round ever since. If I'm seeing an opportunity to climb off the ride, I'm darn sure going to make certain the McBrides take it."

It took all Dair's control not to take a swing at Emma's father. "Haven't you listened to a word I said? I'm not Emma's vigilant and true love. I can't be."

Logan studied his fingernails. "He thinks once he's dead, she'll fall for me, and Emma and I will be the ones to finally break the curse. Tried to tell him she wouldn't go for it, but…well…the man is sick. Guess we have to make allowances for blatant stupidity."

The other men simply stared at Dair. Then Luke asked, "That brain tumor must be parked on top of your good sense, huh?"

"Dumb as a box of rocks. My girls sure know how to pick 'em." Trace drummed his fingers against the table. "So, what's the schedule? We catching the six o'clock train?"

Dair pounded the table with his fist. "Listen to me. We are not doing anything. Logan and I are going after a killer."

"And the knuckleheads and I are going with you."

Dair drained his whiskey, poured another, and drained it. Jake shook his head. "Do yourself a favor, MacRae, and don't try to fight it. He's as stubborn as a two-headed mule."

"Emma gets it from you, then."

Luke sighed. "Maribeth is a chip off the old block."

"Kat is her daddy through and through," Jake added with a grimace.

"It makes a man proud to turn out such fine women," Trace said with a grin. "So, tell us more about this killer. From what I gather from what Emma said, he's evil, cunning, and invisible as a ghost. How do you expect to find him?'

"By finding the Sisters' Prize. If I do that, then I expect he'll find me."

"He has a good head start on you," Jake observed. "Maybe he's already found it."

"Perhaps." Dair toyed with his glass. "If that's the case, I expect I'll find signs of it. With any luck I'll be able to track him from those."

"Luck?" Trace scoffed. "I hope you have a backup plan. Remember who you're dealing with."

"The Bad Luck Brides," Luke clarified.

At that, a frightening thought occurred. "They're not coming along!"

"No!" said Trace.

"Absolutely not," added Luke.

"Over my dead body," Jake declared.

Logan lifted his glass in a toast. "Gentlemen, to hopeless causes."

East Texas

THE PUNGENT SCENT OF PINE swirled in the evening breeze as Hamish Campbell stepped from the cover of the forest and approached the dilapidated cabin. His shoulders were slumped, his footsteps weary following another day of fruitless searching.

He hadn't expected it to be this difficult. He'd thought the engravings on the necklace would point the way. So far, he'd found nothing but disappointment.

He hated Texas. Detested the stifling summer heat. Despised the sorry excuse for shelter this cabin offered. As he climbed the porch steps to the cabin, frustration hummed in his veins. He wanted to throw something, to destroy something, but common sense prevailed. Temper had cost him thirty years ago. He wouldn't repeat the mistake today.

As it happened each time he walked into the cabin, his gaze fell upon a particular spot in front of the fireplace. He could see it all clearly in his mind's eye.

Roslin MacRae sat reading a story to her son as Hamish

stepped inside the cabin. Startled, she stood up, shoving her son behind her skirts. "You."

So, so beautiful. "Hello, luv."

"Get out of my house. Immediately!"

"Now, now, my darling. I've only just arrived. I can't leave yet. Not without what I've come for."

"I'll kill you before I let you touch me."

"Such passion. Such life. You stir me, woman. We'll get to that, but first...I want the Sisters' Prize."

Her beautiful eyes momentarily widened with alarm, though she quickly tried to hide her reaction. With that, any doubt Hamish had of the treasure's existence was laid to rest. He stepped closer, his blood running hot with lust both for treasure and for the treasure's guardian.

The bitch denied him both. When he attempted to use her son against her, seizing him, placing his hands around the boy's throat and squeezing, she used the cursed dagger once again. Fate steered its path and the blade sank into his shoulder, rather than his heart as she so obviously intended.

Pain enraged him. Hamish lost his temper and made a foolish mistake. He'd turned the guardian's dagger upon her and lost his chance at the Prize.

"Until now," he murmured. True, he'd yet to find the treasure he sought, but he had time. All the time in the world. He'd taken care of the only two people who might have interfered.

The Black Widow and the Highland Riever were certainly in the hands of the Scottish authorities by now.

EMMA AND DAIR BOARDED THE six o'clock train headed east along with her parents, her sisters, their spouses and children, and Dair's friend Logan. Tye and Claire cancelled their plans to come along at the last minute when their youngest broke his arm. An hour into the trip, Emma still couldn't believe she was actually onboard. She'd had absolutely no intention of continuing the search for the Sisters' Prize. Nevertheless, here she was.

The following day, she had every intention of staying at the hotel in Nacogdoches to help Jenny care for Mari's and Kat's children while their mothers accompanied their fathers to the cabin where Dair expected to solve the murder mystery. Instead, she found herself riding a rented horse through the Piney Woods of East Texas.

At least she wasn't forced to ride with Dair. After a heated discussion amongst everyone but her, he, Jake and Luke had ridden on ahead. They planned to scope out the situation, and, if necessary, deal with the villain long before the women arrived.

Emma and Dair hadn't spoken since she'd ordered him from Willow Hill the day before. He'd made a halfhearted attempt to approach her once but didn't persist when she turned away. Her attitude frustrated her sisters, she knew, but Emma didn't care. Neither did she concern herself over the men's obvious disgust with Dair's lack of action. She needed all her energy just to keep moving.

With any luck, this misbegotten adventure would end today. Early this morning, Papa found out some interesting information at the café. It seems that a couple months ago completely out of the blue, the owners of the acreage where Dair once lived received an offer for their land well above market price. The new owner was a Scotsman named Hamish Campbell. He'd made a good impression upon the citizens of Nacogdoches during his bi-weekly supply visits. He claimed to be a poet who sought the peace and privacy of the woods to practice his craft. He'd visited town just last week, and as far as anyone knew, he'd be at his new place today.

The closest Emma and Dair came to communicating was the moment her father uttered Hamish Campbell's name. Dair's gaze had flown to hers before he said, "It was his town house I won in a card game. That's how he stole Emma's necklace. The house probably had some secrets I didn't know about. It always did give me some strange feelings."

"What else do you know about him?" her father had asked.

Dair thought a moment, then responded, "Nothing. Other than that card game, I never had any dealings with him."

Her sisters, Papa and Logan had spent much of the ride from town speculating on how Campbell might be connected to the Sisters' Prize. Emma didn't comment. She couldn't bring herself to care.

They found Luke posted as lookout at the turnoff to the cabin. "He's not here," he told her father when they rode up. "He's been here recently, however. The place has obviously been searched."

"Any sign of Emma's necklace?" Kat asked.

When Luke gave a negative shake of his head, Mari glanced at Emma, then asked, "How is Dair?"

Luke hesitated a long moment before replying, "He says he's fine. I have my doubts."

Emma just shut her eyes.

Trace removed his hat, smoothed back his hair, then returned his hat to his head. He and Logan shared a look before he said, "We'll go back to town, then. The women can continue the treasure hunt once Campbell has been apprehended."

"That's a good idea," Luke agreed.

Kat and Mari simply rode on. Logan laughed. "Y'all don't have a lick of say-so over those women, do you?"

"Upon rare occasions we do," Trace protested.

Kat glanced back over her shoulder. "We're not stupid, Mr. Grey. If we thought it was truly dangerous we wouldn't go, but we have plenty of protection. Besides, I still think everything is destined to turn out fine. I still believe my sisters and I are going to break the curse."

They arrived at a small dog-trot style cabin a few minutes later. Jake stood guard on the front porch. Dair was nowhere to be seen. "I didn't figure you'd be able to turn them back," Jake said.

Luke shrugged. "Maybe they'll find the treasure right away and we can get that part of this behind us."

Everyone dismounted while Mari quizzed her husband about the search. "The cabin is small, Mari," Luke told her. "MacRae went over every inch of it and didn't see anything."

"Where is he now?"

"Around back," Jake responded. "He's going over the outside of the cabin with a careful eye."

"So he's not worried that this Hamish Campbell already found the Sisters' Prize?" Kat confirmed.

"It doesn't look like it, honey."

"I didn't think so because we're the ones who are destined to find it." She looped her arms through Mari and Emma's arms. "Right, sisters?"

"That's right," Mari declared. Emma's only response was to ask Jake, "Any sign of my necklace?"

"'Fraid not." Luke scanned the tree line, ever on guard. "I suspect we'll find it on him when we find him."

"All right then, let's get to it." Kat pulled pieces of notepaper from her pocket and passed one to everyone. "This is what the design we're hunting for looks like. It could be anywhere, it will be permanent, but probably obscured."

Dair came around the corner of the cabin holding a small framed picture in his hand. His gaze went right to Emma, then slid away. He spoke to Trace. "I might have found something."

"What is it?"

"A watercolor of a cottage. I think it's my mother's home back in Scotland, but I'm not positive. I just know...there's something about it. It's important. I don't know why and I don't know how, but I feel in my gut that it's something we should pay attention to."

"You think it's a clue to the treasure's whereabouts?" Trace asked.

"Maybe. Problem is I can't see it now and I can't remember what, if anything, my mother said about it."

"May I see it?" Kat asked.

Wordlessly, Dair handed her the painting. Emma couldn't help but glance at it. It was a charming picture, a country cottage with stone walls and a thatched roof. Flowers grew in abundance in the yard. Swirling circles of lavender and pink, yellow and white. Emma studied the painting, and then the dogtrot cabin. She didn't see a resemblance between the two.

Mari peered over Kat's shoulder. "Maybe the clue is something that's missing rather than something that's there."

"That's a thought," Trace said. "What do you think, MacRae? Something missing from the picture?"

"I simply don't know."

"Or maybe it's the brushstrokes," Kat suggested. "I've read about painters who hide secret messages in their paintings by the brushstrokes."

"It's a watercolor, Kat," Mari said. "They don't exactly have brushstrokes like an oil painting does."

"There still could be a hidden message."

Dair shook his head. "I don't think…wait." He took the painting from Kat's hands and stared at it hard. "It's the colors."

He turned away and strode up the porch steps and into the kitchen side of the cabin. Mari and Kat glanced at each other, then started to follow, Kat grabbing Emma's hand and pulling her along, too. Emma considered resisting, but decided making a fuss would only delay matters.

Inside, Dair had hung the picture back on the wall. He stood with his legs spread, his arms folded, studying a blank spot on the wall opposite the cottage painting. "It was here," he said. "A wooden shelf with a plain glass vase and flower."

"Was that the treasure?" Kat asked.

"No…" Dair grimaced, closed his eyes and shook his head. "It's a…"

"Clue?" Mari suggested.

"Key." Dair opened his eyes. "A key. Something about a key."

The sisters remained quiet, giving him an opportunity to think. Dair continued to stare at the blank spot on the wall for a long minute. Finally, he let out a sigh. "I don't know. I don't remember anything else. Look, I think we should keep searching. Maybe I'll find something else that will jog my memory."

Without waiting for comment, he walked out onto the porch and addressed Emma's father. "I've divided up the surrounding property into search areas. There are eight of us. If we search by pairs and have two lookouts at all times, it should be safe enough. Do you agree?"

"Sounds like a plan." Trace looked at Logan. "I reckon our range detective would suit as one lookout. I'll be the other."

Emma sent a pleading glance to Mari who rolled her eyes, then said, "Dair, can I search with you?"

Looking tired and worn, he nodded. "Sure."

Kat snorted with disgust. "Then I get Luke. I'm not very happy with my husband today. I caught him slipping candy to the children last night at bedtime. After they brushed their teeth!"

"One time won't hurt them," Jake protested. "Yesterday was a very long day and they were good on the train. They deserved a reward."

Once the marital bickering eased, Dair pointed out the search areas he'd put together. "In addition to the mark, we are looking for signs of a prior search. We can't neglect the fact that Hamish Campbell might have some information we don't."

Next, the men discussed danger signals and agreed to a rendezvous place and time that would allow Mari and Kat to return to the hotel in plenty of time to feed their children their lunches. Emma intended to go with them. Her sisters planned to return for an afternoon treasure-hunting session if the Prize hadn't yet been located by that time. Emma hoped that could be avoided.

The group broke up into pairs and Emma joined Jake in an examination of the area they'd been assigned. She paid attention and put effort into her search. The sooner the treasure was found or the possibility of finding it eliminated, the sooner she could put this part of her life behind her.

She was studying a carving in the trunk of an old oak tree when she heard Mari's worried voice call, "Jake? Luke? Emma?"

"Yeah," Luke called. "We're here, honey."

Seconds later, Mari rushed into view. "Emma. You have to come. Dair is…hurting."

Her heart twisted. "Where is he?"

"I helped him back to the cabin. I'd stay, but Emma, I have to go back to town." She gestured toward her breasts. "It's time to feed the babies."

Emma rushed toward the cabin, a lump the size of a peach in her throat. She couldn't bear this. She couldn't. She couldn't.

She burst into the cabin. He sat at a wooden table, his elbows propped on his knees, his head buried in his hands. "Dair."

"Go away, Emma. I don't want you here."

The tears now always so near the surface, swelled and spilled. Behind her, her father said, "Emmaline?"

"It's okay, Papa. I'll take care of him. I know what to do."

In short order, her sisters and their husbands left to attend to responsibilities in town. Papa and Logan stayed behind, continuing their watchdog role while Emma did her best to make Dair comfortable. She coaxed him to move to the bed in the other room where she then sat with his head in her lap. She stroked his hair, his brow, his face, whispering in a soothing tone. "Please, God. Protect him. Be all right, Dair. Please, be all right."

"Better with you," he murmured. "Always, better with you."

She lifted her hand long enough to brush away the tears from her cheek. Then, unable to help herself, she leaned over and kissed his temple. "Dair."

He opened pain-clouded eyes. "It's different this time, Texas. Pain is…pressure." Dread filled her as he added,

"If…hell…Jimbo. Kill me if Jimbo. Tell Grey. Want promise."

Emma began to pray. Tears continued to roll down her cheeks as she rocked back and forth. On Dair's head, her touch remained gentle. The hand resting on his arm made a white-knuckled fist.

Then, from outside, she heard a frantic shout.

CHAPTER EIGHTEEN

WITH THE FORCE IN HIS head increasing with every second, Dair needed every ounce of strength and grit within him to remain aware of his surroundings. When the cabin door opened and Logan half carried, half dragged Trace McBride inside, he fought to sit up.

"Papa." Emma scrambled to help her father. "What happened?"

"Cougar," Logan said, sitting Trace on the bed even as Dair struggled to rise and get out of the way. He saw jagged tears in Trace McBride's skin all down his arm and across his back as Logan finished, "Clawed him pretty good. Teeth got him in a couple of places, too."

Trace's voice was labored. "Stumbled across her kits, I think. Wasn't paying attention. Found a knife buried in a tree trunk. Looking at that."

Logan frowned grimly. "He's bleeding badly back here on his shoulder."

"Keep pressure on the wound," Emma instructed as she hurriedly rummaged through a dresser drawer. She removed a fine linen shirt and tried ineffectually to rip it.

"Here." Logan drew a knife from inside his boot and sliced the shirt in two. "Sounds like this helped cause the trouble, so now it can be of some help."

As Emma dampened the shirt with water from a pitcher, Dair noticed the blade his friend set on the bedside table. The pressure in his head escalated as his gaze locked on the dagger.

"Oh, Papa, you're a mess." Emma gently dabbed at Trace's wounds, washing away dirt and blood, wincing at her father's gasps of pain.

The dagger. What was it about the dagger? Some thought, some knowledge, hovered just beyond his reach, but then a great wave of pain washed over him. Distracted him. When he reached for the bedside table to steady himself, Logan touched his arm. "You all right, MacRae?" Then, "Oh, hell. You have another headache."

Dair allowed his silence to answer as he stared down at the knife beside his hand, focusing on its jeweled hilt—emerald, sapphire, bloodred ruby.

Bloodred ruby. The haze over Dair's vision thickened and he swayed. He was vaguely aware of Emma as she wrapped a long strip of shirt around her father's torso and tied it tightly. She stepped away from the bed and stood watching the older man while gnawing at her bottom lip. "He's bleeding too much. He needs a doctor."

Logan rubbed the back of his neck. "He can't ride, and I hate to leave you here. Campbell could turn up at any time."

Dair dragged his gaze away from the knife and worked to force words up through his throat and past his lips. "Go. Take Emma."

Indecision painted Logan's face. He rubbed the back of his neck. "Dair, you're in no shape…"

"Don't waste time, Logan," she declared. "I'm not leaving them. I won't go. You must go. Quickly. Papa needs help fast."

Logan hesitated only a moment before nodding once. "I'll ride hard and I'll be back with the sawbones quick as a minute. In the meantime, y'all keep your guard up." To Dair, he said, "You able to shoot, MacRae?"

Dair gritted his teeth, nodded carefully. Moving his head almost made him pass out, but damn it, he wouldn't let her down.

Once Logan rode out, Emma grabbed another shirt from the dresser drawer and ripped it into bandages also. She clicked her tongue over the bright red blood staining the white bandage wrapped around her father's shoulder. "Oh, dear. Papa, it's not tight enough. I want to tie it again. Dair can you help me? Dair?" She looked over at him. "Oh, Dair. You're no better than Papa. You'd better sit down."

"I'm fine," he managed, barely. "How can I help?"

Her worried gaze searched his face, then she handed him a folded pad of linen. She sounded as if she were far away from him as she said, "Press this against the wound and hold it in place while I tie the bandage tighter around Papa's shoulder, all right?"

Dair did as she requested, and as he stood over Trace McBride, the scent of blood surrounded him, sank into his pores, smothered him. He stood frozen, his brain pounding…pounding…pounding.

"That's good." Her voice was faint against the roar in his head. "Thank you."

He backed away as Emma tended her father and looked at his bloody hand. Instead of a man's hand, he saw the bloodstained fingers of a child.

"No." Dair staggered back another step, then turned away. A roaring sound filled his head. He should leave. He needed to leave here. He glanced around the cabin wildly until his gaze fell upon the dagger. Narrowed to pinpricks on the jeweled hilt. In his mind's eye, he saw a flash of a dark-haired woman. *Pretty stones,* said a boy's voice. *Blue. Green. Red.*

Bloodred.

Bloodred.

God, his head. Pressure. Building. More, more, more.

A woman's voice from far away, "Papa? Papa!"

Mama.

Pounding...pounding...pounding.

Dair brought his hands up, pressed his palms against his temples. *Stop. Please, God. Make it stop.*

He jerked his head around to stare at the four corners of the small room. Where was he? This was right, but still wrong. Acting on instinct alone, he moved from the bedroom across the covered breezeway into the cabin's second room. *You must find her.*

He heard a sound. A scream? Emma!

Safe. She's safe. Tending her father.

A boy cried, "Mother!"

Pounding...pounding...pounding.

The stink of blood beckoned him. Fear fluttered in his knees. He held on to his sanity by a thread. Something was wrong. He needed to protect her. Emma. Mama. He needed to save her.

Use the knife.

A red-tinged mist clouded his mind. Past, present, future, swirling together in the haze inside his head.

Pain throbbed. Pounded. Dair glanced toward the stone fireplace to see the dark-haired woman lying prone on the floor, her blue eyes wide and sightless, a spreading pool of blood beneath her.

Pounding...pounding...pounding.

"Dair! I need you. Dair!"

Emma.

He lifted a bloodstained finger to his temple, traced the faint scar. The knife. Not a knife. A dirk. This dirk. This same Highlander's dagger buried in his mother's heart.

Pressure...building...building...building...

"Dair! Please! Help me!"

Emma. He fought his way through the pain. Back. Back to Emma.

He moved on sluggish feet away from the image in his mind and back to reality in the room across the breezeway. Emma no longer stood beside her wounded father. He jerked his head around, ignoring the crush of pain. Trace, his eyes closed, his body still on the bed.

Emma, her back against the man who restrained her with one arm around her waist and the jeweled dirk to her throat. Gray hair...but that was wrong. Black. It should be black like his. Eyes. Gray eyes. *Mine?* His.

Pain and pressure. Pounding...pounding...pounding.

The Scottish burr flew like an arrow out of Dair's past. "Hold still, m'dear, or I'll gut you like a mackerel."

Burst. Like water through a broken dam, memories gushed into Dair's consciousness. Past and present slipped into their proper places as the mist cleared. The pain disappeared as though it had never been. The memories...the horrible, terrible memories...remained.

Dair met Hamish Campbell's gray-eyed gaze and said, "Hamish Campbell, I presume?"

"Why don't you use the more appropriate term? You should call me Father."

EMMA GASPED. *HIS FATHER?*

Dair entered the room slowly, his expression cold and distant. His gaze, however, was razor-sharp, and Emma felt a rush of relief. His headache must be gone. Good. Although, that changed her plan. She'd followed Campbell's instructions and called him because if this headache had followed the path of the others, he wouldn't have responded. She'd figured Campbell would drag her toward the doorway and thus closer to the rocking chair where Logan had left her father's gun. She'd hoped to distract him with a scream, then lunge for the weapon.

Instead, he was standing tall and strong and stable, not sparing her a glance as he shrugged casually and said, "You may be the sonofabitch who raped my mother, but you are not my father."

Oh, Dair, Emma thought.

Campbell's silver eyes went warm. "You're wrong. It wasn't rape. Roslin wanted me, she always did. Not that brawny farmer she'd agreed to marry. David Gordon had nothing to offer her. Nothing! I did her a favor when I arranged for his accident."

"So you did kill him. My mother wondered about that."

"I loved her, and she'd have loved me, too, if not for him."

"You're insane."

"No. My beautiful Roslin…she's the one who couldn't see clearly. Because of the Prize. Because she was the guardian. She thought I wanted the treasure, but I didn't even know it existed then. It was her I wanted. It was always Roslin. I never quit looking for her after she disappeared from Scotland. I didn't even know about the Prize until I happened across a painting of that unique dagger of hers in a book and asked Robbie Potter to translate the text for me. I was thrilled when I traced her to Texas. I loved her!"

"She hated you."

"No! She didn't understand we were meant to be together. Besides, you can't know how your mother felt. You were a young child."

"I've read the letters she wrote to a friend back in Scotland."

Bess, Emma thought. His mother must have written to Bess.

"I know exactly how she felt about you and about my father."

Emma darted her gaze toward her father. He wasn't moving. Oh, God. She had to get to him fast!

Dair came a step closer and Campbell shifted his hand, angling the knife so that the point rested just above her heart, ready to plunge. "Tell me where the treasure is, MacRae, or she's dead. I've earned it. You know I'll not hesitate to kill."

"Let her go, Campbell. She needs to tend to her father. You and I can discuss this outside."

The villain's hold upon her remained tight. "No, I think we'll do it here." The knife tip poked through her dress, into her skin.

"I don't know where the treasure is," Dair snapped, moving two steps to the right.

"Yes, you do." Hamish shifted also, turning to keep Emma in place as his shield. "Don't play this game, son. It's making me angry. You more than anyone should know what a fearsome thing my anger can be. Roslin would be alive today if she hadn't sparked my anger by throwing that dagger at me, using it against me again, just like she had the night I made love to her."

"The night you raped her. And I am not your son!"

"Yes, you are." The Scotsman smiled and said softly, "She told me so as she lay dying. She also told me you knew how to find the Prize. I suspect she thought the news would prevent me from killing you. She didn't realize I thought I already had. I knocked you hard into the fireplace. Your head hit the stone with a thunk."

Emma's pulse pounded. She glanced significantly toward her father's gun, hoping Dair would get her message and distract him enough so that she could dive for the weapon.

"It was quite a surprise when you sat down at my card table in Edinburgh," Campbell continued. "It was like looking at myself in a mirror thirty years ago. Then when you said your name, mentioned Texas, I knew. You look just like me."

"David Gordon was your cousin. I look like him."

Did Dair see Papa's gun on the chair? She stared at him hard, willing him to see it.

"You lost the town house to me on purpose, didn't you?" Dair asked coldly, taking another step right. "You had me followed."

"Don't move another inch!" The arm holding Emma tightened its grip. "Tell me where the treasure is!"

"Let Emma go." For the first time since entering the room, Dair gazed directly at her. He had a message in his eyes, but what was it?

"That would be a foolish move on my part. You love her, don't you, son? You'll give me the Sisters' Prize to save her. A man will do anything to protect his lover."

"As will fathers," came a pain-wracked voice from behind them.

Papa, Emma thought just as a deafening blast ripped through the air.

Force propelled Emma forward, knocking her to the floor. A silent scream welled up inside her when blood and bits of matter spattered against her like dirty rain. Dazed, trapped by a heavy weight, she couldn't move. What…?

Then the weight was ripped off her, and she was swept up into Dair's arms. His voice shaking, desperate, he demanded, "Emma, are you hurt? Emma? Are you shot?"

Unable to force a word past her throat, she shook her head.

"Oh, God. Thank God." Nevertheless, his frantic fingers searched her. Then the tension he'd held at bay shuddered out of him as he clutched her hard against him. He cursed and groaned and muttered, "I thought you'd been hit…I thought…you went down…oh, God. I love you, Emma."

"Love you." Though it felt like forever, mere seconds passed before panic lifted the fog from Emma's mind and she cried, "Papa."

She and Dair turned simultaneously to her father. Dair spat a curse and Emma's heart dropped to her feet. Her father lay on his back, his eyes closed, his complexion ashen. Blood ran steadily from the wound across his shoulder, turning the bedsheet red beneath him. They flew to help him, working together quickly to staunch the flow of blood. She didn't have time to think or to acknowledge her terror.

She lost track of how long they waited with her father. She blocked out everything but the desperate effort to keep him alive. At some point—whether minutes or hours she couldn't say—Emma vaguely noted the pound of horses' hooves, the thunder of boots on the dogtrot, her mother's frightened cry at her first sight of Trace. When the doctor stepped up to the bedside, Dair gently pulled Emma away. "C'mon, Texas. Let the doctor do his job."

He escorted her toward the door where her sisters hovered, their expressions anxious. Mari took a handkerchief from her pocket and tears spilled from her eyes as she cleaned Emma's face. Then the three sisters fell into one another's arms, crying, questioning and keeping vigil for the first man all of them had loved.

DAIR NODDED TO LOGAN. "Help me drag the carcass out of the way, would you?"

The two men dragged Hamish Campbell's corpse from the room and dumped it on the ground behind the cabin. Logan nodded toward a golden chain that had fallen from the dead man's shirt pocket. "Look at that."

Dair picked up Emma's ruby pendant. The chain was dirty and dulled with blood, and he spared the corpse not a glance as he carried the necklace toward the shallow, clear creek that flowed behind the house. He knelt on one knee and dipped the jewelry into the water, then used a handkerchief from his pocket to clean it with a careful hand.

Jake Kimball spoke from behind him. "You ready to talk about it?"

No. "How is the old man?"

"He's a mess," Luke Garrett said. "Lost a lot of blood. The doctor's stitching him up now."

"He'll make it?"

"Yeah," Jake said. "Too damned ornery not to. But he's weak as a sick kitten, and he'll need to keep his ass in bed. The doctor says y'all saved his life by keeping pressure on the shoulder."

"What happened in there, MacRae?" Luke asked.

For a long moment, Dair didn't speak, but instead focused on the task of cleaning the necklace. He didn't want to talk about what had happened. Didn't want to think about it. Yet he could think of nothing else.

"He put a knife to Emma's throat," he confessed in a low tone. "Demanded I tell him where to find the treasure or he'd kill her."

Luke, Jake and Logan all muttered foul curses.

"Trace played possum on the bed, thank God, and he had a pistol stashed in his boot. Soon as he had a clear shot, he took it."

"As a father-in-law, Trace McBride might be a pain in the ass, but he'll damn sure go to the wall for his loved ones," Jake said.

Luke nodded, then asked, "So who was this piece of vermin? Emma babbled something to her sisters about a family connection?"

"He goddamned wasn't my father!" Dair snapped. "My mother was already pregnant when he attacked her." He told the other men an abbreviated version of the story, completing the puzzle in his own mind as he talked. "I'm not positive how he found us in Texas, but I suspect he tracked us through my mother's family. We lived with her uncle the first couple years, I recall. Then he died and his widow returned to Scotland."

Luke asked about the necklace. "He was able to steal Emma's necklace because he knew the house," Dair replied, rubbing his thumb over the engravings on the stone. *Damned voyeur.* "He admitted to having me watched, which must be how he learned about the Highland Riever. I think he set the law on us because he didn't want us getting to the treasure before him."

"How do you know all of this?"

Dair glanced up at the sound of the voice to see that Logan had joined the other two men in the conversation. He carried a shovel propped over one shoulder and held two others in his left hand. Dair met his gaze and slowly shook his head. "I remembered it, Lucky. Believe it or not, I remembered everything."

"Everything?" the men asked simultaneously.

"Almost everything." Dair nodded slowly. "I need to see that watercolor again."

EMMA SAT ON THE FRONT PORCH steps of the cabin, a sister on either side, eavesdropping on the conversation between their parents as it drifted through the cabin's open window. Now that was a love that was powerful, vigilant and true, she thought as she heard her mother's soft laughter in response to one of her father's silly comments. Theirs was the kind of love she'd always dreamed of having herself.

Concentrating on her parents, she startled when she heard Dair ask, "Will you walk with me, Emma?"

Glancing toward the sound, she saw the other men round the corner of the cabin behind Dair. They must have finished burying the body.

"Walk?" she repeated, her dismay evident. She was exhausted. All she wanted to do was go back to the hotel and take a bath and crawl into bed and pull the covers up over her head.

He offered her a tender smile. "A short walk. It isn't far."

"What isn't far?"

He moved to stand in front of her, then he held out his hand. "Please?"

Still, she hesitated. He had a purposeful look about

him, as if he had something of import to discuss. Emma simply didn't think she had the energy for import. "I'm tired, Dair."

"All right, then. I'll carry you." Before she quite knew what had happened, he'd lifted her up into his arms and strode away from the cabin.

Emma had no more energy to struggle than she did for an important discussion, so she decided she might as well settle back and enjoy the moment. After all, how many such opportunities might she have left?

Dair didn't speak as he carried her through the forest. Emma closed her eyes and rested her head against his shoulder. The anger that had simmered in her heart since their visit to Dr. Daggett had evaporated sometime between the knife and the gunshot. Now she was…empty. No more anger. No frustration. No hope.

"Here we are." He set her down on a patch of green grass no larger than five steps across. It was a curious spot, surrounded by trees but sunny and lush. Patches of wildflowers encircled the circumference of the plot, but other than nature's beauty, Emma saw nothing to distinguish the spot from any other in the forest.

"What is this place?"

"Look at the flowers, Emma. They're the same flowers that are depicted in the painting of my mother's cottage. The same flowers that she always kept in the vase that sat on the shelf in the cabin. Fresh flowers even in winter."

"I don't understand."

"This is a magical spot. A fairy ring. My mother told me that speaking the truth here within the boundaries of the ring will gain me life's greatest treasure."

"The Sisters' Prize?"

"No. A treasure greater than that. I've some things I need to say to you, Emma. Will you listen?"

She couldn't speak past the lump of nervousness in her throat, so she nodded. Dair gave her hand a squeeze, then said, "First I need to explain what happened. Those things I spoke of with Campbell…"

Suddenly, her fatigue intensified. "It doesn't matter, Dair."

"I didn't lie, Emma. I didn't know. I didn't remember any of it until today. Let me tell you what happened."

He told her a fantastic story about the pain in his head and a dam burst of memories. As he talked about his mother's murder, a seed of an idea took root in Emma's mind and grew until it flowered into hope. She drew a shaky breath and asked, "The memories were locked away in your mind all these years?"

"Yes. I guess the events of that night were too much for a child to deal with so I buried them."

Emma's pulse rate doubled as her mind raced. "And you started having your headaches when, Dair? About a year ago, right? After you played cards with Hamish Campbell?"

He hesitated. "Yes."

She clasped her hands. "Dair, what if that's it? Is it possible that the headaches were brought on by the blocked memories trying to get out? What if the doctors were wrong and you're really not dying?"

Hope flickered briefly in his eyes, then he smiled sadly, reaching out to trail a finger down her cheek. "It's a nice thought, Texas, but I'm afraid that's too easy. If it were only a headache, I might buy it, but the tremors, the vomiting, the vision problems—those are all real."

"But—"

He placed a finger against her lips. "Shush, now, and

listen. It doesn't matter. You've been right all along and I've been a close-minded fool. Here's the proof."

He reached into his pocket and drew out her necklace. Emma gasped when she saw it and warmed with pleasure. "Where did you find it?"

"Where doesn't matter. Ask me why I found it and I'll tell you Fate decreed I should. The necklace drives home a point for me. What were the odds that we'd find your necklace after it was stolen? What were the odds I'd meet you and recognize the ruby's engravings when I recalled nothing else about my life with my mother? What were the odds that Jake would dream about Kat's necklace years before he met her, that they'd eventually fall in love? What were the odds that Mari would follow the mention of Kat's necklace in a letter on an odyssey that would lead her to love with Luke Garrett? And going back to the very beginning, what were the odds that you and your sisters would go looking for a gypsy fortune-teller and find a Scotswoman with intimate knowledge of your family's history?"

"You make it sound fantastical."

"That's because it is fantastical. The odds of all that happening are incredibly, impossibly long. Fate had a hand in all of this, Emma."

Her heart quickened. "What are you saying?"

"Outlaws are always gamblers, and I learned early on to figure odds. When I moved past my own fear and really looked at all these long odds, I realized I'd be a fool not to put my money on the trend."

Tenderly, he cupped her cheek. "I love you, Emma Tate. You are the woman of my dreams, the mistress of my heart, the mate for my soul. My past is a swamp of mean motives and dirty deeds, and I'll never be able to atone for the things I've done, but fate brought you into my life, offering me a chance for redemption. Your love can be my salvation, Emma. If I'll allow it to be. That's where the strength part comes in. It takes a powerful love to get me past my fears. But we have that, don't we?"

Tremulously, she nodded. She couldn't get words past the lump in her throat. She didn't want to hope, didn't dare.

"I'm shamed to admit that in that cesspool of my past, I've been less than genuine with women. False words of love and affection tumbled from my tongue with nary a second thought. But with you, Emma, I speak from my heart. My love for you is genuine. It's real. It's true love. As, I believe, is your love for me."

"It is," she insisted, blinking back tears. "It is."

He slipped the necklace over her head and around her neck. The pendant settled between her breasts. He picked it up, held it, rubbed his thumb across the ruby's engravings. "That brings us to vigilant, doesn't it? Vigilant means keeping careful watch for possible danger or difficulties. You've been vigilant, Emma. You did everything within your power to protect our love from the danger that threatens it. I was the one who failed this test. I wanted to be in control. I was wrong and I see that now. From this moment on, I, too, will be vigilant of our love. I will protect it from danger." He paused, sucked in a breath, then blew it out in a rush. "I'll go see the surgeon that doctor of yours recommends."

Emma clasped her hands below her chin. "You'll have the surgery?"

He let out a shuddering breath. "If the doctor thinks I should, then yes. I'll roll the dice, Texas. I'll bet those long odds. I'll put my trust in fate and faith and give up my effort to control. I'll do it for you. I'll do it for us."

"Oh, Dair." She threw herself against him, wrapped her arms around his waist and squeezed tight. "I love you. I love you so much."

She lifted her face for his kiss and their lips met in a melding of emotion, a joining of souls, that wordlessly conveyed the truths in their hearts. They loved. Tears so seldom spilled welled in her eyes and overflowed.

Emma rested her head against his chest, drawing comfort and strength from his embrace. "Your mother was right. This fairy ring is a magical place, Dair. For the rest of my life, I'll treasure the memory of this moment and I'll hold—"

She broke off abruptly. *Fairy ring. Treasure. Hold.*

"What is it, Emma? What's wrong?"

"That woman, the friend of your mother's."

"Bess?"

Emma's heart pounded. Her mouth went dry. "Remember what she said? She said 'Roslin once told me that if a McBride and MacRae ever came to me, I was to pass along this message. The fairy ring holds the key.' Do you think...?"

"The Sisters' Prize," Dair breathed, his eyes alight with speculation. He gave her a quick, hard kiss, then knelt on one knee at the very center of the circle of grass, pulled the Guardian's dirk from a sheath on his belt and started digging.

Quickly, Dair's efforts uncovered a flat rock about the size of a dinner plate. As he brushed away the brown dirt, she spied the carving on the rock. Her hand clutched her necklace. "It's the symbol!"

"It's the X that marks the spot in the 'Land of Beginning Again.'" Dair lifted the rock to reveal a foot-deep hole lined in wood. At the bottom of the hole rested a small gold box. Three jewels decorated the box—a sapphire, an emerald and a ruby.

"The treasure!" she exclaimed, dropping to her knees beside him. "You found the treasure!"

Dair lifted the jeweled box from the cache and handed it to Emma. "Open it, Texas."

Her hands trembled. "My sisters should be here. We all should be together to find the Sisters' Prize."

"Ordinarily, I'd agree, but not today. This was meant for us, Emma. I feel it in my bones."

She sensed it, too, so holding her breath, she opened the box. "A key?"

"And a letter."

Emma lifted the note. "Oh, my. Your name is on it, Dair."

Dair blew out a breath, accepted the envelope from her, and opened it. As he read, a grin spread across his face. "Well, I'll be hanged. The Guardian was no fool. Though she considered a fairy circle secure enough to protect the treasure's key, she thought the wealth itself should reside in a more substantive place. The key fits a lock in a bank box, Emma."

"A bank? Where?"

He rolled his tongue around his cheek. "Fort Worth National."

"Oh, my God. Your mother put the treasure in a bank? What an intelligent woman."

"She was the Guardian." Dair rose, then reached for her hand and tugged her to her feet. Placing his finger beneath her chin, he gazed deeply into her eyes. "She protected that which was important—both the prize and me. I'm taking that lesson to heart. Emma, I need you to do something for me. Something that will be difficult."

Wariness entered her eyes. "What?"

"I need you to recognize that you are on the verge of

breaking the Curse of Clan McBride. You have found a love that is powerful, vigilant and true."

"I have. We have. That's not difficult to admit."

"No. The hard part comes with the task. Emma, on the train ride to East Texas, Mari explained her theory about the tasks Roslin of Strathardle mentioned."

"That she needed to find herself, Kat to forgive herself, and me to free myself." Emma shrugged. "I've done that, Dair. I'm finally free of my past."

"Yes, now you are, but will you remain that way?"

"What do you mean?"

"I think it's possible there might be a final test for your task. If I don't beat the odds…if I have this operation and die—"

"Don't say that!" Emma wanted to reach up and cover her ears. She wouldn't hear that. She wouldn't think it.

"We will still have shared a love that was powerful, vigilant, and true. But for the task to be completed, the Curse of Clan McBride ended, you may be called upon to prove that you've completed your task. You can't close your heart again, Emma. I need your word that if I die, you'll honor our love by remaining open to another love sometime in your future. You have to promise me."

She gave her head a shake. "Excuse me? You're not dead yet and you're telling me to fall in love with somebody else? That's an awful thing to ask."

"Nevertheless, I'm asking."

"Well how could you?" She pulled away from him, turned away from him. "That's just mean." Then she whirled back around and glared up at him. "Would you be so quick to turn to someone else?"

"No, I wouldn't." For a moment, he appeared taken

aback by her expression. Then determination hardened his jaw. "But would you want me to grieve over your grave for the rest of my life, alone and brokenhearted? Could you bear that image? I couldn't. I can't. Please don't do that, Emma. Promise me that you'll live your life to the fullest. I need to go into that operation with that surety, that comfort. I need that peace of mind as I brave my greatest fears to guard the true and special love we share."

She gazed up into his earnest, silver eyes and recognized his pain. Opening her mind, she allowed his plea to sink in.

He was asking her to survive even if he didn't. Since she'd faced such a trial in the past, she knew how desperately difficult keeping such a promise would be.

He'd been right when he said what he was asking of her would be hard. But he was braving his greatest fear for her. Could she do anything less? No. Dair was proving the strength of their love. She must be strong for him, too.

She drew a deep, shaky breath, then said, "I promise you that I will live my life to the fullest, Alasdair MacRae. Without you, I'll grieve, but I'll survive. For I've found my powerful, vigilant and true love. But with you—oh, Dair, with you—I'll live in true happiness and joy. I'll roll those dice, too. I'll put my trust in fate and faith and maybe even fairies. I'll bet that the McBride bad luck is about to change. We'll be happy together for a long, long time." Then she paused, lifted her chin, and added, "On one condition."

Warily, he asked, "What's that?"

"I want you to find a minister and marry me as soon as we get back to Nacogdoches."

A lazy grin stretched his mouth. "Is that a proposal, Emma Tate?"

"No. It's a condition. You're the one who needs to make the proposal."

"I'd like nothing better—if only to get your father off my back." He ignored her punch to his arm and continued, "But are you sure, Emma? You don't want to wait until after the operation and have one of the infamous McBride family weddings?"

"I've already done that once. I'm not nearly as interested in the wedding as I am in the honeymoon. Have you heard about the honeymoon Jake gave my sister?"

"He did mention something about a harem fantasy."

"Among other things. It's a long train ride to Baltimore, Mr. MacRae, and you're a clever man. I expect you can come up with a honeymoon fantasy to rival Kat's."

"Hmm...I'll get to work on it right away."

"After."

"After?"

She sighed and gave his arm another punch.

"For the record, I don't hold with spousal abuse."

"Hit your knee, MacRae."

With that, Alasdair MacRae took her hand in his and in the middle of the fairy circle went down on one knee. "Emma, you own my heart, my passion, my battered and imperfect soul. Will you be my partner in the adventure of life? Will you share the risks and rewards that an uncertain future has to offer? Emma, love of my life, my reason to live, I want to make a formal commitment to a love that is powerful, vigilant and true. Texas, will you marry me?"

She sank to her knees in front of him and stared at him through a shimmer of tears. "Yes, outlaw of mine, I'll marry you. You own *my* heart, *my* passion, and *my* own imperfect soul. I'll be your partner in adventure, in boredom, in life for as long as we have to share. And, if fate decrees the worst, I'll be worthy of you in death. Love with me, Dair MacRae. Live for me."

"I'll do my damnedest, Texas. I'll do my damnedest."

CHAPTER NINETEEN

The Johns Hopkins Hospital, Baltimore

DAIR DRIFTED TOWARD WAKEFULNESS and awareness of an aching pounding in his head. He'd done this before, he thought. Different, though.

He sensed a touch on his hand. The gentle stroke of a thumb. *I'm still alive.* Still alive. For now.

EMMA LOOKED UP FROM HER vigil at her husband's bedside as her parents entered the room. Jenny's brows knotted with concern while Trace's worried gaze scanned Dair's prone body. "How's he doing?"

"Dr. Cushing says I shouldn't worry, that it's not unusual for a brain surgery patient to take so long to wake up. The fever has been gone for twenty-four hours now. That's a good sign."

"His color is good," Jenny offered. "Much improved over yesterday, I think."

"Yes." Emma clasped Dair's hand, stroked her thumb over his knuckles. "I think so, too."

Trace cleared his throat. "I'll sit here with him if you want to go with your mama for a bit."

"You need to rest, Emma," Jenny added.

"I will. Just not yet. I want to be here when he wakes

up. It'll happen anytime now. I'm sure of it." He was going to wake up. He had to. He simply couldn't die, not after all they'd been through. Not when her dreams were just waiting to come true. Not when he had so much to live for—even more than he knew.

Yet, in the deepest, darkest hours of the soul, she faced the reality that she could lose him. It was almost more than she could bear. But Emma knew that if the worst happened, bear it she would. She'd treasure their time together and live her life forward rather than bury it in the past. She had to do it that way. She'd given him her word.

Two days later, Trace and Jenny managed to coax Emma from Dair's bedside only after Dr. Cushing ordered his patient isolated.

The fever was back.

HOT. SO HOT. MUST BE IN the desert.

Can't move. Tied down? Captured?

No. Wait. Honeymoon. Private train car. Arabian Nights.

Flush of pleasure. Emma. Smell her perfume. She must be nearby. She won't leave. So determined.

I'll be determined, too. Need to wake up. Need to see her. Need to live. To have a future. A future with Emma. Wake up. Wake up. Head hurts. Pain too much. Tired. So tired.

Too weak. Not strong enough. Love is vigilant and true but not strong enough. Mama? Mama, is that you?

DOZING IN HER CHAIR AT Dair's bedside, Emma jerked awake. It was late afternoon and the warm sunshine beaming through the window had lulled her to sleep. Why was sitting in a hospital doing nothing more physical than trying her hand at knitting so exhausting? Standing, she stretched as she studied her husband. He'd grown so gaunt since the surgery, and two recent days of high fever had left him looking older than his age.

"Oh, Dair," she said on a worried sigh. What she wouldn't give to see him move, to watch him open his eyes, to hear his precious voice say her name. "Come back to me, MacRae. I need you. Do you hear me? I have news to tell you that is burning a hole in my tongue. You've slept long enough."

She brushed a lock of dark hair off his brow and was encouraged by the coolness of his skin. "I never took you for a lazy man, but I'm about to reconsider. Wake up, MacRae. It's time. I need you to open those gorgeous gray eyes."

WAKE UP, MACRAE. IT'S TIME.

Dair fought his way through the fog of unconsciousness toward the sound of Emma's voice. She droned on and on, scolding him. Cajoling him. *I didn't know I married such a nag.*

His eyelids felt like fifty-pound weights, but he slowly managed to pry them open. At first, the light hurt his eyes. Blinded him. He blinked once. Twice. Then he saw Emma sitting beside his bed. She stared at their hands, linked together. "...all I can do not to tell Mama," his wife was saying. "I think she suspects, but..."

She looked so beautiful. Where was he? Why was he in bed and she not? Why was a tear rolling down her cheek?

It came back to him in a flash. The surgery. Good Lord. He was alive. And thinking! Thinking clearly. Amazing. So why was she crying? Emma never cried.

He croaked out a question. "Texas, what's wrong?"

Emma gasped and their gazes met. "Dair? Dair! You're awake! You came back to me."

She stood and reached for him, clasping his shoulders, laying her head on his chest. She started laughing and crying all at once. "Oh, Dair. You're awake!"

"Sure I'm not dead and gone to heaven?" He lifted a hand and stroked her golden hair. "I've an angel lying against me."

"You can move, too!" She pulled back and looked at him with gleaming blue eyes. "Oh, your legs. Try your legs." He wiggled his toes and she laughed again. "Dr. Cushing didn't anticipate that you would suffer any loss of physical or intellectual ability, but it's wonderful to see. Oh, Dair. You're all right, aren't you?"

Was he? "The tumor?"

"All good news, thank God. Dr. Cushing called it a meningioma and said it was easily removed. It's a benign tumor that probably grew at the site of an old injury. He said you'll continue to suffer headaches until you heal from the surgery, but that those should go away. He'll give you all the details, I'm sure. We need to let him know you're awake. But Dair…oh, Dair…you did it." She paused and her lower lips trembled. "You beat the odds."

"We beat the odds." He levered himself up to a seated position, barely able to take it all in. He was a little dizzy, a little shaky, a little achy, but…he smiled. "I'm alive. I can think and talk and move and breathe and you are here with me. Life couldn't be any better."

Dair drank in the sight of her as Emma smiled a radiant smile. "Actually, it could," she told him, her brilliant blue eyes shining with joy. "It can. It is! Dair, I have to tell you…my hopes…my dreams…you've made them all come true. You've given me a gift I've waited for all my life." She paused significantly before finishing. "Dair, we're going to have a baby."

"A baby?" he asked, hope and excitement and a measure of panic adding a slight tremor to his voice. "We're having a baby?"

She sat beside him on the bed. "Yes. Isn't it wonderful? I'd all but given up on that dream, but now..."

"Our dreams are coming true," he said tenderly.

Emma nodded, gasped back a little sob. "I thought if it's a girl, we should name her Roslin."

Overwhelmed, his heart overflowing, Dair took Emma in his arms and kissed her, pouring all his love and relief and joy and exhilaration into the moment. A baby. Their baby! Life, love and Emma. It simply didn't get any better than this.

From the doorway came the unwelcome sound of his father-in-law's voice. "For God's sake. Can't you wait until you get home to do that?"

Home. Dair broke the kiss, stared at Emma. "We'll need one. A home. We don't have one."

"Don't worry, Robin Hood. I know of the perfect place."

It took him a moment to make the connection. "Sherwood House? You wouldn't mind...?"

She grinned. "What better place to make a home with my very own outlaw?"

Fort Worth

EMMA AND DAIR, KAT AND Jake, and Mari and Luke entered the lobby of the Fort Worth National Bank together. The men drew the stares of the women in the building, while the women attracted everyone's notice. The sisters wore simple gowns of their mother's design that showcased the necklaces hanging around each of their necks. Each of the McBride Menaces glowed with excitement, anticipation and joy.

Flanked by her sisters and with the husbands a few steps behind, Emma approached a teller window, showed the key, and said, "The MacRae box, please?"

The teller opened a leather-bound book and flipped through the pages. Frowning, he said, "Hmm...yes...well...fancy that. Finally. Hmm...if you'll have a seat, my superior will be with you shortly."

"Well, that's curious," Mari observed as the man scurried to an office at the far side of the building.

"You didn't expect it all to be normal, did you?" Kat asked.

"No. I guess not."

Moments later, the teller led them to the office of the bank president himself. "Good morning. Good morning. This is quite exciting. My employee said you have a key?"

"We do."

"Very good. Very good. This account has a special instruction. Along with the key, you are to present proof."

"Proof?" Mari asked. "What kind of proof? Proof of what?"

"I know. Mr. Potter showed me." Emma slipped her necklace from around her neck as she quoted the text from memory. "'The fairy queen gave three stones—blue, green and red—to be presented with the claim that conditions had been met for the ending of the curse.'"

"We have to give up our necklaces?" Kat asked. She frowned at the banker. "Do we get them back?"

"The instructions simply say that they're to be presented."

A man entered the room carrying a small metal box. The president gestured for the man to set the box on his desk, then once he'd departed, the president said, "Ladies?"

The gold chain clinked against the wooden desk as Emma set her necklace beside the box. Mari placed the sapphire next to the ruby, then both sisters looked to Kat. She scowled, then removed her necklace. Once it joined the other two, the bank president invited Emma to try the lock with the key in her hand.

Kat leaned toward Mari and whispered from the side of her mouth. "Do you think the entire treasure is in that little box? Maybe it's not as big as we think."

Emma twisted the key and a lock snicked. She flipped back the lid. "Another key?"

"Excellent." The bank president beamed. "Now, if you'd like to collect your necklaces and follow me, please?" He led them down a hallway to a door at the very back of the building. "This deposit predates the bank building. In fact, the bank's building specifications were altered to accommodate a special vault. The deposit came to the bank from...New Orleans...I believe, when Fort Worth National first opened."

He opened the wooden door to reveal a metal door behind it. "The second key fits this lock. I will leave you to your privacy now." He took two steps away, then paused, dropping his professionalism. "I'll admit to a long curiosity about what's in the vault. If you're of a mind to tell me, I'd love to listen."

The sisters shared a look, then Emma said, "Perhaps later."

She waited until they were alone in the hallway, then said, "Well, this is it."

"I'm nervous," Mari confessed.

"Me, too," Kat agreed. "What do you think we'll find inside?"

"You know, it doesn't really matter," Emma said. She glanced toward Dair and added, "I already have everything I need."

"Or want," Mari added, her gaze on Luke.

"Or dreamed of." Kat smiled at Jake.

"Well you damned sure better hope there's enough money in there for the outlaw to buy a pardon from the governor." Trace McBride's long-legged strides ate up the hallway. Jenny almost had to run to keep up. "I don't hold with the idea of taking my grandbaby to the state penitentiary to visit her daddy. And you'd also better hope the Scottish authorities reply to Luke's telegram explaining that they can stop looking for the Black Widow since the real villain is dead. I don't like having that worry hanging over my head, either."

Jake leaned toward Dair and muttered, "I thought we'd managed to leave the old goat at home."

Trace ignored his sons-in-law, his gaze softening as he looked first at Emma. "How you feelin', sweetheart?"

"I'm fine, Papa."

"Katie Kat? You done with your morning sickness, now?"

"My all-day sickness, you mean?" Kat grimaced. "Yes, Papa. I'm feeling quite well, thank you."

"Mari-berry? Are the twins letting you get a decent night's sleep yet?"

"Yes. They're finally sleeping through the night, thank goodness. I'm glad you and Mama made it, after all."

"It's my fault we're late." Jenny sighed heavily. "Your grandmother wouldn't let me off the telephone. You won't believe what she's gone and done now."

"Shall I go get some chairs so everyone can be comfortable while we share this chitchat in the hall?" Jake asked, his tone dry as July.

"Maybe something to drink?" Luke added.

Dair folded his arms. "A snack, perhaps?"

The McBride Menaces shared a smirk. "Our men have no patience whatsoever," Kat observed. "They probably all rip into their Christmas gifts without any attempt to savor the moment."

"Open the door!" the three husbands cried.

Emma grinned as she fitted the key into the lock. "Mari, Kat—let's do it together."

With three hands giving the key a twist, the lock released and they opened the door. Emma grabbed Dair's hand as she spied the inside of the vault. "My heavens, it looks an awful lot like Madame Valentina's old fortune-teller space."

Plush pillows lay scattered about the floor. The scent of jasmine perfumed the air. A round table draped in midnight blue stood at the center of the room. On top of the table forming three points of a triangle sat three silver chests about the size of a small bread box. In the center of the chests sat a leather-bound portfolio.

"Oh my oh my oh my," Kat murmured.

The vault was large enough for all eight of them to step inside and surround the table. On his way in, Dair grabbed one of the cushions off the floor and propped it in the doorway. When Jake arched a curious brow, he explained. "Any good thief knows to protect his avenue of escape. I'd just as soon not get locked in a bank vault."

Just like they'd done a decade before, Emma, Mari and Kat took a seat on one of the three stools surrounding the table. Their husbands took positions behind them. "This is damned strange," Luke murmured.

"Who's going to open the first chest?" Kat asked.

"Emma picked the first necklace," Mari said. "I think she should go first."

Emma shook her head. "No. Let's do it backward. Mari, you were last. Go first today."

"Which one?"

"You choose," Kat said.

Mari reached for the chest closest to her and flipped open the lid. Sapphires. Dozens and dozens of them. Hundreds, even. "Holy Hannah."

"I'll bet…" Kat flipped the lid on the box nearest her. "Yes." Emeralds filled the box. Kat swallowed hard, then said, "Emma, you know you'll have rubies."

Emma's hand trembled as she flipped back the lid to reveal a cache of red stones. Behind her, Dair sucked in a breath. A bubble of laughter escaped her. "I guess Governor Culberson will be happy. You'll have to quit calling Dair an outlaw, Papa. He'll be able to buy his pardon now so Luke won't have to feel guilty any longer."

"Nah. He'll always be an outlaw to me," Trace observed. "Just like Kimball will always be a scoundrel and Garrett a thief."

"A thief? I wasn't a thief. I was a bodyguard."

"You stole my precious Mari-berry from me."

"Oh, for God's sake."

Jenny interrupted before the men came to blows. "What is in the portfolio?"

The girls looked at one another. Mari suggested, "You look, Emma. You're the oldest."

Emma's mouth was bone-dry as she flipped back the cover to reveal a letter written in beautiful flowing script. Conscious of her family's anticipation, she read aloud:

To my Jewels

You have traveled a long, difficult path to reach this point, but the rewards are great. Through your dedication and perseverance you have earned the right to collect the Sisters' Prize.

My Emerald: Your stone is a power stone for life. It opens the door to the deepest scars of the heart, allowing cleansing and healing and the achievement of greatest heart's desire. You hold the power in your hands. Use it to bring clear vision, tranquility, serenity, faith, inspiration and joy to the suffering. Use your treasure to heal.

My Sapphire: Your stone is a power stone for truth. It draws protection, offers wisdom, intelligence and purity of motive. You hold the power in your hand. Use it to instill hope, encourage faithfulness, focus loving energy and promote sincerity in those in need. Use your treasure to seek what is real.

My Ruby: Your stone is a power stone for light. It illuminates the dark places and helps in the transition from the one of the past to the one meant to be. You hold the power in your hand. Use it to aid in following dreams, searching for wisdom, and finding bliss. Use your treasure to transform.

Remember, my jewels, the lessons you have learned along this long and arduous journey. Never forget those lost along the way. Always hold your accomplishments and achievements in well-earned regard.

You were created in Love. You are meant to be happy. Live it. Believe it. Spread it to every precious life you touch.

The three of you, sisters, daughters of my blood, have proven my word and defeated forces beyond imagining. By the fact of your presence here today, you have ended the Curse of Clan McBride. Look to your hands to prove that you have the promise of

Roslin that from now until the end of time, you and yours will forever be lucky in love.
Ariel MacRae McBride

For a long moment after Emma's voice faded away, no one spoke. Then Mari opened her right hand. "Oh, my."

Kat looked at her right hand. "Oh, my."

Emma glanced from one sister to the other, then stared down at her right palm. "Oh, my."

"Have you noticed how they all say that?" Jake observed.

"What is it, girls?" Jenny asked.

The sisters shared a look, then Mari explained. "It's gone. The mark of Ariel."

"Because you found both Luke and yourself," Kat said. "Mine's gone because I found Jake and forgave myself."

"And I found Dair and freed myself," Emma added. She held out her hand for the others to see. "Our Bad Luck Love lines have disappeared."

Trace studied his daughters' palms, then grasped his Jenny's hand and blew out a sigh. "So. It's done. The curse is broken. The Bad Luck is behind the McBride family now and forever."

Emma, Mari and Kat each smiled at their husbands, and then at their parents. As one, they said, "Amen!"